The Shape of Fear

A Novel of World War II

Charles McNair, M.D.

Trenton, Georgia

Print ISBN: 978-1-959621-45-4
Ebook ISBN: 979-8-88531-866-2

Published by BookLocker.com, Inc., Trenton, Georgia.

BookLocker.com, Inc.
2025

First Edition

Library of Congress Cataloging in Publication Data
McNair, M.D., Charles
The Shape of Fear: A Novel of World War II by Charles McNair, M.D.
Library of Congress Control Number: 2024925161

Dedication

To my wife, Jean and my three children, Annie, Emily and Andrew who were my first and most helpful readers.

Midway in my life's journey
I went astray from the straight road
and woke to find myself
alone in a dark wood. How shall I say
what a wood it was! I never saw so drear,
so rank, so arduous a wilderness!
Its very memory gives a shape to fear.

The Divine Comedy
Canto I, lines 1-6
Dante Alighieri

Table of Contents

The Shape of Fear

Units and Personnel

US Army	Wehrmacht
Infantry	Infantry
8th Army, 28th Infantry Div., 112th Regiment (Pa. N.G.)	272nd Volks-Grenadier Div.
The Keystone Div. (American), The Bloody Bucket	Corporal Hermann Schneider, rifleman
Col. Norman D. "Dutch" Cota, commander 112th Reg. later	
Major General, commanding the 28th Division	
Lt. Judd Barclay, company commander, E Co.	Privat Ernst Locher, rifleman
Sergeant Ted Rosinski, 2nd platoon leader, E Co.	

Private Henry Anderson, rifleman, 2nd platoon, E Co.

Corporal Jeffery Howe, rifleman, 2nd platoon, E Co.

Air Force

100th Bomb Group, 349th bomb squadron

98th Bomb Group, 167th bomb squadron

Joe Hanover: waist gunner, B17F's *Bouncing Betty* &

The Usual Suspects, 349th bomb squadron

Capt. Robert Mullen: pilot, 357th Fighter grp,

363rd, Fighter Sqn. P-51D

Hauptman Jans von Rindel

Lieutenant Joachim Brenner

Jagdgeschwader III/54, D/St, III/St. G77,

"The Green Hearts of Thuringen"

Artillery

229th Field Artillery, 105 mm Howitzers	272nd Artillery Regiment, 88's
Lt. Alfred Moore, battery commander	
108th Field Arty., 155 mm Howitzers	Heinz von Kleist, Oberleutnant
86th Chemical Btn., 4.2" mortars	272 Anti-tank Btn.

Armor

3rd Armored Division, 32nd Armored Regiment	116th Panzer Div. Der Windhunds,
M4A3 Sherman, 76 mm cannon	"The Grey Hounds", Col. Kurt Hindman
Captain Buck Ramsey, Co. A, 707th Tank Btn.	116th Panzergrenadieren
T.Sgt. Enfield Davis. Tank Commander, *Hell's Fire*	Pvt. Klaus Wiesen , sniper
Combat Command B	
893rd Tank Destroyer Reg.	M36 "Jackson" 90mm tank destroyer

Medical Corps

103rd Med. Btn, att'd to 112th Reg.	Der Sanitatdienst des Heers
T.Sgt. Douglas Aiken, medic	Oberstabsartz Genter von Stettgen
Major Albert Brendt, Regimental Surgeon	
Capt. Raymond Hersel, surgeon, Vossenach	

The Crews – B17s
3rd Air Div., 100th Bomb Group, 349th Sqn.

The Bouncing Betty	*The Usual Suspects*
Capt. James Flanagan, Pilot	Lt. Wilson James, Pilot
Lt. Herman Lewis, Co-pilot	Lt. Kenneth Forbes, Co-pilot
Lt. Samuel Topman, Navigator/rt cheek	Lt. Mark Angelo, Navigator/rt cheek
Lt. Stanley Toland, Bombardier/nose gunner	Lt. Norman Ems, Bombardier/nose

TSgt. Joe Hanover, Rt. waist gunner

TSgt. Luis Ramon, Lt. waist gunner

TSgt. Frank Paglia, Belly turret gunner

TSgt. Raymond Gilbert, tail gunner

TSgt. Jason Abrams, Engineer/top turret gunner

TSgt. Paul Phillips, Radio operator/left cheek gunner

The Shy Virgin, B24

TSgt. Jeb Olgilvie, Rt. Waist gunner

TSgt. Thomas Healey, Lt. Waist gunner

Cpl. Randy Payne, top turret gunner

Sgt. Charles Zinn, Rt. Waist gunner

Sgt. Woodrow Eads, Lt. Waist gunner

TSgt. John Payne, Belly turret

TSgt. Harvey Puzio, Tail gunner

TSgt. Fred Lesser, Engineer/top turret

TSgt. Steven Apple, Radio/ left cheek

363rd Fighter Sqn., P-51D Mustangs

Capt. Robert Mulley, *Snafu, Floozy*

Lt. Doug Karnowski, *Slybird*

Cpl. Jack Pander, Rt. Cheek gunner

Pvt. Anton Solario, ball turret gunner

The Crews – M4A3 76mm Sherman tanks
Co. C, 707th Tank Battalion, 3rd Armored Div.

Hell's Fire, lead tank	*Ronna's Revenge, Texas Pride*
T.Sgt. Enfield Davis, commander, 50 cal MG	Sgt. Herman Manns, commander
Corporal Gus Tolliver, gunner	Sgt. Larry Rounds, gunner
Sgt. Stanley Grisholm, bow gunner (BOG), 30 cal MG	Private Robert Smalls, BOG
Private Samuel Peters, loader	Private Sweeny Tuttle, loader
Corporal Roger Emmonds, driver	Corporal Allen Zweiss, driver

Death Wagon

T.Sgt. William Soames, commander

Sgt. Joseph Mac Farlane, gunner

Private Benjamin Johns, BOG

Corporal Dick Holland, loader

Corporal Andrew Stukey, driver

Adolph's Nightmare

T.Sgt. Ramon Suarez, commander

Corporal Cameron Smith, gunner

Corporal Douglas Yates, BOG

Private Martin Jewel, loader

Sgt. Norman Wilson, driver

Chapter One:
The Bouncing Betty

The sergeants came through the 100th Bomb Group enlisted men's tents awakening them in the damp darkness of the airfield at Thorpe Abbotts, Norfolk, East Anglia, at 0300 hours. They were, as always, right on time. The airmen shrugged into their flight suits and trudged to the mess hall.

"Just another day in paradise," said Technical Sergeant Luis Ramon, left waist gunner on the *Bouncing Betty,* as the cook slapped a watery mound of reconstituted scrambled eggs on his platter.

The cook looked up at him. "Three hots and a cot, that's what Uncle Sam promised. Enjoy.'

The 100th Bomb Group, the "Bloody 100th" as it was known, a name earned in the flak- and fighter-filled skies over more than fifty German cities, railroad yards and oil refineries since its arrival from Nebraska a year before, was being roused to do battle one more time. Assigned to the 13th Bombardment Wing with four squadrons, the 100th sustained more losses than any other bomb group. Losses of a dozen planes, each with their ten-man crews, were not uncommon. The worse raid was on Munster, Fall, 1943, when only one plane, the *Bouncing Betty*, of the thirty-four that left Thorpe Abbotts in the predawn darkness, limped home with two smoking engines. The large black "D" in the white square painted on her tail was laced by a Messerschmitt 109's 20mm cannon. Two nearly dead waist gunners lay on the vibrating deck, shivering with cold despite their heated flight suits and jackets. The *Bouncing Betty*, a B17F veteran of twenty-seven missions, more patch than plane, had made it back one more time.

Betty Grable's swimsuit clad image was lovingly painted on both sides of the nose with jiggle lines outlining her rounded parts, denoting her bouncing qualities. A rite of passage for each new crew member of the plane had been established. Before his first flight on the *Betty* the new crew man had to take a running leap and slap his hand on the highest part of Betty he could reach. After the ship returned from that day's mission, the drinks were on the new guy.

Thirty-five crews had ferried the 100th's B17s to Thorpe Abbotts airfield in February, 1943. By the end of the first Munster raid, August, 1943, only five of the original crews remained. It was not only the high loss rates the 100th sustained over targets that awarded them their name. During a return flight from Bremen, a shot-up B17 running on one engine was shadowed by a Focke-Wulf 190. The bomber had indicated it's surrender by opening its bomb bay doors and descending. The German pilot was escorting the bomber to a safe landing and internment in occupied

Belgian. The fight engineer was able to get another engine running making it possible for the plane to get to England. The waist gunner opened fire on the fighter shooting him down. This breach in the rules of engagement so enraged the German fighters that they made the planes of the 100th their special targets. The black "D" on their tails made them easily identifiable.

Now there were near daily long-range unescorted missions with planes and crews lost on each one and no end in sight. So, the major who led the pre-mission briefing was not surprised by the collective groan that arose from the pilots, co-pilots, bombardiers and navigators who faced him in the ready room for the pre-flight briefing.

"The target for today is Munster."

"Oh, come on. Are we the only fucking group bombing that fucking place?" Lt. Toland, the *Betty*'s bombardier, who also manned the right cheek gun, sitting in the back asked in a not so quiet whisper. "What is it? Six or seven times now?"

"Is there a problem with the assignment?" asked the briefing officer, sardonically. "Now admittedly there were three missions scratched over the target due to clouds..."

"Clouds don't stop no radar guided ack-ack fire," another voice called out. "We still lost seven ships."

"It is a tough, but important target. Most of the remaining tank factories are around Munster, it is a major railhead..."

"Yeah, and we got most of them already. How many crews we gonna lose to bomb rubble?"

"That's right," chimed in Lt. James Flanagan, the pilot of the *Bouncing Betty*, "we and the Brits are bombing those sonsofbitches around the clock, all over the whole fucking country and they won't quit. How's rearranging their brick piles going to change their minds?"

The briefing officer realized that a certain amount of grousing about missions was a vital safety valve and tolerated it more than perhaps he should. He also knew he was losing control of the session and what was coming next was not going to make the mission any easier. His empty right sleeve bought him some credibility, but bomber crews had short memories, a necessary world view of "That was then, this is now and 'now' is fucked up".

"You are correct. Most of the hard targets have been damaged, but not put out of commission totally. So, we are changing it up this time." He pulled back the black curtain covering the photo-recon pictures of the cathedral in the center of the city. "We are going after the one remaining major resource left: the workers. Munster supplies the majority of the workforce to the industry surrounding the city. So far, the Eighth Air Force has avoided civilian targets.

That is a nicety that the Germans have never observed. We are hoping to send the message that nothing is off-limits any longer."

"Is that a church?" asked one of the pilots in the front row.

"Munster Cathedral. It is our aiming point for the raid, the front steps, actually. The raid is planned for noon Sunday, when the workers will be coming out, in a state of grace, one presumes. It is expected that with this change in strategy, the German High Command will begin to rethink continuing the war."

"So, let me get this straight. We are purposely targeting civilians," the Sweet Emily's pilot said with increasingly incredulous anger. He had risen to his feet, his face red and veins bulging. "For the first time in the war, the 100th is bombing civilians unrelated to any legitimate war objective?"

"Take a look around, Lieutenant, next time you're in London or Coventry or Bristol or Manchester. Do you think the Krauts took any great pains to avoid civilian casualties? And the objective, Lieutenant, is to end the fucking war as quickly as we can. There is no indication that the civilian population's support of the German war effort is slacking off. The thinking is that if we make them pay a price, that may change."

About half the assembled flight crews saw no problem with bombing civilians, agreeing that there were no innocent German civilians at this point in the war – just abettors.

“Major, if I may,” a voice from the back said.

“'Attention!” the Major shouted.

The men in the room stood as one, staring ahead. Brigadier General Curtis LeMay, commanding general of the 3rd Air Division, strode forcefully to the front, turned to face the pilots, saluted and said, “Take your seats, gentlemen.” LeMay was known as a no nonsense, hard-ass commander who led by example and frequently flew on missions himself. He was the author of the strategy to bomb civilians specifically. He had chosen the 100th BG to lead on the mission because he felt the high casualty rates they had sustained in raid after raid would make them looking for some pay back. He looked over the aircrews as he lit his third cigar of the day.

“Smoke ‘em if you got ‘em.”

“This is an important mission,” he continued, his voice a gravelly snarl, “a change in tactics that the Germans cannot misunderstand. The Major is absolutely correct. The Krauts understand only power and the fact that we have tried to spare the civilian population is interpreted as weakness by them. And you,” he said, singling out the angry

Lieutenant, "are also right. We have destroyed the majority of Germany's industrial base. Now, we are 'bombing rubble', as you say. That makes the civilian workforce as the only significant resource they have left.

"I don't have to tell you men that the Eighth Air Force has decimated their factories so much that they have pulled their anti-aircraft 88mm batteries back to surround the remaining targets, increasing the price we pay to 'bomb the rubble'. It is simply the law of diminishing returns. So, we have to adjust. You all know they are not protecting their cities, cynically exploiting our humanity. That ends today."

Comments like "'Bout time... fucking right...a taste of their own medicine...How does that make us better than the Krauts..." drifted from the aircrews towards LeMay.

LeMay paused, gazing at the mixed reactions to his orders evident in the faces of his command.

"Machts nicht," he thought, "I'm not in the convincing business. I'm in the commanding business."

"I will be flying with you in the *Bouncing Betty,"* he said aloud, "That will be all. See you on the flight line."

"Attention!"

With that, LeMay strode out of the stunned briefing room. The Major took over to finish the briefing, designating the assembly point, a radio beacon beamed skyward called the "Buncher", and the IP, the "initial point" where the bombers would make their turn on the final approach to the target. He noted that the fighter escort of P-47 Thunderbolts would be able to accompany the bombers only to the German border.

"At least we know where the Krauts will be," said Lt. Flanagan, pilot of the *Bouncing Betty.* Flanagan was almost the Hollywood picture of what a pilot should be. He was tall, over six feet, grey-green eyes and the red hair of his Scots-Irish forebears, driven from their homeland by the potato famine in the 1840s to settle in North Carolina. He had joined the Army after one year in college at NC State and was selected for pilot training. He had the trust of his crew because they knew that if anyone could get them home again, it was Flanagan.

The enlisted men had their own briefings consisting of weather information over the target and the most likely times they could expect the fighters and then loaded into the jeeps to be taken out to their planes. Sergeant Joe Hanover loved this period of quiet during the ride. He loved England, the flat green of Thorpe Abbotts, the mist stranding over the fields reminded him of his farm outside of Twin Forks, Indiana. He was stocky, almost square from the work in the fields haying and baling then tossing the hay into the waiting wagon. His black hair and dark blue eyes peering from his open, unlined face were arresting. He had a farmer's tan: face, vee down the front of his throat to his upper chest, both forearms to calloused hands. Under his shirt, his trunk was white as the clouds floating in the endless blue sky over his family's farm. From the first time he saw a crop duster biplane, Joe wanted to fly.

This was his favorite time of day: early morning in the mist before dawn, the silence untrammeled by the great bombers' engines, riding with the rest of his crew in the jeeps out to the flight line. Then looming, out of the ground fog, the sudden, primeval presence of the B17s, pointing skyward, huge birds of prey waiting to start the hunt once more.

Each man had his own pre-flight ritual. Joe's was to formally salute Betty Grable's lovingly painted anatomy. She was painted in her famous swimsuit pose, looking demurely over her right shoulder, hands on her ample hips, positioned just forward of the cheek gunner's window. Twenty-seven yellow painted bombs trailed from her derriere. Fifteen red swastikas swarmed around the cheek guns.

During the night, the ground crew and armorers had prepped the *Betty* for her flight to Germany. Each of the eleven .50 caliber machine guns had 450 rounds. The wing tanks were topped off. There were ten tanks in each wing plus two more in the bomb bay giving a total capacity of 3,700 gallons. The roundtrip flight to Munster would need most of the fuel as it was.

In the predawn gloaming, LeMay's staff car pulled up to the *Betty's* forward hatch. He was thirty-eight years old but took pride in maintaining his fitness. He tossed his flight bag to waiting hands in the plane, jumped up and grabbed the lip of the hatch, and swung himself into the dark interior. The eighteen-year-olds of the crew were impressed. He would be flying in the co-pilot's seat. Lt. Herman Lewis, the usual co-pilot, would make the mission sitting aft of the cabin, ready to fill in wherever a need might arise. The men were at their positions doing their own pre-flight checks during which they let each other know how they felt about LeMay flying with them.

"It's not like it is bad enough flying lead with the Norden, we've got this uptight brass along for a joy ride," complained TSgt. Paul Phillips, radio operator and left cheek gunner.

"And if word got out about it, every fucking Me 109 and FW 190 in Germany is going to be gunning for us," replied TSgt. Luis Ramon, left waist gunner.

"Yeah, you're right. Shooting down LeMay would probably be worth some bratwurst and beer for any Kraut pilot, I would think," finished TSgt. Raymond Gilbert, the tail gunner.

Joe Hanover checked to be sure he had the ammo belt coiled in a plywood box attached to his gun and that it would play out smoothly when he started firing. He pulled back on the retractor slide to make sure of its easy play and fully opened the breech cover. He put the gun through its full range of motion and sighted down the barrel. He had faith in the armorer and ground crew but it never hurt to double check. The flight crew had finished their pre-flight check and waited on the tower to give them the "start engines" signal. General LeMay, seemed relaxed and satisfied with all the activity around him. He competently ran through the co-pilot's pre-flight checks so that even Flanagan began to relax a little.

"Start engines," came the command from the tower followed by a green flare. One by one, the engines came to life belching black turning to grey smoke. It was still dark and fifteen minutes before the *Betty* was to taxi into position at the head of her flight of thirty-six B17Fs. Hanover felt the plane roar into life, shaking and rumbling. Then the jerk forward as she moved down the approach lane and turned to face the two-thousand-yard concrete runway. Flanagan pressed down hard on the brakes as he gunned the four Wright Cyclone engines to full power as one final test of their readiness and to build the power for take-off. One final check with the tower for clearance and the *Bouncing Betty* surged down the runway, gathering speed lifting almost imperceptibly into the air. The entire flight of thirty-six planes was airborne within ten minutes.

The basic formation was composed of groups of three planes flying in a "V" shape. They climbed more than five miles to get above the cloud cover and formed on their usual rally point, "Buncher 28". This was a radio beacon beamed skyward and was the first step in gathering together the 100th Bomb Group. The group then assembled as a wing of seventy-two bombers at "Buncher 23", and finally as a division over Southwold where the entire three hundred plane division would be joined with other divisions from all over England, forming a thousand plane flotilla as a maximal effort to bomb major sites in Germany. It took about an hour of flying time to get the flight organized, even with the experienced pilots of the 100th. This burned precious fuel and added to pilot fatigue but was the most workable system to get the bombers in the best formation for both bombing and defense against fighters. The 100th did not use a "Judas plane", a garishly painted retired B17 upon which the rest of the flight would group. "Judas" because it was leading the bombers to death and destruction which it would not have to face. This time, just the 100th BG was headed to Munster.

When fully formed, the 100th's thirty-six bombers were grouped into three twelve plane groups all flying in a box that was two hundred yards tall by five hundred wide by two hundred-seventy-yards deep. The *Betty* was the lead plane in the center group. She had the target acquisition radar and the Norden bomb site. All the other planes would drop their loads when she dropped hers. This system gave good massed bombing accuracy as well as maximum defensive fire power against fighters while presenting a dispersed target for the flak gunners on the ground.

This tight formation flying required faith in the competence of the experienced pilots flying in clear weather but maintaining it became essential in the shrouding clouds, under fighter attack or the when the flak found them. Formation flying was essential to all the planes' survival. A lone bomber had no chance against fighters and any breaking out of the formation meant almost certain mid-air collisions with the death of the crews. Once formed, the formation had no choice but to fly straight and steady, depending on their gunners for defense.

The bombers joined up with their fighter escorts of P-47 Thunderbolts as they crossed the English coastline and out over the Channel, then across the Netherlands and onto Munster. Flanagan came on the intercom.

"Look alive. We have our little friends with us," referring to the fighter escort. "We've got them until we hit Germany." Hanover looked out over his waist gun to see the Thunderbolts flying in formation. He noted that they had two bombs under their wings. By this time in the war, it was rare to encounter German fighters over France so the Thunderbolts had taken to carrying the bombs for ground targets they encountered on their return flights. If they did have to fight off some German fighters, they would jettison the bombs and engage.

Growing up in rural Indiana, Joe spent a good deal of his time with a twelve-gauge double-barrel shotgun, hunting the ruffed grouse that were in the woods surrounding his farm. Acquiring, tracking and shooting a fast- moving target was second nature to him and made him an excellent waist gunner.

The end of the escort flight over Belgium was signaled by the peeling off of the Thunderbolts near the German border. They had used up half their fuel and were turning for home. Flanagan came on the intercom again.

"Ok, there they go. Look sharp. Permission to test your guns." Short bursts of .50 caliber machine gun fire erupted from the eleven guns on each of the planes, four hundred thirty-two .50 caliber guns in all from the Bloody 100th B17s. Such massed firepower gave Joe Hanover and the rest of the crews some comfort. This would be soon stripped away.

"We have entered German airspace. Should not be long now. Call them out when you see them."

Each of the gunners hunched over their machine guns, squinting into the empty skies, wishing for telescopic vision. Joe was aware of the top turret gunner, TSgt. Jason Abrams, who was also the engineer, turning his turret through its full 360 degrees. He knew that the other gunners at their stations were all moving their guns through their full range of motion. Luis Ramon was the left waist gunner, Lt. Stanley Toland, the bombardier, took his place as the nose gunner crouching ahead of TSgt. Paul Phillips, radio operator, at the left cheek, Lt. Samuel Topman, the navigator manned the right cheek gun and literally bringing up the rear, TSgt. Raymond Gilbert, the tail gunner. All the guns were successfully tested. All waited on their targets.

"All planes," Flanagan called out, "we have reached the IP. Begin your turn now." From here onto the target, the formation would be flying straight and level.

First to engage was a Messerschmitt, bf 109G, nicknamed "Gustav", diving through the formation from out of the sun. He streaked through the middle flight of B17s scoring some hits on aft fuselage of the *Boston's Pride* without doing much damage. He flashed by Hanover's gun before he could even register that he was there. Hanover's quick eyes noted the green heart painted on the side of the fighter. The German fighters now were swooping, diving and turning throughout the tight formations of the bombers. Answering fire streamed from the planes. Inside the *Betty* was a cacophony of noise: voices over the intercom, the deep rapid thuds from the .50s and the metallic rain of the shell casings from the guns. The air battle was now fully engaged. Smoke began to stream from the 17s' engines, 109s disappeared in balls of flame. The

Here We Are began to lose altitude, flames visible from her two outboard engines. She was followed by the *Sheila's Rose, I'm Packin'* and the *Stormin' Norman.* Bombers were dropping out of each of the formations but there were no deviations from the flight plan. Pitifully small white dots of parachutes blossomed from some of them sustaining hope, floating down towards the green earth amidst the plummeting planes trailing fire in which burned the crews of friends and enemies alike.

"Joe, Joe, have you got him? Coming round your side."

The question was answered by a cascade of spent .50 caliber shells as Joe Hanover ran a rope of tracers though the retreating "Gustav". He was rewarded by a plume of smoke then the fire ball that had been the German Messerschmitt bf 109G.

"No 'chute from this one," he thought as he scanned the skies over the barrel his .50 caliber through window of the right waist. It was his fourth confirmed kill.

Joe then picked up the black and white spiral painted nose of an oncoming bf 109, closing fast. The German was firing all he had: the twin 15.1 mm machine guns in the engine cowling and the single 20 mm cannon through the propellor hub. Downing this one would all be on Joe. The 109 was on line with the bomber so the upper- and lower-gun turrets could not engage. The German's rounds went screaming through the quarter-inch aluminum of the

Betty's fuselage and out the other side. Panicked voices filled his headset.

"Do you see him, Joe" …" Sweet Jesus, kill that sonofabitch" …" Fire him up, Joe, fer Chrissake…"

Joe made sure of his aim, knowing he and the *Betty*, had one chance at this bastard.

"Joe…Joe…why aren't you firing?" The voices stopped when he depressed the Y-shaped trigger with both his thumbs, sending a streak of tracers into the 109's engine and cockpit. The fighter exploded 500 yards from the ship, its fragments carrying on to strike the *Betty's* sides without damage. They were not out of the woods. .50 caliber shell casings rained down from the top turret.

Voices called out fighters as they flashed by on all sides of the heavy bombers. Joe watched as smoke began to pour out of the *Sweet Emily's* inboard port engine followed by flames then the wing exploding. No chutes were seen. The 109s were joined by Focke-Wulf 190 Ds, the lethal "Doras", armed with two 13 mm machine guns in the engine cowling and two 20 mm cannons in the wing roots climbing from below the B17 formations, hidden beneath the bombers' contrails. The Doras were the beasts of the fighter squadrons. The huge engine drove the plane at a speed and rate of climb that outstripped all but the newest Spitfires Mk IXs and the P-51 Mustangs. It had a tighter turn radius than either of them as well. The FW 190's engine also protected the pilot from frontal attacks and in crash landings.

Frank Paglia of Little Italy, New York City, was the belly turret gunner and he would have to bring down the Dora on his own. Already, the German had his 20mm rounds screeching through the *Betty's* midsection and out the top, barely missing the top turret gunner. Frank was an ideal belly turret gunner, standing 5'4" and 120 pounds. His small stature allowed him more freedom of movement in the tight turret and more agility in shooting down the attackers.

"Hail, Mary, full of grace, the Lord is with thee; blessed..." Frank prayed as he tracked the German fighter. He was a long way from assisting at Mass on Sundays in St. Patrick's Old Cathedral, back home. Unlike the waist gunners, Paglia had an electronic sighting mechanism. His twin handles with the triggers for his two .50 calibers, moved a lighted box which he could expand or contract to fit the enemy fighters' wingtips. When he had them "lit up", the Sperry aiming computer took over and automatically gauged speed and direction thereby calculating the proper lead distance.

"...art thou among women..." When Frank pressed his triggers, the guns fired. All the gunners were trained in two second bursts to save the gun barrels and ammunition. The approaching Dora was unusual in that Paglia had a few more seconds than usual to track the plane, making a kill all but guaranteed.

"...and blessed is the fruit of thy womb, Jesus..." He liked the belly turret better than the top because the sunlight dimmed the light box gunsight, called the reticle, and he had a harder time aligning it with the fighters which generally slashed through his field of vision in a matter of seconds. That and the fact he was too short for the top turret. The top gunner stood on a platform with his head and shoulders in the turret so height was important.

"Holy Mary, Mother of God, pray for us sinners, now and at the hour of our death."

The twined tracers laced into the Dora's engine and wings, exploding his fuel tanks. There was little left of the plane for Paglia to follow down.

"Amen."

The *Betty* was in the lead box of the thirty-six-plane flight. Paglia had an unobstructed view of the rest of the formation and took comfort in the massed firepower a formation of '17s could produce. When *Sweet Emily* spiraled down, her spot was taken by tightening up the formation to minimize the loss of her eleven .50 caliber machine guns to the formation. Paglia could also follow the burning hulks of all the bombers lost so far. They were still a full hour from Munster.

"Fighters at twelve o'clock!", shouted Flanagan. He had spotted a line of Doras coming straight for them.

The Germans knew that by coming straight at the bombers, the amount of firepower was limited to the nose gun and the two cheek guns. The top and bottom turrets could not converge on the 109s. It was up to Toland in the right cheek, Phillips on the left and Topman in the nose to bring down the attacking Doras. The Germans would try to hit the formation between the IP and before the flak over the target when the bombers were flying straight and steady. There was usually one pass at a closing speed of over six hundred miles per hour. The bombers' single .50 in the nose and each .50 from the cheeks opened up. The *Betty* was responsible for the middle two Doras, her wingmen for the outer two. A total of nine machine guns sought out the German fighters.

The Doras did not try to evade or maneuver. A perfectly straight line of machine gun and twenty-millimeter cannon fire unleashed across their front streaked towards the bombers. There was no time to think, no time to breathe, simply react to the approaching row of death. Tracers laced into the Americans in less than a second taking out the bombers on either side of the *Betty* using their twenty-millimeter nose guns with perfectly aimed hits to the cockpits. The *Betty's* nose .50 took out the Dora to her front. The rest of the flight sped past on either side as well as above and below. Puglia was ready for his Dora which did not continue turning as he was trying to line up a shot on another B17. Puglia's guns turned the fighter into a fireball. After twenty minutes of swirling air combat, the FW 190 Doras and the bf 109 Gustavs broke off their attack. That meant the anti-aircraft gunners surrounding Munster would now take over.

Hanover knew when they entered the flak box because the plane began to buck, shudder and reel from the bursts which were getting ever closer. The news at the base in Thorpe Abbotts was the anti-aircraft fire was so much more accurate because the gunners had radar attached to their 88mm guns making the targeting that much better – good news for the Germans, not so much for the Americans.

"Flak! Flak! Flak! Nine o'clock high and three o'clock low."

Joe Hanover hated flak. He fumed at every irregular black cloud the appeared like malignant popcorn in the airspace ahead, above and below them. They had passed the IP, the initial point, made their turn and now flew straight and level on their bomb runs. They had survived the Gustavs and Doras. Now, there was nothing Joe could do except wait to be blown out of the sky.

"The fuckers have got us bracketed already," yelled Lt. Stanley Toland, the bombardier. He moved from his seat manning the .50 caliber in the nose to his Norden bombsight. The *Betty* was the lead plane in the diminished formation. All the other B17s would drop when she did. There were two other planes in the lead formation with Norden bombsights in case the *Betty* was shot down. Toland adjusted his Norden's gyroscope by touching the knobs with a light touch so as not to accidentally throw off the sighting. The twin square towers with peaked green copper rooves of the Munster Cathedral came into view and crept across the bombsight until they were directly under the crosshairs. Toland flipped up the red guard covering the switch that would arm the bombs. He had control of the plane on this final approach, keeping it level and steady until the target was under the crosshair. At that moment, Hanover hated Toland with all his body and soul. He knew Toland kept them flying straight and level far longer than he needed to out of spiteful bravado. He switched off his throat mic and began to scream into his mask.

"Just drop the fucking bombs, you son of a bitch! It's all fucking Germany down there – just drop 'em. Even you are bound to hit something, you sorry cross-eyed bastard. That way, you might not get us killed, you chunk of officer puke."

Toland pressed the bomb release and felt the *Betty* lighten immediately as the eight five-hundred-pound bombs fell away. Behind him, the rest of the group's bomb loads followed his down on the workers leaving their Sunday service twenty-five thousand feet below.

"Bombs away," Toland shouted into the intercom as he released control of the plane back to Flanagan. Immediately, the wild gyrations began to try to avoid the flak. They made a tight turn to the left and climbed in an attempt to lose the flak. Three more planes fell out of the sky from Hanover's squadron alone. Paglia in the ventral ball turret watched four more bombers begin to smoke, then slow, lose altitude and begin their final dive from twenty-five thousand feet. A few 'chutes appeared but not nearly enough. With the bomb load gone, the *Betty* was livelier and while the flight-maintained formation, each plane had more room for maneuver. The flight, fewer in number by six, soon cleared the flak box and headed at top speed to the border and their waiting "little friends", the Thunderbolts.

"Alright, look alive. We're clear of the flak so that means we'll be picking up the fighters soon. You may test your guns, again." Flanagan knew he had one of the most experienced crews in the Bloody 100th and they knew what to do without him telling them. He did it mainly to calm himself and the rest of the crew. They all knew getting out of Germany was as dangerous as getting in. Like clockwork, the first Dora now refueled and rearmed slashed by the cockpit from out of the sun.

"Jesus Christ! That was close. Abrams," he called the top turret gunner, "anymore up there?"

He was answered by a torrent of shell casings raining down. All the guns were manned and firing. The FW 190s and bf 109s swarmed the bombers, their nose and wing guns aflame as they tried to down as many Americans as they could. They had a closing window of time before the bombers' escort P-47s would re-appear to drive them off.

Now the intercom was alive with urgent voices, strident voices, shouting voices but none betraying fear or panic. They were all too busy for that.

"Comin' round your side"..."Pick him up, pick him up"..."two Me's on the starboard"..."Dora diving out of the sun"..."there goes *'Black Sheep'"*..."any 'chutes?"..."shit,shit,shit get that bastard"..."I see him"..."sonuvabitch, that was close"..."they got *Party Girl*"..."our port outboard engine is smoking"..."extinguisher, shut it down"..."Dora dead ahead"..."Left cheek gun is out"..."Herman get down there and see if Phillips is ok, get that gun back in action"..."Jesus, *Dolly's Car* just blew up"..."got that motherfucker"..."n'other one diving on the port side"..."I got him"..."Christ almighty, come on, guys, we're not the only fucking bomber up here...".

The 109s were from the Jadgeschwader III/54 Staffel or fighter squadron. Their planes had a green heart painted on either side of the engine, marking them as the "Green Hearts of Thuringen" squadron. Unlike their American counterparts, there were no American stars or British roundels marking German victories, just simple vertical lines on the rudders. But there was no doubt of their formidable lethality.

Hauptman Jans von Rindel, a veteran of the fight since North Africa, becoming an ace on the Eastern Front, achieving one hundred-fifty of his two hundred kills against the Russian Air Force during the opening stages of Operation Barbarossa, downing Lavochin, La-5 and MiG-3 fighters over Kursk and Leningrad. But when the Ilyushin Il-2, the Shturmovik, fighter joined the fight in ever increasing numbers, the Luftwaffe's bf 109Gs were finding themselves overmatched. Only the most talented or ruthless German fighter pilots could hold their own. Von Rindel was both. The easy hunting days against the older Yak-1s and slow Yermolayev-2 bombers were gone.

In 1944, Hauptman von Rindel and his staffel were transferred to the Western Front for the "Defense of the Reich". Here they faced the American p-47 Thunderbolts, the P-51 Mustangs as well as the Supermarine Spitfire Mark IXs of the RAF flown by well-trained pilots and in seemingly limitless numbers. They protected the fleets of B17s and British Avro Lancasters which sustained the day and night bombing of Germany.

Captain Hauptman was a classically trained pianist from Heidelberg. His father, a Prussian of the old school, was an ace from the Great War, with twenty-five victories in his Albatross D.2 biplane. When his son, Jans entered the Heidelberg Academy to pursue music, his father disowned him. Von Rindel was of average height, tall enough to see over the engine of his Messerschmitt. His long tapering fingers grasped the joystick lightly and during times when there was no combat, he tapped out Beethoven symphonies in his head. The 7th, the "Pastoral", was his favorite.

Von Rindel's staffel was a combined group of FW 190 "Doras" and bf 109 "Gustavs". The loss of fighters and their airfields meant the Luftwaffe could not sustain individual fighter groups. Hitler prioritized bomber production over fighters so the staffels shrank as a result. The staffel flew out of Elsenborn near Monschau and Aachen. His wingman was a young Lieutenant named Hans Griebel. The nimbler Gustavs protected the Doras which pressed the main attack against the bomber formations. The Germans knew they had only a small window of opportunity between leaving the "flak box" over Munster and reaching the border with France where the P-47 Thunderbolts would re-join the fight to escort the remaining bombers home.

The German pilots were used to flying in loose formations that broke apart when they attacked the bomber formations, each plane becoming a lone hunter. Von Rindel's bf 109 swept under the belly of the *Bombs Away* sustaining some hits from the belly turret and drove up through the formation taking advantage of the stacking of the bombers so that three B17s were in his sights before he broke through the top of the formation. All too soon for the German fighters, the Thunderbolts were back. He peeled away in a tight barrel roll hoping to shake off any P-47 that was waiting for him. Von Rindel looked around as he came out of his roll. Off to his left were two P-47s, known as "Jugs" because of their squat, squared off profiles. They seemed not to have seen him yet. The top turret gunners on three B17s had not lost sight of him, however, and were concentrating their fire.

Lieutenant Flanagan of the *Bouncing Betty* keyed his mic to the inter-ship frequency. "Eagle Flight 365, this is lead ship, *Bouncing Betty,* I've got at least three Doras and four Gustavs on us. Can you give us a hand?"

"Roger, *Betty*, on the way."

One of the P-47s stayed above as the "cap" while four others from "the neighborhood" swept down on the beleaguered formation. On the first pass, one Dora went down in flames. Von Rindel shoved his stick hard to port and down, diving for the deck. Three P-47s followed. Although, the Messerschmitt could out dive the Americans, they had the advantage of already being in their dives and gaining speed. Von Rindel cranked his stick hard to starboard and pulled back, hoping the Americans would fly by him. One of them did, two did not. Von Rindel stayed in his tight roll taking advantage of the shorter turning radius to get behind the Thunderbolts. The two Americans flashed into his gun sight and he let loose with his twin 7.93mm MG17s mounted in the engine cowling. The tracers streamed into one of the Americans which began to trail thick smoke from his engine and almost immediately began his final dive. His wingman climbed hard and to the right but Von Rindel had no trouble staying with him. Short bursts flew passed the P-47 as he engaged in more frantic evasive maneuvers. They dove for the deck together, twisting and turning, the American slowly pulling away. Von Rindel concentrated, trying to anticipate the American's next turn.

"Come right, this time," he said to himself, "and I've got you." The American did pull right, von Rindel slowly squeezed his trigger but his aim was pulled off by the arrival of the other P-47 on his tail. Von Rindel put four to five rounds into the notoriously tough P-47 before a stream of .50 caliber rounds struck his tail and right wing. The Messerschmitt shook, the cockpit began to fill with smoke and von Rindel knew it was time to go. He did not know how much time he had before he exploded or the bf 109 became uncontrollable. He put the nose down and dove for the deck. The P-47 Thunderbolt stayed with him, still firing. Von Rindel pulled his nose up with difficulty and blew the explosive bolts of his canopy. Smoke billowed out around him as he struggled with his harness. Finally, he was free, stood up and jumped out of his cockpit. The P-47 pilot took one more fly-by when Von Rindel's parachute opened, pulling him away from his plummeting plane. The thought that the American might finish him off ran through his mind but the American instead pulled a hard right and climbed back into the fight. Soon the only job for the Thunderbolts would be to escort the remaining B17s back to England.

Von Rindel was uninjured. The sharp upward jerk of his open 'chute was the best feeling in the world. He was unsure how high he was when he bailed out but the frigid air rushing by him and his gasping for breath let him know he was still above eight thousand feet. Far below, he saw black columns of smoke from the crashed fighters and bombers. Now that the P-47s had arrived, von Rindel knew the rest of his squadron would be heading back to their airfields. His job now was to make it to the ground safely and avoid capture by the Free French forces who had no love for Germans generally and flyers in particular. He was more worried about freezing to death during his fall to the ground. His relatively thin flight suit had depended on electric heat from his plane that was now smoking rubble on the ground. He gathered himself into as tight a ball as he could to conserve heat and concentrated on his strategy for evasion once he was on the ground.

As he descended, he began to pick out features on the ground. He maneuvered towards the woods. Landing in trees was very risky but at least offered concealment from the Maquis, the Free French resistance fighters. Trees could beat you up but they did not shoot you on sight. In pre-flight briefings, the Luftwaffe major put particular emphasis on need for caution once on the ground. It was likely that if shot down, the pilots would still land on German occupied territory. But the Maquis fighters were increasingly everywhere, emboldened by the Nazi retreat after Normandy. The trick for von Rindel was to find the German Army before the Maquis found him. He also knew that many sets of eyes were watching what and who fell out of the sky during the air battle.

He landed about twenty feet up in the tree and cut himself free of the parachute harness. Climbing down from the last branch, he heard muffled voices which appeared to be coming towards him. His ears were still blocked due to the pressure change. Von Rindel retreated further into the woods, gripping his 9mm Luger pistol. He finally cleared his ears only to hear, a German voice say, "Hande hoch: Hands up" with an encouraging poke in his back from a rifle muzzle. He dropped the pistol and stood slowly up.

"Oh, excuse me, Herr Hauptman. I did not recognize you. Are you hurt?"

Von Rindel relaxed and smiled at the flustered infantry private. "Don't worry, Private. Can you bring me to your officers?"

They gathered in the parachute and within half an hour, von Rindel was having schnapps and wurst with the infantry company commander. Transport back to his base was soon arranged and he was flying again within a week.

Joe Hanover felt he could relax when the last of the fighters had peeled off. He put his .50 caliber on safe and turned to talk with the left waist gunner, Luis Ramon. Joe had felt the *Betty* take several hits but as there did not seem to be any decrease in her speed, he dismissed them as not serious. As he turned around, his foot slipped on the pile of spent shells, lying in a pool of blood. Luis' head had been taken off by flak sometime over the bombing run. Everyone on the *Betty* was so intent on fighting off the Germans that no one noticed the left waist gun was inactive. Now there was nothing to do but lay Ramon out and cover him. The job of retrieving his head from rolling around the deck was up to Hanover. He tucked it under Ramon's arm and pulled his flight jacket up over his shoulders.

"Everybody call in," said Flanagan over the intercom. One by one the positions reported. Joe came last.

"Hanover, right waist, I'm ok. Luis has bought it."

LeMay chimed in, "Make a proper report, airman. Give his position and nature of his wound." Everyone on the plane was affronted by the rudeness, General or no. It was clear, LeMay had not been a crew member for a very long time. Hanover remained silent.

"Well, report his condition," LeMay persisted with growing anger.

"Left waist. Flak blew his fucking head off," Hanover said angrily, whispering, "You prick."

After a pause during which Hanover assumed LeMay was working on his courts marshal charges, LeMay keyed his mic and said, "That's 'flak blew his fucking head off, Sir.'"

Things began to fall apart, literally, for the *Betty.* She had taken more hits than, in the heat of battle, the crew had appreciated. The port outboard engine was dead, smoke and flame came from the left inboard, which the extinguisher in the wing put out, the tail was nearly shot away and they were losing airspeed and altitude. Flanagan felt it likely they would have to ditch in the Channel, with LeMay on board. Flanagan cared more about his crew than the General but realized losing the commander of the 3rd Air Division would not be a career building move.

"Everyone, we've got to lighten the ship. Throw out whatever you can. Phillips, get on the horn and let Air-Sea Rescue know our position. We're about eighty miles from home. We've been through worse than this." The *Betty* shed her machine guns, extra ammunition, any flight gear and finally the Norden bombsight. They would dump their fuel when they got closer. That only slowed their rate of fall. No one knew if they had bought themselves enough air to make it home over the cliffs of Dover.

The shuddering of the ship worsened, smoke began to stream from the port inboard engine, low oil alarms were going off in the cockpit. Flanagan glanced over at LeMay and was heartened to see that "Old Iron Bottom" seemed shaken. They were now over the Channel with a max speed of one hundred fifty knots but that was dropping. Toland shouted, "There are the cliffs." Their base at Thorpe Abbotts was another ten miles inland. Hope began to rise that they might just make it. Flanagan was fighting the *Betty's* strong pull to the right due to her damaged tail and stabilizer. Their speed and altitude continued dropping raising the real possibility of crashing into the Dover cliffs. They were already too low to safely bail out. It was on Flanagan to get them home. Toland in the nose could see flocks of sheep grazing and small farmsteads that they would plow into if they could not maintain some speed.

They cleared the cliffs by one

hundred feet, scattering the sheep. Up ahead Toland spotted the field. "Thorpe Abbotts ahead," he shouted. Flanagan was pulling back on his wheel and turning it to the left with all his might.

"Wheels down?" asked LeMay, his hand on the levers.

"No, the drag will drive us right into the ground." To the crew he said as calmly as he could, "Prepare for wheels up landing. Brace yourselves."

Throughout the *Betty,* the crew jammed their feet against the bulkheads and wrapped their arms around anything they could. Hanover hung onto his gun mount and braced against the ribbing of the fuselage. They were now at one hundred feet, making barely one hundred knots. The calculation was between maintaining enough forward movement and speed versus hitting the ground so hard that the Betty would flip over. Flanagan cut the two remaining engines, dumped the remaining fuel through the fuel vents under each wing and nudged the stick forward, keeping her as level as possible.

"Brace for impact," he shouted. They were a quarter mile short of the runway, too far for the crash crews to be of any help. The belly turret hit first and was sheared away. The nose dipped and the propellors dug into the soft earth. She bounced twice and skewed to the left before coming to rest.

"Everybody out", he shouted but no one needed any prompting. The crew gathered one hundred yards from the smoking *Betty.* The fuel dump had prevented her from exploding. The fire trucks came careening over the rough pasture land but were not needed. The ambulance collected Luis Ramon. The crew accepted a ride back to the field while arrangements were made to bring the *Betty* in for possible repair or scavenging her usable parts.

Two days later, Flanagan was surveying the damage with LeMay who had understandably taken an interest in the *Bouncing Betty.* She did have an impressive number of holes in her but the repair crew chief assured Flanagan that they could get her flying again.

LeMay made a big show of pointing out all the holes he thought should be patched. The grizzled sergeant leading the repair efforts said, "No disrespect, General, but we ain't gonna patch those. We're gonna up armor the parts not shot up. After all, she made it back here, didn't she?"

Chapter Two: Spearhead

The four Sherman M4A3 tanks idled quietly, separated by ten yards, the barrels of their 76mm cannons barely broke through the tree line and overlooked a crossroad. The tank commanders stood up through their hatches, each scanning with their binoculars. TSgt. Enfield Davis of *Hell's Fire,* in command of the first platoon, Co. A, 707th Battalion, 3rd Armored Division, had landed with his tank on the second day of the Normandy invasion, D-Day+2. He started out as a loader but steadily worked his way through all the positions of the tank until he was in charge of the platoon. Next in command was TSgt. Ramon Suarez of *Adolph's Nightmare,* followed by TSgt. William Soames, *Death Wagon* and Sgt. Herman Manns of *Ronna's Revenge,* named for the lingering, painful, effects of a one-night stand in Paris.

The platoon was formed by grouping the survivors of other platoons soon after the breakout of the French hedgerow country, called the bocage. They were now rolling towards Aachen and the German border by way of the Monschau Corridor along the French-Belgium border. *Nightmare* still had the Douglas hedgerow cutter called the "Rino" jutting out in front of the tracks. These two triangular plates were very effective in ramming through the thick vegetation of the French bocage countryside just inland from Omaha beach. That meant that Suarez was the lead tank, a position, he had mentioned several times, he would be glad to relinquish.

"What is that?" Suarez whispered into his mic.

"Where?" Davis replied

"Left, three hundred yards, just in the tree line. You see it?"

"Oh, shit. That is the barrel of a Panther." Davis notified the other three tanks and they all acknowledged the sighting. "I don't think he's seen us yet." He rotated the turret with the hand wheel until his sight was just a few feet aft of the barrel. The loader, Pvt. Sam Peters, rammed home a 76 mm high explosive, armor piercing, a HEAP, round. The other three tank crews were doing the same.

"On my mark we fire. Three, two, one...Fire!"

Simultaneously the four Shermans fired on the Panther tank which disappeared in smoke and fire.

"Move, move. *Nightmare*, *Wagon* cut down the road see if there are any more. *Revenge*, you're with me." The Shermans burst forth from the tree line and separated as ordered. Enfield Davis in *Hell's Fire* cut across the meadow with *Ronna's Revenge* 20 yards behind him. Both tanks had their cannon traversed toward the hostile tree line, each with a 76 mm round ready to go. The tank commanders were behind their .50 caliber machine guns, scanning the forest's edge.

"Talk to me, *Nightmare*, anything down there?" Davis barked into the mic.

"Negative so far," Suarez answered.

"Nothing here.... Oh, shit," Davis's answer was cut short by the *Hell's Fire* being raked by a MG34 light machine gun from the tree line. Davis dropped back down into the turret even as his gunner was turning the main gun.

"Fire." The main cannon belched smoke and the tank rocked backward. The BOG, bow gunner, TSgt. Stanley Grisham, laced the grass and trees with the .30 caliber coaxial machine gun as Corporal Roger Emmonds, the driver, gunned the tank towards the trees. *Ronna's Revenge* came on line with Davis and it's .30 caliber added to the volume of fire. Her gunner, Sgt. Larry Rounds, replaced the HEAP round with a white phosphorus round and lit the tree line up.

All was quiet when the smoke cleared. Davis scanned the area through his periscope to find any other likely targets. Buttoned up in his turret, he could not hear explosions erupting behind him down the road where *Death Wagon* and *Adolph's Nightmare* were engaging with the rest of the German force trying to retreat. Suarez called in over the inter-tank radio.

"*Hell's Fire*, you flushed 'em. We've got a Panther, personnel carrier and some infantry trying to vamoose by us." The report was interrupted by their main cannon and machine gun firing as well as hits on the American tank.

"On our way, *Nightmare*," replied Davis. Both tanks reversed and turned toward the crossroads. The trees had thinned closer to the road and Davis called to his driver, "Head through those trees, maybe we can cut them off."

The two Shermans crashed through the trees and underbrush, gaining the road beyond where the rest of the tank platoon was heavily engaged with the Panther tank. The personnel carrier was already smoking rubble.

Death Wagon was to the right and a little ahead of *Hell's Fire* so had the clearer shot. A 76 mm HEAP round already in the breach. Sgt. Joe Mac Farlane, the gunner, lined up on the base of the Panther's turret and fired. It was the only place that single round could hope to take it out. His aim was perfect and the Panther's turret blew off, fire erupting from within the tank.

"Great shot, Joe," Davis shouted into the mic. The German infantry seemed to have melted away, but not completely. A parting shot from a Panzerfaust round hit the right track of *Nightmare*, blowing it off.

"*Nightmare*, everybody OK?" Davis called into the platoon mic.

"Yeah, we're fine, just the track."

"We'll form on you." The three remaining tanks formed a defensive perimeter around *Nightmare.* Davis called for a tank retriever to come up from the depot near St. Vith. Each of the tanks' turrets were turning to scan for trouble, their commanders standing to their .50 caliber machine guns. Manns, commanding *Ronna's Revenge,* saw an approaching plane, too far yet for a positive identification but he chambered a round in his .50 caliber anyway.

"Enfield," he called over the inter-tank net, "we've got company closing fast at 3 o'clock. Each commander swung his machine gun around and started tracking the as yet unknown plane.

At one thousand yards, Soames shouted, "It's a Messerschmitt!" and unleashed his machine gun. The others followed suit. Simultaneously, the German fired his rockets and his 20mm nose cannon. He strafed the tanks and passed over them at better than four hundred miles per hour. The rockets missed wide to both sides but the armor piercing 20mm shells made direct, penetrating hits on *Death Wagon* and *Revenge.* The round that hit *Revenge* went through without hitting anything or anybody. *Wagon* was not so lucky. The round was slowed by the one-inch plate, separated by an inch of open space, affixed to the side of the tank. That slowed it enough to enter the tank and ricochet around the interior.

"Get out, get out!", Soames, the tank commander shouted to an already emptying tank. The hatches were thrown open. Stukey, the driver and Holland, the loader bailed out the starboard side, Johns, the BOG and Mac Farlane, the gunner, dove out the port hatch, with Soames launching himself out the top. The 20 mm round struck the 76 mm rounds stored low in the tank cabin. Although they were using "wet storage" with the rounds sitting in a water bath to lessen the chance of spontaneous detonation, the 20 mm's explosive charge lit most of them up and *Death Wagon* exploded, sending spouts of flame through the open hatches. The rounds still remaining cooked off as did the belts of .50 caliber machine gun ammo. *Death Wagon* rocked back and forth in her final death throes. Her crew scattered to the remaining tanks which took off down the road towards St. Vith, leaving behind *Wagon's* smoking hulk.

Lieutenant Kristan Mautel, flying in the same staffel as von Rindel, did a victory barrel roll seeing the American tank explode. As he pulled out of the roll, he noted his beloved bf 109 was sluggish and slow to respond. One of the .50 caliber rounds from *Death Wagon* had clipped the line to his hydraulic stabilizer making turning difficult. He was getting into more trouble as he lost hydraulic fluid and his fighter began to spiral down. He pushed forward on his canopy release handle and then thrust upward. The airstream caught the canopy and ripped it from the plane. Mautel undid his seat belt and shrugged out of his shoulder straps. Freed up from his seat, he fell out of his spinning plane. He fought off passing out and disorientation as he tumbled in the slip stream. Desperately, he groped this chest until he found the ripcord to his parachute.

"Gott sei Dank", he said as his chute opened.

Swinging in a slow descent, he watched his Messerschmitt twist down to earth ending in a violent fireball. He landed hard on his right ankle sustaining a severe sprain which kept him from being able to clear his chute before the French partisans arrived, taking him captive. Luckily for him, rather than shooting him outright, he was turned over to the British. He spent the rest of the war at Eden POW Camp, Yorkshire, tending his garden.

Enfield Davis led his two remaining tanks back to the depot at St. Vith. On the way, they were over flown by a flight of four P-51 Mustangs heading back down the road in search of the remaining German force, hoping to find more Panzers or Panthers. He pulled his tanks into their company area, leaving their crews to see to refueling and rearming. He reported to the company orderly room and his commander to give his after action report.

"Come in, Davis, at ease," said Captain Buck Ramsey, his tank company commander. "I hear you ran into some of our friends back at the cross roads."

"Yes, Sir. Best we can tell it was two Panthers with an APC and some infantry. The platoon took care of the one at the crossroads. They evidently were able to get off a call for air support before we got them. That SOB got some hits on *Revenge* and took out *Death Wagon,* but everybody got out. I think we may have gotten a hit on the Me but can't be sure. Then we rejoined the rest of the platoon who had already taken care of the other Panther and APC. All in all, a pretty good day for our side," Davis finished.

"Indeed," Ramsey replied. "In fact, that Me did crash so you can claim that kill as well. I can't think the Krauts can keep this up for much longer. They seem to be just roving patrols, isolated units, hitting targets of opportunity rather than mounting any kind of coordinated counterattacks. Look at today: two tanks, an APC, a Messerschmitt and an infantry patrol stacked against one Sherman without losing any men. They can't keep that up for much longer.

"Well, not our problem, is it, Sergeant?" his captain continued. "We've got the crossroads covered. You and your men can stand down for a couple of days. Get some sleep and hot chow. We'll fit you up with a new tank and send you out again in a couple of days."

"Sounds fine, Sir."

"Dismissed."

#

The infantrymen from the 112th Pennsylvania National Guard which had been mobilized in 1941, two months before Pearl Harbor and landed two days after D-Day, and by Fall,1944, were patrolling in the Huertgen Forest. The dark, wet forest imparted a sense of dread and impending violence, as if they were watched by a brooding malignant presence. The men walked stooped over and talked in hushed tones as if the forest was listening. The villages on the high ground commanded the road network and views of the surrounding terrain, deeply riven by ravines and the gorge of the Kall River. The steep, heavily forested sides plunged to the narrow, swift river only to climb again to the bald top of the ridge containing the villages of Kommerscheidt and Schmidt.

There were actually three forests: the Huertgan, Ardennes and the Eifel. German artillery observers could watch over the arrival of the American units as they closed on the Huertgan. Lt. General Courtney Hodges, commanding 1st Army, felt he must have the Huertgan Forest cleared to secure his right flank for his advance to the Roer River. To do that, the Americans had to breach the one-to-two-mile breadth of fortifications, tank traps, pillboxes, minefields, of the Siegfried Line which undulated across their path. All while traversing the killing fields of the

German 88mm guns, known simply as "88s". These were magnificent guns: rugged, easy to maintain in the field, lethal against troops, tanks, hardened emplacements, artillery or aircraft. They could be towed, mounted on a truck, installed in a permanent bunker and light enough that four men could position it as the changing battlefield environment required. The "88" became the main gun on Panther I and II tanks as well as the Jagdpanther tank destroyers. It could fire fifteen twenty-pound shells per minute accurately over 14,000 meters. The guns obliterated any hope for safety or even respite for the 112th.

#

"Medic! Medic! Goddam it, Medic!"

TSgt. Douglas Aiken, combat field medic of the 103rd Medical Battalion, attached to Company G, 112th Regiment, Pennsylvania National Guard, 28th Infantry Division, heard the first calls for a medic as if he was in a long tunnel. This was the first sleep of more than two hours he had had since the assault on the Roer River had begun early August, 1944, four weeks ago. It took him a few seconds to orient himself and find where the shouting was coming from, although the cause was well known to him. He pulled himself out of the frigid water filling half his foxhole. He lay flat before moving in case one of the German snipers in the trees had seen him. Scrambling along on his hands and knees, Aiken made his way towards the wounded point man, well into the minefield which engulfed the point platoon.

Aiken pictured the German sniper, felt a tingling sensation which he imagined was the aiming point of the Karabiner 98k sniper rifle's six-power telescopic sight on the back of his head, tracking him through the mines. The sniper hoped Aiken would be disintegrated by one of the hundreds of fatal S-mines sown like lethal wheat along the approaches to the Huertgan Forest, rather than having to shoot him and possibly give away his position. The mines were also known as "Bouncing Betty" mines because they sprang from the earth before they detonated, spewing two hundred ball bearings in all directions. It was very rare for anyone to survive triggering one. Aiken knew he was approaching a very lucky infantryman: one with only his lower leg blown off.

"I am not dead yet," as Aiken thought of the sniper, "because he wants us to be together when he shoots us." He hoped the engineers had cleared the mines immediately in front of the forward foxholes so that he would survive long enough to be shot by the sniper. "This is what my life has boiled down to: waiting to die by at least two different means, probably more, but I'm just not creative enough to think up more ways." Aiken knew what he would find when he reached the man. The S-mines mines were marvels of lethal German engineering, reliable and usually fatal.

Aiken was right in assuming he was in a sniper's crosshairs. Private Klaus Wiesen grew up in the dense forests of Bavaria. He came from a family of skilled hunters. Patience, concealment, silent moving through the trees became second nature for him by the time he was four. His grandfather, himself a renowned and fearless hunter of wild boar, took Klaus on hunting trips with him. The Wiesen family was the main source of meat for the small village of Fussen, Bavaria.

When he joined the Wehrmacht, his prowess with a rifle was noted early on by his instructors and he was assigned to the sniper school outside Berlin. He rapidly went through the four-week sniper course with little needed instruction from the tutors, themselves often invalided soldiers who were no longer fit for the front but had a wealth of experience to impart. By the second week, Klaus was "wedded" to his K98 carbine equipped with the six-power scope. The "shooting garden" was his favorite activity of the entire course. This was a manufactured landscape with miniaturized villages, farms, hills, houses and trenches to give the illusion of distance. Papier-mâché figures of soldiers, jeeps, artillery pieces with their toy crew, all built to scale to appear to be three to five hundred yards away. Down range were instructors pulling the figures along to simulate movement along roads or they could be made to appear or disappear in windows and doorways of houses.

Klaus visited the shooting garden every day making near perfect scores from the first day. His hunting skills fit his training. His instructors made use of them setting Klaus field problems requiring him to remain silent, motionless and concealed for hours before they presented a target for him. He excelled at camouflage and could hit his target from tree, field or trench. Klaus stripped the fabric from an umbrella and attached fresh leaves or grasses in keeping with his surroundings, to the spokes, to create his own shooter's blind. He preferred to hunt alone. Just having another body near him degraded the intense concentration needed for him to be ready when the target appeared. The sniper trainees had access to unlimited ammunition, including the special, very expensive "Beobachter" or observation rounds. These were bullets that were used in place of tracer rounds, exploding on impact. They were extremely damaging to buildings as well as bodies but the advantage of being untraceable back to the sniper more than made up for their expense. They were issued only to the most expert of the snipers. With all his skills Klaus was only a private, two years into the war. His supervisors noted he preferred to wound his targets in such a way that their service was over. His instructors sneered at his "delicacies" and lack of the killer instinct but he was too important on the battlefield to remove him. So, he remained a private, but in the fight.

#

Days and nights of trying to penetrate the dense, dark Huertgan Forest, had made Aiken's sight and hearing more acute. They gave him a sixth sense of when he was being watched as well. This sense was setting off alarm bells in his brain the moment he left his foxhole. He crept forward, wondering if he should probe with his bayonet the uncertain ground ahead of him. He knew the wounded GI did not have enough time for him to be finding mines. Besides, he thought, somewhat giddy with fear, he would be like the car-chasing dog: "What would I do if I found one?" Waiting for the engineers to defuse it would take too long. The best outcome of digging it up himself would be that it killed him outright. Crawling around it made him as likely to crawl onto another one as not. He remembered a crude map of the minefields the engineers did provide, more as a deterrent to anyone wanting to wander around than to inform. It seemed the minefields were laid out in radiating pattern so that there were lanes that were mine free. His wounded man was off a straight line from Aiken and therefore, moving straight ahead might be the best course. Not going after his man was never a consideration. Aiken took a deep breath of the damp, fetid air, rich with rot and death, and scrambled forward.

His helmet with the red cross in a white circle, the arm band and the red cross on his field bag made it clear that he was a medic and no threat to the German sniper. The war for the GI was clearly over, so Aiken hoped there was enough humanity in the sniper to spare their lives.

"Oh, God, you came, thank you, thank you. I've got a little girl I haven't seen and..." the GI cried with relief when Aiken reached him.

"That's ok, save your strength. I'm going to give you some morphine and then get a tourniquet on that leg and get us out of here." Aiken stuck him with two syrettes, then slit the shredded pant leg up, applied the tourniquet. The leg was not completely blown off so Aiken severed the rest of it with his bayonet. He tossed it to one side, triggering a mine. The fatal ball bearings buzzed over their heads.

"Jesus fucking Christ," he said, brushing the dirt off the GI's stump.

He worked quickly, worried that the sniper's patience might wear thin or some other German would spot and shoot them. Aiken applied a field dressing to the stump, securing the ties under the tourniquet. Next, he cut the GI's pack off and his web belt to make him as light and easy to drag as possible. Aiken left the GI's M1 Garand rifle and hand grenades, knowing any attempt to bring them away would get them both shot by the watching sniper. Aiken got them aligned on his tracks and in a half crouch, began the twenty-yard journey back to his waiting platoon, dragging the unconscious man behind him. Still, Klaus held his fire. Through his scope, he could see Aiken's face under his helmet. Already impressed by the American medic's courage, the look of concentrated concern for his wounded man gave him one more reason to hold his fire. Eager hands grabbed them both and pulled them into a foxhole.

Aiken had parked his M29 "Weasel", a small tracked all-purpose carrier about the size of a Jeep, just behind the line of foxholes. The GI was loaded onto a stretcher on the Weasel, then started the rough half mile trip down the valley side to the aide station established at Mestrenger Mill, near the stone bridge across the Kall River.

There had been some sort of mill for grain on the east bank of the Kall River for at least two hundred years. A lazy bend in the river allowed deposition of soil to form a flat plain about one hundred yards wide. The gorge rapidly narrowed upstream and downstream from there. It was natural, therefore, that a stone bridge crossed at that point joining the torturous tracks descending from the thousand-foot heights of the valley walls, topped by tracts of forest and open meadow containing the villages of Gemeter and Vossennack on the west and Kommerscheidt and Schmidt on the east. These towns were sprinkled among the trees of the Huertgan, Eifel and Ardennes forests which formed a nightmare Brothers Grimm landscape. The forest had grown out of a planned plantation of fir trees, long left unharvested. They grew to over one hundred feet with interlocking boughs overhead, blocking sunlight from the forest floor, keeping it relatively clear of undergrowth. Even on the brightest days, which were becoming rare with the onset of fall, the gloom below the canopy was oppressive.

Aiken arrived with his unconscious GI strapped on the litter. More medics came out and brought him inside the mill, placing him on sawhorse litter stands. Very quickly, they had his tattered fatigues off, looking for more wounds. The tourniquet Aiken had applied had loosened in transit and the field dressing was soaked through, dripping blood on the mill's gore-spattered floor. The morphine was beginning to wear off as well, causing moans and cries from the injured man. He was shaking violently, teeth clenched so hard they were in danger of cracking. His breath whistled through them as sweat dripped from his bone-white torso.

The aide station had a surgeon, eight medics, assorted runners and drivers. Triage was conducted without regard to rank, or even which army, only the severity of the wounds mattered. It was sheer chance that the man Aiken brought in arrived during a rare lull. Aiken tried to help but it became clear that he would only be in the way of the well-honed, orchestrated handling of the wounded. This gave Aiken a chance to look around. The former mill, now a forward aide station, had stone walls and floor making up the first floor. The second story was timbered. The waterwheel still turned in the current of the Kall River but was disconnected from the grinding wheel inside. There was a large door for the grain wagons to bring the grain in for milling. The grain elevator was operated by hand and used to get the grain up to the second floor where it was poured down a chute, feeding the grinding wheel. Now, the second floor served as a recovery room and the elevator had been converted to raise stretchers of post-op cases to await evacuation. Any old mill equipment that could be removed had been to allow more space for the incoming wounded. The walls, floor and grinding wheel were all dappled with blood - dried and fresh.

"Krump! KRUmp!! KRUMP!!!"

"Incoming, incoming! Get them down," shouted Dr. Albert Brendt, commanding officer and chief surgeon of the mill/aide station. "Sergeant, get on the horn and let the CP know if they can't suppress that fire, we are going to have to evacuate – again."

The last 8cm GrW 34 mortar round landed ten yards outside the large front doors of the mill, sending frags thumping into the two-inch thick Bavarian oak. They were relatively safe from anything but a plunging round through the wooden roof and upper story but the steep trajectory of the German mortars made them especially dangerous to the aide station and its occupants.

The aide station was currently held by the Americans but had changed hands several times due to the ebb and flow of the battle for the Huertgen Forest. Both sides had made use of the structure for the care and evacuation of their wounded. Inevitably, that meant that the men too grievously wounded to survive the jarring ride up the steep valley sides, Americans to the west, Germans to the east, were left behind. Each side trusted the other to look after their wounded. With time, the number of these resident wounded grew. Unofficial ceasefires were called to evacuate some of the men as well as bring in more wounded from the forest to replace them.

The mortar fire was not slackening and Dr. Brandt gave the order to move those wounded who could be moved onto Weasels and Jeeps for the tortuous ride up the west wall of the valley to a temporary aid station half way up the Kall Trail. Progress up the trail was impeded by rock outcroppings and disabled tanks. These had to be negotiated by the drivers further delaying the transfers. The ride was so jarring that IV lines were pulled out, tourniquets dislodged, men bounced off their litters and were pitched onto the steep hillsides. The same held true for the Germans on the east side of the river. Their road had many sharp cutbacks as it climbed the thousand feet to the ridge line. On both sides the wounded were exposed to cold drizzle turning to sleet or snow heralding the early approach of one of the worst winters in memory.

There were now too many resident wounded in the mill to leave without a doctor. Brandt nominated himself for the job. He looked up from one more amputation to see a German major standing in the doorway. Near panic, Brandt looked beyond him to see if there were German soldiers as well. He saw none.

"Herr Doctor," said the officer, clicking his heels with a slight bow. "I am Oberstabartz Genter von Stettgen, surgeon with the 272nd Volks-Grenadier Division." His English was accented with the clipped cadence of an aristocrat who had been educated in England, possibly Oxford. The major looked every bit as dirty and tired as Brandt did. He was over six feet tall. Three days' gray grizzle coated his firm jaw. His blue eyes were bright, lively and the only things about him that did not speak of over whelming exhaustion. His uniform was stiffened with dried mud and the blood of many soldiers. "May I propose an extended truce? One that will allow us to do our duty to our men?"

Without stopping his work, Brandt asked, "What do you have in mind, Major?"

"You will agree that it is beyond pointless to keep doing as we are doing: evacuating then re-occupying only to retreat again. All the while leaving more of our men behind with gaps in their needed care. I suggest that we simply stay here and try to save the men for whom the war is over but not, hopefully, their lives as well. We pool our resources, personnel and save as many lives as we can."

Brandt severed the last of the tendons and muscle holding the young infantryman's leg to his thigh. It dropped into a canvas bag, blood saturated and already half full. The new blood seeped out of the bag to join the old blood on the stained cement floor of the mill.

"I think that is an excellent idea - crazy, but a welcome relief from the rest of this madness. But I don't think our generals would like it so much."

"True, but you and I are the ranking officers here. When was the last time you saw anyone of higher rank down in this sink of hell? I can tell you my commanders, heroes of the Reich every one of them, are safely installed in deep, dry bunkers well to the rear. I suspect yours are as well."

"Truth to tell, I don't think I have seen anyone recently, now that you mention it," replied Brandt as he secured the dressing to the young man's stump, who began to shake violently as the anesthesia was wearing off.

"It would be simple," continued von Stettgen, "to give status updates to our respective sides, making them think that the aide station is in safe hands. That would make the shelling stop, at least. Under the truce we could evacuate our men much more efficiently and with safety." Von Stettgen moved farther into the room to help transfer the American soldier onto a litter. That act more than anything else convinced Brandt that here was a doctor first and enemy second.

"You've got a deal, Major," Brandt said. "How do you want to get started?"

Between them, the two surgeons had a total of sixteen medics, four vehicles and an ever-renewing supply of wounded. The Americans had two Beecher anesthesia machines which could administer sodium pentothal, nitrous oxide or ether. Ether was probably the best agent in terms of quickly inducing unconsciousness, muscle relaxation and rapid recovery. The difficulty was that gas leaked from the anesthesia masks applied to the wounded men and after a short period of time made the operating teams groggy. It was extremely explosive as well, an obvious draw back as the aide station was frequently under attack. Von Stettgen's truce would lessen that danger somewhat, if the generals fell for the deception.

A space was cleared for a second operating table and the two surgeons were soon working side-by-side, sharing the two anesthesia machines. By being able to stay in one place, the surgical output more than doubled. Evacuations up the steep sides of the river valley greatly facilitated the work as well. The drivers left with a couple of stabilized wounded and returned with supplies. The drivers and medics of both sides were happy to join in the subterfuge and never let on at their respective, larger clearing stations.

Von Stettgen's first case was an American with a partially amputated arm and a gash to his abdomen through which extruded loops of bowel. The medic in the field had done what he could: applied the tourniquet and springled the wounds with sulfa powder. His field dressings were not big enough to contain the bowels so he had wrapped the abdomen with the GI's field jacket and tied the arms across his back. Caring for such extensive wounds was far beyond the capabilities of an ad hoc aide station but doing nothing condemned the twenty-year-old to certain death. In the cold of the converted mill, steam rose from open belly intermingling with Major von Stettgen's frosted breath.

"There is no scent of feces, at least," he thought, "that's something." Then aloud to the nearest medic, "Come here and hold this over his guts." Von Stettgen handed a moist towel from the med kit to the stunned medic. Facing shells and bullets in the field while retrieving wounded men did not faze the medic at all but holding loose intestines was almost too much for him. Seeing this, von Stettgen said, "Steady now. This is the most important thing you can do for your comrade right now."

The feeble grey light that had seeped to the bottom of the Kall valley was now retreating up the valley walls and lingered in the tops of the fir trees. The shortening days of the fall provided scant illumination and little warmth. The station had only a few kerosene lanterns hanging over the tables. The surgeons were constantly leaning into the light, trying to see into the wounds. Major Brandt was trying to clamp a spurting bleeder deep in the thigh of a German infantryman but every time he leaned for a look, his head's shadow blotted out the view. He was just clamping blindly without hitting his mark.

"Goddamit!", he said in mounting frustration, "I don't have time for this shit and neither does he. Here," he said to a medic, "hold the damn light right over the hole. Give me just enough room to get in there." Blood from deep in the leg spurted up onto the hot glass of the lantern, sizzling to a dry, red crust, covering the operating field in a crimson glow. Brandt stuffed some gauze sponges deep into the hole with a Babcock clamp, drying up the field enough for him to spread the wound with a self-retaining retractor. Armed with a long clamp and with the best view of the wound he would ever get, he pulled out the sodden sponges, spotted the bleeder and clamped it. He rocked back on his heels and let out a shuddering sigh.

"Success, Herr Doktor?" asked von Stettgen. He had pushed the bowel loops back into the abdomen and partially closed the wound. The young American had sustained a glancing blow from mortar shrapnel which opened his abdomen without cutting any bowel. In general, the American wounded had a layer of fat which the less well-fed German soldiers did not and this is what proved to be the difference between the young American having a survivable wound or a fatal one. Von Stettgen now could turn his attention to the arm.

The mortar fragment had taken the arm off just above the elbow. The field medic's tourniquet had controlled the bleeding and von Stettgen was able to quickly debride the stump and tie off the major vessels. There would be no evacuation as night descended. The wounded men were transferred to the grain elevator and lifted to the second story of the Mestrenger Mill to await the wearing off of their morphine. At least, the shelling had stopped.

#

The crew of *Hell's Fire* gratefully accepted the three-day standdown in the rear area luxury that St. Vith provided. TSgt. Enfield Davis and his four-man tank crew slept in real bunks in a heated company tent enjoying hot chow and hot showers for the first time since the breakout at St. Lo in late July, three months earlier. In France, the 707th had been held in reserve while the Eighth Air Force had bombed the bocage, the hedge rows which encircled farmers' fields. These were centuries old thickets, impenetrable on foot but provided excellent cover for German snipers and machine guns, planted as they were on dirt mounds and backed by drainage ditches. The American infantry crossing the fields were slaughtered. Stymied, the 707th tanks were fitted with triangular horizontal plates called "Rhinos" with which they plowed through the bocage and created lanes for other tanks and infantry.

The 100th Bomb Group along with others bombed the hedgerows as well. This was the first instance of close air support of advancing ground troops but came at a cost. Some of the bombs fell short, killing or wounding over seven hundred American troops including Lt. Gen. Leslie McNair, the organizational and training genius who was responsible for the make-up of the American Army in Europe.

Freed at last from the bocage, the 707th Tank Battalion chased the Panzer Lehr division across France and Belgium, perfecting the fire and maneuver tactics that allowed the inferior Sherman to hold its own against the Panzer and Panther tanks of the elite German tank division. They pulled up at the Siegfried Line and there they rested. Their tanks needed as much rest and repair as the men themselves. Their mail had also caught up them. Gus Tolliver and Sam Peters' letters contained pictures of their now one-year olds left behind in the States.

"At least some of us had productive last nights at home," remarked Davis.

Ronna's Revenge, destroyed at the crossroads by the Messerschmitt had been replaced by a new Sherman M4A3 tank with the 76 mm cannon. Named *Texas Pride,* by Private Larry Rounds of Throckmorton, Texas. *Ronna's* old crew happily took over. They reveled in the spotless white interior, the easy movement of the turret through 360 degrees, the smooth elevation of the main cannon and the .30 caliber bow gun. The views through the periscopes were clear and not distorted by cracked lenses and accumulated dirt of many battles from North Africa onwards. T.Sgt. Manns, the tank commander, worked the slide of the .50 caliber machine gun as he stood in the open top hatch.

"God, don't you love that new tank smell?' beamed Corporal Allen Zweiss, the driver. "Let's fire this puppy up and see what she can do."

"Well," said Manns, "we should get her filled up, make sure the all the parts are working, I suppose." He got the depot head at St. Vith on the radio and let them know his plans claiming that this was not just a joy ride in his new tank, although he did not expect to be believed. They were a virgin tank meaning they had no ammunition for the machine guns or shells for the cannon.

"OK, Al," speaking to Sergeant Allen Zweiss, the driver, "take us over to the POL and fill 'er up."

The *Texas Pride's* gasoline fueled 450 horse power, V-8 Ford engine roared to life setting off a small earth quake which rumbled inside each man. First black, then grey smoke spewed from her exhaust beneath the rear deck, but soon cleared. Weiss worked the twin vertical steering handles and had her underway. He kept the speed down while in the company area and opened her up a little more on the road to the POL fuel dump. All the hatches were open and the crew had their heads out, enjoying the breeze while they could, for they knew they would be spending many days and nights, buttoned up and stifling.

The tank commander sat in the middle of the turret. The cannon gunner, Rounds, was directly in front of him and the loader, Private Sweeny Tuttle sat to his left. In the belly of the tank on the right was the bow gunner, in charge of the .30 caliber machine gun, Private Robert Smalls, and Zweiss, the driver, was to his left. Each man except the loader, had a periscope with which they would see the landscape. Attached to the left rear of the tank was a field telephone hooked into the tank's intercom allowing ground troops to communicate with the crew.

There were four fuel tanks, two vertical, two horizontal and when they were topped off with 170 gallons, the *Pride* could range about 120 miles. Once Manns received permission to take *Texas Pride* out for a shake-down run, he turned Zweiss loose. There was a large field at the tank depot and they spent the rest of that first day putting the tank through its paces. Next day was live fire drill of the cannon and the machine guns. The periscopes were a composite of wide angle and telescopic sights with cross hairs so aiming the guns was very quick and accurate. After that, the *Texas Pride* was cleared for duty. It was none too soon.

#

The Kall River was the largest but only one of three rivers that divided the Huertgen region into three precipitous ridges, clothed with dense forest, crowned with towns. On the tallest of these was the crossroad town of Schmidt. It had commanding views of the surrounding countryside and controlled the approaches to the Roer River dams. The quickest way to the Roer River and Germany beyond was through the Monschau Corridor, a flat plain flanked by the Huertgen Forest. Lt. General Courtney Hodges, commander of the 1st Army, was convinced that the forest and high ground had to be captured to protect his flank and prevent the Germans from dynamiting the Urft and Schwammenauel dams thus flooding the corridor which would put his plans weeks to months behind schedule. He gave the task of securing the forest, town and dams to Major General Leonard Gerow's V Corps, who then chose as his lead unit the 112th Regiment of the 28th Pennsylvania National Guard Division, nicknamed by the Germans "The Bloody Bucket". This was due to the red keystone emblem of the 28th Infantry Division which to the Germans resembled a bucket. The name also spoke to the high casualty rates of the 112th. The men proudly called themselves the "Bloody Bucketeers".

The 112th had a proud heritage, being the descendant regiment of the 13th Pennsylvania Reserves, nicknamed both the "Bucktails" and the "Rifles". This regiment was the first to cross the Rapidan River in May, 1864, to open the Battle of the Wilderness which introduced Grant to Lee and began the final bloody year of the war. Like the recruits of the 112th, the men of the 13th were from the western Pennsylvania woods and wore in their hatbands the tails of bucks they had shot to prove themselves worthy of joining the 13th. Nicknamed "The Rifles" because they were the first infantry unit to be armed with the Sharps breach loading cartridge rifle which greatly increased their rate of fire over the standard muzzle loaders. They were Grant's shock troops of the Army of the Potomac.

#

Captain Buck Ramsey of Co. A, 707th Tank Battalion, called his tank commanders into his tent as they were finishing their preparations for their next assault. He knew each of them well having served with most of them since landing on D-Day+2 at Normandy. His company had four platoons of four Sherman M4A3 tanks, 76 mm. Along with them came four M36 Jackson tank destroyers with its 90mm gun mounted in a Sherman chassis. The destroyers had arrived just weeks before and Patton made sure that some had been rushed to Monschau Corridor to fend off the Panthers and Panzers that were the principal dangers posed to the inferiorly gunned and armored Shermans. The Shermans were the bait drawing the Germans' fire, revealing their locations so that the M36 Jacksons could finish them off. Ramsey's Co. A, Enfield Davis's platoon in particular, soon became expert at the deadly dance.

"I would say that a couple of days' rest, sleep and hot chow has been good for you boys," Ramsey said addressing his tank commanders. "Sergeant Manns, have you settled into your new tank?"

"Yes, Sir. We took her out and chewed up some ground, a little target practice and we are good to go."

"Good, good. Well, as it happens, battalion has a push planned. We are to support the 112th Regiment in an assault on Schmidt, top of this ridge here." The men clustered around the tactical map spread out on the hood of Ramsey's Jeep. Hodges' 1st Army had been patrolling in and around the edges of the Huertgen Forest but always felt they were watched as the moved. The German artillery fire from their ""88's" had found the 112th and driven them back time after time with ever mounting casualties.

Captain Ramsey explained, "The Krauts have an almost unobstructed, 360-degree view of all the landscape around here from their posts in Schmidt and can call down accurate fire on anything that moves. They are dug in deep and scattered along the ridge line so they are nearly impregnable to our bombers and artillery. They have multiple positions in the town and open ground, all connected by a trench system. So, we are going nowhere until Schmidt is eliminated. General Hodges has devised a combined operation using an armor-infantry assault on the ground and what he assures me will be a massive preparatory air bombardment and rolling artillery barrage on the ridge. That starts at dawn tomorrow with the bombers all day and then the artillery starts overnight. Dawn the second day is when we kick off. We'll be nice and snug right behind the artillery with the infantry right behind us as we proceed up the valley side and over the ridge."

His map shook with the force with which he pointed out the landmarks and routes.

"Any questions?"

"How about some close air support as we saunter on up this hill?" asked Davis.

"We'll have Thunderbolts and Mustangs on station. You mark 'em and they'll blow them to Kingdom Come," Ramsey replied.

There being no other questions, tank commanders saluted their captain and returned to their platoons.

As they returned to their tanks, Soames of the *Death Wagon*, spoke up. "One beat up infantry regiment and four tanks to take what sounds like a fucking German Gibraltar seems a might thin to me. Don't you think?"

Davis had studied Ramsey's map closely and noted the twisting, narrow tract leading up the east valley wall. "I think that's all we get because that's all that will fit up that single road. Let's hope those B17s have some big goddam bombs. Otherwise, it might be a long day."

Chapter Three:
Vossenack

"Incoming! Incoming, get down."

The daily, if not hourly warning of the German 88s named for their 88mm high explosive rounds, landing among or bursting above the American foxholes distributed along and within the sodden muck which was the 112th Regiment, Pennsylvania National Guard's section of the line, barely elicited a response from the men occupying them. Major General Leonard Gerow, commanding general of V Corps, had proposed the 112th as the regiment to secure the heights overlooking the Kall River gorge. Her sister regiments, 109th and 110th, were to diverge around the heights to cut off re-enforcements. The plan also depended on the B17s, Mustangs and Thunderbolts isolating the ridges and eliminating the Germans holding the towns of Kommerscheidt and Schmidt on the east side of the Kall River. The crossroads town of Schmidt was their ultimate objective. It was from there that the Germans were able to accurately target anything moving with artillery fire.

But metal and wooden spike-like shrapnel from the treetop airbursts were not the only things falling on the men of the 112th, the "Bloody Bucket" regiment: freezing rain and snow had been filling their muddy foxholes for days as well.

The 28th Division, of which the 112th was part, had arrived at the outskirts of the Huertgen Forest to relieve the 9th Division. They marched through calf-high sucking mud, churned up by the tracks of the Shermans and Weasels which could barely get through themselves. As they got closer to the dark, forbidding woods, bloated bodies of unrecovered American and German dead lined the logging roads which formed the only ways to approach the forest. And always, the cursed 88s shrieked overhead. The foxholes had overhead cover but that only trapped the stench of the shit and piss in them. The shelling and omnipresent German snipers made leaving the holes to relieve themselves a deadly gamble. Trench foot was a welcome relief as a way to get off the line for a while.

"Jesus Fucking Christ!" shouted rifleman Jeffery Howe, a corporal from Lower Marion, Pennsylvania, as steel splinters from the latest airburst showered down on his roofed foxhole. Dirt, rotting leaf debris and dead rats rained down on him and his foxhole mate, Henry Anderson, a private from East Darby.

"Jeffery, Jeffery, what would your mother say if she could hear you?" Anderson chided. They had gone to opposing high schools and played football against one another before signing up in 1942. Their linebacker builds had been reduced by more than thirty pounds since entering the Huertgen. Chronic draining sores festered over their backs and thighs. Skin from their white mottled feet peeled off with every change in socks. They were last warm and dry three weeks ago in St. Vith and had not had a hot meal in as long. The constant wet and cold, coming early this winter, was eating away at their fighting readiness.

"So, what? You're fine with slowly rotting in this cesspool?" Howe asked. "We supposedly have the air power, tons of artillery, all the tanks a general could ever want and yet they can't seem to knock out those fucking 88s? We're pinned here by them, the snipers, the goddam mud...", his voice trailed off as he used his bayonet to continue working on a firing step that would allow them to at least stand a few inches above the muck filling the bottom of their foxhole. They had dragged some short logs into their hole to try to form a sort of floor which worked for a while but the never-ending rain had again raised the water/muck line.

"And another thing," Anderson groaned softly as his friend continued, "where the fuck are we, anyway? They keep saying we're supposed to take the high ground across the river and hold a couple of towns up there. We're still fighting off the Krauts for the two towns we got on this side. What are they called again?"

"Vossenack and Gemerter," Anderson answered.

"Who gives a shit?" Howe shouted, as he viciously dug at the wall, picturing those generals who kept him here. "Are you telling me if the fucking Germans take back those two shithole towns, that the next thing we know they are goose-stepping down 6th Avenue in Altoona? Go knock back some cold Yuenglings in the Knickerbocker Tavern? Yeah, I don't fuckin' think so."

The two men had soldiered together since enlisting and landing on Normandy two days after D-Day. They participated in the breakout from St. Lo. The drive across France seemed unstoppable and there was almost a giddiness about driving on to Berlin. Then came the Huertgen and the Siegfried Line: the dragon teeth tank entrapments, the pill boxes manned by the old men and boys that Himmler had scoured from the German hinterland and all the open land targeted by the 88s. The early winter cold, continual wetness, fighting against an unseen enemy made omnipresent by the artillery bombardment, cold food, inadequate boots and winter clothing, days of soggy C-rats and cold ersatz coffee and explosive diarrhea preceded by cramps that doubled them over, made getting shot look not so bad.

The arrival of more 88 rounds did not help Howe's mood.

"And my feet! Don't get me started about my goddam feet."

"Alright, I won't," replied Anderson, hopefully.

It was too late. Howe was already unbuckling the two straps holding his cracked combat boot on. There was a slushy, sucking sound as he pulled it off. Muddy water poured out with the remnant of his sock which fell apart in his hands. Patches of dead, white skin adhered to the material leaving behind puckered breaks in the skin around his ankle. The toenails pulled off without resistance. The foot looked like it belonged to a corpse just removed from a morgue refrigerator.

"I cannot feel these motherfuckers most of the time," he said slapping his feet, "but when I can, they burn and sting. I don't have any clean dry socks – haven't had any since we left St. Lo. These fucking woods are eating us alive."

Neither man had been dry, much less warm since rotating back to the line from St. Vith. Any light from a fire, if they could get one going, would immediately draw sniper fire. Anderson's feet were not much better. The only upside to being pinned in their fox hole was they did not have to try to walk on them. They would not be rotated off the line for at least another week. The fight to take the towns on the west side of the Kall River gorge lasted a few days. The German infantry of the 272nd Volks-Grenadier Division, the 272nd VGD, had withdrawn with token resistance into the thick woods that shrouded the steep sides of the otherwise bald Gemeter-Vossenack ridge. The other two ridges, the Brandenberg-Bergstein and the higher Kommerscheidt-Schmidt ridges were all similar. Any troops on top of the ridges had no cover from the German artillery and its endless supply of shells. To try to maneuver brought very accurately targeted shells raining down on them. The town of Schmidt was thought to be where the German artillery observers were stationed. Howe and Anderson of the 112th were heartened every time flights of B17s dropped their five-hundred-pound bombs on the ridge thinking no one could survive that, only to have the damned 88s fall on their positions once more.

"Make a hole!", shouted Sergeant Ted Rosinsky, their platoon leader. He skidded through the narrow opening of the foxhole and barely kept from sliding onto his ass in the bottom muck. "Holy Jesus Fuck!" he shouted, "This place fucking reeks."

"Well, thank you," said Anderson, "we try to make it homey. We're serving cheese and crackers later with some Yuengling. I hope you got our invitation?"

"What in the hell is wrong with you, Anderson? But to be fair, I have been in worse holes.

"Now listen up," Rosinsky continued. "We are jumping off tomorrow at 1000 hours. The 112th has been assigned to take Schmidt on the other side of the gorge. Artillery prep begins at 0600 and will last three hours. This will be followed by close air support by B17s then P-47s. Tanks will lead the way down the Kall trail, across the river and up the other side. We snug up nice and tight to them and all will be well, I'm sure."

He caught sight of Howe's foot. "This will be of little comfort to you, Howe, but I've seen worse feet than that." He twisted around to bring his pack to the front. He had made it waterproof by painting the inside with melted rubber. From it, he pulled out a miracle: a dry bath towel, two pairs of dry socks and a couple of cans of Sterno. "I was able to get these for the platoon. It's not much but since we have a few hours before we kick off, maybe you can begin to get your feet back into shape."

Howe and Anderson were dumbstruck. Rosinsky was right: it wasn't much but it was more than they had gotten from the regiment in weeks. Rosinsky slithered out of the foxhole and onto the next position. The first thing they did was get the Sterno going. After weeks of endless rain, flooded holes and nightly frosts, the small light and the little warmth the cans could give them seemed a roaring fire. Howe and Anderson inverted their boots on their M-1 Garands and bayonets, then dried each other's feet. They shook out the shreds of dead skin clinging to the cloth and left their feet wrapped in the towel. They formed a "V" with their bodies and placed the cans between them, spreading the scant warmth while blocking the feeble light from escaping their hole. It was the best they had felt in the three weeks they had been on the line.

#

Private Klaus Wiesen, the sniper who had let Douglas Aiken, the medic, live was not the only German soldier from the small Bavarian village of Fussen. On Hitler's orders, Himmler had been raking the countryside clean of any male, sixteen to sixty, who could still walk, giving them six weeks, or less, of training before sending them to the Huertgen. Himmler called these press gangs "Heldenklaukom-mandos", literally "hero snatcher commandos". The men were promised uniforms but for the lower ranks, a black armband would have to suffice. They were given new weapons, for weapons the Reich could still produce: it was men that it lacked. The new units were called "Volks-Grenadier Divisions" although they had barely three hundred men per regiment. All ranks were understaffed. The regiment's few experienced officers and NCOs were survivors of Normandy. They were thinly spread among the depleted companies of the 272nd GVD. The code of the German officer was that they led their men from the front. This meant their ranks were rapidly depleted. It was not common practice to do field promotions from the ranks of experienced men like Corporal Hermann Schneider who, due to his longevity, should have been leading at least a platoon, if not a company. He was not, which suited him fine. He knew that at this point in the war, he would be leading men only to their deaths.

Corporal Schneider, a veteran of World War I, was wounded at Normandy and was sent to recover back home in Fussen. In his first war, he had barely survived the gas in the trenches of Ypres as a member of the Fourth Corps when he was eighteen. He was forty-seven when he was drafted into the Volksturm, Himmler's answer to Hitler's demand for fresh fighting blood. Hitler had never fully trusted the Wehrmacht's generals and blamed the war's reverses on them. Hitler envisioned, and Himmler promised, new divisions of fanatically devoted "Uber menschen" - super soldiers armed with invincible secret weapons to throw the Allies back into the sea. What he got were old men and young boys. None of his generals dared to speak the truth to him and Himmler only re-enforced the fables. What Himmler scoured from the hinterland were "heroes" like Schneider and boys like Ernst Locher, barely sixteen when Himmler came for him.

Schneider and Ernst were assigned to the 272nd GVD in August, 1944, joining the Fusilier Company 272 after only two months of training. Schneider had no illusions about this war and planned to use his prior service to his advantage, beginning with the sergeant at the replacement center in Fussen.

"Corporal Schneider, is it?" asked a rotund training sergeant. "I see you have seen action before. We can put your experience to good use to train up these farmers and clerks," he said dismissively.

Schneider began to wheeze and cough. "My apologies, Herr Sergeant. I will be most happy to do whatever I can." He was again cut off with wheezing and racking coughs.

"Just a cold, I presume," said the sergeant. "Let's see about some running."

Schneider dutifully started at a brisk walk, then a saunter before he doubled over with the cough again. It took him five minutes to recover.

"As you can see, Herr Sergeant, I am pretty limited. I was gassed at Ypres and then shot on my way to the rear aide station. I was also shot at Normandy. It still seems to take it out of me. I was told I could do desk duty."

"Well, not many desks in the Huertgen but plenty of Americans. You can maybe be a sniper: not much need to move around since the Americans' advances bring them right to you. Simply shoot them."

The sergeant took Schneider's papers, wrote "Schurtz" for rifleman and stamped it "fit for duty" in red. "Go see the supply sergeant for your weapon. That is all."

He turned to Ernst Locher and stamped his papers. "You go with him."

The two went as directed and both received new Karabiner 43 rifles. Schneider was well versed in weapons of all kinds and appreciated the balance and heft of the rifle. It was semi-automatic, with a muzzle velocity of 2500 feet per second and a 500-yard range. The sights were open and rugged to withstand use in the field. It used either a five-shot "stripper clip" inserted from above into the chamber or a ten-shot box magazine, the latter preferred due to quicker reloading. The two spent the next two days getting familiar with the weapon and sighting them. Under Schneider's tutelage, Ernst practiced sighting, loading and generally handling the rifle. The next night they joined twenty other replacements in the back of a truck and drove through the murk to Schmidt just behind the Siegfried wall where they would be fed into the gaping maw of the Huertgen Forest.

The group was met by a sergeant who would be assigning them to their places in the line that ran along the ridge between the villages of Kommerscheidt and Schmidt. The ridge was bare which bothered Schneider.

"Nowhere to run, nowhere to hide," he said a little too loudly. Ernst overheard him. Schneider saw the look of bewildered fear on his face. "Oh, don't listen to me, Kleine. It's just the muttering of an old man. These positions seem strong and deep, clear ground to fire over. The Americans aren't likely to sneak up on us. We have the best artillery in the world and the Luftwaffe will watch over us. Just stay alert, watch what I do and you'll be fine."

The weather closed in, soaking them in their open fox hole. They could not have a fire to cook a soup or stew so they made due with the grey bread and wurst in their rations and cold coffee. There were two men to each foxhole strung out in a single line. Fifty yards of bare ground lay between them and the battered homes and shops of Kommerscheidt. The rain was soon replaced with a mix of fog and ice crystals. Their visibility was cut to just a few meters. Schneider and Locher each had a blanket which they draped over their shoulders as they huddled together in the foxhole. Ernst was shaking from the cold, wetness and fear. Schneider could do little about the first two but he could possibly help with the third.

"So, tell me, Kleine, where do you come from? What's your family like? Are they farmers or clerks or merchants?"

At first, Locher's teeth were chattering too much for him to speak but the trick of bundling under the two blankets began to have some warming effect.

"M-my f-f-family run a s-small grocery store in Regensburg - that is my sisters and mother do. My father and uncles are all serving in the army somewhere. I haven't had any news of them for months."

Schneider patted Ernst's shoulder. "Well, my family is all gone. There's just me for me to worry about, so, I may have it luckier than you in some ways."

"Before the war," Ernst continued, with less shaking and chattering of teeth, "I worked in the store, mainly stocking the shelves I could reach. I was small and couldn't reach the upper shelves. My sisters used to make fun of me until I hit my growth spurt and grew a third of a meter in a year. By the time I was fifteen, I was the tallest boy in our neighborhood. Maybe that's why the recruiting sergeant did not believe my mother when she told him my age. 'No matter,' he said, 'the Fuhrer likes them big'. And with that, they took me.

"My sixteenth birthday was on the troop train heading to Cologne and then here."

Schneider drew the wet blankets tighter around them. "Well, not much is going to happen in this 'frost und nebel'. They can't see us and we can't see them. Let's try to get some sleep."

"What day is it?" asked Ernst.

"Early November, I think," replied Schneider, already drifting off.

#

"Make a hole!"

"Goddamit, Rosinky," shouted Howe, "we were just getting the first real sleep in days. What the fuck do you want?"

"He really means, 'thanks for the socks and sterno,'" said Anderson.

"You're welcome," he said looking at Howe.

Rosinsky looked around the fox hole. "You've been busy," he said. Since his last visit two days ago, Howe and Anderson had been digging into the wall of their hole and managed to construct a narrow sleeping ledge/firing step which kept them for the most part out of the mire. The dirt from the digging helped to somewhat solidify the muck. At night, they dragged some branches in as well to improve the floor. Those home improvements with the dry socks had gone a long way to healing their trench foot.

"Yeah, well, what the fuck do you want?" groused Howe. 'We aren't getting back to St. Vith, I suppose."

"No, not there, but you do get a change in scenery pretty soon."

Howe muttered "Oh, my sweet Christ. This is not good."

"No, it is not, really," Rosinsky said cheerily. "Regiment thinks the weather is going to clear in the next twenty-four hours enough for our friends in the Air Force..."

"Bunch of pussies," griped Howe.

Rosinsky ignored that comment, "...will be able to begin bombing the shit out of Schmidt across the river in preparation for our little jaunt over there."

"Do we even hold Vosseneck on this side?" asked Anderson. "Shouldn't we clear the Krauts out of there first?"

"Now that you mention it," here, Howe audibly groaned, "the brass is thinking just along those very lines. So, before we go over there, they want us to mop up Vosseneck. We hold most of the town but need to drive them further into the woods. They want us to leave a couple of companies to hold the town and the rest of us get to go on a field trip."

"Well, isn't that nice? At least the brass seems to have a well-thought-out plan to kill us off," said Howe with rising anger. "Haven't any of their efficiency experts suggested just lining us up and shooting us? It will take a lot less time with the same results. Motherfuckers," he shouted.

"Alright, Howe, that's your allotment of bitching and moaning for today. Securing Vosseneck once and for all, shouldn't take too long. Like I said, we hold most of the town and what's left are likely some snipers and such.

"This is how it's going to play out," he continued, "the B17s lead off assuming the weather holds. The hope being that the Krauts will be out and about, you know, sunning themselves and whatnot. If is still socked in, then the artillery will hit the ridge. But as it stands now, the bombers and fighters will bomb and strafe as long as they can, but no more than an hour before sunset. Then the artillery prep beginning at 1800 hours that afternoon and through the night. Then the armor takes over, climbing up the valley side and we will be attached to them like piglets on a hind tit. It should be quite the show. Any questions?"

Of course, Howe had a few. "So, the 112th, already pretty beat up and at maybe three-quarters strength, if that, and leaving two companies behind at Vosseneck and Gemerter to hold those fucking towns against God knows how many Germans that are still hiding out in the woods, then is supposed to trot up the hill side, which is what, eight hundred or so feet, and then take two more towns with also God knows how many Krauts with only some equally beat-up tanks for support? Is that right?"

"Well, we won't be all by our lonesome," answered Rosinky. "The 109th and 110th are going to be sweeping on either side of the ridge to prevent any comings or goings of our friends. We and the tanks follow right behind the artillery as it moves down the ridge and continues to pound the far side of the ridge. And again, weather permitting, we'll have some Thunderbolts and Mustangs on call."

"Do we have any idea how many Germans we're talking about, here?" asked Anderson.

"Well, far be it for me to speculate," said Rosinsky, "and you know my low opinion of the Military Intelligence guys but the XO thinks maybe a division of infantry, a couple of platoons of tanks. The Luftwaffe should be no problem but those fuckin' 88s don't seem to have gone anywhere." And as if on cue, a salvo of German artillery landed along the forest border, showering the men with more debris from their overhead cover.

"God fucking damn!" shouted Howe. "How is it that we have not shut those sons of bitches down?"

"A mystery," commiserated Rosinky. "Anyway, expect a lot of noise over the next twenty-four hours or so and then off we go," he said almost gayly. With that, he slithered out of the foxhole.

"Fuckin' Rosinsky," groused Howe. "Something wrong with that man."

"I cannot disagree," replied Anderson.

At least, Rosinky had gotten one thing right: clearing out Vosseneck was no cake-walk but not too bad. Two companies of the 112th's sister regiment, the 109th had attacked at first light from Germeter, coming out of the woods surrounding the town. They oriented on the

Vosseneck church spire. The 112th, the "Bloody Bucket" regiment, occupied half of the town after enduring nearly constant mortar, sniper and small arms fire for a week. Private Klaus Wiesen, the best sniper in the 272nd had shifted to a tall tree along the edge of the Vosseneck clearing which afforded him an unrestricted field of fire towards the line of American foxholes, including the one occupied by Howe and Anderson. He was intent on keeping the Americans in their holes by harassing anyone who tried to move about. He had had Rosinsky in his sights any number of times but could not bring himself to take him out. With his telescopic sight, Wiesen could easily see the faces of his purposed targets and could not kill them. He stuck to his plan of wounding them instead. Even so, he fired only when there were other Germans around. A fitful night of broken sleep was the best the American infantrymen could expect.

With dawn and the arrival of tank support in the form of the 707th Battalion, the men of the 112th burst forward down Vosseneck's main street behind *Hell's Fire* and *Death Wagon.* The men of the 272nd GVD, fired a few Panzerfausts at the advancing tanks but were driven off by the infantrymen. The Germans had been significantly weakened by long hours of American artillery bombardment. The attacks by fresh American troops of the V Corp, the 109th, 110th and the 112th, were enough to convince the men of the 272nd GVD that it was time for them to go. Within an hour, the towns of Germeter and Vosseneck were in American hands but which was by no means, a firm and uncontested grip. The 272nd withdrew into their prepared fighting positions in the cloaking darkness of the Huertgen Forest which covered the ridge's slopes. A few desultory Panzerfaust rockets were their final shots. Throughout the rest of the fall and into winter, Vosseneck and Germeter were mortared from the woods by the residual force of the 272nd. Their continued presence in the woods threatened the tenuous supply line upon which any further advance across the Kall and then onto the Roer River depended. General Hodge of the First US Army's strategic plan was dependent on this route until the port at Antwerp and the Scheldt delta were securely in Allied hands.

Howe and Anderson were not in the lucky companies, each now reduced to fifty men, to stay behind west of the Kall, guarding the towns. They were back in their hole in time for the prep on the Kommerscheidt-Schmidt ridge to begin.

The fog was light and clung to the ground atop the Schmidt ridge. Private Ernst Locher of the 272nd VGD, looked up after awakening from a miserable night of shivering in saturating, clinging wetness which penetrated to their bones. Schneider, veteran that he was, was still sleeping. Ernst peered up through the mist to see blue sky, the first he had seen since arriving on the ridge. The crystalline, dark blue expanse of the morning sky was something he rarely saw growing up in the Bavarian woods. He was captivated by the pristine purity of it. Even the clouds were so different: long, streaks grouped together, elongating slowly as he watched, blown by the wind, he thought.

"Herr Schneider," he said, loath to waken his fox hole mate but so taken by the scene of such beauty that he felt sure Schneider would want to see it too.

"What is it, Kleine?", the old soldier was instantly and fully awake.

"Look up there. Isn't it beautiful? I don't think I have ever seen clouds like those before."

"Those are not clouds, they are contrails from bombers. Get down, get down," Schneider yelled. He pushed Ernst deeper into the hole and covered him with his body. While not a well-educated man, he understood the physics of dropping bombs. He knew they were released from the bombers with the same forward speed as the planes and continued to fall in an arc that kept them below the planes' flight paths. So, if the planes were directly over them, so, too, were the bombs.

The impacts were furious, tossing Ernst and Schneider up and out of their foxhole. The bombs fell in lines that marched parallel to the ridge line starting at

Kommerscheidt and straight to Schmidt, wave after wave. The ground, so saturated that water oozed from about their boots when they walked on the springy peat, was churned into pudding. Their foxhole collapsed upon their legs, immobilizing them half in and half out. They splayed themselves on the throbbing ground. All Schneider and Ernst could do was cover their heads and pray.

Chapter Four: Kommerscheidt

The *Bouncing Betty* was fully repaired and flight worthy. Besides some local shake down flights and gunnery practice, TSgt. Joe Hanover and the crew had had a few days off and enjoyed more than six hours of uninterrupted sleep, warm tents and what entertainment was to be found in village of Thorpe Abbotts. The daily weather reports were the same: targets socked in; missions scrubbed. Another gift from the enforced inactivity was that General Curtis LeMay had gotten restless and moved on to another bomb group. The "Bloody 100th" was not sad to see him go. So, when the sergeants came through the tents to rouse the men for pre-flight briefings, they were ready to get back up in the air again.

The briefing Major pulled apart the curtain to reveal the target: a narrow ridge deep in the forest along the Belgium-German border. This was clearly not the usual fare for the 100th Bomb Group and there were puzzled mutterings from the assembled crews.

"What the fuck is that?" asked Topman, the *Betty's* navigator from the rear of the room.

"That, gentlemen, is today's target. Although it looks unimpressive, intel assures us that it is vitally important to the continued advance to the Roer River. 1st Army is meeting strong resistance from German infantry, artillery and other obstacles and they feel that this ridge – the 'Kommerscheidt-Schmidt' ridge is key to the entire operation. From the top here, the Krauts command the entire Monschau valley and the approach to the Roer. They also hold some important dams that they can blow whenever they want and swamp the infantry. And besides, it seems to be the only patch of the war with clear skies for the foreseeable future.

"Since it is a small target, we'll handle it with just the 100th BG. The Luftwaffe has been essentially crippled in this sector. It seems Hitler would like as much air cover as he can get to cover his sorry ass back in Berlin, so we do not expect much in the way of Doras and Gustavs. Their groups have been pulled back to Germany to protect the Reich. Escort flights will be on call, so to speak."

This did not sit well with the flyers. "Well, that's sounds just swell," said Lt. Sam Topman, again. The Major viewed him not so much as the Devil's advocate as just the Devil. "A great plan - until it ain't. Did LeMay during his visit with us complain we were wasting the American taxpayers' dollars just sitting around or something?"

"Look, Lieutenant," the briefing Major replied, "all you have to worry about is finding this little bit of the war and bombing the hell out of. It should be..." his voice trailing off before he let slip the fatal words, "a cake walk." He would just once like to get through the briefing without that "wise-ass Topman" mouthing off. It made the stump of his amputated arm tingle.

"Oh, sure," said Topman in his best stage whisper, "'Ours not to wonder why/Ours but to do and die'". The major put up with this manageable amount of insubordination because he knew the *Betty's* crew to be the best in the group and that there was nothing wrong with some pre-flight griping. It calmed the jitters. The rest of the hour-long briefing dealt with start engine time, taxi to take-off, assembly point then crossing the Channel to the IP. All very routine.

"There being nothing else," he said looking right at Topman, "you are dismissed."

The rest of the *Betty's* crew was already at the plane doing their pre-flight. The planes were illuminated by klieg lights, the Luftwaffe's threat having been eliminated from the skies. The last gasp of the Luftwaffe played itself out with Operation Steinbock or as the English called it, "The Baby Blitz" which ended in May, 1944. There was a suspension of the blackouts. Joe Hanover remained at the right waist but could no longer look forward to testing himself against the Messerschmitt 109Gs and Focke-Wulfs 190Ds, the "Gustavs" and "Doras", which were much fewer in number but no less deadly when they did appear. But at least there was the flying which Hanover still loved. Increasingly, however, the flying was into denser and more accurate flak from the radar-guided anti-aircraft guns. The flak guns had been augmented with rockets as well, adding their yellow explosions crowned with black smoke to the murderous skies over Germany. The loss in planes and crews had certainly decreased but was by no means zero. Any number of a hundred things could and did go wrong while pushing the planes to their limits, also causing loss of planes and crews. The bombers were incredibly complicated pieces of machinery maintained mainly by teenagers which made up the bulk of the ground crews. In spite of that, the majority of planes made it off the ground in good enough shape to be shot down over Germany. Many of the men cancelled their free subscriptions to *Readers Digest* after a few missions, doubting they would be around for long.

Hanover knew there were no such things as "cake walks" and he approached this flight to bomb some trees in a forest as he did every time he went up. He scanned the empty skies over the barrel of his .50 cal. He owed his full attention to his crew and himself. Looking out at the thirty-three other B17s that the 100th BG could mount for this mission, without escorts, he felt very exposed and vulnerable. Only fifteen more missions and he was home free.

"We are approaching the target," Captain Flanagan, pilot of the *Bouncing Betty,* announced.

Hanover and the other gunners on the *Betty* pulled back on the charger handle, chambering a round and scanned the skies. Toland, the bombardier, took over the control of the plane as he made his final adjustments.

"Bombs away", he said and the rest of the flight dropped their loads. They all turned for home. Twenty thousand feet below, Ernst and Schneider cowered in their foxhole.

#

Pilot Hauptman Jans von Rindel and his wingman, Lieutenant Griebel, were on a rare patrol on the eastern edge of the Huertgen Forest at ten thousand feet, when he spotted the unescorted B17s starting their turns for their bases in East Anglia, England. He knew they would be out of range soon and it would be now or never if he was to have any chance at them. He signaled his wingman and pulled the stick back. He calculated that he would come up right through the middle of the small formation. By coming up under the thick contrails of the bombers, he could approach the fights unseen until the very end. His wingman separated from him, angling for the rear of the flight. He had a B17 in his sights when he let loose a stream of 20 mm cannon fire. The bomber exploded in a fire ball. Von Rindel continued climbing through the smoke and flame, clearing the flight. He then did a tight barrel roll and dove on a second ship, sending more rounds through the bomber. His wingman accounted for one other B17.

"Jesus F. Christ! Where'd that fucker come from?" shouted Flanagan.

Frank Paglia in the belly turret shouted, "I see him," and unleashed a burst at the rapidly diminishing target. If the German was crazy enough to try another run, Frank would be ready for him.

"I think we have earned our schnapps for today," von Rindel radioed to his wingman. "Let's head home."

Schneider and Ernst looked up through the clearing smoke and dust caused by the bombing run just in time to see the air burst of the B17 high above them.

"Well, it looks like we got one of them, at least," Ernst said.

"Probably so," Schneider replied, "but it could have been one of ours."

They were still shaken and their ears were ringing from the bombing run. They had managed to extricate themselves from their collapsed foxholes. Death raining down on them in the form of bombs or artillery seemed have taken a pause. They used it to get to greater safety.

"Schnell, schnell, get into the trees," an urgent voice from the edge of the trees called out.

"Come on, Kleine, there's more to come." On rubbery legs they ran as fast as they could to the tree line. They were barely half-way there when the artillery shells began to land around them. They were knocked to the ground, stunned, then knocked back up on their feet by the explosive impacts.

Schneider grabbed Ernst's collar and dragged him along. His damaged lungs from the gas at Ypres were giving out fast. The concussion wave from a round landing behind them blew them into the trees where they lay gasping.

"Come on," Schneider said again, "this is not good enough, we need cover." They crawled and scrambled through the splintered trees guided by the shouted encouragement of their comrades. Finally, they tumbled into a concrete pill box.

"Wilkommen, to our humble home," a corporal of the 116th Panzer Grenadiers said, clapping Schneider on the back. Their original unit, the 272nd VGD had become so depleted that they were folded into the 116th Panzers bringing their manned strength up to four hundred men out of an allocated one thousand.

"Many thanks," he said. Ernst was shaking badly and Schneider gathered him to his side.

"We're alright, Kleine," he whispered, holding him tighter to smother his sobs. "We're safe now."

#

The tanks of Company C of the 707th Tank Battalion were topped off with fuel and ammo. Enfield Davis in *Hell's Fire* would be the lead and Ramon Suarez in *Adolph's Nightmare* would be in "drag", the rear position. *Texas Pride* and *Death Wagon* were spaced twenty yards apart. The four tanks lined up at the top of the trail leading down the steep valley side to the bridge across the Kall River some eight hundred feet below. The tankers had watched with amazed satisfaction at the bombing run just completed by the "Bloody 100th" Bomb Group on their proposed target: the Kommerscheidt-Schmidt Ridge.

"That ought to shake the Krauts up some, I bet," said Manns of *Texas Pride.*

"We'll see soon enough," replied Davis.

The tanks were accompanied by the two remaining companies of the 112th. Sergeant Rosinsky had rousted Howe and Anderson out of their holes along with the rest of the men, numbering 120 in all. Private Klaus Wiesen, the sniper, took a few shots at the men as they milled around but drew brisk and accurate fire in response. He dropped from his perch in a fir tree and lay behind its trunk. From there, he could not see any targets and thought that duty had been satisfied.

Rosinsky grabbed the handset on the back of *Nightmare* and called Tech Sergeant Suarez.

"Hey, this is Sergeant Rosinsky, Co. C, 112th Infantry. We're with you on this little excursion."

"Sergeant Suarez, here. Welcome on board, Rosinsky. How many guys you got?"

"About 120. What's the plan?"

"Well, we're going down into the valley, cross the river, climb the other side, join up with the rest of you guys already there and take a couple towns on the next ridge. Keep close and walk in our tracks. Since we're last in line, any mines should be set off before we get to them. Can't say those fucking 88s won't do some damage so were going move as fast as we can."

"Roger, we'll stay nice and close."

On the maps, the trail down the west side of the Kall Valley looked pretty straight. The engineers had walked it and declared it passable by tanks.

Enfield Davis leaned out of his turret and asked one of the engineers walking by. "Just how 'passable' are we talking here?"

"Well, it's no fucking Route 66 but if you hug the wall, you should be able to do it."

"'Should be'? That's the best you can do?"

"Look, Sarge, I measured the width and there is a good foot of road to spare. Just take it slow and easy, hug the wall and you'll be fine."

No amount of arguing with the engineer sergeant would get his tanks across the valley. Davis got on the intercom and relayed the information to his crew. Then he said to Emmons, his driver, "Fire her up and let's go."

Hell's Fire edged slowly towards the drop. For far too many sickening seconds, even Davis standing up through the turret could not see what they were driving into until the nose of the tank plunged over the lip of the valley. For the first twenty feet, there was solid ground on either side but then on the right, everything dropped away into the valley. Emmons kept the left side of the tank pressed against the trail wall, scraping off dirt and rocks as he went. Davis looked over the right side and could not see any road but watched as more of the surface was dislodged and tumbled down into the gorge.

"You guys hold up until we get down, if we get down," he radioed the rest of the platoon, waiting at the top of the valley.

The engineer had lied. The map had lied. This was not a straight shot down the valley wall. There were bends and outcroppings making maneuvering the tank very dicey. Emmons had to periodically kneel on his seat and even with his head out of his hatch, could not see the fifteen feet directly in front of the tank. Davis shouted down steering directions to him. Davis saw it first: a large rock outcropping in the middle of a curve. It narrowed the trail to the point that the tank would become stuck or tumble down into the gorge.

"Hold up! Hold up!" he shouted and *Hell's Fire* rocked to a stop, fifty feet from the obstacle. Davis confirmed there was not enough room the get the tank around it without likely slipping over the edge. He could back up only ten feet. The arming distance for his 76mm high explosive round was fifty-four feet. The other three tanks with the accompanying infantry had made it onto the trail under the cover of the trees. Fearing mines, Rosinsky made sure his men stayed in line with the stopped tanks.

"What the fuck is this?" asked Howe to Anderson as they crouched in place.

"Standard operating procedure – hurry up and wait," Anderson answered.

"Yeah, wait to have the shit blown out of us. That seems to be SOP, too."

Up ahead in *Hell's Fire*, Davis was fuming at the obvious obstruction blocking his tanks.

"I am going to have a chat with that engineer motherfucker if I ever see him again," he thought.

"Alright, Emmons back us up real slow until I say stop."

Emmons was probably the best driver in the 707th and he moved the Sherman at a snail's pace until Davis said, "That's good". They were at best sixty feet now from the outcropping.

"Everybody, button up.

"OK, Tolliver, put a round right at the base of that rock." The gunner centered the aiming reticle on the base and fired. The Sherman rocked back, sickeningly close to the edge. Forward the air was filled with smoke and dust which took some seconds to clear. The rock was still there, but maybe a little dented.

"Another one, same place." They repeated the process twice more before Davis got out to inspect the damage. He saw a crack had formed. He pulled his sweat cloth from around his neck and stuffed it into the slight break.

Back in the tank he said, "Put one right there, Tolliver."

He took his time aiming, making minute adjustments with the electronic controls until the rag was exactly lined up with his sight. He put the round right where Davis wanted and about a third of the rock splintered and fell away over the road and down into the gorge.

"Perfect!" shouted Davis. "Put one more a foot to the left." More of the rock splintered. "OK, let's give it a go. Nice and slow, Emmons."

Hell's Fire inched forward again, scraping the wall on the left and crushing more of the outcropping. Davis watched the right track just barely staying on the road surface but seeing more of the road crumple and fall away. Another ten feet and they were by the rock. Anderson and Howe with the rest of the 112th crept down the trail behind the barely moving tanks.

"What the fuck is going on?" complained Howe. "Sitting ducks have got better cover than we do."

Anderson kept quiet, clutching his M-1 and staying as close to *Nightmare* as he could. At least with the heat coming off the tank's engine, the two infantrymen were as warm as they had been in weeks.

Davis called *Death Wagon*. "Soames, send the engineers down here with some dynamite. They've got some work to do."

Multiple explosions and much cursing, the engineers had been able to gain maybe another foot of width. The entire operation against Kommerscheidt and Schmidt on the east side of the gorge depended on getting tank support for the 112th Infantry's assault. Time and daylight were running out. Finally, convinced that more blasting was not going to be productive, Davis called for *Texas Pride* to make its run.

Following in Davis tracks, *Pride* made it to the bend but the right track was slipping on the road lip and began to slide to the right.

"Back it up!" shouted Davis. "Shit, shit, SHIT!" Davis shouted in his frustration. He and Emmons, his driver, looked the situation over.

"Maybe we could slingshot it," said Emmons.

"What?"

"You know, attach the cable to the front, Zweiss gets to the rock, he guns it, we pull like hell and he slingshots around the motherfucker."

"Really?"

"He sure as hell ain't going anywhere like this, except over the edge."

Davis consulted with Manns, the tank commander and Zweiss, the driver of *Texas Pride*. While they both contained their enthusiasm for the plan, they could not come up with anything better. The cable was attached, slack pulled tight, the rest of the crew got out and they were ready.

"OK, on my count: three, two, one, GO!" Both Shermans lurched forward at maximum power simultaneously and with roaring and grinding, *Pride* was around.

"Jesus Christ, I pissed myself," said Manns over the intercom.

"Thanks for sharing," Davis said. "OK, that's how we'll do it. *Death Wagon*, you're next then *Nightmare*.

The next two tanks made it around but the lip of the road was almost totally gone. Even Weasels with re-supply could not pass the obstruction. Unless the engineers could blast more of the bend, Davis's tank platoon of four Shermans and the two depleted companies of the 112th were the only support the rest of the 112th was going to get.

"Alright, let's get going," Davis said. The way down the valley was rocky with many gullies and boulders. *Hell's Fire* got only one hundred yards along before throwing a track. The rest of the platoon's tanks were idling behind without a way forward. The track would have to be repaired or the tank pushed out of the way. Davis and Emmons got out once again.

"Mother of fucking God!" Davis shouted. "I'm beginning to think we're cursed. Alright, what have we got here?"

Fortunately, the track had come off to the outside of the bogie wheels and would be relatively simple to repair, especially with the extra manpower from the other tanks. The tank was angled downhill which made moving it in a straight line more difficult.

"Get some logs and wedge them between the bogie wheel and the track. Then we back it up real slow-like and hopefully, she'll slip back on."

With Emmons driving and Davis directing the tank inched backward, shading a little to the right, spewing mud, wood chips and crunching stones but the logs gave enough separation of the track from the drive and bogie wheels that it slipped back on.

"Hold it," Davis shouted, "that looks good." He, Tolliver, the main gunner and Grisholm, the bow gunner on the .30 caliber machine gun, soon had the splintered logs removed from the track and the platoon was ready to move down the valley to the Kall River. Despite their best efforts, the tank column began to bunch up on the trail as it threaded its way toward the river. This was not lost on the German artillery spotters stationed in the steeple of the Kommerscheidt church across the Kall gorge and soon 88 mm shells began to rain down on the helpless tank column.

Davis ducked back down in the turret, slamming the hatches closed. The tank began to rock with the close impacts and shrapnel rang off the sides. Howe and Anderson dived under *Nightmare's* rear deck.

"Fire mission, fire mission," Davis shouted into the handset.

"Go ahead," the fire control officer of the 155 mm howitzers, the "Long Toms", of the 108th Artillery battery stationed back at St. Vith.

"We are descending the Kall valley, west side and taking fire from 88s beyond the ridge. I think their observer is in the Kommerscheidt church steeple. Can you take him out? Over"

There was a pause then, "Yes, I see him. Rounds on the way."

Even down in the valley, Davis heard the rounds go overhead. The church was reduced to smoking rubble.

"You got him. Good shooting, thanks."

"Any time, out."

The German gunners continued to fire on the slope, anticipating that the tanks would continue on their course, but were firing their rounds blindly. Davis signaled his tank platoon to move forward as fast as they could. There were several more near misses but the tanks made it to the river and plunged across it, coming to rest by the Mestrenger Mill aide station. Exhausted, the sixty men of the accompanying 112th dispersed along the banks of the Kall River. Major Brandt, the American surgeon, came out to the tanks idling next to the mill.

"Sergeant," he said addressing Davis, "I'm sorry, but you can't stay here. We're using this as an aide station and have a kind of truce with the Germans. If they see tanks or infantry, anything bigger than a Weasel or Jeep, they will assume we are part of the fighting and all hell will break loose. That shelling you guys got coming down the side was close enough."

"Understood, Major, we're headed up the other side and will be out of your hair as soon as we can," Davis replied.

"Emmons, get us out of here."

Hell's Fire erupted into life and with black smoke pouring out her hind deck, lurched forward towards the east wall of the valley. The tract leading up the east side was even more torturous with several sharp switch backs. There was no way of knowing if the trail had been mined. Davis and his tank platoon had to hope the engineers that accompanied the 112th had dealt with them. Leading the way with the best possible speed he could muster, *Hell's Fire* churned up the muddy, steep path. The first switch back nearly had them hung up on the shoulder but Emmons worked the levers and alternated power to the tracks so that he essentially "wiggled" the Sherman over the obstruction. This also broke it down which eased the passage of the rest of the platoon. The rest of the trail up the east side of the gorge was fairly straight and the column made good time to the meadow on top of the ridge. They were now exposed to whatever German guns on the next ridge survived the 108th FA's Long Toms. They still were about a mile from the village of Kommerscheidt. Davis had a feeling their luck was being stretched. The Kraut artillery did not need a spotter to blow them all to hell.

Rosinsky and his men remained within the trees at the top of the east wall. They followed as best they could when the tanks made their run to Kommerscheidt and further secured the town. Exhausted, the grunts and tanks began digging in among the ruined village. Davis jumped down from *Hell's Fire* and found Lt. Judd Barclay, the infantry company commander.

Barclay was tall, spare man with a week's growth on his dirt grimed face. His battle fatigues were muddy and torn. His company was reduced to fifty men due to probing attacks by the 272nd GVD and shelling from the 88s. None of the GIs had slept in two days. Davis saw Barclay's hands shake as he pointed out the German positions, not more than a half mile away. The road between the two towns was straight and uncovered. Davis had to assume the German artillery had its entire length registered for their artillery. The two men gazed towards the town of Schmidt.

"What's the call, here, Lieutenant? Any idea what they've got in town?"

"Battalion says likely a brigade of infantry, supporting mortars, some Panthers, couple of machine gun platoons and all this scenic German meadow between us and them. And, of course those fucking "88s".

"Well, we've got a couple of companies of your guys with us at least, so that's something."

"Yeah, I've been on the horn with Brigade and requested some more artillery on the town through the night and then we kick off at dawn. Seems reasonable to me. Maybe they could drive those "88s" out of here. Brigade said they'd be back with their thoughts on the matter."

Just at sundown, brigade answered in the affirmative, "Rounds on the way." There followed a six-hour bombardment through which Lt. Barclay and his men slept the sleep of the dead. The buildings were all damaged to varying degrees by artillery barrages from both sides. The rubble provided good cover for the riflemen but limited the fields of fire needed for the platoons' four machine guns. The most important road was the one running between Schmidt and Kommerscheidt. It ran between two houses that still had their second stories and it was here that the company's spotter for the heavy weapons platoon set up. Each of the roads leading out of Kommerscheidt had its own .50 cal position.

Rosinsky's squad with Anderson and Howe provided security for the guns. They dug in on either side just beyond the buildings. Further back of the machine gun was the 4.2 cm mortar. Five men entered each of the two buildings for observation and further defense of the town. The push down the road to take Schmidt would be at first light in the morning. Artillery support had slackened off now that the Americans had occupied the town. Air cover was unlikely due to overcast. The 112th settled uncomfortably into their shallow foxholes as the sun set and waited for the night.

"At least this hole is dry," offered Anderson in an attempt to lightened Howe's mood.

"For now," Howe grumbled. He looked to the sky which was darkening with accumulating clouds.

The Germans in Schmidt looked to the sky as well. The cloud cover meant no air support for the Americans still trying to establish defensive positions in Kommerscheidt. The 116th Panzer Reconnaissance Division with its attendant infantry regiment, the 116th Panzergrenadiers, were by this time "divisions" in name only. They had to be combined with the 272nd VGD to have anything near a functioning regimental sized unit. After months of nonstop combat with the Americans, mainly the 28th Division, the "Bloody Bucket", the 116th Panzer, the "Windhunds", was reduced to just twelve Panther IV tanks and three hundred men. These were grouped around Schmidt and in the surrounding forest with a few mortar crews. There was no mistaking the Americans' intention of taking Schmidt. The Panzer commander, Col. Kurt Hindmann, saw that there were only the four Sherman tanks as support for the Americans in Kommerscheidt and knew it was literally now or never for the "Windhunds". He did not know how long the weather would remain socked in, grounding the American fighter bombers or re-enforcements from beyond the Kall River would begin to arrive. He keyed his radio alerting the other five Panthers with which he would make the assault on Kommerscheidt, leaving the other six in reserve.

"Be ready on my mark." Hindmann called in a fire mission from the 88s on the neighboring Brandenberg-Bergstein ridge. They were to shell Kommerscheidt, then walk a barrage from Schmidt to Kommerscheidt behind which the 116th's tanks and men would advance. It was two hours to dawn.

"Here it comes," shouted Rosinsky hearing the screaming shells seconds before they impacted. He was with Howe and Anderson in their foxhole next to the .50 caliber machine gun pointing down the road to Schmidt. No foxhole is ever deep enough when the "shit hits the fan" and that was definitely Howe's opinion.

"God dammit," he shouted as the concussive force of the shells burst threw them up out of their hole. The blinding flash of the shells and the noise of the explosions robbed them of both sight and hearing temporarily. The German artillery dropped fifteen rounds on their positions before stopping.

"Sound off," shouted Rosinsky but no one answered. He crawled out of the hole to check on the other men and found them, miraculously alive, just deafened. Slowly, the men's hearing returned.

"Look sharp. They will be on their way in a few minutes."

Enfield Davis in *Hell's Fire* keyed his mic. "Everybody check in." The other three tanks responded. "*Pride* and *Nightmare*, go left, *Wagon*, you're with me on the right. Move it."

There was a drainage ditch for the road running across the front of the town and this provided some cover for the American tanks. They had armor piercing rounds, a few white phosphorus and anti-personnel fragmentation rounds as well. The walking barrage started just outside Schmidt and came on. The Panzers were five abreast and the infantry arrayed behind them. The smoke and dust stirred up by the barrage and the pre-dawn blackness made accurate aiming for the Americans difficult.

"Tolliver," Davis spoke into his mic to his gunner, "put some wooly pete down the road." Tolliver slammed a white phosphorus round in the cannon and fired. It was point blank, five hundred yards and lit up the center Panzer. With that illumination, the other three American tanks landed their armor piercing rounds on the Panzer's turret. It erupted in flame. In its light, the Americans fired more armor piercing rounds into the other Panzers while their machine guns laced into the German infantry.

"Give them some more wooly pete, hit the infantry," Davis shouted. Three more rounds of white phosphorus burst among the Windhund Panzergrenadiers. Corporal Schneider and Ernst Locher had been following close behind the middle Panzer when it was struck by the white phosphorus. Schneider was familiar with its effects and when Locher was hit, knew he had only seconds to save the "Kleine". The fragment was burning through Ernst's field jacket but had not yet reached his skin.

"Kleine, take off your jacket." The boy was paralyzed with fear. Schneider grabbed the collar and ripped it off him. There was smoldering of his fatigue shirt as the remaining fragment burned ever closer to the boy's skin. Schneider knocked him to the ground, stripping off the fatigue shirt but still a fragment landed on Ernst's skin and he began to scream. Schneider scooped a handful of mud and slapped it on the smoking flesh, pressing down fiercely. Ernst's screaming subsided into a whimper as the burning fragment was smothered. But he was not out of trouble yet. Schneider still had to remove the fragment. It would re-ignite as soon as the mud was removed. The fragment would burn as long as there was oxygen, from air, water, bodies, blood until it had burned completely through.

"Now listen to me, Kleine. Listen! I am going to wash off the mud but the burning will start again when I do. I have to dig it out of you. You must hold still. Do you understand?"

Ernst tearfully nodded. The rest of the German attack flowed around them towards Kommerscheidt and the Americans of the 112th Pennsylvania.

Schneider got his bayonet in one hand and his water flask in the other. "Alright, put your hands under you. Do not move."

He poured the water over Ernst's pale, heaving chest. The hole was already about a quarter inch wide and half an inch deep. The water in the wound began to bubble as the white phosphorus re-ignited. Ernst began to scream again. Schneider pressed down across the boy's chest with his left forearm and with his right hand probed the wound with his bayonet. He felt the tip scrape against the fragment and flicked it out. He poured more water in the wound and sighed with relief that there was no more bubbling from the now nearly inch-deep wound.

Ernst shivered violently with the cold and fear. "I want my mother. Please, take me home. I can't stay here. Please, let me go home." He started sobbing.

"I know, I know, Kleine. Let's get you back to the aide station." Schneider put his field jacket around the boy and the two of them made their way into the woods behind Schmidt.

Col. Hindmann's tank was on the right end of the Panzer line. When he saw the destruction of his assaulting force, he ordered a withdrawal back into Schmidt. The walking barrage of the 88s continued, but was poorly aimed. The American tanks backed further into the ditch and survived the in-coming.

There were two hundred and fifty men of the 112th now gathered in Kommerscheidt. Lt. Judd Barclay of E Company was the ranking infantry officer. He turned to his radio operator, Private Raymond Tuttle.

"OK, Tut, get arty on the horn and tell 'em we want some heavy shit along the road to Schmidt. We've got about an hour before dawn and that's when we'll kick off."

"You got it, Lieutenant." Within ten minutes the 155 mm rounds were on their way.

It was a mirror image of the Germans' barrage. While Barclay took some comfort that his artillery was throwing rounds twice the size of the Germans' 88s, he knew that there would be plenty of Krauts left to deal with once he entered Schmidt. He did not know how many infantrymen or Panzers were left but he could assume that there were some, that they would be pretty pissed and looking for some payback. Barclay looked to the east and saw just the faintest rosy glow of dawn painting the undersides of the clouds.

"Tut, get arty back on the horn and see if they can suppress those fucking 88s and still keep the Krauts' heads down in Schmidt."

"You got it, Lieutenant." After a pause, "Rounds on the way."

Barclay watched with satisfaction as the artillery did its job. He trotted over the *Hell's Fire* idling in the ditch. He picked up the phone on its rear deck.

"This is Lieutenant Barclay, 112th."

"Hi, Lieutenant, this is Sergeant Davis, 707th Tanks. What's the plan?"

"You guys brought some serious shit down on those Panzers. Nice shooting. Let's go see if we can finish them off. Jump off in five minutes. Arty will walk us down."

"Sounds good, we'll be ready. Four abreast at double time?"

"Good to go."

Barclay gathered up his sergeants, gave them the plan and with the 155 mm rounds falling thirty yards ahead, the American counterattack began.

The tanks burst out of the ditch and began firing HE rounds into Schmidt, down its main street and into the remaining houses. Even though their vision was obscured by the dark, the smoke and dust raised by the artillery barrage, they took comfort in knowing that enemy tanks and soldiers were downrange. Barclay's infantry trotted in column behind the four tanks, staying in their tracts in case of mines. There was little return fire as the Americans overran abandoned German positions and pushed through to the end of the town.

Howe and Anderson had been right behind *Death Wagon* which entered the town on the left flank. They took up firing positions next to the tank's tracks.

"Now, see," said Anderson, ever the optimist, "that wasn't so bad."

"Wait for it," Howe replied. "They haven't skedaddled back to Berlin, I guarantee. They'll be back when the rain starts or it gets dark again or both. We haven't seen the last of them."

"Well, aren't you cheery? They left us these nice foxholes, maybe those 88s have been dealt with, the sky will clear and we'll have some nice air cover. Think positively."

Howe scoffed. "We'll see who's right soon enough.

Ahead of them was four hundred yards of meadow land topping the ridge. The ridge dropped away steeply on either side and was blanketed by dark forest. The road ahead entered the forest as well. They could appreciate the commanding views from Schmidt and understood now how the German artillery spotters could call in such accurate fire whenever the Americans tried to move.

"Incoming, incoming!"

"God dammit, I hate to right all the time," shouted Howe as he and Anderson burrowed into their foxholes.

The Germans had simply melted into the dense trees on either side of the ridge and were now using their 81 mm Granatwerfer mortars from both sides of the ridge. The rounds walked right through the town, zeroing in on the tanks.

"Crank 'em up," ordered Davis. The tanks jolted forward, turning to the left and right. They poured machine gun and 76 mm main gun fire into the tree lines and beyond. Tolliver, Davis's gunner, spotted a muzzle flash from one of the remaining Panzers and answered with a round centered on the smoke. His round impacted on the barrel, splitting it two. An inch either way and the round would have bounced harmlessly off the Panzer's turret.

Lieutenant Barclay called in the new position for a fire mission from the 155s and soon the German fire was stopped. The American tanks and their infantry support continued into the tree lines, firing all the way. They encountered no further resistance. As they returned to Schmidt, Barclay ordered more artillery walking down both sides of the ridge for good measure.

"OK," Barclay said to Howe and Anderson as well as the rest of their platoon, "spread out and search these houses for any guests who stayed too long at the party."

"Everyone is a fucking comedian," groused Howe. The preference of the men was to simply throw in grenades and leave it that, but Barclay wanted some prisoners if possible. Anderson entered the first house on his left, through the shattered doorway, illuminated by the coming dawn's daylight filtering through the absent roof. Howe followed, his rifle at the ready.

"Nicht schiessen, nicht schiessen," an urgent voice rose from the cellar.

"Hande hoch, motherfucker," shouted Howe. "Kommen sie raus."

Schneider came out first, making sure both hands were raised high over his head. Ernst followed with only his unwounded hand up. He had tucked the wounded arm into his fatigue shirt as a makeshift sling.

"Show me your hands, show me your hands," yelled Howe, centering his rifle on Ernst's chest.

"Er ist verwundet, er kannst nicht," pleaded Schneider, pointing to Ernst's bloody chest.

Anderson said, "Hold on, Jeff, he's been hit."

Schneider gently pulled Ernst's hand out, who cried out when he let the hand drop to Ernst's side.

"Alright," Howe said, pointing to the floor with his rifle, "on your knees. Search them."

Satisfied that the two Germans were unarmed, Howe and Anderson marched them to the CP in a relatively intact cellar where they joined four other prisoners, awaiting the MPs.

The 112th spent the rest of the day digging in, bringing up more men and supplies from the west side of the Kall valley. The trail was still not open to even Weasel traffic so all re-supply had to be carried by hand. This included the heavy mortar and ammo for each rifle squad's .50 caliber machine guns, along with each squad's bazooka. They set up on the three roads leading out of Schmidt with infantry dug in along the approaches. Davis positioned his tanks on the roads with *Hell's Fire* in the town crossroads to serve as a ready reserve. The harassing mortar fire continued but without much effect.

Col. Hindmann, the Panzer commander, looked over his four remaining, functioning Panther IV tanks. A fifth, while immobilized by a blown engine, could still act as a pillbox with its 88mm main gun and machine guns intact. He had no illusions that would last for long but he would use it as such for as long as possible. His main problem was that his force with the six remaining Panzers was divided by the ridge line. He had lost contact with his own artillery but the four-kilometer range of his tank radio was enough to contact his men through their "Dorette" field radios and the tank command units in his remaining Panther IV tanks.

"Achtung, Achtung, all units. Concentrate your fire on the main road to knock out the Shermans. We will advance under cover of own fire and force them out of the town. We will proceed in five minutes."

Sergeant Rosinsky heard it first: Panther engines roaring back into life. "Here they come," he shouted.

Combined fire of four 88mm main Panther tank guns and eight machine guns laced into the American position.

They fired back with their armor piercing rounds. The bazooka teams scuttled into the ditch running across the front of the town and began to fire on the approaching Panthers. Head-on at three hundred yards the rounds had little effect against the Panther's three-to-four-inch frontal armor but could take out a track. That was the tactic the bazooka teams employed: hit a track causing the tank to swerve then the next team hit the thinner side armor and with luck, taking it out. They did not have the luxury of time as Col. Hindmann had his tanks moving at top speed and would overrun the bazooka teams in two to three minutes. Each team would have one shot but were able to disable one more Panther.

Adolph's Nightmare was the first American tank to engage. The gunner, Cameron Smith, had the stationary tank in his sights and fired an amor piercing round at the turret, followed by a second round before the smoke cleared. The Panther's turret blew off and its remaining crew bailed out.

"Great shot, Cam," shouted Suarez, the tank commander. There were still three more Panthers to deal with. Hindman had not yet committed the rest of his Panzers still in the trees. They went wide of the road using the smoldering buildings as cover.

Davis keyed his mic, "*Pride* go left, I'm going right." The two Shermans sprinted out into open ground, their turrets already traversed to take on the Panthers. The Panther facing *Texas Pride* got its shot off first. The round struck the rear deck and ignited the gas tanks. Sergeant Herman Manns' crew had no chance as the ammunition rounds cooked off. They died in the tank.

Death Wagon and *Adolph's Nightmare*, burst through the buildings which had concealed them and came at the Panther from the side and back. *Wagon* put a round through lighter armor of the Panther's side and *Nightmare* put one through the engine compartment. The Panther exploded. Davis in *Hell's Fire* accelerated at maximum speed to try to circle his Panther. Depending on his maneuverability, Davis needed to get behind the Panther in order to have any chance of surviving the encounter. *Hell's Fire's* speed and maneuverability kept them just ahead of the Panther's rotating gun turret making them try to compensate by turning the whole tank. The Panther was turning essentially in place, trying to get a shot on the Sherman but all he did was dig himself in deeper in the muddy ground.

"OK, get ready, Tolliver," Davis said shouted to his gunner. "We are going to have one shot at this." Davis stood up through his hatch and was working the .50 caliber machine gun, aiming for the Panther's view ports to keep the German's buttoned up and nearly blind.

One more circuit around the now barely moving Panther and Tolliver put a HEAP round into the Panther's engine compartment, blowing its gas tanks. The German crew came out shooting but Davis and Grisholm, the BOG gunner on the .30 caliber, mowed them down. Col. Hindman in the remaining Panther withdrew with the rest of the 116th Panzergrenadiers, melting back into the forest to resume their desultory mortaring of the Americans in Schmidt.

Chapter Five:
Thorpe Abbotts

"You got to love Germany in the fall," exclaimed TSgt. Raymond Gilbert, tail gunner on the newly flight-worthy *Bouncing Betty.* "Nothing but cloud cover as far as you can see. Word is the weather boys do not expect there to be any bombing skies for maybe a whole fucking week which means some passes for us." He fell into his bunk began whistling. "And that hard ass LeMay has moved on so all is good as far as I can see."

The 100th Bomb Group, the "Bloody 100th", had earned a rest. They had been in the lead group in the day after day raids to Marienburg and Bremen, Regensberg's Messerschmitt 109 factory, as well as Schweinfurt's ball bearing plants with little "side jaunts" to Wiener Neustadt with its Focke Wulf 190 fighter factory and the oilfields at Ploesti. These were all thirteen plus hour missions, without fighter escort to very important targets. The problem was that the Germans also knew these were very important targets and had concentrated their remaining fighter assets and flak guns around them. Crews shot down on these runs would not float into the waiting arms of the French Resistance but to assured capture and internment in POW camps for the duration.

Being usually in the lead group of the formations meant that the 100th was first over the target when the anti-aircraft batteries were fully loaded and ready. It meant as well that they were the longest over target. They were responsible to keep the formations tight so that as many planes as possible would spend as little time as possible over the target taking advantage of the time the batteries needed to reload. Most of the losses were therefore at the lead and tail of the formations.

The losses of friends, in mission after mission, ground down the 100th. The fresh faced, eager replacement crews only drove home the pain of missing friends and empty bunks. That was why General LeMay thought the 100th was the perfect group to lead the Munster raid, a chance for payback. The men had mixed opinions about targeting civilians in a relatively undefended city. A few had at first refused to go and relented only under threat of courts martial. Others were very enthusiastic at the chance to finally kill large numbers of Germans. All agreed that the “Mighty Eighth” Air Force, by bombing civilians, would “lose its cherry” in the skies over Munster, skies that the bomber crews waited on the weather to clear.

The reliably available treatment for the fatalistic malaise that had taken hold of the bomber crews - alcohol and sex, lay, for the enlisted men, in the village of Thorpe Abbotts. Officers could commandeer Jeeps and Ford sedans for trips into London. The arrival of the airfield had transformed the quiet Norfolk County village in East Anglia into a good-sized town with pubs and inns to accommodate the needs of the air crews just back from murderous flights over Germany. It had the advantage of being within walking distance of the field. It did not matter that the beer was watered down or the meals were bland. The girls were friendly and no one was shooting at them for a few hours.

"So, what say, Joey?" Gilbert said to Hanover, slapping him on the back. "Off to the 'Fox and Hens' for whatever entertainment we can find?"

"That does sound good to me," replied Hanover. "I have managed to stow away a bike so we can beat the crowd." They had three-day passes, something that was sadly missing in their lives for the past four months, and they had no time to waste. As soon as they had signed out of the company, they turned their backs on the war for seventy-two hours and were the first into the pub.

"Hello, boys," greeted the publican, Horace Standhope, himself a veteran of the Great War, the war to end war, where he lost a leg on the Somme. He had used his benefits and pension to buy the "Fox and Hens" and offer comfort to the new war weary. He had a daughter, Virginia, who helped him and was an additional attraction.

"Oh, Mr. Standhope, you are a godsend, even more than usual," proclaimed Gilbert. "We stand in hope, of your hospitality and more importantly, your bitters." Gilbert was an insufferable punster and this was a well-worn standard. Hanover groaned loudly.

"I don't know this man, really," Hanover said, "we just happened to walk in together. Please don't hold it against me."

"No worries, Sergeant Hanover, I know very well how war throws us together with all sorts. Two pints of bitters, then?''

"And a couple of meat pies as well, if you would be so kind." The two Americans settled into a corner table, facing the door. Soon, Virginia brought them the drinks and pies, steaming from the oven, to their table. Hanover had hoped she would be in the pub. He had seen her only a few times before and found her increasingly on his mind. Ray Gilbert had made a play for her but Hanover saw he was much too forward for her. He took a more circumspect approach.

"Ginny, my girl," Gilbert said in voice much too loud using his best Cockney accent. "Give us a kiss then, darlin'"

"Now, why on earth would I do that, Sergeant Gilbert?"

"Because I am irresistible and I can see you are struggling to contain yourself. Am I right, Joe?"

"No, Ray, I would say you are definitely not. Miss Standhope seems to be containing herself quite well. I apologize for my friend. I think he has suffered oxygen deprivation from one too many flights which has addled his brain."

"I can recognize delusions when I see them and make allowances," she replied. "Will that be all?"

"I guess so, sadly, for now," said Gilbert, head bowed with his hand to his chest.

They enjoyed their meat pies and bitters, leaving Virginia in peace. As they were leaving, Joe went to the bar to settle their tab.

"Once again, I apologize," he said holding out a combination of British pence and pounds for Virginia to pick out the correct amount. He pretended to not know the currency but it was really a way for her to hold his hand to steady it. The touch had been getting longer with time.

"You know, the weather is supposed to be socked in over the targets for a few more days. They gave us three-day passes."

"I will be off tomorrow afternoon," she said. "Perhaps we could see some of the village and countryside." Giving his hand a parting squeeze, Virginia turned to the cash register.

"That would be very nice," Hanover said as he backed out of the 'Fox and Hens'. He nearly fell over his bike and did not remember the short ride back to the field. The memory of the warmth of her hand and her parting smile kept him awake long past “lights out”.

The next day, Hanover rode his bike over to the ‘Fox and Hens’ where Virginia was waiting with her own bike. The sight of American servicemen in uniform with English girls was no longer unusual and the villagers smiled and waved. Virginia and Joe circled the village streets, past the gardens and rose hedges, the small shops and the two churches. They stopped back at the ‘Fox and Hens’ to pick up a lunch basket and rode on into the countryside.

The townsfolk knew the toll that the air war was taking on the bomber crews. The once peaceful farmland around Thorpe Abbotts was now littered with the detritus of crashed bombers. The townsfolk did not begrudge the flight crews what little free time they had. They could now sleep through the roaring engines of bombers coming to life at three in the morning and stopped what they were doing to count the planes home on their return. Nearly every flight had fewer planes than when they took off and always at least one struggling bomber, engines streaming fire, trailing smoke with arcing red flares denoting wounded on board. They all prayed the crews could make it down one more time.

Soon, Virginia and Joe were beyond all sight and sound of the air field and riding along narrow roads, hemmed in by hedges. Virginia turned through an opening and stopped just inside the hedge. They left their bikes there and walked on with the basket between them to an oak tree where they spread out their blanket and laid out their meal of sandwiches, cider and a rare treat, a fresh apple.

"Oh, my God," Joe said, taking in the green and peaceful field. "I never really looked at the country that we fly over. I was always too busy with the plane. I didn't know this kind of quiet still existed. Thanks for bringing me here."

"You know," Virginia replied, "I don't think I really know what you do on the plane. You're surely not the pilot."

"You don't think I could be the pilot?" Joe said, pretending to be offended.

"I do think you could do anything you set your mind to," she answered trying to ease the slight. The last thing she wanted was tension between them. She relaxed when she saw Joe's smile.

"Well, pilot might be a stretch. Our pilot, Captain Flanagan, is amazing. We are usually the lead plane, that's the most dangerous position in the formation, and that's because he is the best pilot. I wish he weren't sometimes so we could hide out in the middle of the pack."

"So, what do you do on the plane?"

"I am a waist gunner, usually the right waist gunner. You know the windows about half way back in the plane? I man a .50 caliber machine gun there." He said this with pride but the look of shock on her face kept him from explaining further.

After a while, she asked, in almost a whisper, "Have you killed anyone?"

"At least five, confirmed." The thought that she would be shocked and no longer want to see him, terrified Joe.

She paused for a couple of minutes, looking over the pasture land before she turned back to him, taking his hands and said, "Good. Filthy Huns. I wish I could kill them myself. They brought this horrible war on us – again. They nearly killed my father in the last one. There have been five boys from the village, boys that I knew, went to school with, killed in North Africa and France. More wounded.

"This can't be over soon enough and if the only way to do that is to kill them all, then that's fine with me."

Joe shuddered being faced with her hatred that he could understand and even experienced himself, but did not expect it in someone with whom he had hoped to escape the war, even if for a little while. They were still until she turned to him and held both his hands.

"I'm sorry. This is not what I wanted. Let's forget about it while we can."

They finished their lunch and laid back, Joe resting his head on Virginia's lap until late afternoon. Very little was said, nothing really needed saying and they parted at the 'Fox and Hens'. Joe and Virginia were able to enjoy the next afternoon as well. The first had been so close to perfect that they repeated it on the second afternoon.

"Well, well, well, where have you been, Joey?" asked Gilbert, leering from his bunk upon Hanover's return after the second picnic.

"Oh, just out and about, you know, hither and yond."

"Yeah, and I know whose 'yond' you were trying to 'hither' into. Any luck?"

"Gilbert, you are a disgusting piece of shit, you know."

"Hey, just asking, no offense. Just curious.

"Anyway," Gilbert continued, "the weather gods have turned against us. Mission to Regensburg in the morning."

"Oh, for fuck's sake. What does this one make? Twenty or so missions?"

"I guess they mean it this time," answered Gilbert. "I hear its maximal effort, three groups at a time, three days in a row: bombs, incendiaries. Should be quite the show."

"Yeah, attracting every 'Messershit' and 'Fucker' they've got left. But, of course, that's part of the plan, isn't it? We're the attraction and as long as we shoot down a few more of them than they do of us, then it's OK with the brass. Never mind there's a ten-to-one difference in crew sizes. They are going to have a field day."

"Ours not to reason why..."

"Shut the fuck up, Gilbert."

#

Deep in Germany were the Schweinfurt and Regensberg factories. Together they represented the majority of ball bearing and Messerschmitt production. For most of the war, these two plants had been too far for heavy bombers. One of LeMay's improvements had been the addition of extra fuel tanks, called "Tokyo tanks", giving them just enough range. They remained out of range of the P-47 Thunderbolt escorts so that all of the flights over Germany were unescorted. Those shot up and could not make it back to England, had to land in neutral Switzerland and were interned or try for North Africa, many ditching in the Med. The 100th Bomb Group earned its nickname, the "Bloody 100th", from making many such raids over targets like Schweinfurt and Regensburg. Losses of over fifty percent were not uncommon. bf109 and FW190 fighters were increasingly armed with incendiary rounds to ignite the bombers' fuel tanks, making even one hit potentially fatal. The unrecoverable crews sharply increased the manpower drain on the Eighth Air Force. By the end of the war, the Eighth alone had lost more men than the entire Marine Corps.

Hauptman Jans von Rindel, flight leader of Jagdgeschwader III/54' squadron, "The Green Hearts of Thuringen", had been transferred to the Regensberg-Schweinfurt air fields to add to the already formidable air defenses. Loss of either Messerschmitt or ball bearing production even for a few months would be a major blow to the Third Reich's war effort. He was hoping for a break from the nearly constant air combat he had been seeing over France and Belgium. He knew the B17s were nearly unescorted due to the limited range of the P-47s. He allowed himself to hope for easy kills. His reputation was a major morale boost for the squadron.

"Gentlemen," he addressed the assembled fighter pilots, "we have a great opportunity here. Our bases are very nearby while the Allies remain at the end of their effective flight times. Our forces can attack the bombers almost over their entire route. Nearer the coast, the P-47 escorts will be more numerous. They have added drop tanks to take us on. Their problem is the added weight reduces their maneuverability, particularly rate of climb and turning. When they engage us, they have to drop their tanks removing any advantage they may have in extended range. That means that for most of their mission, the bombers will be unescorted and that is when we will make our strongest effort.

"Therefore, I have come up with a plan to maximize our advantages: mainly, the proximity of our fields for refueling and prolonged range to intercept the bombers and fighters farther from their targets." He turned to the map on the wall behind him in the briefing room.

"We will divide our flights into two regions: Landsburg and Lechberg. The first will hit them on their way in, passing them onto the second region closer to the targets. Our fighters will break off when the Americans enter the flak boxes over the targets. The first flight will have returned to their fields to refuel and rearm to hit the bombers on their return flights. The second flight will harry the Americans to their targets, then will refuel and rearm when the bombers are over their targets, amongst the flak. For the enemy planes that try to make it to North Africa, our second flight will engage them. By then, there will be far fewer bombers, lower on fuel and ammunition to defend themselves. This should greatly increase our victories and make the Allies reconsider striking this far into the Fatherland."

"Herr Hauptmann," asked one of the pilots, "how many planes do you expect to be available?"

"Along the entire flight line from the coast to us will be about three hundred Messerschmitts and Focke-Wulfs. For us, we will have another one hundred fighters, mainly Messerschmitts."

"When do we expect the mission?"

"They, like us, wait upon the weather. Not too long, I suspect. That will be all. Dismissed."

#

Joe Hanover had given up all thought of living through the war. Once he came to that conclusion, it was as if a great weight had been lifted. Although not really from a military family, all of the Hanover men had fought in whatever war was available to them. His great grandfather had survived the Battle of the Wilderness and the rest of the Civil War. His grandfather was a Rough Rider in the Spanish-American War and his father had been a teenaged Marine in the Argonne Forest, World War I. He grew up with their war stories, tales of near misses, dangerous times, general absurdities. But Hanover knew there would be no little boy, mouth agape, eyes wide, to listen to his stories at family gatherings in the future. The war was his first experience in life as an adult. He had only known high school where the closest thing to "combat" was football. If flying and dying was what it meant to be grown up, then they could shove it. He knew and, did not much care, that he would not be coming home.

But now, there was Virginia.

After one afternoon, he felt they had been together for years. With the second outing the next day, it was like they had known each other all their lives. They had already gone through the awkwardness of beginning, the worry of saying the wrong thing, the anxiety of silent times. As they lay under the tree outside Thorpe Abbotts, looking up at a peaceful sky, her hand absentmindedly stroking his hair, both comfortable with saying nothing, Joe began to feel something return he had hoped he had put behind him: fear. A part of him resented this reason to go on living that Virginia represented. His understanding of where he fit in the war's scheme of things, the tidy finality of his dying, if not on this mission, then the next or the next, had been a great relief to him. Now, Virginia caused the fear of dying to creep back into his soul. Now, he had something to live for.

They stayed the rest of the afternoon of their second day in the meadow before riding their bikes back to the village. As they approached the 'Fox and Hens', Joe felt a shiver run down his spine. There was an MP jeep parked outside the pub; its .30 caliber machine gun cocked at an angle into the cloudless blue sky. One MP stood at the bar as they entered. His gaze was fixed on Virginia but he spoke to Hanover.

"100th Bomb Group?"

"Yeah, I've a three-day pass," Joe said, as he reached into his tunic pocket.

"Leaves are cancelled. Weather cleared for a mission tomorrow and we're to bring you boys back to the field while you're reasonably sober. Sorry, you can hop in the jeep."

Virginia reached for his hand and gave it a lingering squeeze. "Come back safe," she whispered.

The other MP returned with three more crew members and soon they were back in their tents. Gilbert, the tail gunner, had not left the 'Fox and Hens' the entire afternoon. He lay passed out on his bunk, reeking of Barclay's Victory Stout.

"What an asshole," Joe muttered. "He's going to be sharp in the tail, tomorrow." He did not let it ruin the rest of the day for him. Thinking of Virginia, he drifted off to sleep.

The ground crews had been hard at work over the two days that the weather prevented flying. The *Bouncing Betty* was fully patched, one engine and all four propellers, the ball turret all replaced. Thorpe Abbotts airfield had a full repair shop and could get even the most beat up plane back in the air. The Master Sergeant in charge of the shop had one standard assessment of any damaged plane: "No problem, I've seen worse. We'll get her up again, soon enough." That was because any plane in worse condition had not made it back.

Like clockwork, at 0300 hours the sergeants came through the tents and rousted out the reluctant, complaining aircrews. The briefing was barely listened to by the hung-over men, breakfast was skipped and only the bracing early morning air began to bring them back to life – all except Gilbert. Sick call was out of the question. If the docs excused the recovering drunks or the simply hung over, the 100th would not be able to fly half their ships. Cory Standish, Ramon's replacement at the left waist and Hanover got Gilbert dressed, and dragged him into the *Betty* near Hanover's gun. They hooked his oxygen up and by the time the flight had reached "Buncher 28", Gilbert was serviceable once again, ready to man his gun in the tail. In the still dark predawn, Virginia Standhope, through her bedroom window, watched the B17s take off as their navigation lights and flames from the engines marked their upward progress until, one by one, they winked out in the cloud cover. She did know which plane was Joe's so her prayer for safe returns went out to all the crews.

Chapter Six:
Mestrenger Mill

"Kleine, Kleine, time to wake up." Schneider gently shook Ernst Locher awake. They had been captured by the 112th Pennsylvania at Schmidt but were overlooked in their basement when the 272nd VGD had successfully counterattacked and drove the Americans back to Kommerscheidt. He hated to wake Ernst. His shoulder wound had worsened and was now clearly infected. Schneider had used all the sulfa powder in both their med kits and kept washing the wound but there was no mistaking the angry red swelling of the shoulder and the gut-turning rancid odor from the draining wound. Ernst whimpered in his sleep, calling for his mother and was over taken by wracking chills. Red streaks had formed and tracked down his red, swollen upper arm.

"Come, Kleine, we have to get you some help." Schneider half carried Ernst out of their basement to the empty ruins of the house. For the moment, there was no one to be seen but the heavy fire from machine guns, together the chest pounding thumps of mortar rounds, showed the fighting had not moved on. Schneider leaned Ernst against a pile of bricks, covered him with his field jacket and went to find help. He was not sure who held this position – German or American – but at this point, either side would be fine. He hoped to run across the two American GIs who decided to take them prisoner rather than shoot them on sight.

Schneider walked upright, hands out to his side, making it clear he had no weapons. The firing seemed to be around Kommerscheidt and directed into the woods. He saw the three Sherman tanks arrayed in front of the village, their main cannons and machine guns turned towards the woods. No one seemed to be paying attention to the road to Schmidt and Schneider was able to walk up to the tank closest to the woods. Schneider knew enough English to read the words on the tank's cannon: *Hell's Fire.* He tried knocking on the side but that had no effect. He went to the rear deck and saw the field telephone hand set that was used to communicate with accompanying infantry. He picked it up.

"Hilfe, bitte."

At first tank commander, T.Sgt. Enfield Davis thought he had picked up a stray transmission from the Germans in the woods but then he saw the frequency was turned to his field receiver.

"Bitte, hilfen sie mich."

"What the fuck?" he said and rose out of the turret, turning to the rear of the tank to see Schneider crouching there with his hands up in surrender. Davis was horrified to think that a Kraut could get so close to the tank. He could have easily attached a Teller mine and blown them all to hell.

"Emmonds," he said to his driver, currently the least occupied of his crew, "we've got a Kraut trying to surrender to us. Check him out, but be careful." It was Schneider's age as well as his obvious surrender that kept Davis from just shooting him outright. Emmons opened his hatch, slid down the glacis to the front and scuttled around with his .45 trained on Schneider.

"Danke, viele dank. Kommt mit mich, bitte." He gestured toward the house at the near edge of Schmidt, indicating that he wanted Emmons to follow him. Emmonds took the phone from Schneider called into Davis.

"I think this crazy son of a bitch wants to capture the tank and take it back to Schmidt."

Davis actually chuckled at the absurdity of the idea. "That's got to be either the most insane or the ballsiest German we've run across. I'll get the MPs out here."

The sustained tank, mortar and infantry fire from the Americans had suppressed any return fire from the woods causing a lull. Schneider could imagine what the tankers were thinking but the fact they had not shot him outright was encouraging.

"Bitte, Ich haben ein junge verwundert kamarade." He touched his shoulder and grimaced. He made gestures to have Emmons follow him. By this time, Davis had joined them.

"Do you know what he's saying?" asked Emmons.

"'Verwundert' means wounded, I think," Davis said. "One of his guys is hit and he wants us to pick him up, I guess."

"Well, fuck that," said Emmonds. "I'd say one wounded Kraut was a job half finished. Let's put a round in the house and be done with it."

Davis continued to watch Schneider who kept muttering "Hilfe", and gesturing towards the ruined village. Emmons grew more exasperated with each passing minute.

"Jesus Christ, Enfield," he said, "you aren't actually thinking about this, are you? There could be a whole Nazi platoon with Panzerfausts down there just waiting to blow our shit away."

"Yeah, but I don't think so. He's a pretty pitiful decoy. It probably is just a shot up German. Besides, the Captain is always griping about how we never bring in any Krauts for questioning. This could be our chance." Schneider watched the argument go back and forth between the Americans, knowing that Ernst was getting weaker all the time. When he could wait no longer, he gripped Davis's arm. This brought Emmons' .45 pistol up against Schneider's head.

Unfazed, Schneider persisted, "Bitte, sie muss hilfen."

"Easy, Roger," Davis said to Emmons. "Can't hurt to check it out."

He got on the inter-tank net. "*Death Wagon and Nightmare,* stay here and cover the tree line. Emmons, sit him up front between the hatches. Let's go." With their cannon facing the village, Davis manning the .50 cal, *Hell's Fire* rumbled forward.

Schneider sat pointing at the ruined house all the while saying "Danke, danke." When they reached the house, Schneider jumped off, nearly getting run over by *Hell's Fire.* Ernst was unconscious when Schneider reached him. Gently, the old soldier shook him to enough wakefulness to feel pain. He groaned.

"Hier, bitte hilfen."

Emmons and Tolliver, the gunner, jumped down and dragged Ernst up on the foredeck where Schneider held him tightly. Davis radioed ahead to the command post in Kommerscheidt.

"We'll need a Weasel and the MPs for prisoner transport. Two Krauts, one wounded." Davis continued into Kommerscheidt and deposited Schneider and Ernst with the MPs. Ernst was loaded onto Douglas Aiken's Weasel/ambulance and began down the twisting trail to the aide station at Mestrenger Mill.

Hell's Fire returned to the firing line facing the woods. The activity in the town attracted the attention of the German mortar crews and rounds began to land again. The three tanks returned accurate suppressing fire, joined by the infantry mortars in the town.

"Fuck, fuck, fuck," shouted Grisholm, *Hell's Fire* bow gunner, "One Panther, no, two Panthers coming out of the tree line." The German tanks had the Americans in their sights before breaking cover and each got a round off before retreating into the trees. Both rounds missed high but hit in the town bringing down a second story onto the GIs below.

Davis was on the radio for a fire mission before the dust settled. "Tanks and infantry spread out along the tree line." He gave the coordinates for the section in front of him.

"Rounds on the way."

#

TSgt. Douglas Aiken, medic with the 112th, secured the barely conscious Ernst to the litter strapped across the back of his Weasel. He drove to the shattered edge of the town, pausing to see if he had attracted any attention from the German mortar teams in the woods.

"Things seem quiet enough," he said to Ernst who was in no position to hear him. "Off we go, then." There was about twenty-five yards of open ground before he entered the woods. Aiken shoved the Weasel into gear and floored the accelerator. The tracks kept the Weasel from spinning in the mud but Aiken knew there would be no land speed records broken that day. He did get up enough speed to keep the mortar crews from drawing a bead on him and soon he was negotiating the steep, twisting trail down to the Kall River. He pulled up alongside of the mill and was met by German medics.

"Oh, shit," he thought, "the Krauts have taken the mill and now me, too." The Germans did not pay any attention to Aiken and quickly took Ernst inside. Aiken looked around and was reassured by the sight of American medics. Intrigued, he parked the Weasel and went inside the mill.

With the combined German/American aid station established, Major Brandt and Oberstabsartz von Stettgen were able to get two more surgeons and the amount of work they could do more than tripled. Aiken stayed out of the way while still having a clear view.

Ernst was put on a litter rack, his clothes cut off him and his infected shoulder was irrigated again. The sulfa powder was ineffective due to the depth of his wound. Von Stettgen recognized Ernst was in shock, the infection gaining access to his blood stream as well as spreading uncheck through his upper arm.

“Ether and tie him down,” he said to two orderlies. The Beecker anesthesia machines were in use so they had to use open drip anesthesia with ether. This was very dangerous but any delay in treating the shoulder would result in Ernst dying. The last thing von Stettgen did before starting to cut was to inject Ernst with the wonder drug of the war: penicillin.

When von Settgen saw he was asleep and the shoulder wiped down with iodine, he made a sweeping, curved incision from the end of Ernst’s collarbone to his biceps. Immediately, thick green pus erupted from the cut. Von Settgen and the orderlies could not suppress their gagging. The rivulets of pus drained over the front of Ernst`s shoulder and onto his chest, then to the floor.

“Gott im Himmel,” said von Settgen, having to steady himself. “Saline solution,” he said. He irrigated the wound and explored the cavity with his gloved hand to make as sure as he could that there were no more pockets of pus left behind. With his last flushing, he mixed in some sulfa powder with the solution and let it stand in the wound for ten minutes. The combined effect of the ether and the rank smell of the wound had the surgical team reeling and they had to step away while Ernst woke up. He cried out and struggled against the restraints.

"Lie still," said von Settgen. "You are better". They sat him up to drain the wound. "Now this is going to hurt some." Before Ernst could react, von Settgen slid two rubber dams, called Penrose drains, into the wound cavity to allow for continued drainage and irrigation. The pain made Ernst pass out. While he was still unconscious, he was dried off, the drains sutured in place, the wound bandaged then he was lifted out of the pool of blood and pus that collected under him on the litter in the makeshift operating room and onto a cleaner one. Aiken watched in admiration at the smooth functioning of the combined German and American medical teams as they put Ernst on the grain elevator to be lifted up to the second floor for recovery.

Aiken approached one of the medics who was cleaning up for the next one.

"This is a pretty amazing operation you guys have got going here. I thought I was a goner when those Kraut medics came out to unload me." The medic cut him off.

"We don't call them 'Krauts' here. They work alongside us, on our guys the same as we work on theirs. The docs have worked out a truce somehow, so we're not getting shelled or overrun and we just do the work. You bring them in and we patch them up."

"Speaking of which, I'd best be getting back," Aiken said. "I'll see you later."

"Most likely. What's going on out there?"

"We attack and drive them. They attack and drive us and meanwhile, its mortars and 88s all the time. Right now, we have one of the towns, they're shelling us from the woods. They've still got Panthers and God knows how much infantry. Don't expect there's going to be any letting up anytime soon. Take it easy."

"Yeah, you, too. Good luck."

Aiken fired up the Weasel and began the slow climb up the switchbacks and crumbling road edges until he came out in the woods facing the meadow before Kommerscheidt. The two Panthers were back with more than two hundred Panzergrenadieren behind them.

The renewed attack had trapped Schneider with the MPs who had come to take him to the POW pen set up in the woods. For now, they dropped him off in another ruined basement, depending on the heavy volume of fire to keep him there. The American tank line rotated their turrets from the woods back to the road to Schmidt.

"There they are," shouted Davis into the tank net. "*Wagon*, load up some wooly pete for the infantry. *Nightmare*, we'll hit the tanks with armor piercing. Move up and close on them." The optimum range for armor piercing rounds was four hundred yards. The American tanks revved their engines and charged the Panthers to close the seven-hundred-yard gap. Wooly pete was good up to a thousand yards so *Death Wagon* started pumping rounds into the infantry as well as scoring hits on the Panthers. Then they switched to armor piercing shells. The Panthers' sloping front hull, the glacis, had two-and-a-half inches of armor, the turret and sides had three inches increasing to nearly four inches in front of the driver and gunner positions. For a Sherman to take out a Panther from the front was suicide. Most successful attacks were several Shermans ambushing a Panther from the side. That was not likely here. The Panthers' 88 mm cannons were lethal with almost any hit on a Sherman. Davis hoped the white phosphorus hits would blind the Panthers long enough to give them time to maneuver around them.

Nightmare's gunner, Cpl. Cameron Smith had his shot lined up on the nearest Panther's barrel, his loader, Pvt. Martin Jewel, slammed the round home and tapped Smith on the shoulder. Immediately, the round was away, the casing recoiled into the tank between them and Jewel had the second round loaded. Through the smoke of the first round, Martin fired his second. Coming back at them through the same smoke was an 88mm round that glanced off the side of the turret. The entire tank shuddered and rocked. The noise of the near miss was deafening. Smith's rounds struck the base of the Panther's cannon, freezing it in place so it had no choice but to withdraw. *Nightmare* kept after the retreating Panther, putting one round into its track. This caused the Panther to spin around, presenting its side to *Nightmare*'s last armor piercing round which Smith put at the base of the Panther's turret, blowing it off and flames erupted from the cabin.

The line of American tanks had closed to within two hundred yards. Hits from either side would be lethal at this range. All the tanks broke out of formation and were moving independently, trying to get behind their adversary. *Hell's Fire's* two inches of armor would not save them at this range. Mortar crews from the German side fired smoke rounds into the field where the tanks maneuvered for advantage. Davis lost sight of the remaining Panther, assuming he was retreating into the woods. The Americans turned their tanks once again against the tree line. Grisholm, joined the other tanks' bow gunners as they sprayed the wood line with .30 caliber machine gun fire.

"That's good enough for now, *Hell's Fire*," Captain Ramsey's voice crackled over Davis's headphones. He had come forward from St. Vith to coordinate with the infantry and the artillery's forward observer in Kommerscheidt. "All tanks regroup on Kommerscheidt to support the infantry's attack on Schmidt. Well done."

The 112th Pennsylvania National Guard Regiment had only two hundred fifty of its allotted one thousand men with which to attack and re-take the town of Schmidt, much less hold it. This was not lost on Private Jeffery Howe. He and Henry Anderson were helping to man a line of foxholes astride the road leading to the town of Schmidt. He took little comfort in the three Sherman tanks to their front even after the Panthers had been dealt with.

Howe began his assessment of the situation. "We are still going to attack that worthless piece of shit town? With just us? And hold it when the Krauts counterattack and you know they are going to counterattack, sure as hell. The bastards always counterattack. Seems getting us killed is a waste of taxpayers' dollars spent in training us." Howe was only minimally comforted by the effectiveness of the tank platoon headed by Davis. The rest of the tank force and even more infantry remained held up by the poor condition of the Kall Trail behind them. Getting enough ammunition and food up to the forward elements of the 112th was also out of the question for now. The tankers re-distributed what rounds they had between them.

Howe worked the slide of his M-1 Garand for about the hundredth time. It was almost a nervous tic with him. As usual, Anderson let his rants go unanswered.

"What? You don't think this is FUBAR?", Howe continued, using the elegantly accurate acronym for "fucked up beyond all recognition". The arrival of the 155mm fire mission Davis had called in on the tree line just in front of them did little for his mood. "Oh, and right on cue, here is Rosinsky. Fucking hell."

Sgt. Rosinsky, the platoon sergeant, settled into the rubble of the church. He had a bandolier of ammunition and four grenades for each of them. Howe was still not impressed.

"This is great," Howe said, looping his bandolier around his shoulder. "What, now it's 'On to Berlin?"'.

"Jesus Christ, Howe, you are a hard man to please. Our generals are not unreasonable men. 'On to Schmidt' would satisfy them for now. Speaking of which, how are your feet?"

"Much better, thanks," said Anderson. "The socks and getting us above the waterline are doing the trick."

All three men ducked down with the arrival of more 88 rounds from the artillery on the adjacent ridge of Bergstein-Brandenburg.

"Before you start, again, Howe, those guns are being aimed by spotters in Schmidt," who had returned after being shelled by the 155mms in St. Vith, "and they will keep it up until we can blind them by knocking out the observers in Schmidt. Clear enough for you? Wait, I don't fucking care, really. That's the way it is.

"Just like before, the artillery starts, then we follow the tanks. And," Rosinsky had been saving the best for last, "watch your ammo. The trail across the river is still not open so re-supply will be what we can get across with the Weasels and on foot. No more tanks for now." His departure was punctuated by the arrival of more "88s", as he left to check on the rest of the company.

Even Howe was speechless.

#

Only Weasels could barely negotiate the Kall Trail from the east bank, across the river but only as far as the secondary aide station less than half-way up the west side which had been established as a dropping off place for the wounded and was rapidly filling up with both American and German wounded. Douglas Aiken evacuated wounded directly from Kommerscheidt and Schmidt, down the east side to the mill aide station on the river. There he dropped them off and picked up the at least minimally stabilized soldiers to move them up to the aide station half-way up the west side as a way to relieve the main aide station at the mill. The engineers had made little progress in improving the narrow, rock-strewn and crumbling trail with the main obstacle still being the boulder at the bend half-way down the west valley wall and the disabled tanks on the trail. The medics resorted to carrying the wounded on litters from the aide station up to the top of the trail where they could be loaded into ambulances for further evacuation. The ridge had no cover and was subjected to random shelling from the "88s" on the Bergstein-Brandenberg ridge without warning.

Corporal Tom Wilson was the medic in charge of the evacuation and was on one end of the lead litter. He was also the driver and was relieved to see the ambulance still waiting for them, not stolen or blown up. He slid his litter into the back. He knew what an attractive target the litter teams and ambulance made for the German gunners on the Bergstein ridge. He swung around the end of the ambulance and hopped behind the wheel.

The woods around the trail and at the top still had plenty of German patrols. As Wilson began to pull away, a German lieutenant with a squad of four men came out of the trees and stood in the way.

"Halt. I must inspect your vehicle for prisoners." His squad behind him had a maschinengewehr, a machinegun, aimed at Wilson who put his hands up.

"Now hang on there, Fritz. We're medics evacuating wounded, including two of yours. We are unarmed."

While keeping the machinegun trained on Wilson, the Lieutenant and two men went around the back and threw open the double doors. There he saw three Americans and two Germans lying side-by-side. He confirmed there were no weapons.

"You are now my prisoners, and will return with me and my men."

As they spoke four more litter teams came up out of the woods. There was one more German among them. The Germans were getting anxious now that they were outnumbered and even though unarmed, the Americans had enough men to rush them. The German machine gunner nervously swung the barrel back and forth trying to cover the American medics.

"Now look here, Captain," said Wilson giving the German officer a field promotion, "I will be happy to give you your men and litters to carry them on, but my guys are staying with us." He signaled to the newly arrived litter teams to come forward. All the wounded had been given the same level of care for their wounds that the aide station could provide but they clearly needed more.

The German officer looked over Wilson's shoulder and saw another ambulance leave the ruined town of Vosseneck and start toward them. There still seemed to be no infantry so he guessed the Americans had not recognized them as Germans. He knew that would soon change.

"Alright, Corporal, I will take just my men."

"You got it." The three German wounded soldiers, two from the ambulance and the newly arrived one and their litters were transferred over to the five Germans. They needed six men to carry them.

Wilson turned to his medics. "You all get these guys back to Vossenack. I'll help with these litters and you can come on back for me. Looks like we'll need at least two ambulances for what's coming up the trail."

That is how it went for the next two hours until the Kall Trail aide station was emptied of wounded. The litter teams would carry the wounded, now almost all American, to the top and into the waiting ambulances. The few Germans were turned over to their patrol and carried into the surrounding woods.

#

"Feuer!" shouted Oberleutanat Heinz von Kleist and bringing his right forearm down forcefully. His battery of four 88mm Flak PaK 43/41 cannon arrayed on Brandenberg-Bergstein ridge one mile east of the city of Bergstein overlooked all of the Huertgen Forest. Though not as well sited as at Schmidt, the artillery spotters from there could see all the enemy activity and bring down punishing fire on the Americans. The expected loss of Schmidt for their spotters was mitigated by taking Hill 400 which rose up from the Schmidt ridge where it came out of the forest. Spotters placed there could see the American engineers had finally widened the trail enough to allow renewed movement of tanks and men down the west valley wall. The four rounds leapt out of the von Kleist's 88s, on their way to land among the American tanks and infantry bunched up along the Kall Trail with lethal effect. Howe and Anderson in their foxholes at Kommerscheidt heard the vicious whistle of the rounds passing less than one hundred feet over their heads.

"Holy fuck!" shouted Howe to Anderson, "what did I tell you? And you can bet your sweet ass, we are next." They huddled deeper into their holes.

Enfield Davis in *Hell's Fire* spotted the muzzle flashes from the German 88s. He called in new coordinates to the batteries three miles behind him in St. Vith. Rounds were soon on their way to suppress the fire. With the suppression fire from St. Vith, Lt. Barclay quickly realized that there would never be a better time than this to assault Schmidt.

"Alright, 112th, let's go!" With that, Barclay sprang to his feet, assuming his men would follow. Davis and his two remaining Shermans grunted into motion, not strictly in line but slanting to cover the woods and the town. They held their fire to conserve their dwindling reserve of machine gun and cannon shells until needed. The infantry clung to the tanks and double timed across the open ground to Schmidt.

The remaining men of the 272 VGD and 116th Panzergrenadieren returned to the tree line and held their fire until the tanks and men were half way to the town and fully exposed.

"Nichts jetzt, nichts jetzt (not now)," the sergeant from the 272nd said, placing a restraining hand on the shoulder of his machine gunner. They tracked the American infantry and tanks, making their best time across the meadow.

"Jetzt! Feuer!" The Germans opened up with rifle, machine gun and mortar fire. Men began to drop around Anderson and Howe.

"Goddammit," Howe shouted as the rounds began to sing over his bent back and ping off the tanks. "I told you they weren't done with us. Motherfuckers." The natural response to receiving fire in the open was to lie flat and fire back. But they had to keep up with the tanks for any chance of surviving the run to Schmidt. *Death Wagon* and *Adolph's Nightmare* were the trailing tanks. Their commanders, Soames and Suarez, were standing to their .50 caliber guns and began to spray the tree line. Their turrets swiveled adding the coaxial .30 caliber machine gun to the fight. Jewel and Holland, the loaders had the 75 mm fragmentation shells loaded and quickly silenced the German fire from the woods. But the German sergeant had

survived five years of war by quickly responding to changing conditions.

"Get down. Cease fire," he yelled over the cacophony of his platoon's fire as soon as he saw the tanks' turrets begin to traverse and point to his position in the wood line, saving his men from the buzzing shrapnel rounds passing inches over their heads.

Davis slowed his tank platoon only when he entered Schmidt. Anderson, Howe and the rest of the company fanned out among the smoking ruins of the town. Scattered along the open ground between the two towns lay five dead Americans.

The three tanks arrayed themselves as before, one pointing down each of the three roads but without *Hell's Fire* in reserve in the center of town. Davis got in contact with his artillery to give them updated coordinates. Lt. Judd Barclay checked the cover of his men, who had begun to fortify their woefully inadequate positions.

"Dig in deeper, bring those bricks over, set up the .30s along the roads. Conserve your ammo. We've got to hold here until resupply can reach us from Vosseneck."

The cloud cover was what the bomber crews called "10/10", meaning totally socked in. There would be no air support for now.

Davis climbed down from his turret to confer with Barclay.

"How long before they counterattack, do you think?" he asked him.

"Soon, very soon," Barclay replied. "They can see the weather as well as we can and they'll want to push us out of here as soon as possible before we get some air support. Trouble is, we don't know if they are concentrated in just the woods to the east where we know they are, or if they have more troops to the north and west and can hit us from three sides. Are your tanks in good shape?"

"We're short on ammo, of course. I've redistributed it among the tanks but that just means everybody is equally short. For now, we'll have to depend on the arty from St. Vith to keep the Krauts off our asses."

"In coming, in coming!" shouted Corporal Howe. The terrifying high pitch sound - half screech, half scream, of an incoming 88mm round, cut through the Americans' resolve like the wail of a banshee. To hold a position, an infantryman had to believe he could survive. That fragile belief evaporated with the first German salvo.

"Son of a bitch. We are sitting ducks here," yelled Howe. "They've got us bracketed already." The tanks' cannons could not reach the far ridge where the 88s were positioned and the St. Vith artillery batteries had other fire missions. For now, 112th Infantry and the 707th tanks were on their own.

"Dig in, dig in," shouted Lt. Barclay. "We've got to hold here." He kept the squads' .30 caliber machine guns spraying the wood line, acutely aware of his dwindling ammo. He wanted to save the 4.2 cm mortar rounds for if the Panthers made another appearance. The question of whether there were other Germans in the area was quickly answered by accurate and intense fire from their front and east side of the ridge. From out of the woods came the Germans, only two hundred yards away from Schmidt and the pinned down Americans.

"We've got to go, Lieutenant," shouted Howe. Barclay grabbed the infantry phone mounted in a .30 cal ammo box on the rear of *Hell's Fire*, the command tank, which was wired into the intercom.

"Davis, fall back on Kommerscheidt, more Krauts coming from all sides."

"You got it."

The three tanks reversed forming a defensive box and began to make their best time back to the town, leaving Schmidt behind. The most important task was to get the machine guns back as well. Their crews pitched the guns onto the rear decks of the tanks, burning their hands on the hot barrels. The infantry scuttled alongside of the tanks using them for cover. Anderson thought he ought to try to recover at least one of the men killed during the assault on Schmidt but that would slow them down too much. *NIghtmare* ran over the dead man closest to Anderson who, despite the rumble of the tanks and the sound of firing, could hear the crunching of the dead man's bones.

Once back at the shallow ditch in front of Kommerscheidt, the tank platoon lined up and tried to slow down the German assault.

"Fire mission, fire mission, this is 707th tanks" he called into the 108th Field Artillery back at St. Vith. "We've been driven out of Schmidt and have at least a company size infantry attack. We could use some cover fire. Over."

"Sorry, 707th, you'll have to wait a bit. All hell has broken loose. We will send some your way when we can. Over."

"We cannot hold this position, I repeat, we cannot hold here. We are retreating back across the river to Vosseneck with the remains of the 112th Infantry."

"Sorry, we can't help, 707th. Good Luck."

Davis turned to Lt. Barclay. "No arty is coming. We've got to get the hell out of here."

"No argument from me." He turned to the thin line of infantry arrayed behind the tanks and in the rubble of

Kommerscheidt. "Alright, we're pulling back across the river. Withdraw in front of the tanks, keep going no matter what. Move out."

With that the 112th Infantry and 707th Armored retired from Kommerscheidt in good order, across the meadow to the trees at the head of the trail leading down the east valley wall. T.Sgt. Douglas Aiken had just returned in his Weasel with a pitiful amount of resupply including ammo belts for the .30 cals and ten 4.2 cm rounds for the mortar. This allowed mortar and machine gun crews set up a final line of defense just inside the trees. They were just enough to slow down the men of the 272nd VGD and 116th Panzer. The Panthers reversed when the mortar rounds began to fall among them. The American tanks, led by *Death Wagon* inched their way down the increasingly deteriorating east wall trail, followed by the rest of the 112th and finally by the machine gun and mortar crews. The last man to reach the Kall River was Lt. Barclay who stopped at the aide station in the Mestrenger Mill.

"Time to go, Major," he said to Major Brandt. "The Krauts are right on our tail."

"Everyone who could go has been evacuated already. These men won't make the trip. We'll stay here with Dr. von Stettgen and his men. Our medical truce seems to be holding so far. Good luck, Lieutenant." He went back into the mill and Barclay splashed across the Kall.

Chapter Seven:
The Windhunds

Colonel Kurt Hindman, commander of the Windhunds, the Greyhounds, 116th Panzer Division, or what was left of it, sat in the turret of his Panzer IV tank, one of only twelve left to him. He could see the smoke rising from the tank destroyed by T.Sgt. Enfield Davis's Sherman platoon. It is true that they had gotten a Sherman in return, Sgt. Manns' *Texas Pride*, and there seemed to be only three remaining Shermans left facing him. He could not know of the difficulty with the Kall Trail and the hold-up of more tanks and men arriving to re-enforce the small American force at Kommerscheidt that they had just driven back across the river. But he knew whatever it was delaying the Americans on the ground, and the socked in skies which held off the Thunderbolts and Mustangs, would not last much longer: a day or two at most.

Hindman was forty-six, tall for a tanker at six foot-two, grey streaks just appearing at his temples in his jet-black hair, complementing his penetrating, ice-berg blue eyes, which peered above sunken cheeks, wrinkled by four months of a fighting retreat since the American breakout at St. Lo. He was now tasked by the Fuhrer to retreat "not one more foot", accepting he and his men would likely die here defending the Fatherland.

He had earned his silver panzer assault badge and Iron Cross, First Class, on the steppes of Kursk. He wore it on his left tunic pocket. At times when he contemplated his own death or leading his men to their deaths, he would absent mindedly rub the two-and-a-half-inch oak leaf oval with an Imperial Eagle clutching a swastika in its claws at the top and a Panzer IV tank advancing through the center to calm himself. It became for Hindman a talisman of his duty owed to his men and country.

His three hundred remaining men were a mixed bag of many different units. He had his 116th Panzergrenadieren, remnants of the 272nd Volksgrenadeieren, Luftwaffe pilots, mechanics and groundcrew in their blue uniforms and summer boots, even sailors from the Kriegsmarine, some of whom had not held a rifle since their basic training. Most pitiful in Hindman's opinion were the Volksturm: sixteen-year-old boys kidnapped from their families, invalided old soldiers from the First World War; the mentally ill and other defectives that Himmler had somehow overlooked killing while purifying the Reich of such undesirables and were therefore spared until the Huertgen. Himmler had convinced Hitler that the Volksturm were the Ubermenschen that were to drive the Allied armies into the sea. Hitler believed him: he needed to believe him. None of his generals dared to tell him differently.

Col. Hindman had started the war as a lieutenant tank commander with Rommel's Afrika Korps in January, 1941.

He led a squad of four Panzer II tanks armed with a 37.5 cm cannon and two 7.92 mm machine guns, one on the turret and one coaxial with the main gun, with a five-man crew. Even in the early days of the campaign with Rommel's Panzerarmee Afrika, driving the British Eighth Army from Tobruk to Alexandria until finally halted at the First El Alamein then chased back to Tobruk after the Second El Alamein by Montgomery, Hindman had already seen enough war to last two lifetimes. He was a professional soldier, not an ideologue, committed to Germany and his men. His Panzer IIIs were the spearhead of the drive from the victory at Gazala resulting in the capture of Tobruk. His skill in fighting tanks had resulted in Hindman's being noticed. Attrition sped his rise in the command structure.

Those initial glory days of the Panzerarmee in the desert were lost in the fields of Kursk next year where Major Hindman led a reconnaissance tank battalion of twenty-six Panther III's with supporting anti-tank, Panzerjager mobile guns and a regiment of armored infantry in half-tracks. He was able to range between the German front line and the advancing Russians, holding them off by quickly responding to potential break throughs until the start of August, 1943, when the fuel ran out and the Russian Sturmovic II tank killers owned the skies. By then, his battalion was reduced to the size of a re-enforced company with twelve serviceable tanks and less than four hundred mounted infantry.

Major Hindman's tanks had conducted a fighting withdrawal bringing most of his remaining Panther III tanks back to Germany to face the Americans now swarming across France. His Panthers were superior to the Shermans in every way except one: numbers. Germany could produce about seven thousand Panthers while the Americans had fifty thousand Shermans. Their Shermans were far easier to maintain and service in the field and their tank recovery was so efficient that only a totally destroyed tank was left behind. The Germans had no such capability which haunted Hindman as he lost tanks to minimal damage. Any Panzer left on the field was destroyed by the placement of a thermite grenade in its barrel which burned a hole through the steel. To prevent a disabled tank from becoming a pillbox, gasoline was poured in the turret, ignited causing all the rounds to "cook off". The Americans perfected the strategy of the swarming ambush of the always outnumbered Panthers. But one on one, the Sherman was no match for a Panther III or IV and the wise American tank commander knew when to run and fight another day.

Hindman surveyed the land between Schmidt and Kommerscheidt from his Panther IV in the tree line.

"Look, Herr Colonel, the rest of the Shermans are pulling back," Sergeant Hans Strosser, his driver since Kursk. "I guess they didn't like their odds anymore."

Hindman looked to the sky once again. The cloud cover remained unbroken for now but looked to be thinning. He worried about leaving the protection of the forest and exposing his tanks on the open crest of the ridge. He had seen the accuracy of the American artillery stationed in St. Vith and did not want to risk a dash in the open to the Kall River valley. But he knew his chances were never going to better than at this moment. He picked up his radio handset.

Hindman felt hemmed by the narrow ridge, flanked by dense forest. He missed ranging over the North African desert or the wide steppes of Russia. On this ridge, maneuver was restricted to going forward or back, fast or slow. His force was "easy pickin's", he thought grimly, using one of his favorite sayings, picked up from watching American westerns during his university days. He had used it frequently when lining up a shot on a Russian T-26 tank outside of Kursk. It was the T-34 tank and the Sturmovic fighter bomber that drove his Windhunds back to Germany in 1943. He now found himself applying the phrase to his own Panthers all too frequently.

"Achtung, Achtung, all units. We advance through the villages and re-occupy the entire ridge. Do not stop until we have reached the trees beyond Kommerscheidt. We start in five minutes. Acknowledge."

That acknowledgement came in the form of the rumble of Panther engines, a sound that never failed to re-kindle

Hindman's fighting spirit. He knew the war was lost and he saw his duty now to his men and commanding them with honor; to save as many as he could. He would lead the assault.

"Forward, maximum speed." He knew his infantry units could not keep up with the tanks but the Americans would be trying to kill his tanks leaving the men alone for now. The Panthers burst out of the trees on either side of the ridge and sped through Schmidt and onward to Kommerscheidt.

"Tanks in the open," shouted the artillery spotter from his perch in the church steeple of the Lutheran church in Vosseneck. The guns of the 108th Field Artillery were stationed three miles away around St. Vith. The entire length of the Kommerscheidt-Schmidt ridge had been registered with the guns and before Hindman's Panzers were half way across, rounds began to fall to their front.

Oberleutnant von Kleist on the Brandenberg-Bergstein ridge with his four 88s a mile to the east could not reach the American guns at St. Vith. With a light load he could manage six miles with some accuracy but all he could do was to put some shells into the Kall River gorge to speed the retreating Americans on their way.

Major Brandt and Oberstabartz von Settgen, in the aide station, however, could not retreat. When the first shells began landing on the valley walls, all they could do was get their wounded down from the second story and onto the cement floor of the first story. The surgeons and medics covered the wounded men with their own bodies.

The Panther III next to Col. Hindman took a direct hit and exploded, rocking his tank. The tanks were most vulnerable to descending fire through the lightly armored turret top. The use of fragmentation rounds with proximity fuses wreaked havoc on the top of the Panthers and infantry on the ground. The rounds could be set to detonate a few yards above the target and spread a lethal cone of shrapnel destruction upon anything below.

"Evasive maneuvers!" he shouted into his inter tank radio. It would take them a little longer to reach the trees at the top of the Kall River gorge, but it might save some of his remaining tanks. This made the American artillery fire was only slightly less accurate and another Panther was hit. The rest of Hindman's ten tanks spread out along the top of the gorge under the minimal cover offered by the trees. Although the guns at St. Vith were out of range for the Panthers, Germeter and Vossenack were not, nor were the retreating American infantry, exposed in the open terrain between the towns and the gorge.

"Fire at will!" The ten Panthers trained their cannon and machine guns on the American targets with devastating effect. The spotter of the 108th Artillery had lost sight of the Panthers, not sure if they had entered the gorge or were spread out along the top. Then, he saw their muzzle flashes.

"New fire mission. Range: drop 200; round one, wooly pete. Fire."

The ranging round dropped in the trees amid the Panthers. Before Hindman could get his tanks moving again, the 108th Field Artillery had more rounds on the way.

"Sweep 400 yards, fire for effect." The 155mm howitzers of the 108th fired continuously, dispensing fifty rounds before ceasing fire. When they were done, the trees sheltering Col. Hindman's tanks were stripped sticks of smoldering ruin within which seven more Panthers were smoking hulks. Col Hindman and his two remaining tanks that could still move retreated at top speed back to the ridge and plunged over the banks into the dense trees of the Huertgan, pursued by shells from the 108th Artillery. The remaining infantry followed the tanks back into the Huertgan Forest. The "Windhunds" were no longer a fighting force but not completely destroyed. Surveying the carnage, Col. Hindman still had reason to hope, he and the "Windhunds" would be back.

The exchange of fire between the American artillery and the Panthers had stopped. The roar of the rounds passing over the steep gorge had been deafening. There were no new impacts in the gorge itself. The main noise came from Douglas Aiken's Weasel laboring down the east valley wall bringing in the newly wounded resulting from the Panther tanks' fire. He had two men strapped to their litters and two more on the seats in the rear. The months since Normandy retrieving wounded men had made Aiken's triaging ability very astute. He knew who could make it back to the aide station, who were living but hopeless and left behind. For the rest of his life, it was their eyes that Aiken saw before sleep.

The ground between the gorge and Vosseneck was still smoking from the Panther rounds. Aiken's route with the Weasel was a two-way street. He dropped off the wounded at the Mestrenger Mill, rather than risk the run over open terrain, taking unstable wounded all the way to the towns. He picked up stabilized wounded who had been treated at the mill to take back the larger aide stations at Vosseneck and Gemeter. They could tolerate getting bounced around as Aiken drove like a bat out of hell to cross the open area between the gorge and Vosseneck. The more clearly marked ambulances that picked up wounded carried out of the valley by the medics from the small aide station half-way up the west wall offered better protection and a smoother ride than his Weasel.

A POW enclosure had been established in the woods on the west of the Kall River gorge. After Ernst Locher had had his shoulder drained, he re-joined Hermann Schneider with the other POWs captured at Schmidt and Kommerscheidt.

"Kleine," Schneider said, placing his hand on Ernst's back, "you look better." He inspected the dry dressing over his shoulder, even sniffing it, detecting none of the sickening stench of the undrained pus. "Come with me over here. I've saved you some soup although, truly, I never thought I'd see you again."

The POW enclosure was very much a make shift affair. The "walls" were only stacked brush and there were guards every twenty feet. For now, it contained fifty prisoners, most of them wounded to some degree and more than happy to be out of the fight. Schneider got Ernst situated against a tree. Ernst shifted his bandaged arm in his sling and sighed. Schneider handed him a mess tin with cold soup which he took in his right hand and rapidly emptied into his mouth. Schneider gave him his portion as well, not really knowing when or if he might get fed again.

"Now, tell me. How are you feeling?" Schneider asked.

"Much better, thanks to you. I'm pretty sure I'd be dead without your help. I am grateful, thank you, many thanks."

"Think nothing of it. We are comrades, that's what comrades do. Now try to get some sleep."

The fight for the town of Schmidt was not over. The German counterattack led by Col. Hindman's Panzers had driven off the American guards and freed their prisoners, Ernst and Schneider among them. Ernst was seen by medics and cleared for duty. He and Schneider once again found themselves back in the 272nd VGD.

#

The pilots, bombardiers and navigators of the 349th Squadron, 100th Bomb Group, assembled for the early morning briefing in the ready room at Thorpe Abbotts. The one-armed Major pulled back the curtain covering the flight plan map for the day's mission. He expected more than the usual moaning and groaning and he was not disappointed.

"Jesus, that place again?" called out Lt. Topman. "We just hit that place like last week."

"That's right, Lt. Topman, which means a crackerjack navigator like yourself should have no trouble finding it again. It seems the Krauts were not dissuaded by our last efforts and have managed to overrun the entire ridge and taken back the two towns of interest: Schmidt and Kommerscheidt. Our guys were driven all the way back across the river and into Vosseneck and Gemeter." He struck each town as he named them with his pointer forcefully so that the "whack" could be heard all the way to the back of the room.

"Now, intelligence, (Topman snorted derisively snorted), thinks there is a growing Panzer group with infantry support present in the woods on the slopes of the ridge. Their 88s on the next ridge over do not have the range to hit the towns we have. They ran some tanks to the east rim of the gorge to shell the towns but our arty took them out. So, the most likely plan for them is a night attack, across the gorge and retake Vosseneck and Gemeter. If they do that, then all of the Huertgen Forest falls back into their hands. If that happens then First Army's advance to the Roer is in the shitter and our little bit of the war gets that much longer.

"So, we are going to bomb the hell…"

"Once again," said Topman in his best stage whisper.

"Yes, once again and again after that if need be. Not only do we have to keep the Huertgen but also the dams at the head of the valley. These two dams, the Schwamm-whatever," pointing it out on the map, "and the Urft control the flow of the Roer River and if the Germans blow the dams, the valley is flooded, our guys are cut off and, again, we can't proceed for probably a month or more.

"So, a maximum effort:" this time Topman merely mouthed the words, "three flights of a hundred planes each, each day for at least three days has been ordered. The Krauts have cement bunkers scattered throughout the woods on both sides of the Schmidt ridge. Their Panzers can withdraw deep under the tree cover and refit. There have been signs of more Panzer IVs and even a Tiger or two moving into the area. With those leading an attack, it is probable that they can sweep all the way to Vosseneck, move their 88s onto the Schmidt ridge and make things very uncomfortable for our guys in the First Army.

"The plan, then. Is to carpet bomb the living hell out of the Schmidt and Brandenberg ridges, all the forest in between so that the infantry can advance through the Monschau plain, cross the Roer and onto the Rhine. We do that and the war gets shortened by months.

"A worthy goal, wouldn't you say Lieutenant Topman?"

"Absolutely, Major. I couldn't have planned it better myself."

With that, the Major went over the routes, the recall sign, the assembly points for the squadrons, flights, wings, rendezvous with the fighter escorts, the IP and the final bomb runs. They would bomb at eight thousand feet to insure good coverage of the target. Anticipating objections to flying so low, the Major pointed out that the Luftwaffe had been essentially eliminated in the area and the only anti-aircraft batteries were the 88s on the Brandenberg ridge which would be taken care of in the initial bomb runs.

"Let's have a good mission. Dismissed."

#

Col. Hindman and the few remaining Windhunds, had sheltered deep in the forest. His instincts, born of three years of nearly continuous tank combat, warned him that the ridges were going to be very dangerous places and he had to keep his men protected as best he could. He had orders to await the arrival of replacement tanks from Cologne, which surprised him. He knew the tank factories and steel works were prime targets for the American air force so he was not expecting replacements so soon. Clearly, driving the Americans out of the Huertgen and Ardennes forests were top priority for the Oberkommando des Heeres, the OKH, supreme command of the army, led by General Alfred Jodl. But after Wehrmacht's defeat in Russia, Hitler had lost faith in his generals and taken control of planning and strategy. No one dared oppose him, no matter how ill-conceived his decisions were. Therefore, whatever he decided was a priority became the focus of his war machine. He would soon be withdrawing the best troops to launch the "Wacht am Rhein" attack, known in the West as the "Battle of the Bulge". To bring units like the Windhunds to full strength, Hitler diverted manufacturing from aircraft to tanks, essentially surrendering the skies to the Allied air fleets.

Hitler had been hoarding replacement armor and artillery as well as what first line infantry troops he had left for a last gasp effort to break through the Allied lines and sweep up to the Meuse River, thus splitting the American from the British-Canadian armies, possibly even encircle and crush them, then seize the Port of Antwerp. In his mind, that would be such a stunning blow to the western allies that they would sue for peace. He then could turn the full force of the Wehrmacht against the invading Russians and save the Third Reich. No one in the German General Staff said a word against Hitler's delusions.

"Herr Colonel, I have new orders from Panzer Gruppe West," said Sergeant Strosser and handed Hindman a crumpled note on official stationery. Hindman read the note without expression. He picked up his inter-tank radio.

"Heinrich," he said to his one remaining tank commander. "We are to proceed to Aachen to refit. The Fuhrer has apparently pulled some tanks out of Himmler's ass and is giving them to us. God knows where he got the crews and how good they can be, but we'll see. We'll move out after dark. Get some sleep."

The two Panzers had to move on the paved road to make any headway. They drove without headlamps, just barely making out the way forward. The dark, overcast and the fact they were heading away from the Americans did little to soothe Hindman's jangled nerves. His main worry was running out of fuel before he could get to Aachen. If that happened, he would have to abandon the tanks and walk which would be a blow to his already nearly shredded pride and confidence. As it was, the Panzers pulled into the tank yard next to the railhead and shuddered to a stop – out of fuel. They found the officers' billets and slept until dawn.

They awoke to find that an orderly had laid out clean uniforms. They had their first hot shower in a month, a breakfast of sausage and eggs so that Hindman and his fellow tank commander, Major Heinrich Stossen, presented at the headquarters of the 116th Panzer Division in good order. The orderly showed them into the commander's inner office. After crisp salutes were exchanged, General Gerhard Wilck put them at ease.

"Please, gentlemen, sit down. Can I offer you cigars or some cigarettes? Too early for schnapps, I fear."

"Thank you, Herr General," answered Colonel Hindman. "You have been most hospitable."

"Not at all, Colonel. Now tell me what happened at the Kall River?"

Hindman summed up the fighting, the American resistance and their eventual routing. "We were stopped at the gorge and were sorting out how to get across when the American artillery hit us. There was only open ground behind us, no way to get the tanks into the gorge. There is only one dirt track, barely wide enough for a tank, leading down to the river and up the other side. Our 88s firing from the Brandenberg did not have enough range to cover us. Their 155-millimeter guns were accurate and the tree cover was of no help. Major Stossen and I were lucky to have made it over the side of the ridge and into the thicker trees."

Colonel Hindman continued, "I deeply regret the loss of the Windhunds and will submit my resignation." With that, Hindman snapped to attention then bowed slightly.

"Nonsense, Colonel," said General Wilck. "We have more tanks but we do not have the crews, experienced crews to man them. We will reconstitute the Windhunds with Panzer IVs and have them ready for the Fuhrer's plans against the Allies. You should have a few weeks to train and refit. Meanwhile, you and Major Stossen can rest here in Cologne for a few days.

"That will be all." Salutes were exchanged and the two tankers left headquarters.

Colonel Hindman had had his first real bath in three months. He had checked into the Hotel am Augustinerplatz, which had the least bomb damage. It was where the elite of the Wehrmacht stayed when in Cologne. In fact, he had seen two generals and a field marshal in the lobby when he checked in. As he sank into the cast iron footed tub, shivering with the warm water and feeling his muscles unknot, the thought that if the American Eighth Air Force had not slotted this target for more attention, they were missing a tremendous opportunity.

"Just let me finish my bath," he thought, "Then I will happily die, anywhere but in that damned hell hole of a forest."

Chapter Eight: Missing in Action

Virginia Standhope had become accustomed, as had all of the villagers of Thorpe Abbotts, to the sound of the B17s' engines starting up at three in the morning. Most nights she would say a prayer for their safe return as she drifted back to sleep. This night was different. She had not seen Joe Hanover for two weeks after the picnic. He had told her that he flew on the *Bouncing Betty,* but she was too far away from the field to pick it out of the hundreds of planes that came and went on their missions. Her heart was in her throat every time a smoking bomber struggled to make a landing, firing off the red flares denoting wounded on board, and lived in terror until she could hear from Joe again. The 'Fox and Hens' pub was a popular spot for the bomber crews and most of the time, word would be gotten to her that Joe was OK, delivered by sympathetic crewmen on passes.

This night, a frisson of fear ran down her spine, as she heard the planes revving their engines then accelerate down the runway. She threw on her robe over her nightgown and ran outside to see bomber after bomber take off and disappear into the overcast, black night, their taxi lights blinking out in the clouds. She buried her face in her hands, tears escaping down her cheeks and hands.

"Oh, God, let Joe come back to me, please."

The preflight routines had gone without a hitch for the *Betty's* crew. They were flying to a well- known spot: the ridges in the Huertgen Forest to bomb, yet again, as pointed out by Lt. Topman, that miserable plot of Germany. This time, their flight of thirty-two B17s was to concentrate on the next ridge over, the Brandenburg-Bergstein ridge to take out the concentration of 88mm artillery that was plaguing the 112th Pennsylvania National Guard, "The Bloody Bucket", regiment's, attempts at seizing and holding the towns of Schmidt and Kommerscheidt. These towns were vital to the German's stopping the advance of General Hodges' First Army to the Roer River and beyond.

This was the twenty-fifth mission for the *Betty* and except for losing Luis Ramon over Munster during the flight on which LeMay had tagged along, the crew was surprisingly stable. Hanover knew everyone on the *Bouncing Betty* every well. They were closer than brothers, men to be depended upon and protected. Every crew lived with the knowledge that any mission could be their last, that death stalked them wherever they were. Enough planes had exploded on the flight line from faulty five-hundred-pound bombs as they were being loaded, planes flaming out and crashing within sight of the airfield, engines cutting out at any time during the missions and any number of other inexplicable losses that any hopes for their futures were fiercely suppressed. To think of surviving the war and going home made them likely to second guess decisions rather than just acting instantaneously. Death was omnipresent in the form of Messerschmitt 109s, Focke-Wulf 190s, black flak clouds and would not be denied.

Hanover checked his .50 caliber in the right waist and waited for take-off. As the *Betty* rose from the field, he craned his neck to try to see at least Thorpe Abbotts even though it was still dark and he had only a few seconds before entering the cloud cover. He envisioned Virginia safe and asleep in her room in the back of the 'Fox and Hens', a vision that never failed to soothe him.

Ten minutes into the flight, climbing to ten thousand feet and gathering at Buncher 28, Captain Flanagan came on the intercom.

"Look alive. We've got our 'little friends' with us. As you can see, they're P-51 Mustangs, which can stay with us to the target and back. That doesn't mean we get the day off. You can check your guns. We should hit the IP in about an hour. Good hunting."

Each man in the 100th felt a new hope. To have fighters that could stay with them and fight off the Gustavs and Doras, meant that maybe, just maybe, they could live to see their homes again. It did not mean nothing but "cake walk" missions going forward but at the very least, the Mustangs improved the Bloody 100th's chances, and the crews would take any hope they could get.

This was another hundred plus plane mission comprised of B17s and B24s. The 100th BG was again the lead element and crossed into Belgium then turned south at Aachen, descending to eight thousand feet for their final approach. There was some light flak from the city but this intensified quickly as they began their bombing run over the Brandenberg-Bergstein ridge.

Hauptman Heinz von Kleist, who was in charge of the 88s on the Brandenberg ridge, looked up only to confirm what he knew to be inevitable: heavy American bombers overhead and probably having already dropped their bombs. He knew what valuable targets his guns were. With only four of the guns, he had been able to disrupt the American advance through the Huertgen Forest, down the Monschau corridor and delay the capture of Aachen, breeching of the Siegfried Line, the Westwall as the Germans called it, and crossing the Roer River. He had an inexhaustible supply of rounds, dedicated gun crews and the accuracy of the guns themselves. American counterbattery fire was inaccurate due to the extreme range, making aerial bombing the only realistic option.

He saw the bombers were flying below ten thousand feet. He was able to fire off three salvoes of flak before the bombs began bursting on the ridge. He had the satisfaction of seeing two B17s explode and a third begin to burn.

"That's all we can do. Get the guns under cover," he shouted above the cacophony of the bomb strike. He was the last German off the ridge. Due to the superb training of his crews and the mobility of his guns, he was able to move them into the trees and their concrete revetments as the ridge erupted in smoke and flame.

The Mustangs were flying a high cap, not expecting anything from the Luftwaffe and were just as glad to be out of the flak which seemed to engulf the bombers. All the pilots thought it was suicide to fly that low but "theirs not to reason why..." which was the thought running through bombardier Lt. Stanley Tolland's mind as he peered through his Norden bomb sight. The plane was rocked by many near misses and shrapnel began to sing through the plane. Tolland kept the plane flying level through the final bomb run until the Brandenberg ridge was under his crosshairs.

"Bombs away," he shouted and turned the plane back to Flanagan who immediately started to climb and turn to evade the flak. The German gunners on the ground anticipated this move and put a fatal 88 round into the root of the left wing with their final salvo. The explosion of the fuel tanks blew the *Betty* apart killing all the crew except Joe Hanover who was blown through the right waist window into the smoke and flame of the exploding *Betty*. His survival reflex caused him the pull his rip cord and the opened 'chute dragged him away.

Bombers were exploding around him, or had become plunging columns of smoke and fire. A second flight of thirty planes hit the Brandenberg-Bergstein ridge, taking out the remaining 88mm anti-aircraft guns that claimed ten B17s. Flying at eight thousand feet ensured that both sets of combatants hit their targets with devastating effects.

Joe curled himself into a ball as he floated towards a landing somewhere in Germany. He wanted to drop as fast as he could to avoid the fiery debris that fell all around him. He could only hope he would land behind American lines. As the ground grew closer, he saw another threat: he could very easily land in the burning rubble of a crashed B17. He supposed that no one still in the air had to time to look for 'chutes and the way the *Betty* exploded, no one expected to see any.

Twenty yards above the ground, just entering the smoke column of a destroyed B17 and feeling the rising heat of the flames, Hanover made one last desperate tug on his lines on the right, swinging himself just beyond the flames. His 'chute landed in the fire, burning through the lines and allowing Joe to roll clear. He shrugged out of his parachute harness and began patting himself down to check for wounds. Amazingly, he found none. He looked up at the departing B17s and B24s. He spotted a few other slowly descending parachutes. He did not know where the American lines were. He had landed in the trees which had been largely denuded by artillery fire over the last month.

Part of the pre-flight briefings had covered "E&E": escape and evasion. The routes and resources available depended on the flight plan for the mission and had to be committed to memory since if written instructions fell into German hands, whole networks of resistance fighters could be compromised. Hanover now tried to remember his briefing but soon realized that since he did not know where the hell he was, the information was pretty much useless to him.

"SNAFU", he thought. He watched the few other flyers drift to the ground and went to join them. There were only five, all enlisted men.

"Everybody OK?" asked Hanover.

"I think I sprained my ankle or broke it," said a Technical Sergeant from Arkansas named Jeb Olgilvie. He had sandy red hair, blue eyes and freckled. He looked no more than thirteen.

"Can you put any weight on it?" asked Hanover.

"Not much and not for long."

"Alright, we'll get a crutch from one of the branches. Anybody know where the hell we are?"

"Well," said Jack Pander, a corporal waist gunner, "I think our last fix was somewhere over Schweinfurt, just beginning our bomb run when, I guess, an 88 hit us in the tail. We barely got out before we spun in."

"You're all from the same ship?" asked Hanover.

"Yeah, the *Shy Virgin*, 369thSquadron, 448th Bomb Group out of Seething, England, B24s, mainly." Pander said. The rush of being blown out of the sky and living to talk about it spurred his reporting abilities. "We'd only been in England for a few months. We were in North Africa, then Italy and flew a mission the very first day we got to England. We were supposed to bomb Polesti this time but diverted to Schweinfurt due to weather and didn't quite make it. Luckily, we hadn't armed the bombs before they hit us or I think we would have been just a fine red mist drifting down on this little bit of Germany or Belgium or France, wherever the hell this is. You got a cigarette?"

Hanover had been tearing up parachute nylon and wrapping Olgilvie's ankle to try to control the swelling. "Don't smoke, sorry. How's that? Think you can bear weight on it?"

"Gotta a choice? Yeah, it's fine, thanks. Anybody got a compass?" None did.

The *Shy Virgin's* remaining crew were all in the waist when she was hit. It was the fluke of flak that the nose and tail were taken out leaving the wings and fuselage intact long enough for the surviving crew men to bail out. It was terrifying enough to jump out of an exploding plane then drift down through an air battle, knowing that a single bit of flak or a .50 cal round through the parachute canopy would have them plummeting to the ground. The crew had no rations and only their .45 caliber sidearms. They were lost in probably enemy territory, without a compass or map. They could assume that their descent had been seen and a German patrol was headed their way. They moved further into the trees.

Joe Hanover had seniority in that he had been with the 100th Bomb Group longer than the other men had been in England. He was a natural leader as well: assured, never rattled. He feared only for Virginia in Thorpe Abbotts when she heard that he had been shot down. He knew she watched the planes return from their missions, counting them home. She may not know which planes did not make it but he was sure that someone from the group would tell her he would not be returning. Only later did he think of his parents, home in Twin Forks, Indiana, getting the "missing in action" telegram and then nothing until the "presumed killed in action" notice arrived. He put all those thoughts out of his mind and took control of the group of downed airmen.

After the thunderous noise inside a B17 or B24, the quiet in the woods was almost as oppressive. They had not heard birdsong or leaves rustling for so long that it took a while to recognize the sounds. Soon, however, they heard noises that made them quake: human voices. The airmen crept further into the bush, each gripping his pistol.

"What are they saying? I don't think it is German or French," whispered Olgilvie.

"I can't make it out," replied Hanover. The group approaching was armed, seemed relaxed but watchful.

"'Allo, Americains? Are you there?" their leader called out.

"What the fuck?" said Olgilvie.

"Cover me," said Hanover. He chambered a round in his .45 but kept it at his side and slowly emerged from the trees.

"Ah, there you are. Are you hurt? I am Ambroos Hansen, of the *Belgisch Verzet*, the resistance. We saw your parachutes, which means the Bosch saw them, too. We must hurry. Are there more of you?"

Hanover led the five Belgians into the woods and into the fire zone of four cocked .45s.

"Whoa," Hanover said. "They're friendly."

"Couldn't be sure they didn't have a gun to head," said Pvt. Anton Solario, from Queens, the *Shy Virgin's* top ball turret gunner. They all lowered their guns and relaxed.

"Quite right," said Hansen. "But one of you is hurt?" he said, spotting Olgilvie's ankle. "Can you walk on it?"

"I'll be OK, the crutch helps."

"Good, we are not going far. Follow me."

Hansen led them deeper into the woods until he stopped in the middle of a clearing. He made sure that all the men were accounted for then pulled up on what seemed to be a dead bush. This opened a trap door leading into a tunnel.

"Et voila!" he. "Our, how you say, 'home against home.' "

"'Home away from home' is what we say," corrected Hanover. "Looks very cozy".

The Americans followed their Belgian rescuers into the tunnel which soon widened into a chamber large enough to accommodate all of them. Two other tunnels led off into the darkness. Stacked along the walls were captured German weapons. Their Belgian hosts gave them warm soup and coarse black bread.

"You will rest up for the next day," said Ambroos, "while we will discuss how to get you all home." He disappeared down one of the tunnels.

In addition to Solario and Olgilvie, there were Tech Sergeant Thomas Healey from Nebraska, left waist gunner on the *Shy Virgin* and Corporal Randy Payne, of Vermont, the belly turret gunner. They had been flying together for about four months and had formed the tight bond of young men in combat. Now, in the relative safety of the underground chamber, the crews had time to reflect on what they had lost.

"God, Joe," said Healey, "I'm sorry about your crew. Are you sure, you are the only one to make it?"

Joe was quiet for a while, making the other survivors think he did not want to talk about it until he said, "I don't know how I made it. The wing exploded and blew me out of the waist. I don't remember pulling the ripcord but I must have. The whole crew were the best: best pilot, Captain Flanagan, all of them."

"It was the flukiest thing I'd ever seen," replied Healy of the *Shy Virgin*. "Flak took out the nose of our plane with the pilot, co-pilot, navigator, engineer and radio, then the tail gunner. Just like they'd been clipped off with a big pair of shears. We got out just as the rest of the ship blew. Never saw anything like it."

Ambroos Hansen returned with an oil lamp and a pan of what passed for coffee. He also carried a map which he spread out on the floor.

"You men will need to memorize this. The route will get you to the American lines, about fifty miles from here. There will be several stages, different friends who will conduct you further on.

"A group of five is big to move so it is likely you will be broken up and sent on one by one or two at the most. You will be given civilian clothes but keep your rank insignia showing you are American soldiers. If you are captured without that, the Bosch will most likely torture and then shoot you as spies. But they may do that anyway.

"You will move at night and hide during the day in safe places. We will conduct you to the American lines which are currently in the Huertgen Forest, south of Cologne. The Germans are falling back but fighting hard still. The most dangerous part will be getting through their 'Westwall', what you call the 'Siegfried Line.'"

"Why not just sit tight and wait for the Americans to come to us?" asked Salario.

"We can't predict when that will be. The advance may stall due to the Germans' resistance. Their patrols pass through here all the time and if they find us... well, you can imagine. No, it is better to

break up and be on the move. At least, we don't have to get you all the way to Spain anymore."

#

Virginia Standhope was behind the bar at the 'Fox and Hens' when she heard the unmistakable sound of the returning B17s to Thorpe Abbotts field. The near daily missions had developed her ear and she knew from the roar of the engines that this flight had missing planes. She had gotten the ability to distinguish how many planes were coming in on only one or two engines, those that probably would not make the field. She ran out to see the first three planes barely staying airborne, smoke from their engines, red flares arcing away from the battered fuselages. There were more flares from the trailing aircraft but it seemed they could stay aloft longer than the lead ships.

Jeeps, fire trucks and ambulances raced down the airstrip to where the damaged planes would come to an uneasy rest, pulling off onto the grass so as not to obstruct the airstrip if they exploded. Bomber after bomber limped down from the sky until twenty of the thirty-five that had left that had left early that morning were safely on the ground. She could not read the names or recognize the nose art from where she was standing and she certainly could not go the field itself. All she could do is wait for Joe to come into the 'Fox and Hens', home safe again. From times passed, she knew the debrief would take about an hour, leaving only between six and eight o'clock for any of the crews to stop at the pub.

She knew that no matter how tired Joe was, he would at least stop by. So, it was with a hopeful smile that she looked up when she heard someone enter the pub early that evening. But it was not Joe. She tried to hide her disappointment.

"Miss Standhope?", the airman asked, doffing his service cap.

"Yes."

"My name is Herman Pugh. I'm the belly turret gunner on the *Lucky Jane*. We were in Joe's flight this last mission." He stopped, avoiding her eyes, wringing his cap. "We became friends and he always spoke so highly of you."

"Thank you. Will he be along soon?"

Pugh cleared his throat. "Could we sit down?''

Virginia began to tremble. She felt the blood drain from her face and could barely make it around the bar, falling into the nearest chair. "What is it?"

"There is no good way to say this. We were making our turn back north to head for home. We were probably two hundred miles into Belgium when Joe's plane was hit. They chewed us up pretty good. It was flak that hit the wing. It exploded almost immediately. We didn't see any 'chutes. I am so sorry."

Virginia did not hear anything he said after his first sentence. She stared at Pugh who could not meet her eyes.

"No, there must be a mistake. You can't know, you can't be certain." Her voice began to rise. "You're lying for some reason. It can't be true." Pugh rose with her from the chair. She began to beat on his chest. He let her, keeping his arms at his side. "You're wrong, you must be." She was screaming at him, clutching his tunic. "No, no, no." She collapsed in sobs against him. Pugh then held her and they both sank to their knees.

Her father, hearing the cries, came out from the storeroom. Seeing them kneeling on the floor, he knew what had happened. He came around the bar and put his hand on Pugh's shoulder.

"Thank you, Sergeant. I know how hard it must be for you. Please leave us alone."

Pugh helped him pull Virginia to her feet. He turned, closing the door of the pub behind him, putting up the "Closed" sign.

"Come on, my girl," her father said gently, "let's get you some rest."

"Joe...Joe's gone," Virginia sobbed.

"I know." Her father half-carried Virginia behind the bar and into her room.

#

Enfield Davis of *Hell's Fire* led the rest of his Sherman platoon back towards the Kall River gorge, very satisfied with the effect of the artillery on driving off Colonel

Hindman's Panzers and the bombing runs on the ridges. He was to spearhead the drive to retake the towns of Kommerscheidt and Schmidt, once again. Behind him were the one hundred twenty men of the 112th Pennsylvania National Guard, less two understrength companies left behind in Vossenach, which were all that was left of the regiment after only a week of heavy fighting. They were joined by a company of the 110th, making a total of less than two hundred men to retake the Kommerscheidt-Schmidt ridge. The elimination of the 88s on the adjacent ridge made this less of a suicide mission but no means a walk in the park.

Davis led his fully re-armed and re-fueled Shermans back down the west slope across the Kall and up the east side. He noted the marked improvement of the east and west trails the engineers had made and his force made it to the top in half the time as every other attempt. The improved trails also meant there were no thrown tank tracks. But the Trail did remain the only supply route across the Kall. There was no doubt that the Germans had more Panzers and 88s that would be making the trip deadly soon enough. The burned-out hulks of Shermans and Weasels were stark reminders of that. The American artillery had blasted the tree cover and they passed the smoking hulks of ten Panzers, as they continued on into Kommerscheidt, taking up defensive positions there until the infantry caught up with them. Lieutenant Barclay, leading the 112th, grabbed the field phone on the back of Davis's tank.

"Well, Sergeant, what do you think?"

"I am sure glad those 88s seem to be gone and the Panzers seem to be dealt with for now. We still don't know what's in the woods, though."

"I agree," Barclay said, "but there seems to be only one way to find out. We'll kick off in five minutes.''

"Roger." Davis got on the inter-tank com frequency to his other tanks.

"We're moving out in five minutes. Still no break in the overcast so no air support and the artillery can't reach Schmidt, so we are on our own. I'll lead, *Death Wagon*, you take right flank, *Nightmare,* you take the left. The infantry will snug right up behind us so we'll move out at double time speed. Any questions?"

"Yeah, I got one," said Soames. "How sure are we that there's not more arty in the woods, that the Krauts didn't lace the ground with mines and there ain't the whole fucking SS and shit waiting for us in the trees?"

"Well, that's what we are going to find out, isn't it?" replied Davis. "Remember, the US Government gave you that ten-thousand-dollar life insurance policy free of charge? Now might be the time to find out if they really meant it. Button up, we go in three minutes."

Davis stayed standing in his hatch, manning the .50 cal. The other tanks roared to life and started off, their turrets traversing the open ground along the Schmidt ridge. Davis saw a Panzerfaust team pop to his right, just over the rim of the ridge. Too late, he swung his machine gun and fired but it was enough to distract the Germans' aim and the rocket went wide. Another team fired from the left and Saurez in *Adolph's Nightmare* put some wooly pete on that side. No rocket came their way. Lieutenant Barclay deployed fifty men a side to the ridge's edges to try to discourage such activity.

Private Ernst Locher's shoulder was stiff but the sutures were holding and there was no more drainage or redness. Corporal Hermann Schneider hovered over him, tending to the dressing changes, carrying his pack and rifle. They were joined by Private Klaus Weisen, the sniper of the 116th Panzergrenadieren. The three soldiers watched the American advance toward their position at the nose of the Kommerscheidt-Schmidt ridge. They were among the last thirty infantrymen still in Schmidt. They had the unenviable task of holding the American off as long as they could. When the Americans were two hundred yards from the town, Wiesen began his work.

"There you see?" he asked no one in particular. "He must be the officer in charge." He drew a bead on Lieutenant Barclay and gently squeezed the trigger. Two seconds later, Barclay felt the round pass by his leg. As always, Wiesen aimed to wound, not to kill.

"Sniper! Sniper!" shouted Barclay as he hit the ground. The rest of the men did the same.

"Where, Lieutenant?" asked Sergeant Rosinski.

"From the town, I think."

Davis had seen the infantrymen hit the dirt and began to pepper the ruins of Schmidt with his .50 cal.

"Tolliver," he shouted to his gunner. "Put some frag rounds into the town, right, front and center."

"On the way," came the reply. *Hell's Fire* bucked and belched smoke and fire. The shells impacted right on Davis's targets.

Schneider grabbed Ernst and covered him with his own body. The shells impacted feet from their shallow foxhole. They heard the shrapnel buzz over them like a hundred angry hornets.

"What are we going to do, Herr Schneider?" asked Ernst, his voice shaking and filled with tears.

"We are alright here, as long as we don't move. They won't fire if they don't think there is anybody here. Just stay quiet."

"See anything, Tolliver?" asked Davis.

"Nothing", he answered.

"Well, let's get moving." Davis radioed to the other tanks and began to move on Schmidt. Lieutenant Barclay had his men move in *Nightmare's* tracks. With the approach of the Americans once again on Schmidt, the remaining German infantrymen melted back into the trees. The tanks pursued the Germans until losing them in the forest. The following infantry deployed once again in the ruins of Schmidt. Slowly, Schneider raised his hands and rose to his knees.

"Aufgeben, bitte, aufgeben (I surrender)," he said. He kept his gaze down. The nearest GI was Private Henry Anderson of the 112th. At first startled, he trained his rifle at Schneider's chest but when Schneider looked up, Anderson recognized him.

"Sonofabitch," he said. "It's you again." Schneider also recognized Anderson and smiled. "Where's your little friend?"

Schneider rose to his feet as did Ernst, both with their hands over their heads.

Anderson smiled and shook his head. "Well, I guess we get you back to the MPs again." Lieutenant Barclay was two holes over. Anderson scuttled over. "Got some prisoners, Lieutenant. Repeat business you might say."

"What?", then he recognized them as well. "Jesus. We might as well make them mascots."

He had Tuttle, his radioman, call for evacuation. Soon, Sergeant Aiken pulled up in his Weasel. Within half an hour, Ernst and Schneider were POWs again. They began their journey to Patterton POW Camp outside of Glasgow.

Chapter Nine:
Fly and Fight Until Victory or Death

Lieutenant Hans Griebel burst into the ready room of Jagdgeschwader III/54, the "Green Hearts of Thuringen" fighter group based in Elsenborn, near Monschau, close to the Belgian-German border. The group had been moved so as to support the fighting in the Huertgen and slow the northern advance of the First American Army towards the Siegfried Line. It was a mixed squadron of Messerschmitt bf109s and Focke-Wulf 190s with a few bf110, Jabo Nachtjagers, night fighters. The main mission of the group remained inflicting as much damage on the fleets of Allied bombers, Americans by day, British by night, which seemed to increase with every passing day. Griebel was excited to learn that von Rindel had returned after being shot down three weeks before. Griebel had been his wingman and though he knew he had not shirked his duty in protecting von Rindel, he admired and depended so much on him that the odds of surviving the war lessened with his absence. Despite his relief, Griebel knew his place and maintained decorum.

"Herr Hauptman," he said drawing himself erect and with clicking heels, saluted his flight leader. "May I say how very good it is to see you back safe and sound?"

"You may, Griebel but after all, I was merely fulfilling the code of the Luftwaffe: 'Fly and fight until victory or death.'" Already legendary among the Green Hearts, he arose from the deep leather chair from which he had been regaling his fellow fighter pilots with his exploits and heartily shook his wingman's hand. He went to the sideboard and personally poured schnapps into assorted glasses and mess tins which Griebel distributed to the rest of the pilots. Von Rindel noted, without comment, how diminished was their number.

"To our fallen comrades and our future victories. Prosit!" The schnaps was high quality and warmed rather than burned as its effect spread through their limbs. It was getting dark and the Messerschmitt bf110Gs, the "Jabos", night fighter pilots gathered their kits, piled into trucks to be taken out to the flight line. Griebel's plan, assuming von Rindel would not be returning had been to transfer to the night fighters which had both higher success rates and survivability than the daytime fighters. In fact, they had been able to wreak enough damage on the RAF formations, that bombing runs deep into Germany had been curtailed until adequate counter measures were developed.

Although six or more types of German fighters were used as night fighters, this was often due to the attrition of the Luftwaffe than airplane suitability. The surviving planes were fitted with the on-board Lichtenstein radar and used corridors of ground radars that could vector the fighters to the bomber streams close enough that the pilots could spot the British Lancasters by their engine exhausts. Then it was a simple matter to sneak up on the bombers' tails and rake them with twenty-millimeter explosive rounds. The night fighters were soon accounting for as many bombers as their daytime counterparts.

"Well, Griebel, what were your plans when you thought me dead?" von Rindel said jokingly.

"I had considered transferring to the Nachtjagdgeschwader 1, but now that you have returned, I fly with you, Herr Hauptman, if you will have me."

"You were going to become an 'Owl'?" using the nickname for the night fighters. "Weren't you worried your eyes would get big and you could never come out in the daytime? And besides, I have heard the English are dropping tons of aluminum strips to block our radar. The kills are coming down to more like daytime levels. You may as well stay with me and fly during the day and sleep at night." He slapped Griebel on the shoulder and poured another round of schnapps.

"Yes, Herr Hauptman, it is true that the aluminum strips do interfere with our radars. We have to come up on their tails by hit or miss, sometimes nearly colliding with them," said Griebel. "On the scope it is just one big blur. Until we can see the engine exhaust flames from the Lancasters, we often have no idea where they are. By then, all too often, their gunners have us spotted and being so close, we are easy targets. Something must be done."

"Well, Griebel," von Rindel replied, "come back to the light and fly with me during the day. The B17s and B24s are easy to see. And they fly so nice and steady in their formations, bagging one or two is 'easy pickings' as the Americans say."

"But to make matter worse, their escorts, the P-47s, are getting replaced with the gottverdammt P-51s, the Mustangs," complained Griebel with more than an edge of fear in his voice. He swallowed down the rest of his schnapps. The room was silent as the German fighter pilots contemplated not only friends and comrades lost but their own approaching mortality.

Von Rindel looked about the ready room at his flight members. Not only were there fewer of them, there were fewer faces to which he could place names. And they were all so young. He made sure that they had full glasses and mess tins.

"What they do not have are the 'Green Hearts'. Each of us are worth ten Mustangs and tons of aluminum strips." He raised his glass. "To fly and fight until victory!".

"Victory!" the rest of the pilots chimed in. The roar of the night fighters' engine built to a crescendo then faded away as they climbed into the night sky. They remaining pilots broke up and went to their billets. Their day would be starting soon enough.

With the dawn, the "Jabos", having accounted for three bombers, returned to base. Their ground crews turned the planes over quickly and they were ready for the day's flights. The klaxons sounded over the barracks of the "Green Hearts" when it was still full dark. The bomber streams had passed over the Belgian coast and were being tracked by the ground radars. They had turned south over Aachen which meant they were headed to "Green Hearts" territory. Von Rindel and Griebel had only to pull on their boots and flight jackets. They slept in their clothes most nights. Waiting outside was their Kubelwagen, a four-seater with room in the back for their parachutes and flight bags. Their driver delivered them to the flight line where their bf109Gs, the "Gustavs", were fueled, armed and idling. Within minutes of the siren, ten Messerschmitts were airborne, climbing to reach the American bomber formations. They were often accompanied by a "Jabo" which was equipped with on-board radar and could vector the "Gustavs" much more quickly and accurately to the Americans. The "Jabos" were mainly night fighters and could not match the faster and more agile Mustangs. So, once they delivered their Messerschmitts to the air battle, the "Jabos" would turn off and head for home.

When the Luftwaffe first started using this strategy, they were able to counter the escorting Mustangs tactics of flying in front of the bomber formations and to engage the German fighters waiting for them ahead of their targets. Using the Jabo's radar guidance, the bf109Gs could attack the relatively unescorted bombers in the rear of the formations before the Mustangs could return and drive them off. The extended range of the Mustangs meant they could accompany the bombers to their targets and back with enough range to drive off the German fighters and hit targets of opportunity on their way back to base. Von Rindel knew what was coming. As he had against the Russian Sturmovics over Kursk, he used every bit of his skill, experience and cunning to survive in the skies that were increasingly filled with the superior Mustangs and Supermarine Mark IX Spitfires.

The "Green Hearts" were airborne with the first light, vectoring to the Americans. When leading his flight against the bombers he summoned his men to the attack with the same call: "Green Hearts, fly and fight until victory!" He pulled sharply back on his stick and climbed through the concealing contrails of the bomber stream, bursting amongst them with his 20mm nose cannon blazing.

#

Ambroos Hansen with the Belgian resistance returned to the hide-away where the five American airmen were safe for the time being. He had been meeting with the other members of his group, organizing the exfiltration of their American charges.

"Now, we will move mainly at night until we get closer to the American lines in the Huertgan Forest. Then we have to make contact with them when it is light. Generally, we find daybreak is the best time. It is also the most dangerous time, as you can imagine, so we will halt and stay in some safe houses near Stolberg, a village just to the east of the Westwall, your 'Siegfried Line.'"

"How long is this gonna take?" asked Olgilvie.

"Speed is not the issue," answered Hansen. "It will take as long as it takes and depends on many factors: predictable and not. But I would say, on average about two or three weeks."

"Jeez, how we gonna hide out for three weeks?"

"As I said, moving at night, from safe house to safe house, avoiding Bosche patrols, proceeding only when it is safe. We have a network of people who risk their lives, their families' lives every day to help, to keep you safe and return you to your army."

"Don't get me wrong," said Olgilvie, "we are grateful and all. It's just that two weeks or longer seems a lot. But you know what you are doing, I guess. It sure as hell beats rotting in a German POW camp for the rest of the war."

With that, Olgilvie and his crewmates went into one of the tunnels where they bedded down, leaving Hansen alone with Joe Hanover. He was desperate to return to Thorpe Abbotts and Virginia.

"Listen, Ambroos," Hanover said, "I've got to get back to England as soon as I can. Isn't there a faster route?"

"There is," he nodded, "but much more dangerous. We have to get you to the Channel, through Nazi occupied territory, fewer safe houses because of their spies. The closest way is through Antwerp. That is still about one hundred miles. Then we have to get you down the Scheldt estuary and out to the Channel. Then we have to find a fishing boat – can you handle a boat out on the open water, by the way?" he asked. Hanover shook his head. "Ah, well, then, that means we'll need a crew to go along with you."

Hanover was somewhat encouraged that Hansen had not turned him down so far.

"Then, of course, we have to have a way to notify the British air-sea rescue boats to come and get you. They respond to picking aircrews shot down over the Channel, not just single people floating about in a dinghy."

"But you've done that sort of thing before, right? I can't be the only guy in this situation."

"No, but the timing is everything. We will need to join you to a group that has been shot down. You are coming out from the coast in a boat. No telling how you would be received. They will probably just shoot you on sight." Hanover looked distraught. "Let me and my team think about this. Get some rest."

#

Although, the one-armed briefing major for the "Bloody 100" Bomb Group felt the loss of any of his crews, at least with the *Bouncing Betty* out of action, he would not have to deal

with Lieutenant Tolland's sniping at him during the pre-flight. This was fortunate because today's mission was well known to one and all: Wiener Neustadt in southern Austria.

"Neustadt! Oh, for the love of Christ. That fucking place again?" The major knew who this was without turning around. His shoulders sagged and he took in a deep breath. "Is there a problem with the assigned target, Lieutenant Ems?" Ems and Tolland had formed kind of a tag team in the briefings. He was the bombardier on *The Usual Suspects,* a battle-scarred B17 nearing her thirty-five missions and her crew thought, the end of her luck.

"It's just that we hit that place last week, right? And I had a great view of it through my Norden and I can tell you, there ain't nothing left standing to blow up."

"That is not the opinion of our friends in aerial recon and intelligence." The Major threw back the rest of the curtain to reveal photos of rubble.

"There, you see?" Ems said, "Nothing but fuck-all and that's blown to shit. We took care of their ball bearing and Messerschmitt plants months ago."

"Ah, yes, to the untrained eye, perhaps, but concentrate on this bit here."

With his pointer, a seemingly harmless implement but one which the flight crews had focused their hatred upon, because it was what traced their paths to destruction. The Major followed a line of cleared rubble leading into the relatively spared part of town. Magnified views showed a single railroad tract.

Before the major could continue, Ems blurted out, "That's it? A single bit of track? That is worth thirty planes?"

"It is what is at either end of the track, Lieutenant, that is of interest. It seems that the Fritzies have been busy since our last visit. And it is probably just the fact that you have been so effective in blowing their shit up that they thought they could get away with a little unnoticed construction. They figured that we would not think there could be anything worthwhile left and we would turn our attention elsewhere.

"We are sure that they have an underground factory for the manufacture of V2 rockets. The track brings in components and takes out rockets. As you all know, the V2s are really the only effective way they have left to hit English cities since we have taken out their bomber forces. They had been building them along the French coast all of the war until we got France back. Now they moved everything inland and Wiener Neustadt is a major site. For obvious reasons, they have kept the above ground structures to a minimum, hence the single track. But, underground our intelligence tells us, there is an extensive complex of workshops, furnaces and assembly lines. This is the biggest plant that we know of and if we take this out, it should greatly reduce their rocket building capability.

"To that end, all of the payload for this raid will be bunker busters, ground penetrating bombs that will do the job. We will have Mustang escorts all the way to and from the target."

Ems was only minimally placated. There was never a question about refusing to fly, even though Neustadt was a graveyard for bombers and this would be their third long distance mission in as many days. Previous raids had accounted for no fewer than ten planes per mission, especially in 1943, before they had the Mustangs. Even so, the concentration of flak batteries around Neustadt was still harrowing. Every flight crew had in their minds a running tally of missions completed and those remaining, calculating if their time was running out. The rest of the briefing was the usual information about Buncher points, Channel crossing, IP and time over target. Jeeps delivered the crews to their ships. Ems took his place in the nose and settled in for another twelve-hour mission. The taxi and take-off were uneventful and they burst through the thin overcast to a brilliant blue sky of which they seemed to be the only occupants. They were not alone for long.

The "Green Hearts of Thuringen" burst through the obscuring contrails and into the midst of the 100th Bomb Group formation when they were half-way to Wiener Neustadt. Von Rindel had the *Lovely Linda* in his sights and unleashed a burst of incendiary 20 mm cannon fire into her wing tanks. The ship exploded in a fire ball which von Rindel flew through, seeking his next target.

The lead plane was the *Bombs Away,* piloted by Lieutenant Oliver Winston, "Winnie" to his crew. The B17 was rocked by the near explosion as the first Gustav flashed by.

"Jesus Christ!" he shouted, "where did that motherfucker come from? Anybody see the rest?" .50 caliber shells began to rain down on the flight deck from the upper turret.

"It's those fucking 'Green Heart' bastards, again," said his co-pilot, Lieutenant Mike Scavony. "Where are the Mustangs?"

"They're up ahead dealing with our reception committee. Call them back."

Scavony raised the Mustang leader, Captain Robert Mulley. He gave their position and the approximate number of the attacking Messerschmitts.

"On our way," came the reply.

Captain Robert Mulley of the 353rd Fighter Group, the "Sly Birds", pulled up and did a barrel roll followed by six P-51 Mustangs in his group to gain altitude. Their rate of climb was more than 3500 feet per minute and they soon were above 20,000 feet by the time they were over the beleaguered B17s. He dipped the P-51's yellow and black checkered cowling and dove to join the melee. As they approached, Mulley was struck by the almost balletic movements of the German fighters, swooping, turning and diving on the stolid American bombers maintaining their formations. Streams of red tracers arced from the bombers' guns like whips lashing at the bf109s, occasionally striking one of the fighters, turning it into a plummeting fireball.

Von Rindel spotted the attacking Mustangs. "Green Hearts," he radioed, "break off the attack and return to base. Into the clouds." It angered von Rindel that he could not engage the attacking Americans but limited fighters which could not be replaced and his depleted fuel levels meant that the Green Hearts would have to flee to fight another day. Besides, they had accounted for four bombers and the anti-aircraft batteries around Wiener Neustadt would score other kills. He continued his dive through the clouds, reaching clear air at five thousand feet. He continued on to his base.

"They're breaking off," shouted Mulley to the rest of his Mustang flight. "Let's go get them." He notified Winston of the B*ombs Away* that they would be pursuing the retreating Germans.

"Good hunting, the fewer of those 'Green Hearts', the better," replied Winston.

Von Rindel expected the Mustangs to stay with their bombers so he was surprised when a stream of .50 caliber rounds flashed by his canopy.

"Green Hearts, they are coming after us. Engage, engage." He pulled out of his drive, doing a barrel roll to try to shake off the Mustang that was on his tail and possibly come in behind him. But Mulley stayed right with him. Griebel, von Rindel's wingman, saw his flight leader was in trouble and climbed to his aide. He did not see the second Mustang pull up on his three o'clock until the .50 caliber rounds laced through his cockpit, killing him instantly. Von Rindel put his stick forward and to the left as he dove away from Mulley while heading for a cloud bank in hopes of losing him there. Mulley saw the clouds as well and knew he had to down this Messerschmitt before he got there. He unleashed a burst of machine gun fire from his wing guns, seeing it converge on the Messerschmitt just as he entered the clouds. There was no explosion. Mulley pulled back to seek more targets.

Von Rindel continued his dive in the cloud cover until he broke through to clear air again at five thousand feet. One by one, the others in his flight came out of the clouds and joined him and they returned to their base at Elsenborn. They taxied to their revetments. Von Rindel walked down the line, stopping at Griebel's empty spot. Another pilot came up to stand beside him.

"I am sorry, Herr Hauptman, a Mustang got him just before he could get into the clouds. He was a good man, a promising pilot. He will be missed."

"Yes, all that is true," replied von Rindel. They joined the rest of the flight, fewer by three, on their way to their debrief.

#

"Ten minutes to target. Here comes the flak," reported Lieutenant Ems. "At least there really seem to be fewer 109s."

"Yeah, but they still got four of us," replied Scavoney. "They don't seem to be running out of 88s, I see." They could all see the black popcorn shaped bursts of the anti-aircraft batteries surrounding Wiener Neustadt.

Ems hunched over his Norden bombsight as the rubble which was his target, crept across his view. "Alright, I have the ship," meaning he would be flying *The Usual Suspects* until the release point. The penetrator bombs they were using required greater than usual accuracy and all of his concentration. The flak explosions rocked the ship limiting his aiming but he released his four bombs during a fortuitous lull, followed by the rest of the remaining twenty-six planes making up the mission.

"Bombs away, she's all yours, Winnie", he said, returning control to the pilot.

"Let's get the hell out of here," he replied, pulling the big bomber with all his strength to climb and bank to the right. Two more planes were hit and went down. "Jesus, I hope we got that son of a bitch V-2 plant. Ten minutes to picking up the escorts. Keep sharp, we may not have seen the last of our friends from the Luftwaffe."

Mulley, the Mustang leader called in to Winston, the *Suspects* pilot. "I don't see any 109s, so maybe we will see if we can do some damage to those 88s." The extended range of the Mustang made it a triple threat to the Luftwaffe: as an escort, fighter and a bomber. The ability to accompany the bombers all the way to Berlin and back home again, hitting targets of opportunity was unmatched by any fighter except the Supermarine Spitfire XIII.

"Sounds good to me. Good hunting," said Winston.

#

Hauptman von Rindel stood in the ready room of the Green Hearts and raised a glass of schnapps.

"To absent friends."

#

Lieutenant Heinz von Kleist had been watching the air battle, celebrating each downed bomber, mourning each Messerschmitt lost, but did not see Mulley's Mustangs roaring out of the cloud cover to attack his 88s until it was too late to move them. He could only save his crews.

#

The 100th continued back to base at Thorpe Abbotts, steering clear of the guns around Aachen.

#

Virginia Standhope watched the bombers land one by one, hoping against hope that Joe would be on one of them.

Chapter Ten:
Rounds on the Way

The battery of 88mm guns under von Kleist was too important to leave out of action and within two weeks, they had been replaced, for guns the Reich could supply, it was men they lacked.

"Feuer!" shouted Oberleutnant von Kleist of the 272nd Artillery Regiment, brought his right arm down forcefully. His battery of four 8.8cm Flak PaK 43/41 cannon arrayed on Brandenberg-Bergstein ridge one mile east of the city of Bergstein overlooked all of the Huertgen Forest. Artillery spotters from there could see all the enemy activity and bring down punishing fire on the Americans. The expected loss of Schmidt for their spotters was mitigated by taking Hill 400, arising from the trees at one end of the Schmidt ridge, and placing their spotters there. They could see the American engineers had finally widened the trail enough to allow renewed movement of tanks and men down the west valley wall. The four rounds leapt out of the barrels on their way to land among the American tanks and infantry bunched up along the Kall Trail with lethal effect. Howe and Anderson in their foxholes at Kommerscheidt heard the vicious whistle of the rounds passing less than one hundred feet over their heads.

The Oberleutnant was the latest of a long line of German/Prussian artillerymen in his family. He had unruly blonde hair, slightly longer than regulation, high cheek bones and sharp blue eyes. He was born to the sound of guns on an East Prussia artillery base. His family had manned the cannons under Bismarck and Moltke which made the Franco-Prussian war such a brief, one-sided victory. Against all odds, the Oberleutnant would survive the war, emigrate to the US and his son would join the American artillery. He would serve in the "Red Dragons", 13th Field Artillery, on Fire Support Base Blackfoot in Vietnam, twenty-five years later.

The 88millimeter Krupp C64 four pounder was the best artillery piece on that 1870 battlefield. Von Kleist felt a special kinship, knowing that he stood in shoes of his great-grandfather who manned that gun and knew that his 88millimeter guns were the best artillery in his war. The 155s and 105s of the American army could not compare with his guns in terms of rate and accuracy of fire, mobility and reliability. Their versatility was also second to none. The canons could be elevated to take on the endless streams of bombers, but was equally effective against tanks, bunkers, infantry and counterbattery fire. The 88 was the main gun on the King Tiger II and Panther tanks, as well as the Pak 43 Jagdpanther tank destroyer. His battery of four guns were emplaced on the Brandenberg-Bergstein ridge which was the third of the ridges formed by tributaries of the Kall River. His only real fear for them, placed as they were beyond the range of the American artillery, came from the American bombers.

He had played “tag” with the B17s, moving the guns off the ridge when the bombers were spotted. The guns were so maneuverable that their six-to-eight-man teams could have them off the ridge and into their cement revetments within five minutes. When all was clear, it took just a little longer to have them back to firing six to ten rounds per minute again. Corporal Jeffery Howe’s complaint to his sergeant was not idle griping, that despite all the American fire power, they could not eliminate “those fucking 88s”.

Von Kleist had drilled his crews on the PaK 43/41 version of the Flak 88 towed gun. This had a very low profile and could be easily move on firm ground by its crew. The gun shield offered good protection against shrapnel and rifle fire. Its twenty-foot-long barrel added to the accuracy and the high explosive armor piercing, HEAP shell, could penetrate eight inches of armor at one thousand yards, making any tank on the battlefield a potential one-shot kill. The Americans had to take out the Pak 43/41 with the same strategy and care as they used on a King Tiger tank. Von Kleist imbued his crews with the same love of the guns that he had for them. His batteries were always the best wherever they fought.

His guns were equipped with the Wurzburg targeting radar and all of his guns could be controlled by a single gun crew using the "Kommandogerat 40", a rangefinder and mechanical aiming computer which put all four guns on the same target. These two instruments made von Kleist's guns lethal up to twenty-six thousand feet. He had them mounted in his command truck so his entire unit was very mobile. He suspected that his battery had caused enough grief for the American bombers that his guns were special targets for them. That is why he placed such a premium on their mobility.

After pulling back from Kommerscheidt, Howe and Anderson were dug in along the western rim of the Kall River gorge. Howe, especially, reveled in watching the Brandenburg ridge get plastered by the B17s.

"There is no way that those fucking 88s could survive that," he said gleefully. "Maybe we can get some sleep tonight. Those mothers were driving me insane."

"So just the guns, right?" asked Anderson. "Not the cruddy food, the mud, the constant wetness, our feet rotting off, the unending shits, the bugs, the lice? I could go on. But of all that it's the guns that are getting to you?"

"They aren't eating at you? Those screeching motherfuckers flying over at least let you know they missed you this time. But when they land in front or on top of you, there's no warning – just flames and frags screaming all around you. Then you're deaf for a couple of minutes so you can't know if more are on the way. All you can do is try to melt into the dirt, knowing that if they hit you, there won't be enough left to soak up in a napkin. 'Here's your boy, Mrs. Anderson, straight from the front, we mailed him home. You have the heartfelt thanks of a grateful nation.' So much bullshit."

As before with Howe's rants, Anderson let him go on as long as he liked. Whenever he mentioned home, Anderson knew, Howe was scared. Being driven out of Kommerscheidt and Schmidt, pursued by the 88s across the river, had shown how tenuous their grip on their lives had become. Maybe there were to be no Yeunglings at Pirates games in their futures. Exhaustion overcame both of them and they watched in silence with red-rimmed, rheumy eyes, the eastern rim of the gorge and waited for the Germans.

#

"Herr Major, can you assist me with this, bitte?" asked Oberstabartz Genter von Stettgen. He was always polite and proper without being obsequious. The two surgeons had turned the Mestrenger Mill aide station into a smoothly functioning mini-hospital. Their mutual admiration deepened with every successfully treated soldier.

"Sure thing, Major," replied Major Albert Brandt, a surgeon of the 103rd Medical Battalion.

Their medical truce had held through two days of battle. They had come to respect one another's skills which led to a budding friendship. Just as important, they were learning from each other, having been trained under different systems. The speed with which Brandt operated at first had struck von Stettgen as reckless

ness but he had come to see it was efficiency. Brandt admired von Stettgen's clinical assessment skills making him able to rapidly and accurately triage the wounded, giving them their best chances of surviving. His key criteria were if the soldier's bleeding could be controlled and how long the likely surgery would be needed. The majority of successful cases were extremity wounds where amputation was the most effective treatment. Head, chest, most abdominal wounds needed rapid evacuation to a field hospital, if possible. Otherwise, these men would be made as comfortable as possible with morphine and moved to the back of the mill. Sometimes, even morphine was in short supply and the medics had to listen to their screams slow to silence as they bled out.

The case in hand was an American sergeant with both legs mangled. Von Stettgen recognized the leg wounds were immediately life threatening, but treatable.

"You got a real mess here, Major," Brandt said, pulling on fresh gloves. "We might be able to save his left leg, but this right one is a lost cause." The right leg was still attached, although severely mangled to his upper thigh. There had been just enough leg left for the field medic to apply a tourniquet to slow the blood loss. The left leg was chewed up to the knee and would have to be amputated as well. The medic's quick application of the tourniquets as well as supplying a couple bags of plasma had saved the sergeant's life, for now. Post-op infection, bleeding, renal and/or pulmonary failure induced by massive trauma which attended multiple wounds were all still in the cards for the sergeant. As important for him as the timely surgery was rapid evacuation to a post hospital which T.Sgt. Douglas Aiken provided with his medical Weasel. But first, the sergeant had to survive long enough to get off the operating table at Mestranger Mill.

Each surgeon had a medic assisting. Without their help, surgeries would have been impossible. Brandt began with isolating and tying off the major blood vessels he could find in the ground meat that was the sergeant's right thigh. His assisting medic was ready with a canvas bag to receive the leg which Brandt severed with his amp knife. The medic then turned to von Stettgen to receive the left lower leg. The medics had also become knowledgeable about running the Beaker anesthesia machines and monitoring blood pressures.

"Major Brandt, this guy's pressure is barely palpable at 40," the medic said.

"Hang some more plasma and saline. Tell Aiken we have a priority evac for him." The German medic helping von Stettgen hurried out the door after a nod from his surgeon. They finished tying off the bleeders which were slowly oozing now due to the low blood pressure. They bound the leg stumps as tightly as they could and transferred him to Aiken's waiting Weasel. They tied the sergeant on his litter to the back of the Weasel. Another litter case was tied on over the Weasel's hood and one last man sat beside Aiken. One of the medics hopped in the back and held aloft the plasma and saline.

Aiken gunned his engine and the Weasel lurched forward. The trail up the west gorge wall was much improved as a result of the last few days of the engineers' work. Aiken broke through the trees at the edge of the valley rim and did not hesitate as he made his best speed across the meadow heading for Vossenack and its larger, better equipped aide station. The ground had not yet been churned into a boggy morass by the passage of tanks and artillery impact craters.

The receiving surgeon, Captain Raymond Herrsel, at Vossenack took one look at the deathly pale face, lolling head of the sergeant and ordered him into his aide station. Once on the treatment table, the surgeon made an incision over the sergeant's big vessel just under his collar bone and inserted a large IV needle. They had a few units of O negative blood available and as that began to infuse, the sergeant's blood pressure and color improved. With the increased blood pressure, the stumps began to bleed more briskly. O negative blood could be given to anyone regardless of their blood type and obviated the risk of severe transfusion reactions. In dire situations, mismatched blood was given and the reactions dealt with large amounts of steroids. The blood types of all the personnel at the aide station, German and American, were known and they would give emergency transfusions. As a result, all of them were "a pint low" all the time.

"Damn!" said Herrsel as he faced the increased blood loss. "This where an electrocautery machine would come in handy so we wouldn't to tie off each and every one of these buggers. But then, reliable supply of electricity would be handy, too." The aide station's generators were gas powered Onan 120v, 110 amp and very portable. They were able to run for about two hours on a gas/oil mixture but they did cut out frequently due to sludge clogging the fuel lines. They were used mainly to power the lights and radios. But as at the aide station at the Mestrenger Mill, at the bottom of the Kall River gorge, kerosene lamps were often needed.

There now was a steady stream of wounded hit by von Kleist's 88s during the retreat from Kommerscheidt. Brandt and von Stettgen remained in the mill along the Kall River triaging both Germans and Americans based solely on the severity of their wounds. In truth, there was little they could do beyond trying to stop the bleeding. They would do minor abdominal procedures if the bellies had already been blown open. Their evacuation route depended on Aiken's Weasel taking the most unstable wounded up the trail. The medics from the small aide station half way up the western wall carried their litters to the top and the awaiting ambulances, thence to Vosseneck. Even with the efficiency with which the two surgeons worked, the number of wounded waiting to be treated mounted steadily. Supplies, plasma, saline, bandages also were running out. Without saying the words, Brandt and von Stettgen had to send those beyond help and hope to "the back" meaning, the far corner of the mill without treatment to die. Triaging these men was the most brutal thing that either man had ever had to do and would haunt them both for the rest of their lives.

One of von Stettgen's medics hurried into the makeshift aide station and saluted.

"Herr Oberst, a captain with the infantry said we are to evacuate immediately as they are going to be advancing on the Americans. He said transport for our wounded will be provided and the Americans will become our prisoners." There were about twenty wounded, equally divided between the Germans and Americans.

Brandt continued sewing up multiple holes in his patient's, a German lieutenant, small bowel. Von Stettgen visibly stiffened but had control over his voice as he answered.

"Tell that officer that these men are too wounded to be moved now. They are under the command of the 'Sanitatdienst des Heers' and as such are not subject to his orders. None of the wounded nor any medical staff are, actually. We will decide when it is best to move them. You are dismissed."

Brandt, though understanding little German, got the gist of what von Stettgen was saying.

"Well, Major, that is likely to land you, as we say in our army, 'in some deep shit.'"

"What can they do to me? Send me to the front? Oh, wait, they've done that already." He chuckled. "'Deep shit', eh? Is that an official American Army term?"

"It is in the field manual." They continued their work. Soon, they heard the deep rumble of tanks and armored cars followed by tramping boots. A captain of the 272nd GVD looked in on the scene in the aide station mill. He was visibly repulsed by the blood, mayhem and more, the stench of the place.

"Please, Herr Major, I must insist that you evacuate. It will not be safe for you here."

"We are not going anywhere," von Stettgen replied. "These men are our first duty. All those that could be moved, have been moved. Now, you will leave us to our work."

"At the very least, you must stop work on the enemy wounded. You know as well as I that it is forbidden to waste scarce supplies on Americans."

"Hey, Fritz," said Brandt, "what do you want me to do with your comrade here. I figure I've got another hour or two to go."

"This is craziness," protested the infantry captain. "How do you know he is not harming our soldiers under the guise of operating on them?"

"Because," replied von Stettgen, "he is a doctor as am I. We have sworn the same oath to do no harm. Now, again, you are slowing us in our work. You will leave now."

"I must report this," the flustered captain stammered.

"You do that, Fritzy," taunted Brandt. "And on you way out, explain to your Kamaraden out there that you are shutting us down and they can just go ahead and bleed to death on their own sweet time."

The captain turned on his heel, mustering all the dignity that he could and strode off.

"Have you got a lot of those assholes on your side?" asked Brandt. "Because I can guarantee we've got our share on ours."

Von Stettgen laughed softly. "Unfortunately, we do. They seem to be as common as lice."

He turned back to the partially completed amputation and never looked up again.

#

Anderson and Howe of the 112th Pennsylvania National Guard were in the most advanced foxholes of the new position taken after the Americans were driven out of Kommerscheidt. They were there as a trip wire for when the Germans of the 272nd Volksgrenadier Division came storming up the west wall of the Kall Valley. They had a flare gun to fire off when the grenadiers attacked. It was assumed that they would not be in any shape to make a report in person.

"This is great, just fuckin' great." Jeffery Howe began his commentary on this aspect of his particular part in the war. "Are there any other grunts the 112th wants dead more than us? They've got binoculars, right? I've seen them. They can watch the fuckin' trailhead as well from there as we can from here."

"They want us here in case the Krauts come at night," Anderson replied.

"Really? So, the only chance we have of living through the Germans coming up out of the valley is to lay low in our little hole here and hope they pass us by. But no-o-o," Howe said drawing out the word. "They want us to fire a flare just to make sure the Krauts know where we are."

"Don't worry about the Germans, our artillery will get us when we let them know the Krauts are on their way."

"I do love a good back-up plan," said Howe. They were quiet for a while, resting their cheeks on the stocks of their M-1 Garands, watching rim of the Kall Valley.

"You know," said Howe in almost a whisper, "I would've liked to have seen Altoona again and catch a Pirates game."

"Hey, I'm gonna make you buy my ticket," replied Anderson.

#

Lieutenant Alfred Moore, gun captain of a four-gun battery in the 229th Field Artillery stationed outside of St. Vith, was awakened all too soon by his corporal, Lenny

Brink. Moore could not remember his last full night's sleep since leaving St. Lo, three months ago.

"Sorry to disturb you, Sir..."

"But you do it so well, Lenny. Must be all the practice you've had since we landed in Normandy. Never mind. What is it?"

"Recon reports a concentration of Kraut infantry around Kommerscheidt. Intel thinks they're going to make a run across the valley and try to push us out of Vosseneck."

"So, what the fuck else is new? What do they want us to do about it?"

"The old man wants to brief all the gun captains in one hour. He thinks that the Krauts are going to make a night attack soon."

"Lenny, how do you know this shit? It's a good thing you work for our side. Alright, I'm up, no need to hover." Moore crawled out of his sleeping bag, stretched, pulled on his boots. The latrine trench for his battery was thirty yards away and he planned to make that his first stop. His unit had subsisted on K-rations for more than a month. He had had the "shits" for three weeks of that month. He and the rest of his men were losing weight steadily. They had standing orders against foraging among the deserted farms around them. Those orders had been increasingly honored in the breach. The "K-rats", as they were fondly known, had little in them to sustain men in battle for more than two weeks or so. They were originally designed for the paratroops, short term rations for men doing bursts of activity. They had less than three thousand calories per day and no vitamins. They were long on biscuits and short on everything else. The "entrée" was a mushed-up meat-like substance in a small can, opened with a small, easily lost key. Most men used their bayonets. It was inevitable that they would resort to living off the population as have all armies in the field since the time of Hannibal.

The unexpectedly rapid advance of the Third Army across France had out stripped the quartermasters' ability to keep the men fed. Truck transport was shunted aside by tank columns, air drops were often inaccurate and the food took up needed space on overtaxed planes.

Corporal Lenny Brink was an incomparable scrounger and kept his gun crew among the best fed in the 229th Artillery. Farm raised in rural Minnesota, he cast a knowledgeable eye over crops, fruits and animals. No one questioned him when he disappeared for an hour or two as the 229th advanced through the farmlands of France. The Huertgen Forest had little to offer, unfortunately, so the gun crew had to subsist on K-rats, which Lenny took as a personal affront. Moore returned from another "shitter session", his fourth of the morning, and made himself as presentable as possible for the meeting with his regimental commander. He hoped the meeting would not be too long as he already felt rumblings in his gut.

"Do not want to crap in front of the Colonel," he thought.

Lieutenant Moore was in charge of a battery normally consisting of six 105 mm M-1 Howitzers each of which could sustain a rate of fire of six to eight rounds per minute. He had only four guns, having lost two to counter battery fire from the German 88s of the 272nd Artillery Regiment firing from the Brandenberg ridge, commanded by Oberleutnant von Kleist. Moore had not lost any men but had no idea when he would get replacement guns. He planned to take that up with the Colonel, his touchy gut permitting.

He joined the other four battery commanders in Colonel James Mac Caffery's tent. All together, they had twenty-two 105mm howitzers. They had proven their lethality and accuracy when they decimated the "Windhunds". But crucially, they did not have the range of the German 88s.

"Welcome, gentlemen," the Colonel said. "Can I offer you some refreshment, indicating a camp table with an array of tinned meats and vegetables. The sight of the food triggered Moore's gut, causing him to tightly clench his sphincter.

"No thank you, Colonel," the men said at once. All of them had had recent slit trench visits of their own.

"Very well. Let's begin." They moved to the large table upon which a tactical map of the area was spread. There were red circles indicated the latest best guesses of the locations of German assets. The miserable weather with rain and low ceilings had kept any air recon to a minimum. The L-4 Grasshopper observation planes of which each artillery battalion had two assigned and were piloted by artillerymen were invaluable in directing accurate, real-time fire, had been grounded through most of the fall and early winter. The German artillery under von Kleist had the high ground two ridges away and watched the Americans' movements and dispositions making their fire extremely accurate and deadly. The weather negated the Americans' superior numbers in aircraft, artillery and manpower. Even General Patton was praying for clear weather.

"We have radio intercepts indicating the Germans are massing for a go at the Kall River again with the idea of driving us back," began Colonel Mac Cafferty. "The most likely target for them would be St. Vith and its supply depots thus crippling both armor and infantry operations. But I think they have bigger plans: push through to the Meuse and on to Antwerp. Taking St. Vith would be at best temporary victory with no chance of effecting the outcome. But if they could retake Antwerp in a combined Panzer/Infantry strike, splitting the Canadians and Brits thus gaining the deep-water port at Antwerp, that would be a game changer. It could add a year or more to the war. But they have to move through us first. We need to break them up before they can get a head of steam going.

"Now, as always, the weather is not going to be helpful. Regiment is predicting cloud cover from one hundred to eight hundred feet with fog throughout most of the next five days or more – likely more. That means not only will we not be getting any close air support but also little in the way of real time positioning reports and on target results. But it is perfect conditions for the Krauts to attack. So, we will have to start with their last known positions and just blast the hell out of them. We will be using fragmentation rounds set to twenty-foot air bursts. Each battery will be assigned a sector and your jobs will be to make your sector a living hell – real Dante's Inferno stuff. We will have P-51s from the 343rd squadron on call if there is any break in the weather but I think for now, the mission will be blind saturation fires. Any help from anyone else will be gravy.

"Any questions?" There were none – not due to the clarity of the briefing so much as the urgency the gun commanders were feeling from their guts. "Good. Your ordinance supply is underway and final sector assignments will be distributed this afternoon. We hope to have more accurate targeting information by then.

"Dismissed."

The gun captains moved with clenched cheek alacrity to the nearest slit trench.

"God almighty", said Moore to his fellow battery commanders, clearly relieved that he made it to the trench just in time. "It's like the Germans are cooking for us. What do you think – spoiled K-rats, dirty water? Anybody really piss off the cooks in the officers' mess? You think they spiked the Spam stew? Who could have that big a grudge?"

They all agreed that once their guns were placed and the fire missions began, they were not going to be moving around a lot so access to a "shitter trench" should not be a problem.

#

"Fire mission! Set HE rounds for fuze time thirty seconds, azimuth 12 degrees, elevation 45 degrees. Number Three, one round. Fire!"

Lieutenant Moore waited for word from his FO, forward observer, for the impact of the ranging round. It soon came.

"Adjust 200 yards right and lower 50 yards. Air burst at twenty-five feet."

Moore gave the correction. "Round on the way"

His FO radioed back in thirty seconds, "Right on target."

Moore gave the coordinates to the rest of the gun crews. "Volley fire" and after confirmation from his FO, "Fire for effect. HE, air burst, twenty rounds."

Fire and smoke erupted all along the gun line landing among the two hundred men of the 272nd VGD grouped near the trail head on the east valley wall. The ranging shot had given some warning and the men had begun to scatter but still twenty of them were killed or seriously wounded.

"Check firing," Moore called out causing the guns to go silent. It took thirty seconds for the smoke and dust to clear the target before the FO could report. From announcing the fire mission to its completion, five minutes had elapsed. Lieutenant Moore had one of the best trained artillery platoons in the Huertgen.

"That's chased them," came the FO's report.

"Any tanks?" asked Moore.

"No, I guess they don't want to risk them or they don't have anymore," his FO answered.

"Either way suits me," Moore answered.

Van Kleist soon had his 88s in action, using counterbattery fire to try to silence the American guns. Through the rest of the afternoon until dark, the guns engaged in a kind of "call and response" like a deadly Southern Baptist tent revival. Then the darkness, bringing with it the surviving men of the 272nd VGD and the ten surviving tanks of the Windhunds moving towards the Kall River gorge.

Chapter Eleven:
The Usual Suspects

The men of the "Bloody 100th" Bomb Group had finally caught a break after near daily missions ranging over central and southern Germany. They had been confined to barracks allowed out only one day in every three to lessen hangovers and possibly going AWOL to avoid the ten-to-twelve-hour flights. The only good thing to be said was that everyone's mission counts were mounting steadily to the golden number of twenty-five when they were to be rotated home. Then the number rose to thirty, then thirty-five. The only thing preventing a revolt among the crews was that the rate of attrition of the old crews was so great that the new replacements came in not knowing any better.

A twenty-two-year-old veteran waist gunner, S.Sgt. Woodrow Eads, of El Paso, Texas, manning the left waist on the B17G, *The Usual Suspects*, summed it up neatly on one of the nights off in the "Fox and Hens". He was surrounded by replacements hoping to glean some hope from the seasoned airman that they could possibly live through the war.

"We heard about the increased number of missions, Sergeant? Do you think it is fair?"

"Fuck it," Eads answered without hesitation. "It don't mean nothing. They can raise it up to a hundred missions if they want to. Ain't none of us gonna live to see the twenty-five anyway." No one could argue with him.

Virginia Standhope was behind the bar. She still looked up with every opening of the door, hoping to see Joe Hanover walk in. It had been a month since news of the *Bouncing Betty* being shot down. None of the rest of the crew had returned. There had been no further news which was not unusual. If a plane did not return, there was no one left to grieve, except the ground crew. By 1944, the planes and crews were replaced by a seamless conveyor belt from the factories and training bases in the U.S. The quality of the crews was undiminished despite their ever-increasing numbers and decreasing ages. Pressing the attacks farther and farther into Germany made each mission last more than twelve hours, exhausting the men.

The Luftwaffe had been driven from the skies for the most part. Hauptman Jans von Rindel's "Green Hearts" were forced to fly cannibalized 109G Messerschmitts. The Eighth Air Force had smashed the airfields, fuel depots and refineries, factories and assembly plants. His Jagdgeschwader III/54 was limited by lack of everything: planes, fuel, ammunition and pilots. There were no more random patrols just waiting to happen upon the bombers. Now he and his pilots waited in their planes at the end of their runways until the bombers were spotted, their altitude and routes plotted, then be guided by the most direct route to intercept. Their attacks were like slashing saber cuts, roaring through the formations, turning to streak through them once more and return to base. They could not engage with the escorting P-51 Mustangs, only evade them.

Still, von Rindel would lead his men into the sky to face the endless American bomber fleets. He would note and mourn each newly empty revetment at the Green Hearts' base. He accepted that the defense of the Reich fell to the pedestrian but still deadly 88millimeter anti-aircraft guns ringing the ever-decreasing number of targets. But his spirit and courage remained undiminished as he toasted the remaining few fellow pilots.

"To fly and fight until Victory or Death".

#

Sergeant Eads was nursing his third pint at the "Fox and Hens", the surrounding FNGs, "Fucking New Guys", undeterred by his hostile silences.

"But we heard that the Luftwaffe is pretty much finished," said a novice gunner who looked to be fresh out of grade school.

"Don't believe that bullshit," growled Eads. "All we've done is sort of cull the herd, as we say in Texas. There may not be the hundreds of 109s from last year but that just means the Kraut pilots now are the survivors, the best of best. I figure we still lose about a plane for every one of those fuckers that get to us. They know how to blast out of any cloud cover, dive straight out of the sun. Those sons of bitches are on us before we know they are there. They are not afraid to fly through their own flak. They've started to hit us on the bomb run when we're flying nice and straight and level, after the Mustangs and Thunderbolts have peeled off. They use exploding 20millimeter rounds that if they hit the fuel tanks, can take a Fort down with one round. And every plane that goes down takes ten good men with it."

"Wait, what's a 'Fort'?" asked the child-like FNG.

"Oh, fer Chrissakes!", Eads shouted, "does your momma know you are out this late at night? A Flying Fortress, the B17 that is going to be your new home or more likely your grave for however much time you've got left."

Eads took a long pull at his beer and motioned to Virginia to fill him up again.

"Thanks, darlin'" he said in his west Texas drawl that became more pronounced with every pint of stout. He looked morosely down at the tan foam topping his beer. The FNG knew enough to keep his mouth shut for now.

Eads burped and continued. "Yeah, the 109s ain't what they used to be, but don't kid yourself, they'll kill you just as dead. Nowadays, it's more those fuckin' 88s. They're radar aimed, can shoot in any kind of weather and all they need is to be nearby you when they go off. Jesus Christ, over Frankfurt or Schweinfurt, or any other fuckin' '-furt' you can name, you can get out and walk on the flak – it's that thick. And they don't waste any time finding you. They've got you bracketed as soon as you turn on the IP and begin the bomb run. And there ain't nothin' you can do but scrunch up into a tight ball, sit on your flak jacket so they don't shoot your balls and pecker off and wait it out. All you can hear are those frags screaming through the plane, the men screaming when they get hit- slipping on the blood, watching Forts spiral down or blow up, full of your friends. All the while waiting for some cock-sucking Kraut ack-ack gunner to put an 88 right up your ass."

Virginia slid Eads' beer away and patted his arm. She smiled at the ashen-faced FNGs.

"You've got to fly tomorrow, don't you, Woodrow?" she asked. He nodded. "You'd best be off, then. Get some sleep."

Woodrow Eads sighed deeply and looking into Virginia's eyes, patted her hand.

"I'm sorry about Joe, Ginny. I truly am." He lurched towards the door and into the night, still feeling the warmth of her hand on his arm.

Luckily Technical Sergeant Woodrow Eads' liver was as battle tested as the rest of him and after five hours' sleep, but skipping breakfast, he loaded into the jeeps with the rest of *The Usual Suspects'* crew and rode out to his B17G. This was his twenty-fourth mission and just three months ago, would have been his next to the last. Now he still had eleven more to go to make his thirty-five flights. He had become numb to the danger, stopped worrying and barely listened to the four AM briefings. All the missions were the same. Only the pilot and navigator really had to know where they were going. His job was the same regardless. That did not mean that he took his job any less seriously. He was there in the left waist to protect his plane and crewmates. The rest was just so much noise.

He climbed out of the jeep under the plane's nose. He thought *The Usual Suspects'* nose art was clever: three furtive looking men with five o'clock shadows, in black fedoras and khaki trench coats, each holding a bomb. He swung up into the belly of the plane and took his place at his .50 caliber machine gun in the left waist. He nodded to TSgt. John Payne, the belly gunner. They had become friends through the ten missions they had flown together. The target for today was some "-furt" or other, Eads did not care which one. He was not entirely happy about the decreased Messerschmitt attacks, because they at least gave him something to do. He was impotent against the 88s that raked through their formations, bringing down Fortresses, killing his friends.

He pulled back the charge handle of his .50 caliber to ensure its free play, cocking the empty gun then pulling the trigger and opened the breech to make sure the armorer had cleaned and oiled the gun. Like every other waist gunner in the squadron, he put his .50 through its full range of motion and checked that he had a full ammo box. With this activity, his pre-flight jitters were calmed. They were a young crew, all lieutenants and sergeants, reflecting the high turnover that the "Bloody 100th" sustained.

The pilot was Wilson James from Jackson Hole, Wyoming. He grew homesick every time he flew over the Bavarian Alps, missing the Grand Tetons. Kenneth Forbes, co-pilot from Sacramento, California, spent most of his growing up fishing the Sacramento River delta and still snuck away to do a little flyfishing around Thorpe Abbotts whenever he could. The navigator/left cheek gunner was Lt. Mark Angelo from just outside Boise, Idaho, where he had become an expert elk hunter. He wore a highly polished antler tip around his neck to replace the crucifix he had thrown away after the first Munster raid. Lt. Norman Ems was the bombardier and nose gunner from Bend, Oregon. Unlike Angelo, he wore a crucifix and a St.

Christopher medal that he promised his mother would stay with him. All of the officers were in their mid-twenties.

TSgt. Fred Lesser, the engineer and top turret gunner, hailed from Hanover, New Hampshire. TSgt. Steven Appel was the radioman and right cheek gunner, a top football recruit for UCLA, from El Cajon, California, but was drafted before he could take a single snap. TSgt. Harvey Puzio, the tail gunner from the Bronx, because, he claimed "every crew needs a guy from the Bronx." Why this may be was never questioned. He had accounted for five kills from his lonely outpost in the tail. The right waist gunner was TSgt. Charles Anderson. At twenty-five he was the oldest member of the crew and slated to rotate home to Baltimore, if his luck held.

The *Suspects* was his third ship, joining the Eighth Air Force when it was the VIII Bomber Command in Langley, Virginia, before shipping out to England in June, 1942. His longevity was the leading mystery of the "Bloody 100th". All he wanted now was to re-join his father on their crab boat on the Chesapeake and spend his days on the water, hauling up blue crabs. Fishing the Chesapeake was a family tradition. His great grandfather, Archibald Anderson, started crabbing after surviving the Civil War as a member of the 13th Pennsylvania at the Battle of the Wilderness, May, 1864.

TSgt. John Payne was small and compact as befitted a belly turret gunner. He was friends with Woody Eads and tried his best to slow Eads' unravelling. He was, unfortunately, claustrophobic and delayed getting into the belly turret for as long as he could. All his requests to be transferred to any other position in the plane were denied since nobody liked the belly and he fitted it so well. The turret easily jammed if hit and he had seen one too many trapped gunners washed out with a hose after wheels up emergency landings. He welcomed the onslaught of the bf109s because it took his mind off being trapped in the turret.

The ten men of the *Usual Suspects* formed a close-knit group. They were all nearly the same age so informality was the lubricant that made them a smoothly working bomber crew. They wrote about each other to their families and circulated pictures, shared care packages from home and got anyone drunk who needed it for whatever reason. Although they had their share of tough missions, testified to by the patched 20mm holes and gashes caused by the "88s", they had not suffered a fatality. Their ground crew, eighteen-year-olds for the most part, always found a way to get them back into the air for their next target.

#

"Alright, gentlemen," said Ambroos Hansen as he entered through the trap door into the underground hide.

The five rescued American airmen, including Joe Hanover, had been joined by two British flyers. All told, the men had been underground for two weeks. T.Sgt. Jeb Olgilvie's, of the *Shy Virgin,* sprained ankle had nearly mended and all of them were getting antsy.

"What news?" asked Hanover, still the unofficial leader of the group.

"Good news," Hansen answered. "I have heard from our network that the way to the American lines is relatively clear. They are still fifty miles to the south but the Bosche have been taking a severe beating, thus keeping to their bunkers and not patrolling as much. That being the case, Sgt. Hanover, I don't think the far riskier channel crossing is worth it."

"How long do you think it will take to get to our lines?" asked Olgilvie.

"To cover the distance, moving mainly at night, depending on the patrols, I think it is a matter of maybe two weeks. You will be given identity papers, civilian clothes, cover stories but the hope is that you won't need them. Again, making contact with the Americans and crossing into their lines will be the riskiest part of this whole venture. We approach their lines through the woods east of the Kall River. We must go slow and silent because the Bosch also use that route. That is why we have to risk it now because they seemed to have beaten back a bit. Still, it is very risky, very dangerous."

"How many guys have you gotten across like this?" asked Solario, the top turret gunner on the *Shy Virgin.*

"We haven't had the route up that long, but we have more control and so far, we haven't had any problems. Like I said, the Americans on the front line are getting used to seeing us." That seemed to placate the nervous airmen and the newly arrived British.

"I started doing this business three years ago with the 'Comet Line'", Hansen said. "Those days we had to get your predecessors all the way through Belgium, France and to Spain. From there, the British consulate would get them to Gibraltar and home. As the Germans became less effective at stopping us, we would get to Paris then to Brittany and across the Channel. Betrayal by collaborators was an ever-present danger. The men were often hidden people's homes or apartments until they could be moved. When the filthy Bosche found a hiding place, the people were tortured for days or even weeks. A favorite technique was to shoot a child in front of the parents to begin their interrogations. After that, any survivors were sent to concentration camps. I, myself, have lost two cousins this way, both girls of eighteen." The men were silent but with a new admiration for the Belgian strangers risking their lives to return them to the fight.

The newly arrived Brits were Flight Sergeant Neville Church and Lance Corporal Brian Grieves who had been on board a Lancaster Avro heavy bomber that was shot down by a "Green Hearts" Messerschmitt, floating to earth just inside Nazi occupied northern France. In the hours spent underground, awaiting exfiltration, the Allied airmen began to compare notes on their planes.

Looking around at the Americans in the flickering lamplight, Church said, "You know, there's a reason that there are, what, six of you Yanks and only two of us. The main reason is that one can exit either a B17 or B24 much more easily than one can from a Lancaster. I swear if there was ever a plane designed by a committee, a committee, truth to tell, that never flew in one, it's the Lancaster."

"What makes you say that?" asked Joe Hanover. "It seems big enough, carries a good bomb load, including torpedoes and can take a lot of punishment."

"All true," replied Grieves, "But there is no ventral machine gun turret. We don't have any defense against Messerschmitts coming up from below. We don't even know they are there until they blow us out of the sky. They even have modified some 'Gustavs' with an upward pointing 20millimeter cannon they call 'Schraege-Musik', so called 'Strange Music'. They don't even have to climb up to us. It took them maybe five minutes to figure that out.

"And then, if you don't immediately blow up, there are only two undersized escape hatches and the bomb bay. You will never meet a living Lancaster tail gunner whose plane has been shot down. Those poor buggers can't fit their parachutes down the tunnel to the tail. They have to crawl back to the bomb bay where they have hung their parachutes, get into them and bail out, while the plane is on fire and diving, twisting and filled with smoke.

"We've got six .50 caliber guns to your eleven and no waist positions. Flying mainly at night is some defense but now the Germans have airborne radars, in addition to the ground radars, so they find us without a bother and their fighters home in on our engine exhaust flames. And the Spitfires aren't really night fighters, so we lack the escort protection that your bombers have."

"And there is even a psychological bit to all this", continued Church. "During the day, your lot can see all the other bombers and escorts making the raid. It must be a grand sight, very comforting. Flying at night, we get the sense that our plane is the only one up there. At best, we can see one or two other planes in our flight. We become aware of the rest of our mates only when they blow-up."

Joe Hanover could sympathize but grew defensive, thinking the Brits might have the opinion that the Americans have it safe and easy.

"Yeah, well, seeing everything isn't such a great thing. Knowing which plane got hit and seeing them spiral down, looking for parachutes and now the Germans don't seem to worry about their own flak. They follow us all the way to the targets and back out again. We're taking hits from the ack-ack and the Messerschmitts all the while flying nice and level until we make the drop."

"Agreed", said Church said. "it's all a total cock-up, what you Yanks call a 'snoofu'?"

"SNAFU: situation normal, all fucked up," corrected Hanover.

"Quite so, an elegant and comprehensive term. Ah, but the 'Lanc', she's a tough old girl. She'll get you home, more times than not. Not so much with us, this time, I admit, but still and all, she stayed up long enough for us to get out."

"But you have to admit," rejoined Grieves, "the bloody bastards that designed her thought more of bomb load than the crews living long. What is it? Maximum load is twenty-four thousand pounds? We can drop the 'Long Tom' bunker buster that will take out any amount of concrete the Jerries can pour. We have the ability to drop torpedoes, huge bomb loads and incendiaries, so, I agree, the 'Lanc' is a beauty, until the Huns find us."

"Just like the bleeding 88s, more and more of the searchlights are radar guided," continued Grieves. "So, whereas before, it was more or less bad luck when they pinned you with one light, now they light you up with three or four lights at a time. And just like you Yanks, we've got to fly nice and level while they chew us up. The 'Window' helps quite a bit. You Yanks call it 'chaff', the aluminum strips that we drop to cloud the radar. Now, the Jerries just seem to aim for the middle of the window cloud but more of us do make it through."

Church was suddenly quiet, staring at a wall in the dugout.

"What's up, Churchy?" asked Grieves.

After a shuddering inhalation, he said, "I was on the Hamburg raid about a year ago. The second night we were dropping incendiaries into the flames from about two thousand feet. One of my jobs was to get photos to assess the damage, so I was leaning out the open bomb bay doors with my camera. The heat from the fires was so intense, even at two thousand feet, that I couldn't stay there. My oxygen mask got sticky from beginning to melt.

"Of course, the toffs running the show, safe in London, thought it was a 'jolly good show' and ran newspaper reports, describing in great detail the results. There were some Swiss business men, evidently, who reported on the destruction. The Swiss like to be precise but even they couldn't come up with numbers of the dead so our lot just made it up. But I saw one report in the *Times* that the

Germans found a bomb shelter filled only with ashes, no bodies, just ashes. They calculated one cubic foot of ash per adult and one-half per child to get the number of people in that shelter. The papers had quite a time of it."

"I guess you can't be blamed after the blitz and all," said Hanover, trying to make Church feel better but the British flyer went silent again and stared straight ahead. Soon, the words started coming from him in a flat monotone.

"That heat that nearly melted my oxygen mask was part of the firestorm. I could see a twirling column of flame that nearly reached up to our plane. It had gale-force winds with it. This *Times* article said that people were swept off their feet and sucked into the flames, pavement was ripped up and whole buildings were blown down into the fire. Your lot bombed during the day and we bombed at night. The light from the fires made it so bright that it was hard to look directly at it. The post-action reports that the toffs held for the bomber crews, to congratulate us, I suppose, called the strategy a huge success of joint British-American science. They had planned to start a firestorm, you see, and researched for months the mix of bombs and incendiaries to create it and the combination of buildings in a city that could support such a huge fire. Hamburg was a legitimate military target but clearly the plan was to kill as many civilians as possible."

"Hey, it's war, you know?" Private Anton Salario, of the *Shy Virgin,* spoke up. "We are told that our job is to inflict as much damage on the Krauts as we can to end the war as soon as we can. They say that will save more lives in the long run. They obviously aren't ready to give up since here we all are, hiding out in a hole after being shot down, a whole year later. Yeah, I wouldn't feel too bad for the fuckin' Germans."

Church almost whispering, replied, "It's just to be able to literally create Hell on earth is sobering, I guess. But, as you say, here I am, a year later, knowing all that and still in Lancs, aren't I?"

Ambroos Hansen let the men settle into a contemplative silence before he spoke.

"We leave tonight. It is going to be the dark of the moon and overcast. The expected rain will keep the Bosche in their holes so we can make pretty good time. Also, rather than break into small groups, at least for now, the plan is to move all of you together to at least the first of the safe houses about ten miles from here. So, rest up, gentlemen, we leave in two hours."

Chapter Twelve:
Attack Across the Kall

"Here they come!" shouted Corporal Jeffery Howe of the 112th Regiment, E Company, Pennsylvania National Guard. He leveled the .50 caliber machine gun at the rim of the Kall River valley and began firing. Private Henry Anderson called in the attack and fed Howe's .50 caliber the rapidly diminishing belts of ammo. Their foxhole was thirty yards from the valley rim. They were the trip wire to begin the artillery barrage once the Germans showed themselves. No one, including themselves, expected them to live through the attack.

Howe watched with some grim satisfaction as German heads were transformed into red puffs with each hit of his rounds. That slowed them down. Soon enough potato masher hand grenades and rounds from the five-centimeter Granatwerfer 36 mortar, the light mortar which was the favorite of the German infantry, were landing around their hole. All they could do was hunker down and hope the artillery missed them.

Their lieutenant, Judd Barclay, watched through binoculars as his most forward position was enveloped in smoke. The artillery barrage soon lifted and the three remaining tanks of Company C, 707 Tank Battalion, led by

Enfield Davis in *Hell's Fire* roared into action, moving at double time speed followed by the rest of the 112th with the idea of pushing the Germans back beyond the Kall River, once again. *Adolph's Nightmare* and *Death Wagon* lined up beside Davis's *Hell's Fire* along the western rim and poured their machine gun fire into the Germans. There was still 10/10 overcast, grounding all air support.

Anderson and Howe were deafened by the competing barrages and choking on the smoke and dust which they raised. But they gripped each other's shoulders to confirm they were still alive. They could not hear the approaching tanks, firing as they came or the shouts of their fellow "Bloody Bucketeers" charging to the rim of the valley. Lieutenant Buckley slowed to look into their foxhole, expecting to see only the mangled corpses of the men he felt he had placed as a trip wire only to see them looking up at him. He laughed with relief as he shouted, "Come on, let's go. Still some work to do."

Howe and Anderson could not hear what he said, deafened as they were by the explosions, but figured out what he wanted as Buckley reached down into the hole and grabbed Anderson by his field jacket.

"Not done trying to kill us yet, Lieutenant?" shouted Howe but he could not hear any reply. They carried the .50 cal with them to the rim of the valley. From there, they could fire down on the retreating Germans. Slowly, their hearing returned but any orders shouted at them were drowned out by the crescendo of tank and machine gun fire. The tanks could cover the infantry as far as the other side of the valley. Davis did not want to commit to the arduous track leading down the valley side, which would make them helpless against the 88 fire that would soon be headed their way. His decision was confirmed by the arrival of von Kleist's 88 rounds from two ridges over beginning to impact in the valley, trying to support his infantry's retreat.

The retreating Germans had reached the far rim and were beyond Howe's .50 caliber range. He ceased fire. Only then did he have time to take a breath and look around at the headless German bodies blown on their backs just down from the rim. He counted six of them. Lieutenant Barclay came back to them.

"Good job you two. You stopped them cold and drove them back. I am putting you both in for Bronze Stars. You deserve them," he said. "Stay here, re-supply is coming." With that he followed the rest of his Pennsylvanians down into the Kall River valley. Von Kleist's deadly 88millimeter rounds were landing along the western valley wall, guided by his forward observer who had re-established his post in the Kommerscheidt village ruins.

In the Mestranger Mill aide station at the bottom of the Kall valley, the two surgeons, Brandt and von Stettgen, continued to work on the wounded of both sides. They stopped ducking with each over flight of either the 76millimeter tank rounds or the 88millimeter artillery shells until the impact explosions began to march down the valley wall and once again towards them.

"Aiken," Brandt called out for his medic and Weasel driver. He had become a lifeline for the aide stations at the bottom of the valley and the smaller one half-way up the western wall. Aiken was either fearless or suicidal in making his runs back to Germeter with wounded but stabilized men and returning with supplies.

"Yes, Sir," Tech Sergeant Douglas Aiken answered.

"It looks like we are going to have to evacuate again if that shelling gets any worse." They all ducked down when a close hit threw dirt and shattered rock against the walls of the mill. "Goddam it," Brandt shouted. "You think you can continue to make the runs up the valley?"

"We'll give it a try, Major."

Von Stettgen called for his medic/radio man. "Corporal, call the company and tell them we are still here and they are shelling their own wounded. They can kill the Americans when they get to the other side of the valley. Until then, they are only going to kill us."

"Ja, Herr Oberstabsartz." It took an impossibly long five minutes before the barrage stopped.

Aiken had loaded three litters onto his Weasel and sat two men on the back deck, one on the forward deck clinging to the spotlight. "Hang on," he shouted as he rammed the control levers forward and the tracks dug into the mud. Lurching forward nearly dislodged one of the litters but the riders on the rear deck grabbed the litter handles just in time at the cost of opening their own wounds, starting the bleeding again. They were about a mile from the evacuation station at Germeter and most of that over open ground. Aiken had to take it slow and easy, without any evasive action so as not to throw off any of the wounded he carried. Brandt and von Stettgen notified their respective sides to try to keep the Jeep from being fired upon but the distances were great, the red crosses on the jeep were small and covered by wounded. Aiken knew they were a tempting target; non-combatant rules be damned. The newly wounded from the American counter attack across the Kall valley were beginning to arrive at the Mill.

Men from the 112th Pennsylvania stopped to catch their breaths along the eastern rim of the valley, having double timed across the Kall and up the east wall. Howe, Anderson and their lieutenant, Barclay, lay on their bellies, sweat stinging their eyes as they watched the retreating soldiers of the 272nd Volks-Grenadieren Division. The Germans were disciplined in their retreat – no panicked running, maintaining an orderly firing line to slow the American pursuit. They took up positions in Kommerscheidt once again. Soon, mortar rounds began to rain down on the Americans along the eastern rim of the valley.

"Christ!" said Howe. "Here come the fucking mortars and now we've got to clear them out of there one more time, I suppose."

"They really should make you a general, Howe, with your grasp of the combat situation," joked Barclay. "The good news is the tanks are going to try to make a run across the valley and give us some support. We'll kick off when they get here." He slid down the valley side to check on the rest of the 112th as they came up.

"And that's the fucking 'good news'? How about a plan where we don't get killed? That would be good news," Howe muttered.

Enfield Davis in *Hell's Fire* did one more inventory of his ammo. On the inter-tank network, he checked in with *Adolph's Nightmare* and *Death Wagon.*

"OK, here we go, once again," he said into the microphone, trying to sound relaxed and confident. "Follow me, twenty-yard intervals."

Hell's Fire was in the lead and jolted forward as Emmons, the driver, nudged them over the brink then faster down the slightly improved trail. They cleared the bend without having to slow down and were climbing the eastern wall before the first of the 88s hit. They all sighed in relief upon gaining the top of the valley. Lieutenant Barclay picked up the infantry phone.

"Hey, Davis, good to see you. The Krauts are set up in Kommerscheidt and are mortaring us pretty good."

"No problem, Lieutenant. We'll clear them out for you." With that, Davis gunned his tank toward the ruined town.

"Tolliver, put some HE rounds on the town." As they approached, his other two tanks joined in and with their combined fire power, quickly drove the rest of the 272nd GVD back into the woods one more time. Von Kleist's forward observer radioed the loss of the town to the battery of 88s just before he evacuated. Von Kleist soon had his guns back in action battering the Kommerscheidt-Schmidt ridge.

"Cease fire, cease fire," shouted Davis. They were low on ammunition and all operations east of the Kall River still depended on the single tract trail crossing the river. The engineers had improved both sides but Davis doubted that it could withstand heavy re-supply traffic of Weasels needed to rearm his tanks and the infantry. He cast an eye to the overhead clouds and realized they were still on their own. No air support was likely after the one bombing run earlier that day. He called into the depot at St. Vith and got Captain Ramsey on the line.

"Captain," Davis began, "a little update for you. All three tanks and all of the 112th are across the Kall, once again. The Krauts are back in Kommerscheidt and are mortaring our positions, once again. The bombing run earlier did not seem to take out those 88s so we are hearing from them as well. We are low on everything: .50 cal, .30 cal, HE and wooly pete rounds, smoke rounds. The infantry is in no better shape and since there does not seem to be much hope for any air support, we are pretty much shit out of luck if they decide to come at us again." The call was interrupted by the arrival of more mortars.

"Look, Davis, I hear you and now that the trail is improved, we'll be getting you some re-supply," Ramsay replied. "I am rounding up more Weasels to get it all to you. Right now, I've got the one Weasel that is doing double duty as medical evac and re-supply. It's coming your way. Give the 229th Field Artillery your new position. They've moved forward and can reach Kommerscheidt now. Let 'em know what you need. Out."

Ramsey turned to Technical Sergeant Aiken who had just dropped off his last load of wounded.

"Sergeant Aiken, I need you to get over to the ammo dump." He gave Aiken the list. "I'm looking for more Weasels to help you out but you're it for now. Good luck."

Aiken loaded up his Weasel and a small trailer with all the ammo he could carry and started back across the open area to the valley. He knew he was out of range for the 88s until he descended the west valley wall but that did not mean that the forward observers for the Germans did not spot him and his cargo. There was little doubt that some "hot shit" was headed his way soon. He knew it was pointless, but Aiken tried to make himself as small as he could and still see over the Weasel's hood. He hoped he had adequately tied the ammo in the trailer that was bouncing around behind him as he made his best speed across the open space stretching out before him. He hoped to make it across the Kall before the 88s found him. So many hopes.

#

"Diesen verdampte Wetter!" shouted Hauptman von Rindle, slamming his flight helmet onto his bunk. "It has been three days now and no sign of letting up. Meanwhile, the Americans are flying over us on their way to Berlin or Breman or Stuttgart, beyond our reach. Even six months ago, we could have gone after them. We had "Jabos" with their radars then, and could find them at night, in any kind of weather and attack! Now, we are short on everything, except Americans and British, and we have to wait for the perfect time. 'Oh, no, Herr Hauptman, we can't have you just take off and fly around until you run into someone. You just taxi out to the end of the runway, nice and slow, shut down your engine to conserve fuel, until we tell say you may take off.' By the time we can climb to them, their bombing runs are done and we have to deal with their

Thunderbolts and Mustangs." Here he lowered his voice and looked around the barracks tent he shared with three new pilots. Their ashen faces were no deterrent to his tirade.

"And it seems Goering keeps telling the Fuhrer that all is well. The Allies are no match for his Luftwaffe. 'Give him a little more time, he says, and we will sweep them from the skies'. Quatsch (bullshit)! He hasn't been able to get his fat ass in any plane smaller than a transport for years.

"Time after time, we climb into our patched up Messerschmitts and Focke-Wulfs to fight brand new Mustangs, Thunderbolts and Spitfires. We lose irreplaceable pilots with every sortie. And Goering slaps us on the back, hands out a few Iron Crosses and retreats back to his biergarten. I can tell you he will run out of chests to pin them on before he runs out of medals."

Although he did not know the new pilots well, or at all, really, he did not fear they were informers, ready to report to headquarters his political blasphemy. They were clearly shaken to see their Staffel leader so irate. The rate of loss in planes and pilots meant he no longer bothered to learn their names. The key to surviving in the hostile skies above Germany was experience and none of the quaking "kinder" listening to von Rindle's rant would be around long enough to gain that. The Jadgeschwader III/54, "Green Hearts of Thuringen" would continue to live up to their motto of "Fly and Fight until Victory or Death", but increasingly what they found was death.

#

Davis and his fellow tankers were buttoned up, returning the fire from the 272nd GVD currently holed up in Kommerscheidt. He did not hear Aiken approach in his Weasel with its meager but still welcome ammunition supply

Aiken pulled up behind *Hell's Fire* and opened up the .30 caliber ammo box mounted on the right rear deck which contained the field telephone wired into the tank's intercom.

"*Hell's Fire,* I've got some re-supply for you," said Aiken.

"Thank God," replied Davis. "Be right out." He opened the top hatch and tumbled onto the rear deck and then to the ground.

"We were almost out and would have had to withdraw. Anymore headed our way, do you think?"

"They are trying to scare up some more Weasels but for now, this is it. No good news about the weather, either. They expect cloud cover for the next twenty-four hours, at least," Aiken reported. "And the trail through the valley is open but I don't think it is going to bear up under much traffic. So, even if we had the Weasels, the trail may not last too long."

"Jesus, you are just a fount of good news, aren't you? Well, I suspected as much. With what you brought, we can probably sustain this position if the Krauts attack, but no way we are going to be pushing them out of Schmidt anytime soon, especially without any air cover."

Aiken helped distribute the ammo he brought, then turned the empty Weasel and its trailer to head back for more wounded. Van Kleist's 88 rounds began to land on Kommerscheidt once again.

#

Mustang pilot Captain Robert Mulley stretched himself awake in his bunk at the USAAF base, Leiston, Sussex. He rolled to his right where he could look out the tent flap to see that the overcast, was still 10/10, but had gained some altitude, about ten thousand feet was his guess. He remembered the weather briefing from last night that all of England and most of western Europe was similarly socked in.

"No bombers today," he thought and rolled onto his left side, pulling up the covers.

"Excuse me, Sir. It's Hammond, Sir, briefing in 30 minutes." Jimmy Hammond was his impossibly young crew chief for his P-51D Mustang, named *Snafu*. Mulley was convinced that Hammond went straight from the Boys Scouts to the 357th Fighter Group, by-passing his senior year in high school, shaving, his voice changing and almost certainly, sex. What he did have, somehow, was an almost mystical connection with the inner workings of the Mustangs. Crew chiefs years his senior learned to consult him if they were having trouble with their planes.

"Its 10/10 overcast, Hammond, from here to the end of the known world," he said, rolling over and pulling his blanket more firmly over his head. "No escort today. Go away."

"If you please, Sir..."

"Nothing to shoot down, either."

"I think the brass wants just the Mustangs to sortie and shoot up what they called 'targets of opportunity'".

"Like what the fuck what?"

"They didn't say, Sir. That's what the briefing is for, I guess." Duty being satisfied, Hammond beat a hasty retreat.

"Oh, sweet mother of God," he moaned. "They do not pay me enough for this shit."

He threw off the cover and immediately began to shiver. Hammond had taken his long underwear, thick socks, lined flight suit to have them cleaned in the village, thinking they had a day off. Before waking him up, Hammond had retrieved them and the items were neatly folded on the camp chair near the end of his cot. Every morning the group had a mission, which were most mornings, Mullen re-thought his decision to extend his tour another twenty-five missions. He was not prompted by patriotism but knowing by doing so, he would be discharged upon his return home. Otherwise, he had been looking at eighteen months of flight instructor in New Mexico. At the rate of the missions, he'd be home and out of the Army in two months. He just had to live through those two months.

He groaned as he rolled to a sitting position and stood unsteadily. Hammond, "God bless 'im", had a lukewarm basin of water along with his shaving kit. He shaved and dressed quickly knowing that at least there would be hot coffee with the briefing.

The briefing room was in a Quonset hut next to the base hospital. He joined the stream of other, barely awake Mustang pilots, each looking up at the 10/10 cloud cover and wondering. They entered into the blessed warmth and coffee scented briefing room.

"Good morning, gentlemen," Lt. Col. Abrahamson said with some faint attempt at welcoming them. He waited patiently as his thirty pilots of the 357th Squadron settled into their seats, cupping their steaming cups of coffee. Captain Mulley as squadron leader for the 357th sat on the left of the front row.

"Now, as you can see," the Colonel started, "there will be no escort duty for today or the next two to three days. But you all remember that the P-51 is a fighter bomber aircraft and therefore we have the opportunity to expand our activities." His aide drew back the large curtain covering the map of Belgium and northern France. Clearly marked were rail lines, marshalling yards, depots and the few remaining airfields still in German hands. There was a murmur from the pilots at these prospective "targets of opportunity", when they realized that they would be able to generally run amok.

"You will be able to range as far as Aachen to the north, Cologne and Schmidt to the east, Bastogne to the south. Hit any targets of opportunity. We have word the Germans are planning to try to break through, we just don't know where. Anything you see moving is fair game. You will have three 500-pound bombs and full ammo. The third bomb will replace the Texas tanks as you won't be ranging that far. We do not expect much from our friends in the Luftwaffe. Intelligence informs us that they are restricting patrols due to fuel and pilot issues. There is a chance that you might be able to surprise them on the ground as an added inducement.

"As you can see, our main targets will be the rail lines and marshalling yards. Follow the roads and take out any trucks or tankers you can find. We hope to have two or more days of this weather, so make the most of it.

"Good hunting."

The pilots finished their coffee and headed for the jeeps that would take them to the flight line. This type of mission where they could call their own shots, appealed to every desire that made them want to be fighter pilots in the first place. The need for more sleep was instantly swept away as they jumped out of the jeeps to do their final pre-flight. Mulley knew that he could trust Hammond and his ground crew to have *Snafu* prepped and ready to go but the plane was his responsibility, one that merited his highest respect.

Mulley had been in the Army Air Force for three years. During that time, he had flown in the P-39 Aircobra, the P-47 Thunderbolt, the "Milk Jug" or just plain "Jug", which he loved due to its size, survivability and sheer power. He resisted changing over to the Mustang for a while, thinking it was too lightweight to go head-to-head with the FW 190 Doras which had overtaken the 109 Messerschmitt as the main killer of American and British bomber fleets.

His reluctance diminished when Mulley was assigned to the 357th Squadron and trained on the Mustang. The squadron's nose art made him feel that he would fit in with this group. On the fuselage just ahead of the cockpit was a bullet-riddled skull sporting a Hitler mustache with a bloodied bayonet stabbed from the occiput and exiting through the left eye socket.

Mulley was completely won over the first time he flew the Mustang. He felt that he became a part of the plane. He settled into the cockpit as a hand would into a killer's glove. The speed, agility, range and the lethality of the Mustang meant that the fighter escorts could range ahead of the bomber streams in "fighter sweeps" to clear the hostile skies of Germany and still get back in time to provide the close escort needed if the Luftwaffe did appear. The six .50 caliber machine guns in the wings allowed the Mustang to "punch above its weight". The German attack tactics had changed as well. Often the bf109s would run interference for the heavier FW190s in grouped attacks on the bombers. Or they would form up in a single line behind and below the bombers and close at high speed, slashing through the formations then disappearing.

The 357th could put thirty Mustangs into the air for the mission. They could launch three abreast from the field at Leiston, Surrey. They were soon all airborne after which Mulley and his wingman, Lt. Doug Karnowski split off from the main group as they crossed the Belgian border and descended to four thousand feet. Their hunt began.

They first encountered three coastal radar installations near Audembert and Marck, France. They made short work of them with their .50 caliber fire. Next, they swept on to the airfield at Marck and caught three bf110s on the ground and two Messerschmitts as they climbed to meet them. They used one 500-pound bomb each to crater the air strip. Staying low and fast, they followed a main road to the railway marshalling yard outside Marck and strafed the warehouses. They were rewarded with secondary explosions. They flew further inland finding a truck convoy protected by a Mobilwagen half-track mounting four 20mm Flakvierling cannons on a converted Panzer chassis. Mulley and Karnowski dove down from five thousand feet, approaching the convoy from the rear, Mulley in the lead.

Their strafing run took out four of the trailing trucks before the Mobilwagen began to fire its quad cannons. Both the Mustangs flew down the line of trucks before the German gun could traverse and follow them. The two Mustangs pulled up, did barrel rolls and returned for a second run. The German gunners were facing in the right direction this time and began firing. Mulley and his wingman released their remaining bombs at the head of the convoy, stopping it dead in its tracks. The Mobilwagen was still intact and followed the two Mustangs more accurately. Karnowski took a hit in the port wing which blew apart. He had no chance and flew straight into the ground, ending in an immense fireball. Mulley pulled sharply left and began his evasive climb. The two-centimeter shells streaked on either side of him as he pulled up hard and to starboard. They did score a glancing hit on his port wingtip and the tail. Although handling and speed were impaired, he could stay airborne. He turned for the coast and radioed the convoy's position to the rest of his flight.

Mulley started to talk to his plane, trying to convince the *Sanfu* to get him home. He figured he needed only thirty minutes air time to get over England. He thought he could make the field at Thorpe Abbots and headed there. The hit to his rudder was significant, making control of the plane increasingly difficult. To make matters worse, it seemed more of the tail was falling off as he flew. The white Dover cliffs came into view and Thorpe Abbotts was only ten miles inland. His best option was to land the plane, next was to get over land with enough altitude to bail out and worst case was an uncontrolled crash landing.

He fought the increasing shaking and yawing of the Mustang. As more of the tail came off, the ship became more unmanageable. He cleared the cliffs but was having more trouble keeping aligned on the runaway at Thorpe Abbotts.

"Tower, Thorpe Abbotts. This is Mustang flight 357. Requesting emergency clearance for landing."

"Roger, Mustang 357, you are cleared for main runway. Cross winds from the west at 10 knots. What is the nature of your emergency? Trucks are rolling."

"Thank you, Tower. My rudder is shot nearly away and I have a hole in my port wing tip."

"Roger, Mustang 357, we have you in sight. Put down your landing gear now."

"Christ! I thought it was down, indicator lights show wheels down." Mulley tapped his indicator light to see it go out. He reached down to his left and pulled up on the landing gear release lever. His indicator light showed green again but switched off when he tapped it again.

"How about now, tower?"

"No gear visible."

"Well, shit. It'll have to be a gear-up landing."

"Roger, Mustang 357. Make your best approach on main runway. Trucks have rolled. Good luck."

Mulley was losing control of the plane with every chunk of tail rudder that fell away. He was approaching from the east and more or less aligned with the main runway at Thorpe Abbotts which ran east to west. Two shorter runways which ran southeast to northwest and southwest to northeast were out of reach for him. The stick was shaking violently, requiring all his strength to keep the plane centered on the runway. He continued to drift and yaw as he descended towards the east end of the runway. He saw the flashing lights of the emergency trucks lining up three-fourths of the way down the runway. It was anybody's guess where *Snafu* would come to rest, if it would explode or careen into the trucks. The last thing Mulley did was to dump his remaining fuel at about two hundred feet. The lighter Mustang was even harder to control now that it was essentially a glider.

The ground was coming up fast. He was at fifty feet when the rest of his rudder shredded away. The plane yawed sideways and hit the ground doing one hundred-fifty miles per hour. Sparks and flame erupted from the undercarriage, the port wing sheared off and the fuselage canted to port, threatening to flip over. Had Mulley not emptied his tanks, he certainly would have exploded. *Snafu* began a slow spin toward the grass infield before coming to rest a two hundred yards from the rescue trucks. Mulley took a deep breath then cranked his canopy open with his right hand and he undid the seat belt and parachute. He scrambled out the right side of the plane, onto the remaining wing and jumped onto the grass, running toward the approaching emergency trucks.

He looked back at the smoking wreck of the *Snafu.* "What do they say? Any landing you can walk away from is a good landing," he mused. As the fire crews hosed down his plane, Mulley gratefully accepted a ride back to Thorpe Abbotts' officer's club and within a few hours the short hop to Leiston was arranged. He entered the 357's ready room for debriefing.

"Bobby, Bobby, Bobby," said his group commander, Lt. Col. Abrahamson, "always the big entrance with you, isn't it?" He handed Mulley a cup of coffee. "Sorry about Karnowski and the *Snafu.* I wish we could give you a little time off but there seems to be big doings and Group wants every pilot and plane up. Get debriefed and we'll see about a new plane for you."

Captain Robert Mulley managed to contain his enthusiasm. He was also not looking forward to facing Jimmy Hammond, his barely pubescent crew chief who thought of the *Snafu* as more his plane than Mulley's or even the USAAF's.

Chapter Thirteen:
Home Again

A wing of B24 Liberators had been added to the Thorpe Abbotts air field due to the losses sustained by the B17s. First to arrive was *Hell's Here*. Her nose art was Satan wreathed in flames throwing balls of fire. There was a small group of nose art connoisseurs who would critique the renderings and offer unwanted remarks. These sessions took place in the Officers' Club with faux artistic erudition enhanced by inebriation.

"Well, I for one, find that *Hell's Here* presents a welcome change from the usual barely clothed pornography of most of the group," stated the navigator of the *Popped Cherry,* Lt. Hiram Conners.

"You're a fine one to talk," replied Lt. Herman Swank, co-pilot of the *Catastrophic Cathy*. "*Cherry's* nose is adorned with a brunette smiling contentedly. I wonder why."

"Well, who decides on the nose art, anyway?" asked a new pilot.

"I think it's the enlisted man who does the painting, an inventive but rather dirty minded individual, it seems."

"Well, be that as it may," said Capt. Mark Regan, captain of the *Catastrophic Cathy,* "we better wrap this up. Mission tomorrow. See you all at the three am briefing." Drinks were finished, final complaints voiced and the assembled flight crews of the 343rd Squadron, 98th Bomb Group, went their separate ways to the tent barracks at Station 111, Thurleigh, England. The majority of the B24 Liberators of the 100th bomb group were divided between the airfields at Seething and Thurleigh in addition to Thorpe Abbotts.

#

"Regensburg, not that fucking place again," *moaned* Lt. Benny Ulan, bombardier of the *Hell's Here*. The assembled flight crews at Seething, Thurleigh and Thorpe Abbotts were at the three am briefings, all looking at the same map of northwestern Europe. These three flights would be joined by three others, gathering on Buncher 28, then forming on the routes for the three flights that differed slightly and were indicated by a red ribbon thumb tacked to the large maps. It was hoped that the multiple groups coming via different routes would stretch the Luftwaffe, reducing the number of attacking planes per group so that the bombers' own armament could handle them. Each of the briefing officers had their pointers and droned on about Bunchers, IPs and times on target. The one-armed Major at Thorpe Abbotts saved the best for last.

"Now, gentlemen as you can see, this will be a maximum effort with three strike forces arriving via three different routes and times on target separated by no more than an hour." The Major using whacks of his pointer for emphasis. "It is expected that this scheduling will not allow enough time for the 109s to re-fuel and re-arm and the 88s on the ground to re-plenish their rounds."

"That's the good news?" asked Lt. Wilson James, pilot of *The Usual Suspects.*

"Are they gonna shoot down the 88s as well?" asked Lt. Norman Ems, the *Suspects*' bombardier.

"Well, no, actually. But the lead plane in each group will be dropping chaff which has been shown to throw off the gunners' aims pretty well." There was muted joy from the assembled crews.

"As for the target, yes, that fucking place, Regensburg, again. It seems that the Krauts have re-built, resurrected enough of a factory to turn out about 100 Messerschmitts a week. And I am sure you all remember Schweinfurt fondly," he paused to allow the groans to subside. "I thought you would. And I am also sure that you all recognize the critical nature of the humble ball bearing to the war effort. Well, it seems that has also been revived. So, you can appreciate the need to hit these targets and hit them hard, once again.

"This will involve almost four hundred planes from sixteen different groups. We will have P-47 escorts to Eupen on the border. But that will leave still an hour of unescorted flight time to and back from the targets. Success will mean that the German war industry will have been significantly crippled for at least six months."

"Any sign of us getting Mustangs for escort. Aren't they in England by now?" asked Lt. Ems.

"They are arriving but too late for this mission. They are not yet here in sufficient numbers to do us any good. Then there is the training up of the pilots and getting them familiar with our little neighborhood so, like I said, it will be a while. Any other questions?"

There being none, the crews were dismissed. They boarded the jeeps and trucks to ride out to the flight line and their waiting B17s and B24s. Each man felt their guts beginning to turn over and once again wished they had visited the head one more time before their eleven- to twelve- hour flights.

#

"Be alert", said Lt. James Wilson, pilot of *The Usual Suspects,* the lead plane of his group. "Because the nation needs more 'lerts'" thought Ems, his navigator.

"We just crossed over Eupen. We'll be making our turn for Schweinfurt in 30 minutes. Bombing altitude will be ten thousand feet."

In addition to his bomb load, Wilson had the chaff, strips of radar-confusing aluminum, to be dropped when they were over the target and upon which the hopes of his flight members for survival were pinned. As flight leader, he could talk to the twenty-six other B17s that the 100th Bomb Group contributed to this mission.

"Tighten up the formation. They ought to be hitting us soon. Good luck."

The day was clear with the sun glinting off the wings of the bombers. It was diving out of that sun that the first bf109Gs dived on them. Hauptmann Jans von Rindel of the Stab III Geschwader #77, his new "Green Hearts of Thuringen" since his previous flight had been destroyed, led his depleted but still fearsome flight of Messerschmitts to attack the bomber stream. His twenty-millimeter nose cannon stitched through the center of the *Special Delivery*, taking out the top turret and exploding the wing tanks. The plane disappeared into a ball of flame. Soon, the rest of his flight engaged the unescorted bombers. They fought back with their own machine guns. From the deadly ballet of bombers and fighters, planes pirouetted down to the green earth below.

Technical Sergeant John Payne, the belly gunner on the *Suspects*, from Philadelphia, Mississippi, watched the blossoming white parachutes from the stricken planes, German and American, massing over the green land of Germany and was reminded of the cotton fields back home. He was curled in the fetal position, feet in their rests. The right pedal controlled the gunsight, the left was the intercom switch. The joysticks by his head swiveled the turret and controlled elevation of the guns. Each joystick had a thumb trigger to fire. The aiming window and gunsight were between his knees. There was not enough room for a parachute. His back and butt had an armored plate but everything else was plexiglass. His feet and hands were numb due to position and the cold. Next to his skin he wore the "Blue Bunny" suit, named for its color, which contained the heating wires. Over this was his thick flight suit, then his fleece-lined flight jacket and gloves. All this would not prevent him from freezing to death in minutes if the turret windows were shot through. It was minus fifty degrees at the 25,000 feet they were flying.

He was responsible for the lightly armed, highly vulnerable belly of the plane. The Luftwaffe pilots knew this, too, and most of their attacks came from that quarter. One advantage was that he did not have to fight the sun so his reticle sight was bright and sharp. Once the target was acquired, the Sperry computer dialed in the speed and calculated the bullet drop, greatly increasing the gunner's accuracy. Payne was not completely sold on turning everything over to the "machine" as he thought of it. He was a good shot from his days hunting in the Mississippi woods around home. He could manually override the computer and his kill rate was as good if not better than the other gunners. Each kill was certainly more satisfying to him. There were five swastikas stenciled on his turret. He planned for more.

He kept the turret in constant motion to supplement his scanning the skies. He could quickly identify friend from foe, engaging them at a greater distance. The two guns were fed by small ammo boxes containing 450 rounds each sitting atop the guns. These were replenished by belts fed to them by chutes from reservoirs inside the plane.

"Well, hello, darlin'" he said as he sighted on a fast-approaching bf109 Messerschmitt. The sighting reticle dot within the aiming circle covered exactly the Messerschmitt's nose cannon flashes when Payne depressed both triggers. The 109 disintegrated in fire. He did not pause to celebrate his sixth kill. He continued scanning the skies looking for his seventh. The 100th continued its mission to Schweinfurt.

The intensity of the Luftwaffe attacks only increased as the 100th approached Schweinfurt. They broke off only when the flak gunners took over. The 100th had lost five bombers already since the turn over Eupen. *The Usual*

Suspects' chaff was released as a countermeasure to the gunners' radar. The chaff were strips of paper about ten and a half by 2/3 inches with one side coated with aluminum foil and one-pound packs were shot out the flare chutes alongside the fuselage at timed intervals. This not only opened the packs but electrostatically charged the strips so they repelled each other rather than clumping. The resulting cloud rendered the ground radars blind so that the antiaircraft rounds became inaccurate. The effectiveness of chaff was one of the few hopes the aircrews had of actually surviving the war.

"Five minutes to target", called Lt. Wilson, the *Suspects'* pilot, "descending to ten thousand feet". It was hoped that the new altitude would throw the gunners off and make the chaff more effective. Lt. Ems, the bombardier, hunched over his Norden bombsight. "Ship's all yours, Norm," Wilson said, turning over the flying of the plane to Ems on the final part of the bomb run. Through the sight, Ems could see the buildings of the Schweinfurt ball bearing factory, spread out below. As lead bomber, he would release his bomb load over the first set of buildings with rest of the flights "walking" their bombs through the complex.

"Bombs away," Ems said.

Sprouts of grey-black smoke from the explosions erupted from the factory buildings as the bomb loads landed. There were no secondary explosions. Payne, looking back could see there was good coverage of the building from the rest of the flight. Time over target was less than fifteen minutes before the bomber could turn for home and back to the waiting Messerschmitts and Focke-Wulfs.

"Here they come," shouted Captain Wilson. The re-fueled and re-armed fighters were split in two groups, the FW190 Doras coming straight on and the bf109 Gustavs diving down out of the cloud cover.

The unescorted B17s fought back as best they could, but John Payne in the belly turret, watched plane after plane either explode or plummet trailing smoke and flame to the ground. He had no illusion that he was going to live through the mission. His only plan was to take out as many fighters as he could. His only hope was a quick death. He feared burning to death more than anything else on or above the earth.

A Focke-Wulf 190 was driving upward toward the B17 formation. Fully re-armed, he was sparing no 20mm cannon fire. Payne swung his turret to face the oncoming fighter. Their rounds passed each other as they tried for a kill. Payne's twin .50s found their mark and the FW190 exploded. The German's rounds passed through the *Suspects'* fuselage wounding the left waist gunner, Sergeant Woodrow Eads. They had thirty minutes flying time before they got back to Eupen and the escorting Thunderbolts. The Luftwaffe knew that as well.

Hauptman Jans von Rindel of the "Green Hearts" rallied his remaining fighters.

"Green Hearts! Break off and re-group on me." He pulled hard on his stick and made his bf109 scream as he climbed to twenty thousand feet. Within minutes the rest of his Staffel joined him. There were only fifteen of the thirty who had begun the fight. A mile below them the B17s remained in their defensive box but, to von Rindel's satisfaction there were far fewer of them, most streaming smoke and struggling to maintain their formation.

"Green Hearts, we will have one more go at them before they pick up their escorts. Let's make it count and teach them the cost of attacking the Fatherland. 'To Victory or Death!'"

The mixed flight of bf109s and FW190s peeled off, following their leader and attacked the bombers from above. Each fighter picked out a single bomber to attack, lacing into the planes with their 20mm nose cannons and the two 20mm cannons in the wing roots. Von Rindel could claim another kill and his group two more with hits on at least ten of the B17s before they broke off the attack.

"There the motherfuckers go," said Lt. Kenneth Forbes, the co-pilot of the *Suspects.* "Maybe five minutes to Eupen and the Thunderbolts. Report damage." All told, the Suspects had five wounded out of her ten-man crew. One engine was out and another smoking heavily. She struggled to maintain speed and elevation.

"Alright, toss out everything not bolted down," said James, the pilot. "Ken, go back and see what you can do with the wounded." From the cockpit, James surveyed the survivors of the flight. They were down to eighteen of the thirty-six planes that left Thrope Abbotts and most of those had some degree of battle damage. James switched to the flight frequency in order to talk to the rest of the flight.

"Report casualties." One by one the bombers answered with their body count. By the end of the butcher's bill recitation, there were fifteen dead, forty-eight severely wounded. Not a plane escaped. Giving those remaining forty-eight flyers any chance of surviving meant getting back to Thorpe Abbotts and landing as best they could. The order of landing was a sort of honor system, each pilot estimating how long the plane and crew could last, then taking a place in the landing order based on how many working engines they had left.

"Thorpe Abbotts ahead, about ten minutes," reported Lt. Mark Angelo, the *Suspec*t's navigator.

Gradually, the flight elongated out of the box formation. James contacted the tower and gave them a status report. Every available ambulance, fire truck, Jeep prepared to off load the planes as they came in. Red flares began to sprout from the sides of the bombers on their final approach. There were flares from each of the bombers struggling to stay aloft long enough to make the field.

TSgt. John Payne, the belly turret gunner on the *Suspects,* attempted to rotate the guns to the rear in preparation for landing. He could not. He found he could not rotate them downward either so his escape hatch door would open into the ship. The turret was jammed and immobile. The B17's landing gear gave enough ground clearance so that the turret did not have to be retracted as it would in a B24. It was standard procedure that the gunner would vacate the turret before landing for safety but not absolutely necessary as long as the landing gear was intact, which it was not. Payne was trapped.

"Confirm landing gear down," said James, the pilot.

"It most certainly is not fucking down," yelled Payne. "The turret is jammed and won't move. I can't get out."

"It's alright, John," said Wilson James, the pilot, trying to project a calm he did not feel. This was every crew's nightmare. "We'll get you out."

Within a minute, Payne could hear thunderous hammering on the turret from the rest of the crew. Looking up he could see dents appearing as they used hand sledges to try to dislodge the turret. It was made of quarter inch steel so the process was going to be slow. They lacked chisels or axes, something that might cut through the turret wall. They disconnected the ammo chutes that fed the magazines atop the .50s. With all the hammering, they did not want to accidentally cause a round firing in the plane or the turret.

Payne saw they were approaching Thorpe Abbots. The escorting P-47s had peeled away and the flight was aligning behind the *Suspects* so that he had no visible companions to lessen his overwhelming sense of being alone. Lt. James called into the tower.

"Tower. Mayday. Mayday. This is the *Usual Suspects.* We have a gunner trapped in the belly turret and three wounded on board. Request permission to pull out of formation and circle while we get him out. Over."

"Roger, *Suspects,* you are cleared to leave formation. Proceed northwest on heading 045 three miles and commence your circle. We have no incoming traffic in that direction. Good luck."

The return of the 100th from any mission always attracted all the eyes on the base. Word spread of the trapped gunner ensuring everyone not actively involved in landing the rest of the flight, watched and prayed. The remaining seventeen B17s aligned again. The first five in line barely maintaining air speed on at most two engines. They had already fired their red flares. Landing rank was determined by the number of working engines and how much of the plane was on fire.

"How's it going back there," called James on the intercom.

Knowing that Payne was able to hear everything going on, TSgt. Fred Lesser, the engineer, called back, "We're making some progress. We've knocked off the ammo chutes and trying to expand those holes." The chutes entered the belly turret on either side and were the weakest part of the metal turret. The escape hatch was blocked by the turret frame and could not be pried open.

Lt. James tapped the fuel gauges for the remaining engines. They had another five minutes of flight time before they would have to belly in. Norman Eads, the left waist gunner, lightly wounded and Payne's friend, pounded with fury, trying to knock the turret loose. Charles Zinn, the right waist was making his last flight before going home. He pried at the turret frame with a crowbar also to no avail. The rest of the crew were trying to get the landing gear down. One of the 20mm rounds striking the ship had smashed the controls, immobilizing the turret. The gear was jammed by another hit.

Payne tried to remember the Southern Baptist sermons of his youth, trying to remember prayers of hope. None came. He prayed his own prayers for forgiveness, he closed his eyes and shut the intercom off. He did not need to hear the final order to prepare for a crash landing. The pounding on the turret stopped.

Lt. James made his last turn for his final approach. There was nothing he could do. He had to land the plane to save the rest of the crew, three of whom were badly wounded and running out of time. He lined up on the runway, noting the emergency vehicles lining the tarmac.

John Payne could feel the final turn and descent.

“Our Fa....”.

The belly turret sheared off. The fuselage ignited; flames spewed along its length. *The Usual Suspects* careened and twisted down the runway until coming to a stop half-way down. Ems grabbed Harvey Puzio, the tail gunner and Eads dragged Fred Lesser, the top turret gunner out through the side windows. Lt. Mark Angelo, the nose gunner/navigator had bled to death before the landing. James and Forbes, the pilot and co-pilot had to break out their side windows and slide down the *Suspects'* nose to the ground. Puzio and Lesser were loaded into ambulance and taken to the base hospital. *Suspects*' flames were extinguished and the wreck was hauled off to the side of the runway to join the other hulks that would never fly again but got their crews home one last time.

Chapter Fourteen:
To Care for Him Who Has Borne the Battle

The fall weather of 1944 in East Anglia, England, had been glorious: warm, misting in the mornings, clearing in the afternoons. The countryside around Thorpe Abbotts remained green longer than the locals could remember in some time. Perfect weather for the bombers of the 100th Bomb Group. There were no scratched missions. The pace ran to three missions a week, more than two hundred planes each. The work of Station 139, Thorpe Abbotts base hospital had been equally steady as a result.

Captain Luther Haynes, chief surgeon of the hospital had taken to sleeping late, once the night's cases had been dealt with. The mild weather made for comfortable sleeping and Haynes was making the most of it. Until his surgical orderly shook him by the shoulder.

"The 100th just got back..." said Corporal Victor Hume.

"Oh, God, that is never good," Haynes said. He rolled out of his cot, pulling on his blood- soaked boots and stepped outside. He arched his stiff, aching back, feeling years older than his 33 years. He was five years out of his surgical residency at Chapel Hill, North Carolina. The experience he was gaining at Thorpe Abbotts could not be reproduced anywhere else. He worked on an endless stream of horribly wounded young men, trauma that he hoped he would never encounter again once the war was over. Haynes worried about returning to peacetime surgery when he realized he had forgotten how to do a simple hernia repair or an appendectomy.

The arcing red flares from the wavering bombers signaled wounded aboard. The flames and the smoke streaming from engines made clear the stricken B17s had one shot at making their landings. As far as he could tell, none of the planes had all four engines working, some only had one still sputtering and belching fire. One by pitiful one, most without intact landing gear, the bombers crashed landed on the main runway, skidding and swerving onto the grassy borders. Two exploded before their crews could get out.

The crash trucks sped down the run way to help even as more planes bellied in. The fire suppression teams began their work, spreading foam over the wrecks. Only ten of the thirty planes the 100th was able to contribute to the Schweinfurt raid returned. It was the raid that became known as "Black Thursday".

Thorpe Abbotts, Station 139, began as a Royal Air Force field but during the build-up of 1942-3, the US Eighth Air Force took over the field for its 100th Bomb Group (Heavy) which flew B17s. The hospital was originally in tents but grew into a complex of Quonset huts housing the receiving ward, where initial evaluations were done, the surgery suite of six operating tables, recovery beds numbering fifty in all and a short-term ward for medical cases. The wounded were stabilized then evacuated to larger hospitals for tertiary care. Messerschmitt and Focke-Wulf machine gun rounds, flak and burns accounted for the majority of wounds handled at the hospital. Upon arrival, all the men were in some state of shock from blood loss and hypothermia. The number of wounded was unpredictable. Each raid was different in the losses sustained. The raids ranged from the French coast to Bremen, Berlin, Schweinfurt and other cities, as well as railway depots, oil refineries and German airfields, all of them guarded by the radar guided 88mm anti-aircraft guns.

Haynes watched as the ambulances, jeeps and trucks sped toward the hospital loaded with the wounded. The rest of the surgical staff, orderlies, nurses came running. How long they would be there was anyone's guess. Haynes turned to watch the last of the B17s make its landing before entering the receiving ward. Stretcher bearers dragged the first of the airmen into the ward and the twenty litter stands began to fill up. At this stage of triage, the most important medical instruments were bandage scissors. The heavy fleece lined flight jackets, then the flight suits, boots gloves all had to be cut away before evaluation of the wounds could begin. No morphine had been given and the screams of those unlucky few that were still conscious, soon filled the ward. The men were moved as little as possible but still it was torture for them.

Haynes began his evaluation of the men lying on the litters. The first three he came to were dead. The fourth's intestines spilled out when his flight suit was opened. He tried to scoop them back only to have them slip through his fingers and onto the floor.

"Morphine," he shouted. An orderly arrived with the shot which Haynes administered then covered the doomed airman's belly with a sheet. He moved on the next litter. The orderlies that preceded him had already cut away the flight suit and given morphine.

"At last, something I can do," thought Haynes. The waist gunner's left arm was barely attached to his chest. He called out, "Amp set." Each litter stand had a side table next to it. Corporal Victor Hume, his surgical assistant, pulled on his gloves and rapidly unwrapped the set. It contained sterile drapes, bowls and all the instruments needed to take off an arm or a leg. Hume washed down the airman's side and half of his mangled upper arm with an iodine solution. Haynes picked out some sterile towels to drape the shoulder. The airman was unconscious from the morphine and shock so they would not have to wait for anesthesia. Hume held the arm while Haynes selected the large amp knife, similar to a carving knife one would find in any kitchen, and deftly sliced through the shoulder joint, allowing Hume to take the arm away.

This started the bleeding from the large axillary artery and vein. Haynes, sponging with one hand and clamping with the other had controlled the bleeding to the extent that the airman would live long enough to be moved out of reception hut into one of the surgical huts where his wounds would be further stabilized, fluids and blood administered, sulfa powder sprinkled over the wound giving him some hope of surviving.

The rest of the reception ward was now filled with wounded and surgical teams. Triaging the crews from the 100th as they arrived from their burning planes became a matter of the skill of the surgeons and the luck of the wounded. Balancing the severity of the wounds versus the time and resources needed to treat them decided who would receive lifesaving surgery and who would not. The screams began to subside due to the number of men receiving their first morphine doses. The floor became slick with blood, littered with flight suits, boots, arms and legs. Other orderlies gathered up the detritus, dumping the debris into wheelbarrows and taken to the burn pits slowly filling just beyond the hospital huts. One hundred octane aviation fuel was poured over the mounting pile and lit on fire. Soon, black smoke filled the air around the hospital and the stench of burning flesh drifted back inside to the operating rooms.

All of the 100th's planes that could make it back had landed and their survivors picked up. The unwounded lucky went back to their barracks to collapse on their racks. The hospital dealt with the wounded and Graves Registration crews gathered the dead. Haynes and his colleagues had another long night ahead of them. A thought passed through his mind as he faced a nineteen-year-old with burns to his face, hands and most of his body, that maybe the 100th had lost so many planes this time that they could not fly again for a few weeks until replacements - planes and crews - could be found. Maybe it was a sliver of silver lining to this black, stinking cloud that hung over Thorpe Abbotts.

The burn case that faced Haynes, a corporal with the unlikely name of Gene Autry, but the inevitable nick-name of "Cowboy", could not even scream as his flight suit was cut away. His hoarse cries died away in wet gurgles indicating that he had inhaled if not actual flames, then at least super-heated oxygen. His mask had melted to his face. His body had baked within the smoldering flight suit. His skin adhered to the clothing and tore away leaving pink, glistening tissue that blistered when touched. Serum seeped from the surface like a roasted Thanksgiving turkey. He was losing precious milliliters of fluid every minute. He smelled like bacon.

"More morphine and an endotracheal set. We've got to get this boy an airway before we can do anything else,"

Haynes told Hume. Hume had already opened the trach set and had the ET tube ready for Haynes. He then injected five ccs of the morphine. The onset of the opiate was delayed because Autry had swollen so much that the needle barely reached the muscle. Haynes could not wait. With his left hand holding the laryngoscope and the tube in his right, Haynes hooked the blade over Autry's tongue and pulled up. He then slid the tube down through the exposed vocal cords, swollen and red, and into the trachea, which was filled with bubbling fluid. The boy gagged and coughed up blood-tinged fluid, covering Haynes' face. Hume handed him the suction tubing with which Haynes began to try to empty the frothy mess welling up from Autry's lungs.

One of the anesthesiologists began probing in Autry's groin to find the femoral vein which lay just to the inside of the pulsing artery. They had to establish a way to give Autry fluids to replace what was oozing out from all over his body. Adding to the necessary torture of simply trying to treat the badly burned airman, he was strapped to a back board to prevent his thrashing about.

"Got it," the anesthesiologist said. He threaded the long needle into the vein and normal saline began to flow in. The back board would keep the airman from bending which could puncture the femoral vein with the rigid IV needle. There were twenty wounded in the reception ward, eight of whom were badly burned. Between the smoke from the burn pit wafting into the ward and the smell of over cooked bacon coming from the burn patients, it was all the doctors and medics could do to keep from retching.

"Silvadene, lots of it," called Haynes. This was a sulfa based cream that was used on burns as a dressing, antiseptic and, by protecting the burns, a pain killer. One of the main tasks in treating the burns was to debride the surface of dead skin. This was largely done by simply peeling off their flight suits. Haynes and Hume scooped the cream with their gloved hands and spread it on the burns. The men were then wrapped in sterile sheets This began to reduce the pain and fluid loss but dehydration and hypothermia remained major risks. Once the initial treatments were done, the burn patients were transferred to a heated Quonset hut and readied for evacuation to a larger, more capable hospitals outside London. Many more surgeries lay ahead for "Cowboy".

The surgical cases were receiving stabilizing operations. There was no telling the extent of their wound from initial quick evaluations. Emergency treatments revolved around control of bleeding, amputations, placement of chest tubes which drained blood from the chest cavity and re-expanded lungs. For those whose bellies were already opened by their wounds, simple resections of perforated bowels were done to try to minimize contamination of their abdomens. Once the initial rush of the wounded passed through the receiving ward, Haynes and Hume began to attend to the surgical cases.

The primitive X-rays available at Thorp Abbotts could roughly locate where bullets and frags were but not what surrounding tissue damage was done. The bullets had entered through the thick flight suits, carrying cloth, leather and lamb's wool into the wounds with them. These did not show up on X-rays but still had to be removed entirely. The hospital was set up for six surgeries at a time but there were only four surgeons available. Two were on leave to London and it would take time to locate and recall them. For now, triage meant some airmen would live and others would certainly die. The wounded were sorted according to injury, not rank. Men assigned to the base and not directly involved in the recovery and turnaround of the planes, came to the hospital to offer whatever help they could.

The medical teams wore no masks and breathed through their mouths to minimize the sickening effect of the crematorium stench which was trapped inside the huts. There was no real escape: what they did not inhale, they tasted. The teams knew from multiple mass casualty situations, their clothes became so impregnated with burned flesh and blood, all their uniforms would be thrown into the burn pits anyway.

"Sweet Jesus! Captain Haynes, over here," shouted Hume. He had moved on to the merely grievously wounded that were on other litters within the receiving hut. Hume had moved a blood-soaked pad from an open abdominal wound and blood immediately began to spurt into the air.

He grabbed a fresh abdominal dressing and pressed onto the wound.

"What have we got?" asked Haynes.

"Judging from the height of the squirt, I'd say a nicked aorta," naming the main, garden hose-sized artery lying in the back of the abdomen.

"Suction and a vascular set," Haynes called to another medic. The set was thrown open on the bedside table and Haynes rooted through it to find a long-curved Kelly clamp.

"Ok, Victor, keep sucking right there," he said, indicating the bottom of the bloody hole that was the airman's abdomen. Haynes in his right hand held the clamp and a sponge in his left which he pressed against the large artery. He quickly lifted the sponge to identify the bleeder and just as quickly clamped about half the artery, stopping the bleeding but still allowing some blood flow to the boy's legs and kidneys. With the major bleeding controlled, Hume shifted over to the surgical set and assembled a curved needle called a French eye atraumatic on a long needle holder with silk thread to close the hole in the aorta.

"You are the best, Victor," said Haynes, taking the instrument and closed the rent in the artery. The major bleeding being controlled, Haynes began to explore the rest of the abdomen, to "run the bowel". Each inch of the small intestine, about thirty feet, and the large intestine, another five to six feet, were inspected for any holes. He found some and these were closed with the more silk thread. He closed the abdomen and then had the airman flipped onto his stomach to inspect the back. Fortunately, no penetrating wounds were found. After a three-hour operation, the man was allowed to awake and was transferred to the post-op hut.

Other surgical teams were working on the rest of the wounded from the 100th's disastrous raid on Schweinfurt. Burn patients were slavered with the white Silvadene cream and wrapped in sterile sheets, amputations, minor procedures done in reception while the more serious cases moved into the OR hut. By nightfall, the wounded of the "Bloody 100th" were cared for. The rest of the crews were drunk or asleep. Though the 100th would not be flying for a while, the crews would be dispersed as replacements among the other squadrons and many would be in the air the next morning.

#

"Fire mission!" barked Lt. Alfred Moore of the 229th Field Artillery (FA) to his crews manning the 105 Howitzers recently moved forward to within a half-mile of the Kall River's west rim. The only closer American position was Anderson and Howe's foxhole. They rattled with every over pass of the shells. Moore's guns which should have been a source of re-assurance to Howe, only deepened his foul opinion of his part of the war.

"Jesus-Fucking-Christ! Just when I thought those shit-for-brains generals had thought of all possible ways to get us killed, they move prime targets right up our asses so the Krauts will think there is something here worth blowing up. It wasn't enough for them to move us all the way across the fuckin' river, just to be pushed back here, 'to re-fit' they said, so they can shove us back into Kommerscheidt again.

"Oh, yeah last time worked real well. Fucking Krauts didn't seem to have any trouble getting our asses out of there."

"Well," answered Anderson, "last time, we just had those three chewed up Shermans. I guess they see having a 105 battery to back us up will give us a bigger punch." Anderson had no illusions about cheering his friend up, he just wanted to break up the tirade before Howe got so pissed off, he might go after their lieutenant, Lt. Barclay and get himself put in the stockade. Throughout their exchange, the 105s raged just yards over their heads, shaking them in their foxhole. The barrage had been going on fifteen minutes when Lt. Barclay came up over the rim to their position.

"Anderson, get on back to the CP, get a new radio and batteries and the official kick off time for the counterattack. What I know is we start moving just after sunset. We'll move across the river and regroup on the other side. With the night time barrage and the Shermans, the brass is hoping for better outcomes. Re-supply by Weasel will be going on all night, so we should be in good shape by the dawn. Got it?"

"Yes, Sir," replied Anderson.

On his way back, Douglas Aiken in his Weasel with a load of wounded from the aide station at Mestrenger Mill slowed beside him.

"Got room for one more if you need a lift," he said. "Can't recommend that you dally out here."

"Thanks, heading for the CP." Anderson had seen enough dead and wounded to last him ten lifetimes, but to be riding with these mangled, silent men, to embrace them to keep his tenuous seat in the bouncing Weasel, brought him face-to-face with his likely future. He had been successful thus far in putting off thoughts of what could happen to him.

"Food for worms," he remembered from his twelfth-grade English class's study of Ben Franklin quotes. "Jesus, was that really only two years ago?"

"Got to swing by the aide station and drop these guys off," yelled Aiken to be heard over the Weasel's engine. He swerved sharply to avoid a shell crater. Aiken grabbed one of the wounded to keep them from sliding off.

"Christ!" Aiken said, "Nearly dropped one off too soon. Thanks. Good save. I'm Doug Aiken, who are you?"

"Henry Anderson, 112th."

"Glad to meet you. This is some shitshow, ain't it? More to come, I hear."

"Always seems to be"

They arrived at the aide station. No one came out to meet them.

"Huh, no one home, or they're on a fucking lunch break. Bunch of REMFs. Help me with these guys."

Anderson was covered in blood from hanging onto the wounded man. He supported the wounded man as they stumbled into the aide station at Vosseneck.

"Hey," shouted Aiken, "somebody want to give us a hand here?"

A medic appeared from behind a tent flap and hurried to take the man from Anderson. "You can come with me," he said to Anderson, thinking he was also wounded.

"No, I'm OK," Anderson said. "I'm just here to some things from the CP. My unit is the 112th up at the Kall and we need new radios with batteries. Where should I go for those?"

The medic directed him to a tent further back from the aide tent. The CP tent was in chaos. Curriers came and went, orders were being shouted by harried officers into field radios. Over laying all of this was the blasting of the field guns shaking the tent and deafening all within the CP. Anderson stood there to one side of the tent opening, occasionally being bumped into by messengers rushing out or coming in. Finally, someone noticed this bloodied infantryman standing by the opening.

"Are you OK?", asked one of the orderly room clerks. "Are you hit?"

"No, I'm fine. I got this from holding on to a guy who was pretty shot up. I'm from the 112th along the Kall. I need some new radios, batteries and the kick-off time for our next little adventure". Anderson was aware of the crinkling of the dried blood on his fatigues and chest. He was suddenly aware of how hungry he was, unable to remember the last time he ate.

"Supply tent is two down, should be able to get what you need there. As for when we start all the fun, your guess is as good as mine."

"Can I get something to eat, too? We ran out of K-rats a while ago."

"Mess tent is three down. That all you need?"

"Yeah, thanks."

"Good luck. This fucking weather is still grounding the air support and we are a battery down, so looks like you all will be on your own."

"Well, the Krauts call us the 'Bloody Bucket" for a reason, I guess. Thanks for your help."

Anderson found what he needed and was munching on a sandwich with one for Howe in his pocket, as he started back across the field towards the Kall.

"Hey, you looking for a ride back?"

Anderson turned to see Aiken with his Weasel loaded with mortar rounds, .30 and .50 caliber belts, several ammo cans and a box of grenades.

"Absolutely," Anderson replied. "Looks like we both did a little shopping. Any idea when the shit is supposed to hit the fan?"

"Soon, I would think. They've got me making ammo runs out and bringing in wounded pretty much non-stop. Today's daily rumor is that midnight tonight is likely. I've heard that twice which makes it as reliable as if I heard it from Eisenhower himself. Sounds like plenty of shit hitting a mighty big fan."

Aiken dropped Anderson off at the foxhole he shared with Howe. Anderson dropped the sandwich to Howe then delivered the radio and batteries to Lieutenant Barclay.

"Any news," asked his lieutenant.

"Rumor repeated twice is that we go tonight. Aiken has been ferrying ammo up and wounded back all day. The 109th is supposed to join us. No more tanks than the three we have and no air support due to the weather," Anderson answered, still chewing on his sandwich. He was unfazed by the blood covering his fatigues and hands although Barclay was getting a little queasy watching him.

"Well, I expect we'll be getting the word soon enough. I can at least get in touch with somebody in the rear, now that I have the radio. Aiken is getting us pretty well re-supplied. But it is only a matter of time before the Krauts spot him and blow him all to hell.

"Sergeant Rosinski, spread the word. All men to have full ammo, water and rations for three days. Kick off may be as soon as tonight."

#

The arrangement between Brandt and von Stettgen continued to work. The number of wounded they could treat was limited only by supplies. Aiken kept them stocked as well as he could. He was their lifeline since they were so deep in the valley, radio contact with either of their commands was spotty at best.

Aiken sought out Major Brandt while his Weasel was getting loaded with fresh wounded.

"Major, just a heads-up, but rumor has it that the counterattack may kick off as early as tonight. Anything that you need?"

"Yeah, like fuckin' every-goddam-thing," he replied. Since Aiken had last seen him two days ago, Brandt looked ten years older. Blood crusted his fatigues, smeared over his forehead and clotted in his boots. Only his hands were somewhat clean.

"We need blood, gloves, dressings of all sizes, more IV bottles, sutures, plasma, some more medics and any surgeons that are just hanging around. We can't evac to either side without becoming somebody's prisoners. Our only choice is to lay low here and keep doing what we're doing. The German medics have been great and Major von Stettgen is as exhausted as I am. But we need whatever you can bring in."

His desperation was evident and punctuated by the opposing artillery rounds streaking overhead.

"We are one short round from being blown all to shit. You tell them back in Vossenack that we are still here."

Oberstabsartz von Stettgen looked up from his eighteen-year-old infantryman from Munich.

"Sergeant, whatever you can bring in will be greatly needed and appreciated. I have not been able to convince my commanders that we are not aiding the enemy so they are not as forthcoming, unfortunately. It is 'eklig', disgusting, but true." He finished the amputation he was working on.

"OK, Aiken," said an aide station medic, "you are loaded up and ready to go. Good luck."

Chapter Fifteen: Infiltration/Exfiltration

It had been four months since the *Bouncing Betty* did not return and was presumed lost with her whole crew. Each night when the flight crews from the 100th BG came into the "Fox and Hens" pub, Virginia Standhope stopped what she was doing and examined each face. Joe was not there but she refused to believe that he would never be there again. It would feel like a betrayal if she stopped looking, waiting for him. The airmen had stopped trying to win her over and were now protective of her. They worried as she lost weight, lost interest in their stories and banter. She had also lost Norman Eads, the last crew member who remembered Joe, when the *Usual Suspects* went down. Now there were always new boys, from new planes passing through the pub, full of life, excited to be doing their "bit". All of them doomed.

Although she was only twenty-two, all the airmen who came into the pub seemed impossibly young to her. She did not want to get to know them fearing their losses as well. Virginia stopped going outside when she heard the planes returning. Only her father was of any comfort to her. He heard her crying herself to sleep every night. Virginia's grief made him miss her mother desperately. She had died giving birth to Virginia, something he had never told her. He lived in the hope that Virginia's life would go forward with a man she loved and who loved her. Now he felt he was living with ghosts: the girl Virginia used to be, his wife and now Joe Hanover, he had given up all hope that Joe was still alive. Something else he kept from Virginia.

#

Ambroos Hansen was the life line and only contact with the world outside the dugout that housed the downed airmen. He came at irregular times, sometimes gone for days and now at the end of their third week underground, the men were at the end of their endurance. They had lost weight, become pale as wraiths and were now paranoid about Hansen's actual aims for them. Joe Hanover still had some sway over them but that was loosening. The trap door opened and Hansen descended into the hole, dragging a sack behind him.

"Hallo, my friends. I was able to get some nearly fresh vegetables and dried fruit. The black bread is not too stale." He dropped the sack in the middle of the gathered flyers. He sensed the frustration of the men.

"Yeah, thanks," said Olgilvie bordering on anger, "but when the hell are we going to get out of here? We've gotten so weak that there is no way we could make it a half-mile let alone the five you say is the first stop. We might as well turn ourselves in to the Krauts as rot away down here."

There were murmurs of assent from the other men.

"I understand, and I have some good news. There is going to be three nights of storms which is also during the time of the new moon. We will not have such favorable conditions again for some time. My friends running the escape route say that they think it is so safe that we can use the roads rather overland through the woods. That will be easier on you and we can make good time. The German patrols have decreased so much that there are days when they don't leave their bunkers. In short, everything is, how you say, "Coming up daisies." Ambroos smiled having used a new American saying that he had just learned.

"'Roses', the saying is 'roses'," Hanover gently corrected him. "So, what is the plan? When do we go?"

"Tonight, two hours after dark. I will be joined by another member of the resistance who is very skilled, fearless and knows this area like no one else. When she arrives, she will give us the all-clear," his rising slightly at the end to confirm he used the right idiom. Hanover smiled and nodded.

"Wait, 'she'? A girl is going to come along?" asked Olgilvie. "What good is she going to be if the shit hits the fan?"

Although he took exception to Olgilvie's doubting tone, Hansen controlled his voice. "She is a veteran of two years of fighting the Nazis. We met when we were running the Comet Line, two years ago. It was a very dangerous route that went through the woods to safe houses in the towns. With it, we got our guests through Belgium, France and on to the Spanish border. From there, the men were picked up by sympathizers and sailed home from Gibraltar. Most recently, we were able to use safe houses in Paris, which she arranged and monitored. She escorted the men to Brittany and across the Channel. She has led four groups of your comrades through the lines without losing anyone this year alone. She knows the American positions in the Huertgen and has made contact with the front line there. Word will be gotten to them when to expect you men and they will be on the lookout for you. She speaks German, is local and can dissuade even the most suspicious Bosche from interfering. If that fails, she has killed two of them with her knife. You are going to be in good hands.

"Now get some rest."

#

"Make a hole," Sgt. Rosinki of the 112th shouted as he slid into the still fetid darkness of Anderson and Howe's foxhole, along the margin of the Huertgen Forest. The last German counterattack had driven the Americans back to their starting point when they took over the area from the Ninth Division two months ago. It was all Anderson could to keep Howe from sinking into irretrievable despair. Howe had even discussed staying above ground during the unrelenting artillery barrages of von Kleist's 88-millimeter guns.

"You know, fuck this shit," he had said to Anderson on more than one occasion. "Next barrage, you can have the hole all to yourself. I'm going to stay topside and see if I can't get me a million-dollar wound. You know yourself, the regiment sees us as expendable and they'll keep us here until we're dead so they don't have to scare up any replacements. Well, fuck 'em. I'm going out on my own terms."

Rosinski brought a change in plans.

"Alright," he said as he pulled new dry socks out of his pack. "It is a definite 'go' for tonight. We, some of the 109th and assorted others, are going to hit the Krauts starting at 0300. No air cover, no artillery prep. The idea is total surprise. Besides, with our air recon grounded, we don't really know where the fuckers are. Any prep would just warn them. Now, once we do know where they are, we can call in all the heavy shit we want.

"So, noise, light and fire discipline will be key to this. Form up at the CP at twenty-two hundred hours. Final details will be gone over then. Lt. Barclay will be leading us. Hold your questions for the meeting. See you then." With that, he slithered back out of the foxhole.

Anderson and Howe were quiet until Howe growled, "Tell me again why we even have a fucking Air Force. They've been AWOL through this whole clusterfuck. My next war, I'm signing up with them."

Another twelve rounds from von Kleist's guns arrived to put an end to their speculations. Howe stayed in the hole.

#

It was just as well that the night was so dark, wet and miserable when the men of the 112th gathered at the CP. That way they could not see what a disheartened, beat-up group of soldiers they had become. The regiment would normally have one thousand men divided into three brigades. It had been months since the 112th could field even four hundred men able to carry on combat actions. Weeks of constant wetness, cold, poor rations and disrupted sleep had sapped their physical reserves to the point that they could have easily been mistaken for invalids, if not for their armaments. Major General "Dutch" Cota addressed the officers of his regiment who would then spread the word to their men. The regiment was assembled so that there would be a coordinated attack across the Kall Valley. While the officer's meeting was taking place, the men received their first hot, or nearly hot, meal in weeks. This was not enough to cheer up Howe.

"Oh, Christ, they are fattening us up like lambs for the slaughter," he groused to Anderson. "This is going to be bad."

"Oh, come on, Jeff," said Anderson, "was there ever a gift horse's mouth that you did not look into? Just enjoy it while we can."

Lieutenant Barclay gathered with the rest of the what remained of the 112th's officers in the CP tent. Major General Cota stood on a field desk to address them.

"Welcome, men. Regiment has ordered us to attack and drive the Germans out of Schmidt once and for all. I know we are all tired of this back-and-forth bullshit that has been going on these past few weeks. And as you know, the reason that the Krauts have been able to target us so effectively with 88s is the observation points in Schmidt and Hill 400. As long as they hold those two positions, we ain't going anywhere.

"So, the new plan is to essentially sneak up on 'em. You've seen what effect having bombing runs, artillery strikes and armor has had on driving them out of their positions. All that 'sturm und drang' seems to have done is let them know we're coming. The time used to traverse the Kall Valley gives them plenty of notice and all the time they need to blow us all to hell.

"Lieutenant Barclay, your platoon will lead point on this. If you make it across without difficulty, then the rest of the regiment will follow. I cannot emphasize enough this must be done with the utmost stealth and silence. Once the regiment has crossed, we will advance on Schmidt and re-take the town. When and if we hear firing, then the tanks will cross as fast as they can and when we have coordinates, the artillery will support you. Weather remains problematic so we cannot expect air support.

"Any questions?"

"Yes, sir," Lieutenant Barclay stood, "two if I may. How many tanks are we talking about? And, as we have seen in the past, those 88s can be brought into action pretty damn quick. When we engage, it will probably be no more than five minutes before they start shelling the living hell out of us. How soon can we expect some counterbattery firing. The far ridge is out of range where our guns are positioned now."

"We will have the three tanks from the 707th that have great familiarity with the terrain and have proven themselves. As soon as the regiment moves forward, the artillery will be right behind them and set up along the western wall. We already know that the 'Long Toms' can reach the far ridge from there. Their first priority will be the 88s and to take them out. The plan is we will hit them unawares, hard and fast and get them on the run before they can mount a defense. Any other questions?"

"Very well, you have been given the line of march and order of advance. Return to your units and brief your men. Have them rest, fed and ready to go by 0300 hours. There being no other questions, you are dismissed."

Ruefully, Barclay thought, "I should have brought Howe along. He would have plenty of questions." He did not look forward to briefing his men, especially given that they were to run point on this operation.

#

Joe Hanover did not know if it was the long weeks passed since he last saw Virginia Standhope and could not accurately picture her face anymore but he gasped at the resemblance when he first saw Camille Renard who was going to lead the downed airmen on the first leg of their journey home. She was tall, thin with shoulder length auburn hair and blue-green eyes the color of the sea like Virginia's. Her excellent English made her orders clear. Jeb Olgilvie of the *Shy Virgin* was equally taken with her.

"There is no fuckin' way she knifed two Krauts," he muttered to Joe.

"Well, if she did, they had a much better last vision on earth than we are likely to have. Damn, man, she is something."

Camille was well aware of the effect she had on men and knew from the start that she had to take charge of the group to be taken seriously. She settled in the hideout with an air of familiar authority. She eased her pistol, a .32 caliber semi-automatic, nicknamed "Ruby", from her belt and placed it on her lap. Olgilvie wondered where her knife was.

"Hello, men. My name is Camille Renard, but I should say, that is not my real name, but the one chosen for this mission. It changes each time for security reasons. I know Ambroos has told you a little of the journey ahead. Last report had the American lines eighty kilometers from here. Unfortunately, the Bosche were able to push them back across the Kall valley again to their lines along the Huertgen Forest. This does not bother us too much since the last three months have shown this back and forth is typical of the fighting here. Now, we also know that the Bosche troops are mostly old men and young boys of the 272nd VGD. They have little armor, mostly mortars and are armed with the Karabiner 98k and the MP40 submachine gun.

"As Ambroos has explained, the conditions are the best they are likely to be with terrible weather and dark nights. We start tonight. You must obey my orders without question and immediately. We do not expect to meet any Bosche but you never know. Unfortunately, we won't be able to arm you. Amboos and I will have the only weapons but our goal is to not need any. We won't survive any fight with the Bosche so our plan is to avoid them. I have made this trip successfully four times and know how to approach the American lines. I will be in the lead and Ambroos will be at the end.

"Now get some rest."

Ambross' return was heralded by the smell of hot soup. Where this miracle came from was unfathomable. It was the first hot meal the men had had in weeks. Camille and Ambroos hoped it would help fortify the men for their challenging trek ahead of them. At the appointed time, Ambroos, armed with a MP40, pushed up the trapdoor and peered out into the dark rain. He turned his wet face into the dugout.

"All clear, we go." He moved to the side and as each airman climbed out, put his hand on their back, "Stay low, go about twenty feet and wait for the rest. Camille followed Joe up into the blackness of the rainstorm. She had her knife, MP40 and her "Ruby" pistol. When they were assembled, Ambroos led them off. To maintain the line, each man kept his hand hooked in the belt of the man ahead. Movement over the field was slow and clumsy but soon they gained the road. Ambroos halted them there, each lying in the ditch while he reconnoitered the road ahead.

"All clear. We go."

Jeb Olgilvie was right about them being out of shape. Even the half mile or so they traversed over wet, broken ground before they reached the road had the airmen panting and holding their sides. Any stoppage caused them to bend forward with their hands on their knees. The hot soup had made this much progress possible but how long they could hold out was clearly not going to be enough. Camille at the end of the line, through hoarsely whispered encouragement tried to keep the men moving but saw their frailty. Making the five miles to the first farmhouse seemed impossible. During one of the increasingly frequent rest stops, she caught up with Ambroos.

"This looks bad, Ambroos," she said. "I don't know how long they can keep going tonight."

"We have only gone a mile on the road and only three hours till daylight," he replied. "I don't think any of them will survive a night outside in the woods.

"I will go ahead to the Villiers' farm," he continued, "and get their wagon to bring them in. It is very dangerous and if I am not back in two hours, assume the Bosche have me. Which of the men is in charge?"

"I think the American, Hanover. They still seem to listen to him, but everyone is so poor."

Ambroos handed Camille his MP40. "Give this to him and have him take over the lead. All he has to do is stay on the road and listen for any noise. I will hurry as fast as I can. Bon chance, my dear girl," cupping her face in his hands. He disappeared into the black night at a trot.

Camille returned to the men and found Joe. "Come around me," she said, keeping her voice low.

"Ambroos has gone ahead to get a wagon. He wants Joe to take the lead," she said handing him the MP40. "All you have to do is stay on the road and listen. He hopes to be back within the hour with a wagon that can take us the rest of the way."

"And if he don't come back?" asked Olgilvie.

"It means he is dead. We stick to the plan. Let's go." She gave Joe's shoulder a pat and led him to the front. Olgilvie was next in line and hooked his hand in Joe's belt. Moving on the road was easier but only a little and they still had to stop every quarter mile.

#

Corporal Herman Schneider and Private Ernst Locher having re-joined the 272nd GVD were back in their shallow foxholes in the ruins of Kommerscheidt. The counterattack which drove the Americans back across the Kall had brought a lift in their spirits.

"Well, Junge," the old soldier said, "it looks like there is still some fight in us yet, eh?" Ernst managed a wan smile. "The cooks will be coming soon with something warm to eat and maybe we can dry out a little. There won't be any more fighting for a while, I think. They'll let us alone while the higher ups come up with a new plan."

Ernst's shoulder wound, under the close attention of Schneider had healed well. Schneider made sure Ernst kept it moving so the joint would not freeze up.

"Does this mean maybe we will be rotated to the rear sometime soon?"

"All in good time, Kleine, it is not for us to say. Meanwhile, look what I have here." Managing what flair he could, Schneider pulled out some biscuits and a round red and white tin of Scho-Ka-Kola chocolate which was a combination of chocolate with roast coffee and kola nut. There were two layers of eight wedges of the dark hard chocolate. Ernst's eyes grew wide at the sight.

"How did you get this?" he asked as he took a piece in his mouth which was so dry that it took a while for the candy to melt.

"When you have been around as long as I have, Junge, you know where to look. I have been saving this for a special occasion. This is as good a one as any."

Unspoken was his thought that special occasions were not going to be of the good kind in their futures. He had been a soldier for over two decades. He knew when offenses, even successful ones, were too costly. The Wehrmacht had exhausted itself hammering against the Americans in the Huertgen. A few new replacement Panthers had come and gone. The new faces beside them in the 272nd were old men or young boys just like himself and Ernst. He had not seen any sign of the Luftwaffe to drive off the endless assaults of the American and British bombers that hung over them like a lethal ceiling. He had heard the rumors of Hitler hoarding super infantry, unstoppable tanks and secret weapons for a massive push to drive the Allies back to the Channel and bring peace on his terms. Schneider had heard it all before. He had served in German's past and now his duty was to save her future by saving Ernst. His own life did not matter and had not mattered for some time. If he could save Ernst then that was justification enough. He enjoyed the look of surprised delight on Ernst's face as he ate the chocolate. They looked across the Kall Valley towards the Americans and waited.

#

"Sergeant Rosinski," Lieutenant Barclay called out from the edge of the pitiful group of men that comprised the 112th Pennsylvania National Guard. Everyone was getting antsy about being so exposed at the CP, even given the near impenetrable darkness.

"Yes, Sir." Rosinski trotted up to his platoon leader.

"Gather the platoon." In a few minutes, the eight surviving men fit for duty in second platoon, Company E, assembled on their Lieutenant and moved out of earshot of the captain. "OK, here's the word. We kick off at 0300, make our best time across the Kall and up to the other side. The sarge will have the radio and will stick to me like white on rice. We are the point platoon on this little shindig. We are to go quick and quiet, sneak up on the Krauts and then radio their position back to regiment. The rest of the regiment will follow us across and be lined up along the eastern wall of the valley. We are to hit the Germans hard and fast. We are depending on the element of surprise to bring sufficient amount of shit to bear on them.

"Now, you may have noticed the lack of artillery prep. That is because we want to ambush them. In the past all the artillery has done is to let 'em know we're coming. This way, we are going to be on them and kicking some serious butt before they know we're there. Their artillery probably won't know what's going on because of the distance and darkness. That will buy us some time before they start in.

Again, they probably don't know where their guys are and may hold off firing, at least for a while. Meantime, our artillery will be up on the western wall. They know where the Kraut guns are and at the first hostile round fired our way, they are going to blow them all to hell."

Barclay did a good job of selling the plan by not emphasizing his platoon's near suicidal role in it. "Any questions?"

Above the muttering coming from the platoon rose Corporal Jeffery Howe's voice.

"Permission to speak freely, Sir?"

"Of course, Howe," replied Barclay, realizing Howe was the safety valve for the platoon. Rosinski braced himself.

"Well, Sir, it's not the absolute worst plan I have heard since we've been here. That's a mighty low bar, mind you. But, if I understand it correctly, we're supposed to stumble along in the dark towards what could be the whole fucking Wehrmacht until we trip over them and hope we have time to let someone know we found them?"

"Basically. As soon as we have made contact, we'll draw back, call it in, at which point the rest of the regiment will join us in the attack."

"We could be some way away from them, right, In the dark and rain? So, we don't know how long it will take them to get to us to join this attack. And what's to say that they don't just shoot us all to shit while they are 'joining the attack'?"

Here, Lieutenant Barclay remembered why he shouldn't ask for questions and he began to improvise.

"We make contact, call it in and pull back. The rest of the regiment will be coming forward and when we meet up, we can guide them to the Krauts. They won't be firing until the meet them. That will increase the impact of the ambush. The Krauts will be following after what they should think is a probe by a recon patrol and walk right into the rest of our guys.

"Alright, get some rest. About three hours until we go. Dismissed."

As Howe and Anderson made their way to their foxhole, Howe said, "I take it back. It is the worst fucking plan I've ever heard."

#

Ambroos Hansen ran the three miles to the Villiers' farm. He had encountered no German patrols on the way. Francoise Villiers was an active member of the resistance, using his farm and outbuildings to hide and rest up the exfiltrating American and British airmen that were being escorted. He was used to Hansen arriving at all hours and was ready to help.

“Ambroos, my friend, what have you got for me?” he said handing him a cup of tea to let him catch his breath.

“I have six men about three miles down the road. They are in pretty bad shape and I will need your wagon to bring them in.”

“Of course. Those ‘anusridder Fockes’ (assriding fuckers)’, his favorite name for the Germans, “don’t seem to be around in this weather, but still, we should take some precautions. I’ll wrap the horse’s hooves in burlap to deaden the noise. It won’t take a minute.” That accomplished, the two men set off back down the road.

Joe Hanover and the rest of the airmen, with Camille bringing up the rear, had gone less than a half mile down the road when the wagon appeared around a bend in the road. They were in such poor condition that even at a slow walking pace, they had to take breaks. Camille ran to the front.

“Any problems?” she asked Ambroos who shook his head. “Hello, Francoise, thanks for this.”

“Don’t mention it,” he replied. “Are we all here? Well, then, let’s proceed.”

He turned the wagon around quickly and the weakened airmen struggled into the back.

"Hide yourselves under the hay and be still", she said.

Ambroos took the MP40 back from Joe and stationed himself just behind Francoise. Camille was in the back facing out, next to Joe.

"Here, take this," handing him her pistol. "Pray God, we don't need it."

They set off at a slow trot. The dark and rain had not let up which gave Francoise some hope. This was dashed when he saw the dim headlights of an approaching "Maultier", a half-track utility truck with a two-man crew.

"Schijtlius! (shit)" Francoise whispered. "Bosche. Stay quiet, maybe they have somewhere to be."

The Germans slowed to a stop, pulling across the road, leaving the truck idling. "Halt, what are you doing out this time of night and in the rain. All your hay will be ruined."

One man dismounted with his own MP40 pointing at Francoise. His partner remained in the half-track with his machine pistol covering the wagon as well.

"I had this covered in the field," Francoise answered, "and thought I could get back to the barn during a break in the rain but got caught. I would like to keep going, Mein Herr, bitte."

The dismounted soldier walked around to the back of the wagon and began to poke the hay. Camille fired directly into his chest, killing him instantly. Ambroos rose up beside Francoise and killed the other German before he could fire. All the airman sat up, Joe with the pistol pointing at the dead German. Camille took charge.

"Come, move this piece of shit off the road, into the ditch and cover him. Bring me his weapon."

Ambroos and Francoise climbed into the half-track and threw the driver over the side where, Olgilvie and Hanover dragged him into the underbrush.

"Let's see if we can hide this somewhere and come back for it." They drove the truck as far off the road as far as they could, quickly looked over the supplies it carried.

"We'll have to come back for this if we can. Meantime, let's get it covered up. It was expected somewhere and the Bosche will be coming for it soon, I should think."

He lifted the hood, took out the distributor cap and finished covering it with brush.

"Best we can do, let's get out of here."

He rejoined the group at the wagon. Stealth was no longer a safe option and Francoise urged the horse forward. Within another half hour, they pulled into Villiers' barn.

"I am afraid you will have to go back underground for a while, but not until dawn, I think," Francoise said. "Meanwhile, let me get us some food."

The exhausted airmen laid back on the wet hay of the wagon and were asleep. Before Joe dozed off, he felt the warmth of Camille's hand on his shoulder. In his dazed state, he was back in Thorpe Abbotts with Virginia for an instant. Even looking into her face, he almost called her "Ginny".

"Joe, you did very well, you all did. But I must have the pistol back."

Chapter Sixteen: Counterattack

Enfield Davis gathered his two remaining tank crews in the dark rain. Douglas Aiken and his Weasel, having nowhere else to be, joined them. They all drank the rapidly cooling soup from their canteen cups. Davis had met with his company commander, Captain Ramsey and received the unpleasant news that his tanks were to lead the attack once contact had been made by the 112th Pennsylvania, the "Bloody Bucket" regiment.

Davis had definite concerns about the emphasis on stealth that underpinned the attack plan. His depleted tank platoon was to wait along the trailhead on the western edge of the Kall Valley while the infantry advanced across the valley until contact was made. Davis stood up in his turret, despite the rain, to watch the silent, sodden men flow around the quiet tanks like an outgoing tide. He looked down on the rain-slicked helmets, field jackets strung with bandoliers of ammunition and grenades, shouldered rifles. The scene was no different from any infantry advancing since the Trojans against the Achaeans: only the weapons changed. None of the men looked up, even to see where they were going, only followed the man in front of them.

"Jesus, Enfield, button up, will you?" asked Corporal Roger Emmons, his driver. "This ain't a bathtub. We'll be floating soon."

Reluctantly, Davis took a last look at the advancing infantry then sunk back into the commander's seat and pulled the hatch closed.

When the firing began on the eastern side, his tanks were to make their best speed across the valley and support the infantry. Davis and his remaining tank commanders, Suarez in *Adolph's Nightmare,* and Soames in D*eath Wagon,* had traversed the trail several times and the engineers had been hard at work widening and improving the surface, but the unremitting rain and snow had undone much of their work. Crossing in the rain, in the dark under the pressure of getting to the other side to support the 112th's attack was going to be difficult if not impossible. Still, they had their orders.

Lieutenant Alfred Moore of the 229th Field Artillery (FA) also had his worries about his assigned part. He had to move his 105mm howitzers right up behind the tanks, then move them into final position to be ready to bring suppressive counterbattery fire on the 88s of the 272nd Artillery Regiment commanded by Oberleutnant Heinz von Kleist, as soon as they joined the party. As best he knew, Moore thought those guns were still two ridges away but the horrific weather had grounded all recon flights by the attached L-4 Grasshopper observation planes, so Moore had no recent confirmation of von Kleist's guns' location. He had decided to attach a forward observer to the 112th to try to spot the 88s' muzzle flashes and direct return fire. But in the murk of the continual rain and snow fall, even that was not a sure thing. In short, the opinion of all the commanders to whom the execution of the attack was entrusted was unanimous: FUBAR – "fucked up beyond all recognition". But they, too, had their orders.

Howe and Anderson set about preparing for the recon patrol – "death march", in Howe's mind. They taped their dog tags together, tightened up their web gear and canteens, even jumping up and down to make sure everything was secure. Last thing to do was to smear black mud on each other's face. Rosinski came to their foxhole.

"Give me anything you are leaving behind and I'll get it to the CP for you. You can pick it up when we're done with this op."

"You have my mother's address, right?" asked Howe. "'Cause I don't see anyway we are going to be around to collect it after this shit-show." He did not look up from sharpening his bayonet. The forceful strokes of his whetstone were the only sign of his fear.

"Look, Howe, we have as much, if not better, chance of getting through this as we do sitting here waiting for an 88 to blow us all to hell. Aren't you the one who can't understand why we haven't shut those motherfuckers down? Well, now's your chance to help out with that. I, for one, would rather be taking the fight to the Krauts then just taking their shit in this fucking forest."

"Great, you can have my spot."

"Are you refusing to go?"

"No, he's not," Anderson spoke up. "We'll be there."

Rosinski grunted and went to find Lieutenant Barclay who was along the rim of the valley.

"Hey, Lieutenant, the guys are almost ready. I'll check out the walkie-talkie and then we should be good to go."

"I'm going with you," Barclay said.

Rosinski knew his lieutenant and anticipated this. "Begging your pardon, Sir, but do you think that's a good idea? If we both buy the farm then who's going to run the company? We get some shavetail replacement who doesn't know shit from Shinola and there go the rest of us. I think you'll be more useful organizing the company's part in the counterattack after we have found the Krauts."

Barclay wrestled with his answer. If he agreed too quickly, even though Rosinski was right, it made his offer look like empty bravado. If he argued and then gave in, it could erode his standing with the sergeant. He really did want to go, he thought it his duty as platoon leader but he had to admit to himself that Rosinski, having more combat experience, would be more effective on this patrol.

"Alright, Sergeant, you have a good point. Your job is to find the Krauts and not get killed. Do not engage if you find them. Just return and report their location. Do a radio check now and when you are across. I'll see you over there."

Rosinski had confidence in his ability to lead the patrol and that his men would do well, even that pain in the ass Howe. He joined them at the most forward foxhole which was Howe and Anderson's.

"OK," he said, "Anderson, you take point. We are on channel five for the CP. I'll take the radio with me but if I buy it, the first thing is to secure the walkie-talkie. We lose contact and the whole plan is in the shitter." Their faces and hands were coated with dark mud. They carried only water, ammo and their M-1 Garands, bayonets fixed.

Rosinski keyed the radio. "We're setting out."

Silently, he led them to the valley rim and over the side. They crossed without a problem and Rosinski keyed the radio again. He motioned the patrol forward. He expected there would be an outpost at least in Kommerscheidt but they passed through without making contact, then across the shallow ditch and toward Schmidt. They moved in a shallow "V" formation with Anderson on point, separated by about five yards which was as far apart as they could be and still see each other. Behind them, Lieutenant Barclay was organizing Company E to lead the rest of the regiment across the Kall Valley. Lieutenant Moore of the 229th Field Artillery moved his four-gun battery up to the western edge of the valley. His forward observer had gone ahead with the patrol and climbed up the highest mound of rubble that was left in Kommerscheidt. He hoped he was high enough to spot the muzzle blasts from von Kleist's 88s, two ridges over. The rain falling on the churned mud of the Schmidt ridge was all that was heard. It was cold. The men's teeth chattered, their breath smoked and their hands shook. They kept their fingers off the triggers for fear of an accidental discharge. At least there was no wind, but there was lightening.

Further down the ridge, unaware of the approaching patrol, Schneider and Locher of the 272nd Volksgrenadier Division huddled in their foxhole. "How are you doing, Kleine?" he asked. Theirs was the most advanced of the German position. "We seem to always be in the wet hole, like our betters think we are ducks or something." He gathered the shivering boy closer to him and tightened the sodden blankets around them both.

"Do you think we will ever be warm and dry again, Herr Schneider?"

"Ach, naturlich, Kleine. We do our shift out here and then it's back to the company tent for some soup and dry clothes. There won't be anything happening in this weather. You know the Americans like their artillery to make some noise before they try anything. So, as long as it's quiet, we should be fine. Duck under the blankets. I'll keep watch."

Anderson felt they were as noisy as a herd of cattle moving through the ankle-deep, sucking mud. The rain had washed off all the carefully applied mud on his face and when he looked back towards the rest of the patrol, he saw their white faces bright as headlights when the lightening flashed.

"Sweet Jesus, we are goners," he thought.

The low cloud cover made flairs ineffective but there were increasingly frequent lightning flashes, making the patrol very visible. Howe was on the left end of the "V", Rosinski on the right. Watching the men ahead of him, Howe was reminded of the strobe lights in the few dance clubs he had gone to before shipping out. It was mesmerizing to watch their herky-jerky movements as they moved towards the German positions. He was brought back to reality by the first rifle round speeding through the formation. Schneider had spotted them.

Anderson dropped as did the rest of the patrol but held their fire, waiting to see what the German had in mind.

They daubed their faces once again with the mud. After no further firing, Anderson motioned his patrol forward, crawling this time.

"What was it, Herr Schneider?" asked a frightened Ernst Locher.

"Maybe nothing, but I thought I saw something in the lightning flash. Like I said, the Americans aren't likely to attack in this weather, without artillery and no planes for spotting." This was mostly for Ernst's benefit. Schneider chambered another round and squinted into the black rain. He saw nothing in the next flashes and chided himself for being an old, nervous man.

Anderson crawled through the gelatinous mud. He tried to keep his Garand out of it but that was futile. Behind him, the rest of the regiment was assembled at Kommerscheidt and Davis's tanks were creeping down the steep western wall of the Kall Valley. The runoff sluiced down the trail surface, causing the tanks to fishtail dangerously near the edge.

"There is no fuckin' way one of us doesn't go over," thought Davis. "This is insane."

At that point, Captain Ramsey called Davis. "Give me a progress report, Davis."

"Well, Sir, the infantry's across but I don't know their disposition. We are sliding our way down the west bank and I gotta tell you, it will be a miracle if one or all of us don't fall into the valley. The trail surface has basically washed away on this side and I doubt the eastern side is any better. Over."

"You've got to get those tanks across. The whole attack depends on that. As shitty as the conditions are, we are not likely to get any better and if this attack fails, we are all back to square one."

"Yes, Sir," replied Davis, "we'll get over there. Out."

Anderson crawled slowly forward, looking for where the rifle shot had come from. The rain falling hard on the mud threw up a screen of spatter which limited his already poor visibility. He knew he had to find out how close the German shooter was before he could report their position. The intermittent flashes of lightning only made his night vision worse. But the same was true for Schneider who regretted his shot. Anderson decided to chance rising to a half crouch to increase his forward speed. He had only gone ten feet when another lightning flash exposed Schneider's foxhole not two yards away. Anderson lunged forward with his bayonet. Schneider covered Ernst's body with his own and took the glancing thrust of Anderson's bayonet.

Having found the German advance position and remembered his orders not to engage, Anderson turned back and motioned to the rest of the patrol to head back. Rosinski fell in beside Anderson.

"What have we got?"

"Just a forward listening post, I think. Only two, maybe three guys. I stuck one of them. Didn't see any heavy shit. It may keep them from reporting us for a while, so maybe we can still get the jump on them."

"Here's hoping," replied Rosinski.

The patrol made their report to Lieutenant Barclay who as ranking, surviving officer of the depleted 112th, down to only 300 men, was in charge of the counterattack.

"Sir," Anderson began, "we ran into probably a two-man listening post 800 yards down the ridge. I think I bayoneted one of them which is why they didn't fire us up."

"Any idea how far ahead of their main element they were?"

"Sir," answered Howe, "we couldn't see shit beyond maybe five yards, if that. There was just that one shot which probably was a mistake since I doubt they could have seen us."

"Anything to add, Sergeant?"

"No, that's it."

"OK, I'll call this in. Then, we go."

#

Ernst Locher was panicked. "Herr Schneider, are you hurt?"

"Just a cut, Kleine. He missed my lung. We have to get back to the company and report."

With much painful grunting, Schneider was able to climb out of the foxhole and leaning on Ernst slowly made their way to their company. Using a trick he had picked up on the Western Front when moving in open terrain in a lightning storm, with each flash, the two comrades froze with their eyes closed until darkness returned. Soon enough, they heard the sentry's challenge.

"Halt, wie gehts dort, (who goes there)?"

"Corporal Schneider and Private Locher, from the listening post. The Americans are across the valley and are advancing," said Schneider.

"Kommt mit mir, (come with me)."

The sentry led them to the command bunker just inside the woods on the far side of Schmidt. Schneider could barely walk by the time they arrived. He did collapse when the company commander walked in.

"What is this man doing, sitting in front of his company commander? Get to your feet, immediately."

"Excuse me, Herr Oberst," Ernst spoke up, "but he is wounded and has lost a lot of blood. The American cut him with his bayonet. We came straight here to report."

The captain motioned to one of the medics in the bunker to see to Schneider but no less gruffly to Ernst said, "Well, then report. What are you waiting for?"

Ernst recounted their encounter with the American patrol but could offer little information since he was in the foxhole, covered by Schneider's body.

"Well, that not of much use to us. You don't know how many there were, how were they armed, just probing or the advance of a main attack. We'll have to send out a patrol to find out what you should have. Corporal, put this man on report."

Somewhat revived, Schneider was able to speak up, haltingly. "They were only a six-man patrol, probably trying to find out where we were. Their point man nearly fell into our hole. They retreated as fast as they could. By now they have reported back to their superiors."

The German captain took this in. "Well, if they are crazy enough to attempt an attack in this weather, we can expect their artillery preparation soon. We will be ready for them if they come.

"You two get some rest, dry clothes and food. The medics will look you over.

"Dismissed."

#

"Well, what's the plan, Lieutenant?" asked Anderson.

"Unchanged. They are probably thinking it would be insane to attack in this storm – no air support, inaccurate artillery direction because nobody can see shit, but they have to prepare for us just the same. They expect us to hold true to form and are holed up in their bunkers waiting for the artillery prep before we hit them.

"Lucky for us," at this point, Howe snorted loudly. Barclay ignored him. "We are going to oblige them. We've got five hours to daylight. Be ready to move out in 30 minutes. Remember, noise discipline is going to be the difference between us counting their meat or them counting ours.

"Get some chow and rest. Good hunting."

Anderson and Howe walked back to a little lean-to fashioned from the rubble of Kommerscheidt by any of the many previous tenants – American and German.

"What was that 'meat' talk?" he asked Howe.

"I think it is carved on the front door of West Point: 'Sometimes you count the meat, sometime the meat counts you'."

"Lovely," replied Anderson. They opened the "B" unit of their C ration which contained crackers, sugar and dextrose tabs along with a lemon powder which they mixed with their canteen water. The "M" unit which contained the actual meal, they thought would take too long to eat and they were looking for a "sugar hit" for quick energy.

"Who needs home cooking, right?" said Anderson. Howe grunted.

They used the rest of whatever time they had before the attack to clean their Garands and rechecked their ammo and grenades. That done, they settled in to wait.

Rosinski came around.

"Company E, on me. Time to move out. The rest of the men will follow us."

"What 'rest of the men?'" groused Howe. "I've seen Boy Scouts troops with more guys than us."

He and Anderson took point with Barclay and Rosinski and the radio five yards behind them. The regiment was splayed out in three columns moving as quietly as they could. The lightning flashes betrayed them for seconds at a time. Each man was sure that the ensuing darkness would bring German bullets. Anderson led them past the empty listening post. Looming ahead in slowly revealing detail was the ruins of Schmidt.

"Feuer!" and immediately the dark was cut through with MP40 and K94 tracers. How the Germans had seen them or heard them or was it just blind luck, Anderson had no idea. He dropped and return fire into the blackness sparked with muzzle flashes. The rest of the 112th broke their columns and deployed in a firing line.

Davis shouted to Emmons, his driver, "Let's go. Best possible speed."

The three tanks roared to life and headed down the ridge and up the east wall. Davis could not believe they all made it. Each tank took a sector of Schmidt and covered their area with 76 mm cannon fire. The advancing infantry heard them coming and cleared lanes for the tanks to advance, forming up around them as they went.

Not really expecting a counterattack, the Germans had only deployed in a thin skirmish line which rapidly gave way to the 112th's assault. Schneider and Ernst had been sleeping in a tent. They stumbled out into the confusion of the building rout of their company. Schneider knew they could not stop the Americans and soon, the enemy artillery would be in play. He grabbed Ernst by this collar and dragged further into the wood. The 272nd was a seasoned combat unit and their non-coms had organized a line of resistance just inside the tree line.

Panzerfausts and mortar rounds began to find their marks. Men began to drop around Anderson and Howe. Lieutenant Barclay radioed Moore of the 229th FA on the far side of the valley with coordinates and soon 105 mm rounds were landing on the shattered remains of Schmidt.

"Come on, come on, let's move it!" shouted Barclay, knowing the American incoming would keep the Germans in their holes. Two ridges to the east, Oberst von Kleist saw the shell bursts and began to return fire, targeting Moore's guns. Moore's forward observer in Kommerscheidt picked up the 88s' muzzle flashes and called it into Moore who was then able to return fire, changing his target from Schmidt.

Company E, led by Barclay, took advantage of the chaos and stormed into the remnants of Schmidt. As the Germans began to return fire, Howe and Anderson, along with the rest of Company E, dropped down among the shattered buildings and returned fire. No one could see their opponents, merely firing at muzzle flashes and noise.

"Keep it up, men," shouted Barclay. "Anderson, Howe, take the platoon, move right and try to outflank them."

Keeping low, firing from the hip, the platoon scuttled to their right but found the German line extended further than they thought. Peeled off from the main body of the company, they also found themselves outgunned. They had only their Garands and some grenades. The Germans soon had them pinned down and without artillery cover, the platoon was at a grave disadvantage. The Panzerfausts and mortars, firing from the safety of the woods landed accurately among the Americans. Casualties began to mount.

"Rosinski, get arty back on the line. We've got to get some rounds. Move the bazooka teams up here and tell them to get on those mortars. Keep it up, men, move forward, move forward!"

Technical Sergeant Douglas Aiken, the medic with Company E, moved forward into Schmidt with his aide bag. The first man he came to had half his face blown away but his gurgling, choking breathing forced Aiken to try to do something. He turned the man on his side, and applied a field dressing. As he held the man's head, his fingers slipped into the back of his skull, feeling the overset jell-o consistency of his brain. Still, the man struggled to breath. Aiken took the morphine syrette from the man's aid kit and two of his own, then injected them into his shoulder. The man shuddered once and stopped breathing.

Aiken had only to roll to his right for his next man who was already dead. He scrambled forward to a man calling for a medic. His left arm was partially detached at the elbow. Aiken applied a tourniquet, springled on some sulfa powder and gave the man his morphine. After he had wrapped the arm in a field dressing, Aiken secured the arm to his side with the man's field jacket. German rifle and machine gun fire began to pick up once the American artillery was diverted to deal with the 88s.

"Son of a bitch," said Aiken as a K94 round passed just over his head. "This is a fine shit-show." Caring for the wounded kept him from being panicked. He had long ago given up thoughts of survival and home. If he was going to die, he would die trying to help others.

Hell's Fire was the lead tank. Davis shouted down to Emmonds, "Gun it, head for the tree line."

He popped open the hatch and began firing the .50cal. The 76mm main cannon was firing high explosive rounds along the tree line as well as the .30 cal. Rounds began pinging against the turret and cutting through Davis's field jacket.

"Goddam it, Enfield, get the fuck back in here, ya goddamed idjit", shouted Emmonds. He pulled on Davis's leg. All that could be seen of the German line through the dark rain were a line of muzzle flashes and occasional Panzerfaust blast.

Death Wagon and *Nightmare* were firing as well and soon, combined with the fire from the 112th, the German resistance melted away. The tanks continued through Schmidt to the end of the ridge where it entered the trees. Barclay's bringing up the bazooka teams was the deciding factor in driving off the infantry. Davis wondered where the Panzers were, not knowing that the artillery had taken them out earlier in the fight. A stillness settled over Schmidt. Only the artillery duel between Moore's 155 "Long Toms" and von Kleist's 88s lingered for a while until they, too, grew silent.

Barclay radioed the CP that they had re-taken Schmidt and would need re-supply. Aiken brought his Weasel forward to collect the wounded and start back to the aid station at the Mestrenger Mill where he dropped off the freshly wounded, picked up the semi-stabilized wounded to get to the main aide station at Vossenach. There he would load up on re-supply and make his way back to Schmidt. The whole round-trip, assuming von Kleist's guns did not blow him all to hell would be well over an hour. The whole operation across the Kall depended on the one trail and the one Weasel for now.

Chapter Seventeen: Thorpe Abbotts

From Villiers' farm to the American lines was twenty miles by road. The airmen had recovered pretty well with the regular hot meals, dry, warm sleep and exercise. Ambroos and Camille felt by the fourth day, they were ready to set out again.

"We have two days before the moon is bright enough to be a problem," Ambroos said. "The Bosche have increased their patrolling since their truck went missing but we have seen this before. They know the Resistance is active in this area and will go back to their usual routines in a day or so. As we know, most of them are Volksgrenadier divisions, understrength and mainly old men and boys. We have good intelligence that Hitler is saving his top troops and armor for a final, how you say, 'last hole'..."

"'Ditch', we say ditch" Joe gently corrected him.

"Ah, yes, 'ditch' effort to breakthrough, to split the Brits and Canadians and retake Antwerp. Then he thinks he can dictate peace plans on his terms. All a fantasy, of course, but useful to us in that it keeps his best troops away. Fortunately, any generals that would oppose him with the unwanted truth have been cowed or killed. Strategy, it seems, has been replaced with vengeance and killing. Again, good for us."

T.Sgt. Jeb Olgilvie, waist gunner on the *Sly Virgin,* a B24 stationed at Thorpe Abbotts, had grown used to life on Villiers' farm and the frequent presence of Camille. His thirst to get back to England and behind a .50 caliber, freezing in a roiling bomber, had been subdued.

"Again, why wouldn't it be a good idea to hole up here until they push the Krauts back?" he asked.

Camille confronted him. "Every day you are here increases the danger to us and our operation. More downed airmen like yourself will be coming and need our help. We cannot, how you say, fill up with men who can move on. We must move you on. Tonight." She turned on her heel and left the barn.

"Jeez, just askin'" said Olgilvie.

"Don't make her mad at you, Jeb," said Hanover, patting him on the shoulder. "Two Krauts with a knife, remember."

Ambroos figured two nights' travel on the road to Schmidt would get them there. They would stop in the trees to see who held the destroyed town. Even so, the woods blanketing the sides of the Kommerscheidt-Schmidt ridge still held plenty of Germans. Finding that the 112th was holding Schmidt for now was fortunate but complicated at the same time. When the American lines were stable along the edge of the Huertgen, Ambroos knew how to approach them and what units there were. Now, he had to make contact with probably new and trigger-happy GIs in a hyperalert state of mind.

"We have some luck and not, I think," he reported back to the group. "The Americans hold Schmidt but I don't know which Americans. They may not know me. I am used to dealing with, what the Germans called 'The Bloody Bucket'". I will have to approach them on the road, during daylight and hope they will think I am a local looking for help and not just shoot me. Or the Bosche may beat them to it. But it is the only way to proceed that I can see." He looked to Camille's whose frightened face almost made him falter. "Once I have made contact and still live, I'll let them know about the rest of us and see what happens."

"Outstanding plan," whispered Olgilvie.

"He's got us this far, right? Have a little faith, Jeb-boy," Hanover said encouragingly.

At first light, filtered through mist, Ambroos embraced Camille and set out. He emerged from the woods with his hands raised, carrying Camille's white handkerchief.

He whispered, "Holy Mary, mother of God, look down on this poor sinner in mercy and let me bring these, thy servants, to safety."

Anderson poked the sleeping Howe next to him in the most advanced foxhole on the road out of Schmidt.

"What? What the fuck?" Howe said irritably. He was instantly awake with his Garand M-1 pointing directly at Ambroos' chest. "Who's this motherfucker?"

"Re-enforcements, I bet," kidded Anderson. "Cover me."

Anderson motioned to Ambroos to continue forward and when he was ten feet from the hole, quickly grabbed him by the arm and pulled him into their foxhole. It was awkward and cramped but Howe kept his rifle on Ambroos.

"Thank you, thank you," stuttered Ambroos. He spotted the red keystone of the 112th Pennsylvania on Anderson's shoulder and said, "Ah, you are 'Bloody Buckets'. Fabulous.

"My nomme de guerre is 'Ambroos'. I am with the Belgian Resistance in this area. I have some of your compatriots with me in the woods: shot down airmen – British and American. I would like to give them to you."

Both the Americans were amused by Ambroos' presentation. Howe shifted his Garand.

"And we would be pleased to have them," answered Anderson lightly. "The question is how to get them. I don't think the Krauts will let us parade up and down the ridge again. The airmen are pretty mobile, active, yes?"

"Mais oui, but I don't think they can run the whole way here. I worry waiting until dark because we have seen evidence of the - 'Krauts', you call them?"

Anderson nodded.

"'Krauts', yes interesting, how did you come to call them that?"

"Jesus, Henry, enough with the chitchat," interjected Howe. "We've got to get this guy back to the company. They can figure out something."

"Sure, right, I'll take him, unless you'd like to."

"Again, with this fucking 'after you, no after you, no, I insist' bullshit. You take him and get back here, pronto."

Anderson and Ambroos scuttled bent over back through the ruins of Schmidt to the company CP and Lieutenant Barclay.

"Hey, Lieutenant, I've a local here who says there are about six downed airmen in the woods he'd like to hand over," Anderson explained. Ambroos drew himself up and gave a jaunty palm out salute to Barclay, which he returned, smartly.

After learning the details, Barclay recognized the difficulty.

"You're right about the Krauts. They may have let him pass thinking he'd get some of us to return with him and hit us then. So, sending a patrol to get them is suicidal. I'll talk with our friends in the 707th Tanks. They might like to go for a drive."

As it happened, Doug Aiken pulled up in his Weasel with resupply and looking to see if there were any wounded needed evacuating.

"Outstanding timing, Sergeant," Barclay beamed and slapped Aiken on the back. "We have need of your truck."

He quickly explained the situation and Aiken, with much misgiving, agreed. Next, Barclay talked with Enfield Davis of *Hell's Fury* and a formation was soon decided on. The three tanks would proceed in echelon, Davis in the lead, the other two tanks off to either side and Aiken's Weasel in the middle. They would take no infantry with them, needing all the spare room for the airmen, and make their best time through the deepening mud to the woods, snatch the men and return the same way. Only Ambroos sat up top with Davis. Barclay arranged for covering artillery on their return trip after he cleared it with Captain Ramsey, his CO.

"OK, button up, here we go," Davis said over the inter-tank channel. The Shermans and the Weasel set off to cover the about eight hundred yards of bare ridge line to the woods. They were half-way there before the Panzerfausts, small arms and mortars opened up. Their best defense was speed but that was reduced due to the mud. Davis felt they were standing still as the German small arms and Panzerfausts began to register some hits. These were not effective due to the distance from the woods to the tanks. Suppressing fire from the Shermans' .50 calibers and fragmentation rounds kept the Germans' heads down.

"Give 'em some wooly-pete and smoke," shouted Davis into the mic.

Soon, the crossing was made without damage. The tricky part was stopping to pick the men up. The three tanks rotated their turrets to keep up their fire. Aiken In the Weasel hunkered down as low as he could, hoping the tanks would block most of the German fire. He knew the return trip would be even hotter.

"You can drive into the woods quite aways," shouted Ambroos to Davis. "My Camille will have them ready." Once there, Ambroos jumped to the ground and urged the airmen onto the tanks and into Aiken's Weasel. He remained behind with Camille. Then with much gear grinding, smoke belching, the small rescue party reversed and drove back onto the ridge.

Plumes of white exploded along the tree lines. The clouds of obscuring smoke covered the rest of the retreat, defeating to some extent the German fire which was much more accurate on this return run. All breathed easier when the suppressing artillery from the 229th FA arrived and silenced the German guns once and for all.

Quiet descended once again and Howe and Anderson settled back down in the hole at Kommerscheidt. Anderson waited for Howe to say something.

"Some set of balls on that little guy, I've got to admit," he said and turned on his side to finish his sleep.

#

Oberst Jans von Rindle and his "Green Hearts of Thuringen", formerly of the Jadgeschwader 54/III, the remnants, at least, no longer had a base from which to mount into the skies and attack the Allied bombers in their ever-increasing hundreds. His Staffel was dispersed among the roads and trees of the Ardennes-Huertgen forests. Their runways were either the roads or fields. Their ground crews were marvels in keeping the mixed bf109 and FW190s repaired and aloft. He had seen no decrease in the ardor of the impossibly young and undertrained pilots that Goering fed into the slaughter pens. They arrived borne on the wings of lies about "wunder flugzeugen" that would sweep the Mustangs, Tempests, Thunderbolts and Typhoons from the skies of Germany. There were the rumors of their best pilots training on the ultimate fighter: the Messerschmitt 262 jet that could wreak havoc on the Allied Fortress and Liberator formations. The planes were so fast the there was no defense against them. Soon, the fields of Germany would be littered with the bodies of the bombers and their crews.

Von Rindle knew better, of course, as he awoke once more in his cold tent to the sound of the Kublewagen sounding its horn to warn of the Americans' arrival over his sector. They were drawn back ever closer to Berlin in their "Defense of the Reich" duties. As one of the few remaining aces of the Luftwaffe, von Rindle had a new "long nose" bf109G. The long nose of the fighter housed a bigger engine and cannons. The German aircraft industry, despite the near round-the-clock bombing by the Allies had continued to not only maintain production above replacement levels but introduce innovations as well. The problem was the lack of skilled pilots and fuel.

Von Rindle and his "Hearts" were deadly none the less. His mixed group of bf109s and FW 190s had accounted for five Fortresses, two Mustangs and three Thunderbolts this month alone. It was cold comfort to him as he wrapped himself in his blankets and flight jacket to snatch a few shiveringly cold hours of sleep before the Kubelwagen's horn would wake him. Each sortie saw American bombers fall in fireballs but at the cost of unsupportable losses to his beloved "Green Hearts".

Each morning, he found himself ruminating over the same problem. "If only, I had a month to train these children 'Der Dicke (The Fat One)'", meaning Goering, "sends us, we could stand a chance. As it is," he thought as he shaved with the cold water in his mess tin, "I might just as well shoot them on the ground and save fuel at least."

Orders had come from Allied Fighter Command. The sole target of the Mustangs was the Luftwaffe. The fighter escorts were freed up from shepherding the bombers to their targets and back. The German fighters were growing ever fewer and Fighter Command wanted to finish them off, once and for all. That is why Captain Robert Mulley of the 363rd Fighter Squadron, could not believe his luck as he patrolled with his ten-plane fight of Mustangs over the Huertgan Forest to see at least fifteen 109s and 190s lined up on a road below him, readying for take-off. He had flown over this patch of Germany several times hunting the Staffel he knew had to be based in the area, given the speed with which the fighters attacked the B17s, rising from below to lance through the formations and then disappear, always taking some Fortresses with them. They sheltered under the trees and camouflage nets rarely coming out to oppose the Americans fighters.

"Bandits, bandits, on the ground, three o'clock low." He needed to say nothing more. One by one the silver birds of the 363rd, peeled off and descended. Mulley led them in, his six fifty caliber machine guns firing taking out two of the rear planes. The rest of his flight followed him down and within less than two minutes, the last of the "Green Heats of Thuringen" were smoking piles of wreckage. Von Rindle had been in the lead plane, taxiing for his take-off with his canopy open to enjoy the last few breaths of clean air, when he felt the fatal vibrations. He had no time to think about his reaction for if he had, he might just have stayed with his plane and died with his Staffel. But years of combat reflexes propelled him out of his cockpit. The force of his exploding Messerschmitt blew him clear of the fireball.

"OK, boys," Mulley said into his mic., "let's get back to our day job," surveying the smoking rubble below with satisfaction.

The 363rd Squadron, climbed through the thin overcast and re-joined the 100th Bomb Group bombers making their final turn to target the Messerschmitt factories at Regensburg, fulfilling their new purpose: to clear the skies of the Luftwaffe. The P-47s, the "Jugs", did not have the range for bomber escort all the way into Germany, but as close air support for the poor, bloody infantry, slogging its way across France and Belgium, the Thunderbolts were deadly: attacking troop concentrations, railheads, bridges and any barge traffic. German movement was now impossible in any but the dirtiest weather or darkest night.

While thousand plane sorties were still common, the Eighth Air Force had shifted their tactics somewhat. With the Mustangs arriving in ever increasing numbers, it became reasonable to be nimbler in targeting. Smaller sorties going to more diffuse targets stretched the Luftwaffe and ground defenses, exhausting supplies and crews. The Germans countered this by dispersing their manufacturing and assembly sites, hiding them under trees, in barns, caves to try to improve their survivability. The logistics of servicing the sites and collecting their products was nightmarish. Nighttime bombing by the British, daytime by the Americans on the plants and the continual sniping by the P-47s and P-51s was grinding the German war industry to almost a halt.

Captain Mulley gasped, as he always did, when he broke through the cloud cover and saw the eighty bombers that the 100th BG, "the Bloody One Hundredth" had put into the sky for this raid. The ordered boxes of the big planes, the shining silver fuselages appearing motionless from the ten miles' distance the Mustangs still had to cover before re-grouping, hanging in the firmament like puppets: so beautiful and so perfect - a tableau of slaughter.

"OK, look alive, with have our little friends back with us," said, 1st Lieutenant Liam Graham, flying the lead in the

Lillies of the Valley, a B17G. "Thirty minutes to Germany. Hopefully, the Mustangs have scared the Krauts off. Look alive to stay alive." This was his signature sign-off and was greeted with groans from his crew.

The relative calm was shredded by 20mm cannon fire and a streak of flame ripping through the lead formation, striking the *Lillies,* midships causing it to fold in on itself and plummet towards the ground.

"What the fuck was that?" shouted Graham's second in command, Lieutenant Horner in *Rum Runner*. Mulley was laying a mile off the bombers and out of the corner of his eye caught sight of the silver streak streaming flame just before it vanished in the overhead cloud cover. Seconds later, the apparition re-appeared taking down two more Fortresses and was gone. No one had seen anything like it but Mulley had heard rumors.

One of Hitler's "wunderfleugzeugs", a new fighter powered by jet engines, which the Germans called "Die Schwalbe", "the Swallow" had made its debut. Momentary fear rippled through Mulley as he realized what he had just seen. The Me262 was undoubtably a game-changer in the air war. He knew the Fighter command had nothing that could possibly match "Die Schwalbe", making the bombers essentially defenseless against them. If the Germans had managed to manufacture the planes in large numbers, the war would become much longer and more deadly.

The bombers with their escorts proceeded to plaster the factories at Regensberg with renewed urgency. The 262nd had opened a new window of threat, one that Americans had to close as soon as possible.

#

Von Rindel and the ground crew caught a ride with the Kubelwagen to the collection of shacks and revetments that formed the forward base for the "Green Hearts." It was purposefully low key to avoid attracting attention. He slammed down his flight gear and slumped onto his bunk.

"Well, that's that," he said to his crew chief sergeant as he fished a flask of schnapps from under his mattress. He took a swallow and offered it to his sergeant.

"That's the end of the 'Green Hearts'. Those were the last of the planes that we had cobbled together from the 'walking wounded.' I cannot see where any more will be coming from, fighters, at least. Der Fuhrer continues to insist on building bombers at the expense of the fighters to flatten England. Well, that dream has gone up in smoke with the rest of the Luftwaffe. That fat fuck, Goering," no longer keeping his voice down, "keeps feeding Hitler lies about how his planes are sweeping the skies. It's amazing Der Fuhrer can hear anything Goering says when his nose is shoved so far up Hitler's ass."

The sergeant got up and quietly closed the shack's door. The SS or their spies were everywhere. As if confirming his worst fear, a fist hammered on the door.

"SS, open up." Von Rindel barely noted the intrusion.

"Oberst von Rindel, I am Lieutenant Janner, SS. You are to come with us." After a pause, "Bitte."

Von Rindel smiled at his sergeant and followed the man out.

"What is the meaning of this?" finding it always good to take the offense against the SS.

"You are to report to headquarters. That is all I know."

The ride was a short one and von Rindel delivered as respectable a salute as he could manage to his Gruppekommandor.

"Ah, my good von Rindel, have a seat. I am sorry to hear of your Staffel but of course, happy to see you escaped without injury."

"Thank you, Herr Gruppekommodor," he replied, keeping his eyes three inches above the shining bald head in front of him. Framed pictures of Goering and Hitler were on the wall behind him. "I, of course, take full responsibility for the losses and tender my resignation effective immediately."

"What is this nonsense? Of course, you are not going to resign. The loss of your Staffel is certainly regrettable but it is a fact of war. No one could have known the Americans were patrolling in the sector instead of sticking close to their bombers. We will have no more talk of resignations.

"Now to the point. You have no doubt heard of the Me262. It is the weapon we have been waiting for. Don't ask me how, but the Ministry of Munitions has stockpiled over three hundred, three hundred! Can you believe it?", slamming his hand down on his desk. "With these new Jadgeschwaders of jets, we will be unstoppable. High Command has decided to give you command of JG27, eighty jets to take the fight to the enemy. What do you say?"

Von Rindel had come fully expecting to be relieved of his now destroyed command and possibly shot. He took a moment to overcome his surprise.

"A great honor, Herr Gruppekomodor. I have never flown jets, of course."

"A trifle to a man of your talents. You shall learn with your flight. We need you on the attack in a month. In fact, pilots who have converted to the 262 report it handles so well and is so easy to fly that only a few training flights are needed to achieve competence. Can you imagine a weapon like this in the hands of Luftwaffe pilots, the finest in the world? We will drive the Americans and British from the skies in their antiquated propellor driven heaps.

"You leave tonight for Lechem and from there to the attack!"

"Herr Gruppenkomandor, I have not been home for almost a year and a half. Might I have a three-day pass to see my wife and children en route?" asked Von Rindle.

"Has it been that long? But yes, of course, the Reich owes you at least that." He wrote the pass himself and handed it over. "Good hunting, Herr Oberst." They exchanged salutes and von Rindle was gone.

The thought of flying in a new airplane was exciting to him. He had wrung every ounce of performance out of both the bf109 and FW190s. He had heard through the pilot grapevine of the 262, also known also as the "Sturmvogel" or "Storm Bird". These reports emphasized the ease of flying the new bird but, he knew that could lead to overconfidence and stupid mistakes. Once airborne, he knew the 262 was formidable but as had happened to his Staffel, helpless on the ground, during take-offs and landings. And fuel, always the fuel problem. He had heard the planes drank fuel like Goering gobbled schnitzels.

"Ah, well," he thought, "it will be good to see Katcha and the kinder again. That will be worth it."

#

Jeb Olgilvie and Joe Hanover were soon on their way back to Thorpe Abbotts. Olgilvie had been transferred to the 100th Bomb Group to help replace that unlucky group's steady high losses. He regretted losing any, however imagined, chance with Camille in the forest but not as much as joining the ill-fated 100th Bomb Group.

"Don't worry, Jeb-boy," said Hanover light heartedly, "there are plenty of lonely women in England. One will be near-sighted enough to fancy you, I bet."

"Easy for you to say. You think your girl in Thorpe Abbotts you keep going on about has been waiting for you. She probably heard you were dead anyway. There are plenty of better-looking airmen at the base than you to occupy her time."

"Just you wait until you meet her. You will eat your words, I guarantee it."

They were soon back at the billets. The first night they had off, they headed for the "Fox and Hens". Joe's heart was pounding through his chest. Had Ginnie been waiting for him - still hoping against hope that his long, silent absence had not meant he was dead on some German field, burnt to ashes along with his plane? After some advances from the men stationed at Thorpe Abbotts, all but the newest of the replacements had given up on winning her over and respected her grieving.

Joe slowed as he approached the familiar door of the pub. From inside came music and raucous singing, the aircrews making the most of their time away from the war. Ginnie had stopped looking up at the opening door, no longer expecting to see Joe enter. But this time she did glance up at the sound of the bell. There stood an airman, paler and thinner than most but so familiar. Her heart had fooled her too often before for her to believe this was Joe. For his part, the thin, sad girl behind the counter could not be the Ginny he remembered. The life seemed to have been sucked out of her, hope dashed and her future forsaken. They stared at each other as the sounds and smells of the pub faded away.

"Joe?" she whispered. "Joe?"

"I'm back, Ginnie, if you'll have me."

Running into each other's arms, Joe ran his hands over her thin back, feeling each rib and bump of her spine. Her warm breath on his neck, the kisses amid the sobs, more than answered his doubt.

"Oh, God, Joe, I thought you were dead, that I'd never see you again. I had almost given up hope and now, here you are."

Horace Stanhope, Ginnie's father, put his arms around them both and led them into the back of the pub.

"Most welcome home, Joe. My, God, it's good to see you. How long do you have?" Ginnie shuddered at the question.

"We have a mission tomorrow, weather permitting." Ginnie gasped and clung to him tighter.

"Well, then, not a moment to spare, is there?" He guided them to the stairs leading to Ginnie's room and closed the door behind them.

Joe awoke from habit at three in the dark, cold morning. Ginnie lay cocooned in his arms. As quietly as he could, Joe parted from her and dressed outside her door. Though awake, Ginnie stayed in bed, unable to face another leave-taking. She heard him tip-toe down the stairs, the bell ring and the door of the pub close behind him. An hour later, the roar of the bombers rattled her windows.

Chapter Eighteen: Schmidt Again

"Goddammit, goddammit, goddammit!", shouted Enfield Davis over the inter-tank frequency. "Lay some heavy shit on those Panzers."

He had just seen *Adolph's Nightmare,* commanded by Technical Sergeant Ramon Suarez, explode in a fireball which rocked *Hell's Fire* from fifty yards away.

"Get that son of a bitch," he screamed. His gunner, Corporal Gus Tolliver had a HEAP round all loaded and the retreating Panzer VI in his sights. He squeezed the trigger and the round was on its way. Head on, even a HEAP round fired from a thousand yards had no chance of taking out a Tiger but it was turning to re-enter the woods on the slopes of the Kommerscheidt-Schmidt ridge so that the round hit the thinner armor on the side. It did its job. The turret blew off in a volcanic blast, leaving no doubt of any survivors.

There was no jubilation in *Hell's Fire,* only stunned recognition of the loss of five close friends. *Nightmare, Hell's Fire* and *Death Wagon* along with the original *Ronna's Revenge* had come on shore at Normandy on D-Day+2 as part of the 707th Tank Battalion (Medium). Until *Revenge* was lost to a bf109 strafing run, her crew transferred to the replacement tank, *Texas Pride,* they had stormed across

France from the break-out at St. Lo until the mud stopped them before the Siegfried Line and the Huertgan Forest on the German-Belgium line, winter of 1944. The platoon had lost *Revenge's* replacement *Texas Pride*, commanded by Sergeant Herman Manns, to another Panzer. Now only *Hell's Fire* and *Death Wagon* remained of the original four remained.

There could be no time for grieving. The diminished tank platoon would still have to spearhead the attack on Schmidt. The attack force of the decimated 112th Pennsylvania National Guard comprised of less than three hundred men along with some engineers, dragooned from their task of trying to keep the single-track trail across the Kall River valley open, were all that were available to take Schmidt. That trail was the lifeline for the American advance onto the Monschau plain and the Roer River. The deadly back-and-forth of the battle for Schmidt was in its third month. It had been fought in the worst weather imaginable. There were endless days and nights of rain, sleet, icy mist which precluded any air support or accurate artillery fire. The tracks of tanks and Weasels which were the only vehicles that could move, spun impotently in the knee-deep mud that made up the fighting terrain in the battle for Schmidt. Movement was possible for the tracks only because "grouser pads" which were attached to the tracks to dig deeper into the mud. With these, progress was still slow, and on any incline, the tanks would drift sickeningly downhill until traction was regained.

Davis looked around until he found Lt. Judd Barclay, now the commander of the 112th, due to the unrelenting attrition of its officers.

"So, Lieutenant, ready when you are," Davis shouted down to the infantryman.

Barclay cast an eye skyward to the unbroken cloud cover. Anderson and Howe were standing next to their lieutenant and looked skyward as well.

"Meaning no disrespect, Sir," Howe began with uncharacteristic deference, "but we are pretty much dead men walking now. You attack that town again without any air support, we will be for sure dead men and no joke."

"We've got the tanks and artillery has the town locked in. They are just waiting on our call. With the engineers, we have more bodies than we have had since arrived here. Their artillery has been neutralized for the most part and have the same shitty weather we do. So, I would say this is as good as it is likely to get.

"Mount up." Barclay turned and climbed up onto *Hell's Fire*. "Let's go, Sergeant." He pulled back the cocking handle on his Thompson and braced himself.

"Oh, for Christ's sake," muttered Howe but he fell into line behind Davis's lead tank. The tracks threw up so much mud that the men had to fall back another ten feet to avoid being completely caked and blinded with it.

The light rain had lessened to an icy mist which now had turned to dense fog, completely obscuring their way forward.

"I can't see shit, Ensign," shouted Emmonds, the driver.

"Just keep it straight as you can and make your best speed," replied Davis.

Soon all cohesion of the combined infantry/armor attack was lost. The following infantry wallowed through the mud, the tanks becoming mere suggestions of something massive ahead of them, making the men follow the tanks by their noise alone.

Lieutenant Barclay could barely see the end of the tank. "There is no fucking way, I can call in any artillery in this shit. I have no idea where the hell we are," he shouted to Davis over the tank's rumble. He had taken a compass reading before setting out but that was mainly guess work as well. Only when they began to receive random fire from the Germans did he have the sense that they were getting close. The three hundred or so infantrymen strung out behind his tanks, struggling through the gelatinous mud, could only see the man in front of him and if he went astray, there was no getting them back. They had four hours to take Schmidt, dig in and prepare their night positions before dark and the certain counterattack.

"Ok, where the fuck are we?" asked Howe, hanging onto Anderson's field jacket. Pulling up his foot up through two feet of mud to plunge it back into the muck once again. Step after trudging step was exhausting all of the men. They could barely see the tanks ahead and guided on them by the sounds of their engines and smell of their exhaust.

"Now, remember, we have the element of surprise on our side," joked Anderson. "Except the surprise will be if we find anything in this fuck-fest. The Germans probably can't find us either."

That hopeful note was terminated by rounds from a MG34 machine gun rippling through the tanks. The shrill whistle of the ricochets rang by their ears.

"Oh, fuck," shouted Howe, "we're in for it now." He started to return fire but Lieutenant Barclay shouted, "Cease fire, cease fire. We can't see shit in this much less shoot it."

"Well, what are we going to do, Lieutenant?" asked Howe. More rounds snarled passed them. "They seem to be able to see us."

"They are just firing on the tanks. Form up behind them, stay with the tanks.

"Sergeant Rosinsky."

"Yes. Sir."

"Keep the men behind the tanks, in their tracks. Otherwise, we'll lose half the force."

The small attacking column had no idea where they were on the ridge and had to use the German fire to guide them. If they started receiving flanking fire, the tanks would turn into it and the infantrymen would follow. Progress had almost ground to halt when the Panzerfausts arrived. The harsh, guttural sound of a round passing over their heads shook them to their bones.

"Jesus Christ, Lieutenant, what do you want us to do?", Howe called out.

"We gotta stick with the tanks," Barclay shouted down from his perch on *Hell's Fire*. There was some reassurance from the fire of the 76mm cannon and the two machine guns each *Hell's Fire* and *Death Wagon* poured into the fog. They slowly pushed forward until Gus Tolliver, the gunner on *Hell's Fire* spotted the flash from one of the Panzerfausts. Without hesitation, he put a fragmentation round into the dark space and was rewarded with a secondary explosion, signifying the end of at least one of the fire teams.

After that, the German fire slackened as they pulled back.

“Keep moving forward, men,” shouted Barclay. The tanks decreased their rate of fire to conserve ammunition. Re-supply in these conditions was impossible.

The ground underneath their feet became firmer and actually turned into a paved road: the main street of Schmidt.

“Holy shit, we’re here,” said Anderson.

Barclay jumped down from the tank and stood between the stumbling columns of his men. “Alright, spread out among the ruins and move forward until you reach the edge of town. Dig in there. Sergeant Rosinsky, you take the left flank, I’ll take the right. I’ll keep the radio.”

Davis in *Hell’s Fire* and Soames *in Death Wagon* separated in the destroyed town, Davis to the left, Soames to the right. Their turrets rotated through 360 degrees, assuring full fields of fire. They shut down the engines to conserve fuel. Soon the tanks felt like freezers.

Barclay keyed the radio. “Objective has been secured.”

"Roger. We'll try to get some re-supply up to you," replied the CP.

#

Deep, racking coughs doubled Privat Ernst Locher over and cut off his breath. Corporal Hermann Schneider, covered him with his own sodden blanket and hugged him to provide what body warmth he had left. His bayonet slash was healing slowly and miraculously was not yet infected. It had been two days since their last hot food. The Americans had driven them out of Schmidt back into the trees. Schneider had noted where the headquarters tents were and instead of following the rest of his platoon, he guided Locher to the medical tent which, given the lack of snow on the canvas, promised some heat and maybe food. Ernst continued his coughing, bringing up bloody, green sputum. He shivered uncontrollably though his forehead was hot to Schneider's touch. A medic came out from the tent.

"Excuse, me, Herr Doktor," Schneider spoke up.

The medic turned angrily on Schneider. "What you talking about, I am no doctor. What do you want?"

"This boy is sick, pneumonia, I think, and needs your attention."

"This is a surgical unit, not medical. Bring him back when he is shot or take him five tents to the rear where the medical tent is."

"I doubt he can make it that far, nor me either. Can't we come in for a few minutes to get a little warmth and maybe one shot of penicillin?"

"Listen, old man, do as I say or I will shoot you both as malingerers." He made a motion to draw his Walther P38 pistol.

An officer came out of the tent, drawn by the noise and the need for a cigarette.

"What is going on here, Corporal? Doing the Americans' job for them?"

"No, Herr Docktor," the flustered medic said, drawing himself to attention. "These men are malingerers, I suspect. Anyway, they claim to be sick and I directed them to the medical tent."

The doctor looked over Ernst and saw how ill he was.

"Bring them in. I think we can spare some light and warmth while I see what the matter is."

None too gently, the medic dragged Ernst inside. The tent reeked of blood, feces, chlorine solution and dirty, wet men. There were litters supported on barrels or crates.

Moans and cries of the wounded men rose into the fetid air. The floor of the tent was churned into mud ankle deep and littered with boots, filthy uniforms and occasionally, an arm or a leg. What little heat there was came from a rusted conical shaped stove with a pipe chimney reaching through the low canvas ceiling. Schneider thought that Ernst was probably putting out more heat than the stove.

The medic roughly pulled off Ernst's fatigue shirt, ripping the buttons in the process. The doctor stepped up.

"I am Doktor Ermenger. He has been wounded, I see. Not too long ago by the look of the incision. Not one of ours, either. Where was he treated?" He rapidly moved his stethoscope over Ernst's chest then percussed over the lungs. "Hm, right upper lobe consolidation."

Schneider explained how they had been captured by the Americans, treated at an aide station and put in a POW enclosure but escaped when the German counterattack occurred.

"Quite commendable, wouldn't you say, Corporal? Not malingerers at all."

"Yes, Her Doktor," he replied through clenched teeth. He remained irrationally angry at Schneider and Locher for embarrassing him in front of the doctor.

"Now, draw up two grams of penicillin and find another shirt for the private."

The doctor injected the antibiotic. The medic returned with a bloody shirt he had found in the pile of discarded equipment taken off other wounded or dead men.

"There," continued Ermenger, "we'll keep him here for a few days to complete the treatment and see that he recovers. Meanwhile," turning to Schneider, "here is a pass and meal ticket for you. You can take him back to your unit when he is ready."

"Thank you, many thanks, Herr Doktor," said Schneider and saluted.

"Nonsense, the least I can do. It is so horrible here in this wood, I am glad I can help someone."

#

The weather forecasters for once agreed with one another. Both the American and Germans called for clearing skies over the Huertgen Forest. This was received as good news by the bored flight crews on both sides. The pilots of Jagdgeschwader III/54, von Rindle's flight, as well as the 363 Squadron, 357th Fighter Group where Captain Robert Mulley had been longing to get into the air with his replacement P-51D Mustang, which he inherited from a pilot who had rotated home.

The strategy for the Mustangs was the obliteration of the Luftwaffe. The Thunderbolts were tough, durable fighters but the Me109s could outclimb and out turn them. The kill ratios for the two planes were pretty equal. The expectation was that the nimble Mustangs could deal with the Luftwaffe thus freeing up the Thunderbolts for ground attacks at which they excelled. Since D-Day, the Thunderbolts concentrated on railroads, road junctions and convoys to clear the way for the advance to the Siegfried Line.

This suited Captain Robert Mullen. He felt his P-51D fit him like an assassin's glove. This was the third P-51 variant and clearly the best. From the bubble canopy allowing much improved visibility, the silver of the unpainted fuselage gleamed in the revetments, to the red rudder, everything about the plane made his heart beat faster. Thirteen pounds were saved by leaving the planes unpainted. The red-yellow-red lines on the spinner, the retained white and black "invasion stripes" on the under carriage, the red and yellow checkerboard of the cowling complimented the 363rd squadron's insignia: a bullet-holed skull pierced by a bayonet blood dripping from the tip. Mullen had a Hitler mustache painted on it as a final touch. The Mustang's name, *Ain't Misbehavin'*, was perfect he thought. That was good since it was considered bad luck to re-name a plane. There were seven swastikas painted on the side under the cockpit. He had been flying for a year in the Thunderbolts and was an ace with five kills in that fighter. It took him just a month to chalk-up his seven kills in the P-51. Sliding into the cockpit was almost sexual for him. The roar of the supercharged Packard-Merlin engine coursed through him, re-enforcing the sense of being one with the machine.

There was thin cloud cover at five thousand feet and clear above that. The 100th Bomb Group was heading for the Huertgan. Mullen felt like he was going to meet with old friends. The bombers were led by the *Loosey Lucy,* piloted by Lieutenant Carl Stanley of Detroit. This was their fifth mission together as a crew. They had followed the "Judas plane", brightly painted green with red and purple spots, to the assembly point, "Buncher 28". The Judas plane was usually a B-17 taken out of combat but used to quickly assemble flights. Its garish paint job made it easily identifiable. Named "Judas" because it led the flights into danger but peeled off for Thorpe Abbotts once the fighter escort arrived.

Mullen flew up level with the *Loosey Lucy* to make eye contact with her pilot.

"*Loosey*, this is *Ain't Misbehavin'*, of the 363rd. And how are you all this lovely morning?"

"We are doing just fine. What do you hear about running into any Krauts on this run?"

"Seem to be fewer and fewer which is just fine with me. But some of us will go on ahead see if there is a reception committee waiting for us."

"Roger."

Mullen keyed his mic on the inter plane frequency. "Section one and two, on me. Section three stay with the bombers." With that he goosed his supercharger followed by ten fighters and soon the bombers were diminishing specks to their rear.

JG III */54,* Hauptman von Rindle's reconstituted fighter group, still bearing the "Green Hearts", had been warned of the approaching bombers, flying at only ten thousand feet to concentrate on hitting Schmidt and the ridges. They were to try to drive the Germans out once again. The town had changed hands so many times that von Rindle hoped the B-17s would be hitting their own troops by mistake. In any event, his flight of eighteen 109Gs and 190Ds' mission was to thin out the bombers, regardless of their target. Each of his flight carried a Werfer-Granate 21 rocket launcher under their wings. These had enough range to bring down the bombers without getting into of the B-17 gunners' kill zones. On the down side, they were bulky and cut their airspeed and maneuverability.

"Green Hearts, stay alert. We should be meeting the Americans very soon. To Victory." They were flying at twenty-five thousand feet and von Rindle spotted the bombers below him. He also saw bright flashes of the P-51s climbing up to meet them. This would be their last sortie in 109s before transitioning to the jet powered Me262 Storm Swallow.

"Mustangs climbing at eight o'clock. Engage, engage!" The Staffel fired off their rockets in the general direction of the 100th BG bombers without much hope of a kill. They then jettisoned the empty rocket tubes and turned to face the 363rd Squadron. He put his stick hard to port, aligning himself and his following flight to dive at the Americans out of the sun.

Mullin saw the last Messerschmitt before being blinded by the sun.

"Split up, engage individually."

The first 109 flashed by Mullen who rolled into a dive to follow him. He recognized the "Green Heart" insignia on the Messerschmitt's fuselage. The German pulled up and to starboard hoping to make Mullen overshoot him. Mullen did not. The two planes continued their deadly ballet in the hope of getting behind the other. This put Mullen at a disadvantage in that the 109 could outturn him. 20mm canon rounds began to sing by him. He put his plane into a steep dive then pulled back to do a vertical roll. The Mustang had nearly twice the fuel capacity of the 109 and could support a longer fight until the German ran out of fuel. Mullen just had to either shoot him down or survive his attacks. Either way, he knew he was up against a damn good pilot. Beyond that, the Germans outnumbered him almost two-to-one.

"Section three, section three," Mullen called to the remaining P-51s protecting the bombers. "We've got a bunch of Gustavs and Doras up here and could use some help." Another string of 20mm rounds streaked just over Mullen's port wing.

"On our way", came the reply. The remaining Mustangs peeled away from the bombers and hit their superchargers.

Joe Hanover in the right waist of the B-17 *The Usual Suspects* watched with some fear as the last of the escorting Mustangs shot up to join the dogfight. He nervously pulled back on his charging handle and moved the gun through its full range. He hoped the Mustangs would take care of the German fighters but it never hurt to be prepared.

Von Rindle saw the rest of the Mustangs, the sun sparking off the polished aluminum fuselages climbing to join the fight which to his mind was no longer winnable.

"Green Hearts, more Mustangs at eight o'clock. We must disengage." He noted his fuel was running low but had enough to return to base. He assumed the Americans would break off and rejoin the bombers. Those were not Mullen's orders.

"They're making a run for it," he called to the rest of the flight. "Stay with them."

A shudder ran down von Rindle's spine when he saw the Mustangs giving chase. More combat flying would almost certainly run them out of fuel before they could reach their base. Off to his left he saw a Dora explode and a Gustav begin to trail smoke. He realized that today was truly the last day of the "Green Hearts". He had served his country honorably. The last trip home to see his wife and children was more than he had hoped and saw it as a gift from his commander. There was only one thing left for him to do. With one last glance over his shoulder at the Mustangs killing his flight, he pushed his stick hard down and to the left, diving on the bombers.

Joe Hanover watched fascinated by the deadly choreography of the dogfight above him. One by one, German fighters fell past him. Only one Mustang was lost. He picked up one bf109 approaching. He thought this one was taking its death dive as well but saw no streaming fire or trailing smoke. Then the plane's nose spat out a stream of 20mm rounds, striking just aft of his window. Hanover had less than a second to react.

"Oh, shit," he said, swinging his .50 caliber upward. The 109 filled his sights and Joe depressed the triggers, sending red tracers into the attacking Dora.

Hauptman Jans von Rindle hummed the final notes of the "Pastoral" as he was engulfed in flame.

Chapter Nineteen:
Huter des Jagers (Hunter's Hut)

The hut was more than one hundred years old. It had been built and improved upon by generations of hunters. Its solid log walls, caulked with moss had two shuttered windows for light and air. The stone fireplace still drew well, keeping the one room dry and warm. It was a place of shelter and rest for the hunters of the Huertgan Forest.

Since the war came to the Huertgan, the hut was largely forgotten. It was reached by a narrow track which had been overgrown by young fir trees. The nearest passable tract was about a quarter of a mile away. There was nothing to frighten the deer and bear which roamed freely among the dense trees.

Until the war.

Frau Frita Rudin, was a widow for the past two years. She and her thirteen-year-old son, Hans, lived in Aachen when her husband had been called up, sent to the Eastern Front and died in Kiev. He had been a hunter and knew of the hut. He and his son had spent several happy days there. Now, in the summer of 1944, when the increasingly desperate Reich came for her son for the Hitler Youth, she remembered the hut, deep in the forest. She knew she had little time to save her son.

The bombing of the city was becoming more frequent and she sensed that time was running out. The authorities had said the civilians were to evacuate. Frau Rudin understood this meant that anyone unable to fight were to be turned out into the countryside. It was a very efficient way to screen the population and cull out all the males, age twelve to sixty-five, for the army.

To her neighbors, she spoke with pride that soon her Hans would be joining the fight to defend the Fatherland. At night, after he had gone to sleep, she collected as much clothing, coats, food as the two of them could carry. On the day of their departure, she explained to her neighbors that she was taking some things to relatives south of Aachen that she no longer needed now that her husband was dead. They set off early in the morning. Only when they were safely out of the city did she reveal to Hans they were starting a new life in the forest.

"But, Mother," Hans protested, "I want to fight for Germany, like Papa did. He would be proud of me, wouldn't he?"

"Our family has given enough to Germany already. You must live to help re-build Germany when this terrible war, this Wahnsinn (madness), is finally over. Besides, I need you to do what Papa can no longer do. We must survive. In the forest, you will hunt like you did with Papa to keep us alive. Now, we walk."

It took them three days to reach the hut. German patrols were all heading south to meet the Americans who were rapidly advancing across northern France with Aachen as their goal. Soon, the Hurtgen Forest would be embroiled in some of the worst fighting of the war.

They entered the dark forest in a rain storm. Hans knew the track and found the path leading to the hut even though it was overgrown with new growth trees. Frita had never been to the hut and had to trust her son to find it. As they stumbled on through the dark forest, the path being more a suggestion than a clear route, her panic grew. What good was it to save her son from the Nazis only to watch him starve to death in this trackless wood, she thought.

"Here we are, Mother," Hans said with more than a little relief in his voice. The hut was barely visible in the dark storm. But when Hans struck the door with his fist, Frita's fear began to melt. She hugged her son then followed him into the dry main room.

"Your father would be so proud of you, Hans. You are truly the man he had hoped you would be."

There was dry wood stacked in a corner. The window shutters were closed and Hans soon had a fire going, He and his mother huddled in front of the blaze as the chill of the journey and months of fear fell away. They swept out the hut and made the bed ready. Hans went to a makeshift cupboard and found some canned beans, a pot but more importantly a hunting knife and his father's Mauser Gewehr 98 rifle passed down from his grandfather's service in World War I. There was a full box of shells and the rifle had been left wrapped in oiled rags. Hans worked the bolt and clicked the trigger. There was a ramrod with oiled cleaning swatches which he passed through the barrel finding it clean.

"There, Mother, we have all we need. There is a brook out back for water and fish. I will go out tomorrow to see what I can find for us to eat. Now lie down and get some rest."

#

Schneider and Locher had spent the past week in the snow, shivering with only their worn overcoats for protection and cold rations to eat. Ernst was still weak having incompletely recovered from a badly infected shoulder wound followed by pneumonia. Doktor Ermenger, the compassionate surgeon who had taken him in at the aide station had planned on keeping until both problems had resolved but that had changed with the arrival of an imperious infantry captain.

"Herr Doktor," he said clicking his heels and giving the Sieg Heil salute which Ermenger barely acknowledged. "My orders are to return to duty all men capable of fighting or at least assisting the fight. This man looks well enough, wouldn't you say?"

"No, I would not," replied Ermenger. "He needs to recover from his infected wound and pneumonia. He needs at least five more days of antibiotics."

"Yet, he sits, he eats. Our medic can change his dressings if needed and continue the antibiotics. Most importantly, he can contribute to the fight. I can assign him as a machine gunner's mate, that's not heavy duty. Come with me, Private."

Corporal Schneider came into the tent and saw what was going on. He knew the infantry officer's type and that no appealing to reason or mercy would prevail.

"It is alright, Herr Doktor, I will go with him," Schneider said.

"Ah, excellent" said the sergeant, "how you say 'Two for the price of one.'"

They moved from the relative protection of the camp in the trees back out onto the open Schmidt-Kommerscheidt ridge. The fighting had continued to ebb and flow over the contested ground. Currently, the Germans held it. Ernst and Schneider re-occupied their old foxhole. Schneider had "appropriated" new, dry blankets, a capital offense if discovered. He wrapped the shivering young boy in both of them.

"Ah, home sweet home, eh, Ernst? Not much has changed – maybe a few more bomb craters, a wrecked vehicle or two. This weather should keep the bombers at home for a while at least. If only we could get a fire going, but can't have everything, I guess. I did get us a little something from the supply tent." He twisted around and from his pack produced six inches of wurst, half a loaf of hard bread and a can of beans. "Now, we can eat like the generals back in the rear."

Ernst ate most of the beans and wurst. Schneider finished their scant meal. Ernst sighed and was soon asleep. Schneider absent-mindedly stroked the boy's shoulder glad he could do something worthwhile for him. He turned his mind to their escape. The short time with the Americans and their treatment of Ernst convinced him that the dire warnings given by his unit's information officer was nothing but lies and propaganda. Surrender at the first available chance was their only hope for surviving. He waited on the next American counterattack. Meanwhile, he curled himself around the sleeping boy for shared warmth.

#

"Motor stables, you've got to love 'em," said Ensign Davis from deep in the belly of *Hell's Fire.* After a month of hard fighting, his depleted platoon had been pulled back to St. Vith for some maintenance and refit. He was hoping to be off the line through Christmas. The mechanics would see to the engine and drive train. The armorers would take care of the main gun and the machine guns. All they had to do was clean out the inside and maybe re-paint. The had their nights free to see what St. Vith had to offer, which was not much. The town was a commercial hub for centuries but the village had remained small with two churches, an inn and a pub along the main, the only street. Villagers lived in scattered cottages. The main Army facilities were outside of town to the east. The Luftwaffe made a few raids when “the boys were in town” as the villagers thought of the Americans. The main attraction for the raids were the tanks and trucks undergoing repair and maintenance. P-51s were based at YAAF-729 air base near Maastricht, Belgium, and were able to scramble and drive off any Doras or Gustavs that were foolhardy enough to sortie. Even so, Staffels like the “Green Hearts” did make early morning raids from time to time. The main difficulty for them was, as always, fuel.

The five-man crew of *Hell’s Fury:* Gus Tolliver, gunner, 76mm cannon; Stanley Grisholm, bow gunner, .30 caliber; Sam Peters, loader and Roger Emmonds, the driver, had been together since D-Day+2. Of the original platoon the only loss was *Rhonda’s Revenge,* but without loss of crew. *Texas Pride* and the rest of them had some dings and gashes but were intact and serviceable. The refit at St. Vith was just what man and machine needed.

“Oh, man,” exclaimed Gus Tolliver, “I could definitely get used to this. This is the first time I have been warm, dry, well-fed, well-rested all at the same time since we left England. And we get to stay here through Christmas?"

"That's the current rumor," replied Davis. "I've checked in with the mail tent who said there has been Christmas mail expected for the last week. That means, as we all know, maybe here by Easter but it is the thought that counts."

The five-man crew of *Hell's Fury* were luxuriating in new fatigues, socks, boots and field jackets. They had been relieved of all duties not strictly related to their tank and had even been able to sleep through the outgoing H&I, harassment and interdiction, rounds which were fired intermittently whenever there was not a fire mission in support of the 112th Pennsylvania along the Kall River gorge.

"Just ten days to Christmas," Emmons, the driver mused as he rolled over to get more sleep. "1944 overall was a real motherfucker but is ending pretty nice after all."

#

"Feuer!" shouted Oberleutnant Heinz von Kleist of the 272nd Artillery, based in Blankenheim five miles from the front line. His target was St. Vith and its repair facilities. He had a full complement of new 88s and intended to use them. The 1st Panzer SS division supplemented with ragtag elements of the 272nd VGD, the 5th Fallschirmjager (paratroopers) and the 116th Panzergrenadiers, even some plane-less Luftwaffe troops and Kriegsmarine sailors with no ships, had managed to struggle up to eighty percent strength, Ernst Locher and Schneider among them. Under cover of darkness and the fire of the 88s, they had advanced to the east wall of the Kall River gorge and only awaited orders to attack the Americans scattered through the ravine and up the western bank. Howe and Anderson manned their usual foxhole and watched the east rim of the valley.

"It's those fucking 88s, what did I tell you?" Howe shouted to be heard above the screams of the shells flying over their heads.

"I know," replied Anderson, "but at least they are going somewhere else, for now."

"This cannot be good," Howe said. "Where's the Christmas lull they keep talking about? Where's our goddam counter fire?"

More rounds began to impact behind them but closer each time.

"The Krauts are trying to sterilize the ground before their big push," Howe continued. "They're done pussyfooting around. They've got to make their move before the weather breaks."

They curled up as tightly as they could, trying to meld with the mud of their foxhole. They pressed their heads further into their helmets. Each impact bounced them almost out of the hole and struck them like a kick in the ribs, knocking the air out of their lungs. Half an hour later and it was over. Experienced infantrymen like Howe and Anderson knew what that meant. They checked their Garands, ammo and hand grenades and watched the rim.

"Son of a bitch," shouted Davis *Hell's Fire,* "I knew it was too good to be true. Mount up, mount up." He and the rest of his crew rolled out of their sacks and sprinted to the tank, tugging on boots on the way. The German fire was erratic and poorly aimed due to the same lack of forward observation as the Americans. They jumped in their tank and within a minute were rolling forward towards the Kall. The tanks were fully fueled and had their full complement of seventy high explosive rounds and five white phosphorus shells. Chatter over the radios was confused with contravening orders from multiple sources. But the pattern was unmistakable, one that the crews recognized from fire fights too numerous to count.

Speaking on the inter-tank channel, Davis began directing his platoon. "Fan out along the rim, I'll take the trail head. No one enters the valley unless ordered. Be alert for any of our guys getting flushed out of the gorge."

Davis was not happy about sitting in the midst of the 88s' field of fire but was counting on the German ground attack that he was sure was headed their way to keep the Germans from firing. He had four Shermans. Each crew chief stood to his .50 caliber machine gun. The bow and main cannon gunners and loaders were ready as well. Behind him, Davis was aware of the 112th men moving up as well. Eyes strained against the darkness, looking for any glimmer, spark that warned of the German attack.

Fired from deep in the rear a white phosphorus shell exploded one thousand feet above the Kall and drifted lazily down under its parachute. Its light revealed eight hundred soldiers of the German attacking force were storming across the Kall River.

Frau Rudin and her son, Hans, could hear the sounds of the battle which waxed and waned but did not consistently advance on their hut. Hans crept out and circled the hut as he brought in more fire wood, satisfied that no light escaped. Only the smoke from the chimney betrayed their presence but there was nothing he could do about that. The snowfall helped to limit the spread of the smoke. He sat next to his mother with the Mauser on his lap.

Chapter Twenty:
The Bulge: Day One

"Rosinski, Howe, Anderson", shouted Lt. Judd Barclay, "move left and try to get behind that son of a bitch machine gun. We aren't going anywhere until you take him out." With that, they all had to duck behind the snow and shattered log parapet hastily thrown up as the platoon tried to advance.

"Oh, shit," moaned Howe. "He does know there are other guys in the platoon, doesn't he?"

"Seriously, Howe?" Rosinski said. "We haven't been shot at for fifteen minutes. Come on, leave time is over."

With Sergeant Rosinski leading the way, the three men began their slow crawl, taking a wide arc to out flank then get behind the German machine gun crew. They did not know how many Germans there were and only knew the machine gun's position but not if there were any other enemy in support. Occasionally, they could see the loader's helmeted head pop up as he directed the gunner's fire. Rosinski had first heard the distinctive sound of the Machenengewehr 42, the MG 42, when he landed in Normandy. Some described it as cloth ripping. Rosinski preferred the American nickname: "Hitler's zipper". He had seen the fearsome effect of the gun in the hands of a well-trained crew of anywhere from two to six men. It was light weight so that even one man could carry it in attack but was usually used with a bipod, greatly increasing its accuracy. Because it was so mobile, it was hard to determine how many guns were in action as crews would frequently shift firing positions. The MG42's main weakness was that it had to change barrels every two to three minutes of sustained firing due to rapid overheating. This took about ten seconds during which Rosinski would move forward. He knew what he was up against, which is why he took the lead.

When they had gone twenty yards, he said, "Howe, you wait here and cover us. Anderson, follow me at about ten feet. Have a grenade ready." The two infantrymen made their way closer to the machine gun.

"Next pause, I'll toss my grenade and you shoot anyone who pops up. If I miss, it's your turn." Anderson nodded his understanding. Rosinski took one more look, then a deep breath, pulled the pin and tossed his grenade towards the Germans. The explosion was muffled by the deep snow filling the gun pit but did not quiet the screams of the crew. Howe, Anderson and Rosinski rose to their feet to finish off any survivors. There were none.

"Nice work, Sarge," Anderson said.

"Can we go..." Howe was cut off by the scream of incoming 88s.

"Hit the deck," shouted Rosinski, though no urging was needed. The three Americans dove into the pit with the destroyed gun and its mangled crew. It made no difference if this was targeted fire or simple harassment: either one could kill.

The barrage lasted ten minutes until the American counter-battery fire quieted the guns.

" 'Bout fucking time," snarled Howe with the arrival of the friendly rounds. "Let's get the hell out of here."

The forest was hard to navigate in the best of times. The back and forth of the fighting along the ridge and into the woods had completely disoriented the three soldiers. They also did not know who held the ridge. They did know that the woods were still in German hands and their chances were fast dwindling the longer they stayed. The heavy combat and the general destruction caused by multiple artillery barrages, made finding their way back to their own lines guesswork at best. Rosinski led off in what he thought was the right direction. What few landmarks there had been were obliterated by the shelling. Their tracks had filled with snow. Rosinski had a clear remembrance of the tactical map but that was of little use in the featureless forest. All he could remember and hoped to find was a narrow track near some sort of hut which he guessed was off west somewhere. He hoped to find the track and follow it back to his own lines.

"Alright, follow me," trying to sound more assured than he felt.

#

"Mission for tomorrow," said the one-armed major as he walked the black curtain to the side revealing a map of southwest Germany, red tape tracing the routes in and out. A groan rose from the assembled pilots as they homed in on the endpoint. He was briefing the 357th fighter group by itself instead of the usual 100th Bomb Group. After the last raid on Regensburg, the 100th was down to its last serviceable plane, the *Bouncing Betty.* They left Thorpe Abbotts with seventeen planes, one hundred-seventy crew men. Two other planes had barely made it back with wounded on board but one crashed and burned on the runway without anyone escaping. The other one made it safely down but would be salvaged for parts. The group awaited replacements on their way via Greenland but that was a week off. It was thought by the "higher ups" hitting Regensburg so soon after the mauling the 100th received, that a single flight of thirty P-51 fighter-bombers could slip in unnoticed to finish the job.

Almost in unison with the major the Mustang pilots said, "Regensburg", followed by muttering that the major was just as happy not to hear clearly.

"Yes, Regensburg. We are going for surprise and hopefully bring some real shit to bear on the Messerschmitt factories there. In preparation, the 98th and its Liberators will take out the coastal radars an hour before the 357th Fighter Group crosses and fly like bats outta hell to Regensburg. You will be carrying three napalm cannisters each. As you know the March attack on Berlin was very successful for its first use. Since then, napalm has been used in Italy, France and the Pacific. This raid made by p-51s will deliver a knock-out blow to the factory for some time to come and will be the prototype for more raids like it.

"With the coastal radars taken out and by flying low and fast, the 357th should be in and out before the Krauts know you were there. Captain Mullen's 363 Squadron will be the lead element. Any questions?"

There were none. Beyond the briefing hut, the engines of the 98th could be heard warming up. The plan was for the fighters to leave one hour after the 98th's destruction of the coastal radars so there would be no warning of their taking off. For this mission, two squadrons of twelve planes each were assigned. The 363rd Squadron commanded by Captain Robert Mullen would be lead. The final plan was to have the twenty-four Mustangs fly abreast and drop their cannisters as they flew over the factory. This way they would not be flying through the flames and smoke of the napalm and have clear vision of the target. Other bomb groups would hit Schweinfurt to the north about an hour before the 357th hit Regensburg to further draw off and confuse the German fighters. The Mustangs carried extra fuel to compensate for the weight and drag caused by the napalm.

"I don't know, Bobby," radioed Lt. Henry Jones to his squadron leader, Capt. Mullen.

"What among the many things you don't know, Hank, is it this time?"

"Very funny. It just seems so strange to be up here without any big fellas. I don't know, I just feel so exposed, like we're out on an excursion."

"Well," replied Mullen, "that is all about to change. Ten minutes to the drop point. Form up on me."

The rest of the flight of twenty-three P-51s came on line with their flight leader, separated by two hundred feet and dead level. They all saw the factory complex at Regensburg, scarred and smoking in spots but still ringed with deadly accurate 88s. They hoped that the P-51s, flying low and fast, unheralded by radar contacts would remain unnoticed for just a few minutes more.

"On my mark...five, four, three, two, one...DROP, DROP, DROP."

In unison the twenty-four fighter/bombers dropped their seventy-two canisters of napalm, blanketing the Regensburg Messerschmitt factory in a single hellish fire ball. The pilots could not help but look back over their shoulders as they pulled away. They had no doubt that their mission was accomplished and there would be no bf109s coming from Regensburg to contest the skies over Germany for some time to come.

Unburdened by the extra fuel carried in tanks in the rear of their fuselages and the drag of the napalm cannisters, the Mustangs fairly danced in the clear skies as they turned for home. They still had their full ammunition loads for their six .50 caliber machine guns, three per wing. Realizing that his flight might relax thinking the mission was over, Captain Mullen got on the radio.

"Look alive, if the Krauts didn't know we were here before the run, they sure as hell know it now. There are plenty of airfields between us and home. They'll be looking for some payback."

Mullen was proven all too prescient. The Messerschmitts that had turned north to attack the bombers hitting Schweinfurt had returned to their fields to re-arm and re-fuel. They swarmed into the skies to meet the Mustangs. The Germans had not counted on the P-51s having their full complement of ammunition and were hoping for a one-sided contest.

"109s six o'clock low," shouted Mullen. "Pick 'em up, pick 'em up." He and the rest of the flight turned as one to face the Germans and then broke apart to engage them separately. The two flights of fighters passed each other at four hundred miles per hour. The tracers racing by, each side scoring one victory apiece. The tighter turning radius of the Messerschmitts meant that they could get behind the Mustangs as they tried to recover. The P-51s could outclimb the 109s and so hope to shake them off.

Mullen had a 109 on his tail, tracers streaking by on both sides. He put the stick sharply down and engaged his turbocharger, pulling away from the German. He turned hard to port and had a 109 in his sights. A short burst and the 109 exploded. He still had a 109 on his tail, although not as close. Mullen's wingman pulled up and downed that Messerschmitt. Freed up from immediate combat, Mullen and his wingman climbed into the swirling fighters, the air laced with red and green tracers, explosions rocking them as those rounds hit home. The Mustangs had about four times the fuel capacity with its drop tanks and internal tanks: 380 gallons versus the Messerschmitts' 85 gallons. Mullen missed the extra gallons in the drop tanks left behind to accommodate the napalm cannisters. The extra weight and drag of all that fuel cost them maneuverability versus the 109 but the Mustangs could stay in the fight far longer than the 109s.

The Germans had the advantage of more local fields to support their fighters which proved pivotal in the early phases of the air war. The Mustangs were used for long range support. They were designed to escort the bombers all the way to Berlin and back. The Messerschmitts were quick hit, slashing attackers against the Allies both outbound and return flights. Their pilots were fresh while the Allies were fatigued by constant vigilance during the ten- to twelve-hour missions. The attrition of the Luftwaffe by late 1944, meant that escorting bombers became a less vital mission. The P-47s and P-51s had free range over Europe and destroyed German airfields, fuel depots and factories. By 1944, the Allied pilots had every advantage over the Luftwaffe, in planes, experienced pilots, superior fighters and maintenance. The Luftwaffe pilots that remained to "Fly and Fight until Victory or Death" could read their doom in the contrails of combat and the smokey pyres of their comrades. It was only a matter of time.

#

Oberleutnant Heinz von Kleist surveyed his battery of six new Pak43 88mm guns. As important as the excellent guns were the full crews he had under his command. With these assets at his disposal, he knew he could rain down death and destruction on the seemingly unstoppable Americans just two ridges over. He did not know that his opening volley would open the "Die Wacht am Rhein" operation. This was to become known to the Americans as the "Battle of the Bulge". His first targets were the Sherman tanks lined up along the rim of the Kall River gorge. He already knew two important facts: the aiming coordinates and the cloud cover making bombing runs at best unlikely and at worse inaccurate. It was with a certain contentment that he raised his arm, bringing it sharply down.

"Feuer!"

Immediately his six guns roared forth fire, smoke and destruction, his rounds only ten seconds from striking the American tanks. Heinz had overestimated his range by fifty yards. The rounds fell among the foot soldiers of the 112th Pennsylvania as they moved forward to enter the gorge.

"Son of a bitch," shouted Sergeant Rosinski. "Move it, move it. Into the gorge."

"You see where those rounds came from?" shouted Sergeant Enfield Davis of *Hell's Fire*.

"Can't see shit," replied Corporal Gus Tolliver, his gunner. "But sure as fuck better get the hell out of here."

Davis had positioned his tank at the trail head entering the gorge and led his tank platoon down the steep side as more of von Heinz's rounds landed. The soldiers of the 112th received the brunt of the artillery strike. However, Lt. Alfred Moore commanding the "Long Toms" of the 108th Field Artillery had a good idea of where von Heinz was. He ordered a counterbattery strike which silenced the German guns for the time being. Another illumination flair shot up and drifted lazily down over the gorge showing the 272nd GVD soldiers beginning to fall back.

"That's got them running," shouted an exuberant Lt. Judd Barclay, commanding what was left of the 112th. Normally E Co. platoon commander, the 112th was reduced to Just two companies and he was the ranking officer.

"Come on, let's get after them," he shouted, leading Corporal Jeffery Howe, Private Henry Anderson and Sergeant Ted Rosinsky into the gorge. After the shelling, there were no more than two hundred men left in the 112th. They sprinted down the trail and around Davis's Shermans in pursuit of the retreating 272nd GVD. The fading light of the illumination flare made picking targets difficult. The flare's white light swaying under its parachute made the infantrymen crossing the gorge look like dancing ghosts. Davis radioed for another flare but by the time it arrived, most of the 272nd had climbed eastern wall, turned and fired down on the Americans. Its light gave the Germans all the targets they needed.

"Son of a bitch," shouted Rosinski, "find some cover until that flare burns out." Ten more men of the 112th were wounded out right. They had made it a little way up the eastern wall.

Agonized calls of "Medic, medic" rang out. The aide station at the Mestrenger Mill began to receive wounded. The American and German medics ventured out to retrieve men from both sides. Sergeant Douglas Aiken parked his

Weasel alongside of the mill and began to assist with the wounded.

Barclay saw some of his wounded being taken by German medics into the Mill.

"Howe, Anderson, come with me". The three American infantrymen burst into the mill through the half open oaken doors thinking they were on a rescue mission. Instead, they found a room filled with wounded from both sides. Major Albert Brendt looked up from a shattered German soldier.

"Put down your weapons. We're an aide station and we already have more than enough business without you cowboys breaking in here."

It took Barclay a few seconds to realize what he was seeing: medics and surgeons working on more wounded men than he had seen in his entire time fighting. Every one of them were mauled beyond his comprehension. The cries, screams, whimpers, the sight of severed arms and legs, intestines oozing out of torn open bellies, blackened holes where eyes had once been, some eyes dangling onto charred cheeks by their optic nerves, brains bulging into helmets held on only by their chin straps. The smell of blood, urine, shit, mud filling the entire main room of the mill. Then in the far end of the room, the dead, stacked like howitzer shells. It would have been better to carry them outside to freeze in the snow, but the needs of the living outweighed that nicety. Barclay, Howe and Anderson reeled backwards out to the mill.

The final flare had at last burned out, plunging the gorge into darkness.

"Come on," shouted Barclay, as they re-joined the remnants of the 112th. "Get up the trail."

Von Heinz and Lt. Moore continued their exchange of artillery. Shell after shell arced over the Kall River gorge screaming on their way to deliver destruction. No one bothered ducking anymore.

The 112th made their best speed up the eastern wall, slowing only as they approached the top, expecting at any minute to be mowed down by the 272nd GVD soldiers. But they had pulled back in the darkness to the ruins of Kommerscheidt waiting to receive the Americans.

"Hold up here. Spread out to form a firing line, dig in while you can", said Barclay.

"Rosinsky, take Howe and Anderson and do a little recon on our German friends. See where they are. Do not engage unless you have to."

This time, Howe did not even bother to groan. The three men moved forward as silently as they could toward the Germans awaiting them in the darkness.

Corporal Herman Schneider and Private Ernst Locher had moved into the basement of one of the destroyed houses in Kommerscheidt. Locher's shoulder was only minimally stiff and ached in the cold. Schneider's plan was to try to wait out any attack in the basement and see what developed. He still hoped to be able to surrender to the Americans.

The destroyed town was only a black mound against a dark sky. Rosinsky in the lead, Anderson to the left, Howe to the right, their bayonetted M-1 Garands at the ready. The sounds of distant impacts of the artillery thudding in their chests in time with their heartbeats. The sucking mud had frozen into sharp, irregular ridges making quiet progress impossible. Their breathing sounded thunderous to them and each awaited the fatal bullet. Anderson remembered the last recon they did and nearly fell into a foxhole full of Germans. So, he was in no hurry to push their luck. Three days later, 112th was to be pulled back to a rest area near St. Vith. They just had to survive the next forty-eight hours, east of the Kall.

#

Col. Kurt Hindman of the 116th Panzer Division, the "Windhunds - Greyhounds", brought his new Panther IV to a rocking stop inside the tree line facing the American 28th Division. He had new tanks, a full platoon and new crews. He had new "gerucht" or rumors about the Americans facing him: three depleted regiments partially filled with new replacements. The 112th, 109th and the110th Pennsylvania National Guard were recently pulled out of the Huertgen Forest and the ravines surrounding Schmidt. Hindman did not know much about the American National Guard as a fighting force. He assumed that they would be "junior Schulteam", the junior varsity to the regular American army. He held the Volksgrenadier Divisions in equally low regard, filled with kidnapped old men and teenagers. He and other remaining elite units of armor and infantry had been held back from the fighting of the winter of 1944, so far, to refit, re-equip and train for the final German offensive that would, Hitler assured them all, smash through the depleted American lines to the Meuse then turn north to split the Canadians and British armies with the final objective being Antwerp.

No, it was not the Allied armies facing him, nor the lack of air support, nor his own depleted Grenadiers that worried him. It was fuel. He had less than half of the amount needed to move his Panzers to Antwerp. His first objectives were the American fuel dumps which he had to capture intact if there was any chance for Hitler's fantasy to come true. He also knew there was no chance in hell that the Americans would let that happen.

He took off his cap and headset, sighed deeply and tried to rub the fatigue from his face. Nine days from Christmas and he was waiting for the artillery barrage which would, he was told, blast the ragged American line of infantry in front of him into oblivion. He ordered his tank platoon to shut down their engines to conserve fuel.

Right on time, 5:30 am, Oberleutnant Heinz von Kleist's 88s let loose. The rounds screeched over friend and foe alike to shatter the thin line of Pennsylvanians in their path.

Chapter Twenty-One:
The Bulge: Day Two

"Goddamit, goddamit all to hell," shouted Corporal Jeffery Howe. "What the fuck is this?" Most of the 112th Pennsylvania along with rest of the 109th and 110th had been pulled out of the Huertgen to a quiet sector where the generals did not expect the Germans would be able to mount much of an offensive. All but Co. E of the 112th which had been left east of the Kall as a "trip wire" for when the Germans attacked. They were to delay them as long as they could before retreating across the river. It was hoped that the re-deployment of the regiments would allow them time to assimilate green replacements, get new equipment issue, dry their feet out and have three hot meals a day for a while. Instead, they were the aiming point for the "Wacht am Rhein": Hitler's illusion of a final offensive to drive the Allies back, split the Americans from the British and Canadian armies to the north and to make them sue for peace. Then his Wehrmacht would turn to confront the Russians pressing in from the east. He had committed most of his armor and best troops to the effort. He attacked under the clouds to prevent the Allied air forces from intervening.

All Howe knew was that he was watching his last hope of every seeing home again blowing up in his face.

Von Heist's barrage lasted ninety minutes. In the stunning silence after it, cries for medics rang out. But everyone's hearing was so deafened that no one responded for a good ten minutes during which time was lost and lives bled out.

"What's that?" asked Anderson when quiet and hearing was restored to their immediate world. They strained their hearing to make out the slightest sound. There was a merest rumble.

"It's fucking tanks," shouted Howe. "Get the bazookas up here."

75 mm rounds from the Panzers began to impact around them. Von Heinz's guns continued to pound the valley rim where the 112th clung to fading hope.

"Jesus Christ, we can't stay here. We've got to fall back," Howe looked around for Lt. Barclay. There was no question that he was right but to do so without orders to coordinate movement, the withdrawal would soon turn into a rout. Their only safety lay in being able to have a disciplined retreat, allowing squads and fire teams to support each other. Finally, the order came.

"Able, Baker Companies, fall back," shouted Lt. Barclay but without a hint of panic. "Easy Company, lay down suppressing fire."

The two bazooka teams had just climbed to the top of the gorge and fired their rounds into any group of Germans trying to form an assault. Hinman watched from the open turret of his Panzer IV tank as the bazooka teams tore up his infantry until he figured they had exhausted their rounds.

"Now, get after them," he shouted and his row of Panzers exploded into life, accelerating towards the thin American line.

"Shit, shit, shit, Lieutenant, we have got to go now!" shouted Howe.

Lieutenant Barclay called into the 229th Field Artillery which was still near the western rim.

"Two-two-niner, field artillery. We've tanks and infantry in the open advancing, on Kommerscheidt. We could use some help."

"I see them," answered Lieutenant Alfred Moore. "Hunker down, rounds on the way."

Moore had two of his five guns fire wooly-pete rounds to discourage the infantry and HEAP rounds in the other three for the tanks. Under their cover, Easy Company with Howe and Anderson retreated back across the Kall. Once again. After the fight for Kommerscheidt, the 112th was down to barely two hundred men.

#

The ready room of the 100th Bomb Group at Thorpe Abbotts was filling with the one hundred forty officers – pilots, co-pilots, navigators and bombardiers – that were available to man the thirty-five B17s the Group could get airborne for that day's mission. As the only group rested enough to fly, the planes had been scrounged from other groups to replace the 100th's Regensburg losses. The one-armed Major in charge of the briefing waited with growing impatience as the barely conscious men found their coffee and settled into their seats. The missions had increased to five per week, deep into Germany, bombing a decreasing number of targets, it was true, but those targets were heavily defended with deadly radar-guided 88mm antiaircraft guns. The loss of planes had decreased with the advent of the P51 Mustang escorts but the Major looked out at the group of men, dotted with unfamiliar faces. He no longer wanted to know their names or backgrounds. He had tried but only became confused, calling them by dead crewmen's names. This was seen as a bad omen by the remaining men, further unnerving an already jittery bunch.

The Major had gotten his twenty-five missions in earlier in the war, participating in the raids of '42 and '43. He had lost his arm to a frag that had decapitated his co-pilot over Bremen. The torniquet his top turret gunner applied had saved all their lives as he was able to fly the plane back to Thorpe Abbotts. He felt the loss of each of the crews. His despondency grew with each mission he had to brief. So far, he had hidden it from the crews, projecting a confidence and calm that he no longer felt. How much longer he could do this was anybody's guess. He could request rotation back home and no one would dispute it. But he continued briefing as he felt no one understood what he was asking his crews to do better than he. The drinking on off-mission days helped. By the time of this briefing, December 18th, 1944, word was coming from Belgium and northern France of a new German offensive which looked increasingly dangerous.

"It looks like the Krauts mean business this time," the Major said pulling aside the black curtain. The hated red lines leading from Thrope Abbotts to somewhere along the Belgium/Luxemburg border and the Ardennes Forest.

"We are two days into a major offensive. Don't ask me where the hell they got the men and tanks, but they did – lots of them. They are essentially re-tracing the 1940 Ardennes Offensive route. Hitler must have remembered it fondly from back then. The objective this time is not Paris but the fuel dumps around St. Vith. The Panzers can't run on Hitler's hot air and we have pretty much destroyed his fuel supplies. So, the thinking is that they are making this last, desperate lunge to get fuel. Then, probably turn north towards Antwerp. They are doing this depending on the cloud cover to hide under. It is true that the weather has kept us grounded but our weather boys assure us that the clouds will disperse beginning this afternoon allowing some recon P51s to fly over and see what they can see. If the weather does break, our weather wizards assure us that skies will be suitable for bombing run through Christmas at least.

"Therefore, gentlemen, the plan is the have the 100th BG, gassed, armed and manned, ready to go when we hear from our recon. When they confirm sighting the Krauts, hopefully in their holiday finest and multitude, we will launch and bomb the hell out of them. Now it is not just us on this jaunt but at least five other groups. They will get their assignments and times so as to minimize us running into each other. We will have P51 escorts. The 359th based in East Wretham, the 357th from Leiston and the 356th coming out of Martlesham Heath. We will rendezvous at Buncher 28, rallying on a Judas Plane. It should be pretty crowded at the Buncher so watch out.

"We have infantry in the area from the Huertgan blocking the Monschau corridor. Our targets are the troop concentrations, rail yards and supply depots which have been moved up in anticipation of this Kraut operation. That is why accurate recon is essential as we expect the bomb line to be only one mile from our forward positions.

"It all depends on the recon and the weather. Any questions?"

Every morning, afternoon and evening from the 18th to the 24th was socked in by dense, clinging, yellow tinged sulfurous fog preventing the 100th from taking off. Even the recon P51s could not get to the end of the main runway at Thorpe Abbotts, let alone to Belgium. The news from the Ardennes was growing more desperate with each passing hour. The crews were frustrated and sought what distractions they could. Joe Hanover was not as distraught as other members of his crew. He found the extra time spent with Virginia at the "Fox and Hens" were the best hours of his war.

The village had been getting ready for Christmas, their fifth since 1939, and they all prayed it would be their last in wartime. Festive lights, decorated trees and streamers festooned all the cottages, hedges and pubs. A big Christmas party was planned for Christmas Eve. Even the mission lights over the bar in the EM club seemed brighter. The had been steadily green for more than a week - no mission today. Then on the 23rd, the light switched to yellow – standby for a mission and by early on the morning of Christmas Eve it turned red – mission scheduled. The MPs scoured Thorpe Abbotts for celebrating airmen, officers were re-called from London and by 10 am December 24th, the thirty-five planes of the 100th fit for duty were filled with their slightly less than fit for duty crews. Their target was the Luftwaffe base at Babenhausen. *The Usual Suspects* was to fly lead. Hanover had been a late addition to replace Charles Zinn at the right waist. He had his thirty missions and got to sit this one out.

As soon as they crossed into Germany, the flak had found them. The clear skies made the accuracy of their "enfernungsmesser 1-meter" range finders deadly, more so than their radars and planes began to explode leaving no chance of survivors.

"What the hell is this?" Joe said into his throat mic. "I thought we had taken out their AA batteries."

"Well, it's Christmas for the Krauts, too, you know," said Lt. Forbes, the co-pilot of *The Usual Suspects.* "Maybe they got some new 88s from Papa Hitler in their stockings."

"You know," said Captain Wilson, "as a new little wrinkle, they have been lining up their Tiger tanks which have 88s of their very own. Those sons of bitches can fire straight up to twenty-two thousand feet, and they move around. That may explain their renewed interest in us."

More Fortresses fell victim to the 88s, a total of four before they reached the IP. Then the Gustavs hit, swarming like bees protecting their hive.

"Shit, there goes *Lonesome Ranger.* Any 'chutes?"

"Nope," said Payne, the belly turret gunner. A bf109G, a Gustav, flashed by Payne and he trained his twin .50 cals on the retreating fighter. He was rewarded with a thickening trail of black smoke.

"Here come our Little Friends," shouted Forbes.

The Mustangs combined from three fields, gathered at Buncher 28, had arrived. Now the lethal ballet of air-to-air combat began. The Germans had their own "Little Friends" only these were not so little. The FW 190 D, the Doras, heavily armed and armored used the Messerschmitts to fend off the Mustangs as they concentrated on the bombers. The German fighters combined with the unrelenting flak began to tear apart the B17 formations.

Joe Hanover in the right waist of *The Usual Suspects* seemed to have either a Dora or a Gustav in his sights all the time. He barely had to track them without scoring some hits. Shell casing rained down, 20- and 30-millimeter German rounds sang through the fuselage.

Finally, the words all the crews were waiting for, "I have the ship. Bomb bay doors open", Lt. Norman Ems the bombardier, said. An interminable minute later, "Bombs away".

The Usual Suspects, freed of her two-thousand-pound load, sped up and began to rock with every close explosion of flak. Payne in the belly turret took his eyes off the swarming fighters to watch the bomb loads impact on the ground: nice, green German farmland.

"Fuck! We're short, about two miles short," he shouted into his mask. "What the hell."

Being the lead ship, the rest of the 100th dropped their bombs harmlessly on the farmland as well. Babenhausen could relax, for now. The 100th would have to return another day.

"Shit, Ems," said Captain Wilson, the pilot, "What happened?" There was no answer. Ems had moved back to his gun position in the nose. That explanation was for the debrief – if they got there. There was the lethal business at hand of getting out of Germany and back home.

Captain Robert Mullen of the 357th Fighter Group, Leiston, serving as close escort, saw the bombs fall short as well. He was not sure if the Gustav pilot in his gunsight had noted the mistake as well. Mullen half hoped the Kraut had as that might ease his passage. His .50 caliber rounds ripped into the plane ahead. He flew through the smoke and flames.

"Four bombers, two fighters, forty-two guys lost to bomb a fucking field," thought Mullen. "Jesus Christ, there better be a good explanation for this."

#

"Not for us this time, it seems, Kleine," said Corporal Schneider as they watched the air battle pass above them.

"At least not this time," he thought. They were back with the 272nd GVD and back in the holes at Schmidt that they had been driven out of days before. With the unrelenting cloud cover, there had been no American planes for a week. But now the clouds had parted and almost immediately, the Americans were back. There was no letup in the artillery barrages. Between their own 88s and the American 155s, Schneider mused that nothing could get through the shells passing overhead to harm them on the ground. He knew that was nothing but wishful thinking.

The Volks-Grenadier Divisions like the 272nd had been relegated to rear area security while the Fifth Panzer Army of General Hasso von Monteuffel swept by them to attack the center of the thin American line held by the 112th Pennsylvania National Guard. Von Monteuffel held both the Americans and the VGD in contempt when compared to his Panzergrenadieren. His mission was to move through the American line quickly and seize the American fuel depots around St. Vith to feed his hungry tanks.

The element of surprise was his greatest strength. Not only had the cloud cover kept the Allied air reconnaissance in England but the strict radio silence imposed on the army had actually worked. Most of the communication between commanders was by land line and therefore could not be intercepted by Allied intelligence. With these factors in his favor, von Monteuffel felt confident that his Panzer IV and Panther tanks would make short work of capturing the fuel.

There would then be no stopping him. Delay, the German commander knew, was his most formidable enemy. Every hour of delay meant he was burning fuel he could not spare.

"Anderson and Howe, come with me," shouted Sergeant Rosinsky.

"What the fuck is it now?" whined Howe.

"We're supplying security for the engineers while they lay some mines in front of our position. It'll be a nice break from digging foxholes, don't you think?"

"Aren't we supposed to be in the quiet section of the line?" asked Anderson.

"Yes,' replied Rosinsky, "but what is to our rear?"

"A bunch of REMF pussies," muttered Howe.

"Besides them: the fuel dumps at St. Vith. Intel is sure that the entire Wehrmacht is running on fumes and they have got to get some gas from somewhere. St. Vith is the closest spot."

"You mean there ain't a plan to blow that shit up if there is even one Kraut nearby?" asked Howe. "Let 'em come, I say and torch it in front of their faces."

"You see, Howe, that's why you're still not a general. Any number of things could go wrong and if the Krauts get the fuel, the war goes on for another year or so. Intel is pretty sure that this is the Krauts' last gasp. We stop them here and that is the ballgame for them."

"But we don't know for sure the Krauts are coming our way, right?" asked Anderson.

"Not for sure but it can't hurt to be ready, right? So, let the nice engineers lay as many mines as they want. We will get lots of bazookas up here for you all. The job is to delay the Panzers, kill as many as we can but keep them out of St, Vith. Got it?"

The barrage signaling the start of von Monteuffel's attack began early in the morning of December 16th. There had been no air recon due to cloud cover so the extent and size of the Panzer attack was unknown. Howe and Anderson were dug in as deep as they could. Howe handled their bazooka with Anderson loading him. The minefield began one hundred yards to their front and extended another three hundred yards beyond. The mile and a half beyond the mine field was all pre-registered by the 229th Field Artillery. Even Howe had to admit that there was some "heavy shit" in front of them. It was still cold comfort for him.

Von Monteufel's Fifth Panzer kicked off when the final artillery barrage had finished. The heavens remained overcast. The artillery had opened holes in the minefield in front of the 112th. He did not know the depth of the minefield and assumed that before the field was pre-registered by the American artillery. Speed was his only hope. He would have to leave his Panzergrenadieren behind, to follow as best they could. He had already commandeered as much of the 272 GVD. Locher and Schneider included, he could find. Even though, he did not agree with Hitler's planned breakout to the Meuse, he had his orders and would carry them out.

"Angreifen, angreifen, (attack)", he shouted into his Funkgerat or FuG5 intertank radio. Hauptman Kurt Hinman led his line of ten Panzer IVs forward toward the 112th's line of foxholes. The rest of the sixty tanks he had available followed close behind. The front line of tanks was essentially sacrificial lambs to clear out a path through the mines. Von Monteuffel knew he had only minutes before the American artillery would begin to decimate the rest of his force.

"Schneller, schneller, (faster)," he shouted into his FuG5. Hinman was through the open ground in front of the minefield before the artillery could arrive. He felt it was his honor and duty to lead the attack.

A Panzer next to him hit a mine and exploded. One to the left and behind hit another mine, blowing its track of and sending it careening into the path of a third tank. Von Kleist's artillery had done a decent job on the mine field so that von Monteuffel lost only two more tanks and the follow-on force with the 272nd GVD got through relatively intact. That was bad news for the 112th, Howe and Anderson in particular.

Their bazooka rounds were of little use against the thickly armored glacis of the Panzers. They tried for the tracks but von Monteuffel's strategy of maximum speed meant that they would overrun the advanced American positions in a matter of minutes.

"Fall back, fall back," shouted Lieutenant Barclay. "Back to the secondary positions." These were trenches and tank traps again meant to slow, not stop the Panzer onslaught. Despite the snow cover, the 112th's position was engulfed in dust and smoke. Visibility was cut to ten yards. The continuous explosions had deafened everyone so shouted orders had little effect. Lieutenant Barclay went from foxhole to foxhole to signal the men to withdraw. The retreat was orderly without panic but with as much speed as they could muster. Still, the bazooka teams stopped and fired at any visible tank. Another Panzer was knocked out.

The men of the 112th, the "Bloody Bucket Regiment" added to their reputation. Men were falling all around Howe and Anderson. The Panzers had two MG34 machine guns and these did most of the work. The 75mm main gun were being held in reserve for use against pillboxes and command centers. The retreating men of the 112th did what they could, stopping every twenty yards to fire their bazooka rounds against the oncoming Panzers. Howe and Anderson dropped into a trench and turned to face the tanks.

"Make this one count," Anderson shouted to Howe. "It's the last one."

Howe calmly lined up his sight on the right track of the nearest Panzer that appeared out of the dust and misting snow. Anderson tapped him on the helmet and their last round was away. It struck the track and the tank swerved to the right exposing its relatively lightly armored side to a second bazooka team who took it out.

"Alright, let's get the hell out of here," Howe shouted. They made their best speed over the uneven ground, carrying the bazooka tube in the expectation there would be more rounds to be had from less lucky bazooka teams. Howe and Anderson with the rest of the skeletal 112th scrambled through the tank traps that were being made as the retreat progressed. None of the barbed wire, fallen logs that made up the traps would stop a Panzer. They were more means to hang mines on which would detonate when a Panzer hit them.

Despite these efforts, the Fifth Panzer Army rolled forward, pushing the American line ever backwards towards St. Vith which was taken in two days of hard fighting. What fuel that could not be moved back in the retreat was blown up almost in von Montueffel's face.

Bastogne had held until relieved by the 101st on Christmas. The attack on Bastogne had drawn off enough men and tanks from the main thrust against the three Pennsylvania regiments' fighting retreat further slowed the tanks, burning through their fuel. The Fifth Panzer's assault ground to a halt short of the Meuse River. Realizing his entire force could be cut off, von Monteufell ordered his own retreat. One by one, his tanks and armored personnel carriers ran out of gas and had to be abandoned. By January, 25, 1945, the Fifth Panzer Army returned to their original lines.

Chapter Twenty-Two:
No Respite

"Tell me, Herr Major, how did you end up here?" asked Oberstabsartz Genter van Stettgen. They were in their third day of their informal joint venture and had become comfortable with each other.

"Well, I was drafted out of my second year of surgical residency at the University of Illinois in Chicago. That was two years and a lifetime ago. They ran me through the medical officer training course at Ft. Sam Houston in Texas and six weeks later, I was on a transport ship landing three days after D-Day. After that it is kind of a blur, just small tent hospitals following the fighting, especially after St. Lo until we got here, wherever 'here' is."

"So, not a career officer? You have plans after the war?"

"I try not to think about 'after the war'. Just seems like bad luck. How about you?"

"I am originally from Heidelburg, I did all my training there at the University of Heidelburg and was slotted for a professorship. My family descended from the aristocracy which made us suspects. I was in college when the 'Night of the Long Knives' in '34 happened. It was Hitler's attempt to purge the upper ranks of the military, which at that time was predominantly drawn from the aristocracy, and replace them with his nonentities. I was a junior grade officer in '38 when 'Krystal Nacht' happened and the hunting of the Jews began in earnest. I and my family evidently did not show adequate enthusiasm and we lost our home in Heidelburg to a Nazi functionary. All hope for my advancing in the Heer is gone. I was fortunate to be allowed to remain a doctor.

"I, too, have no thoughts for after the war. Hitler and his madmen will not allow Germany to exist if they lose the war, which they almost certainly will. I see your bombers every day to which we have no answers. The rapidity of your army's advance after Normandy was slowed only by logistics, not our forces."

"You guys still seemed to be able to push us out of the Kall valley and put up some hard fighting."

"A dying spasm, I fear... I hope. I have no personal knowledge, of course, but this last offensive will finish us, I think. Talking with our wounded, they tell of tanks running out of fuel, bullets, shells. They speak of the necessity of capturing the fuel dumps around St. Vith to sustain our efforts. That is a slender thread from which to hang the Third Reich. The Luftwaffe is nowhere to be seen. Our artillery is the only branch that is capable of making a show but, as you know, without infantry to back up their efforts, they are only making foxholes for your troops."

As if he had been listening, von Kleist's 88s arched, screaming over their heads to continue their chase of the Americans. Soon, Alfred Moore's 105 counterbattery fire answered and after half an hour, quiet returned.

"It's like they are keeping up appearances, just phoning it in," remarked Brandt. "I have long ago stopped trying to see any sense in this. It makes you think someone, somewhere: Hitler, Roosevelt, God had a number of dead in mind and we just have to keep up the killing until we reach it."

"As good an explanation as any I've heard. But we are doctors and therefore suspected of insufficient ardor by our military betters."

They were working side-by-side on horribly injured soldiers; they often did not even know which side. The mill on the Kall River was a life-saving way-station for these wounded boys. The two surgeons worked without ever knowing the ultimate outcomes for their patients. It was enough for now that they were giving them a chance. Evacuation remained the biggest challenge. They were still dependent on Douglas Aiken and his M29 Weasel. He had been assured at the main aide station near Vossenach that help in the form of more medics and Weasels was coming but he grimly thought to himself that he would believe that when he saw it. For now, he made the run with wounded to Vossenack and returned with supplies. There was often ground fog and overcast so he felt concealed from von Kleist's guns for now. The rumbling sound of his engine was well known to the medics and willing hands met him at both ends.

"Hey, Major," he called through the doors of the mill. "I was able to get more sterile supplies, plasma and even a couple of not too old O-negs. There is also a case of K-rats."

"God, Aiken, you are a wonder," said Brandt.

"Many thanks, Sergeant," said von Stettgen. "Can you tell us what are the chances of our having enough time to eat today?"

"No guarantees, Sir. Still plenty of action. Your boys," when speaking to von Stettgen, he had stopped calling them "Krauts", "are pushing us pretty hard to the west, trying for a break-out I presume. Meanwhile, Bastogne is still a bastard but I hear the 101st and Patton are coming to relieve them. The only thing preventing us from being up to our asses in blown up boys is the overcast keeping the fly-boys grounded. The 112th Pennsylvania, my boys, by the way, are hanging on by their fingernails for now."

"I didn't know you were a Pennsylvania man. What part?" asked Brandt.

"Out Lancaster way. Family's been there since the Revolution. Long line of Amish folk which explains my medical slant."

"Oh, why is that, Sergeant?" asked von Stettgen.

"Pacificists, don't fight for nobody or nothing."

"Well, may your kind grow and spread. That may be our only hope."

"It'd be nice, but don't seem likely. Gotta go."

"Geht mit Gott," whispered von Stettgen.

The shelling had slackened to the point where the bodies inside the Mill could be moved outside into the snow for collection by Graves Registration companies for both sides. They stacked the Americans to the left, the Germans to the right, the unidentifiable were evenly divided between the two piles. The unrelenting cold and snow helped only the dead. The detritus of the operations which filled the canvas bags, were dumped outside in the snow as well, making their own growing piles.

#

Aiken had three litters on his Weasel as he bumped his way to the top of the Kall River gorge. With each jarring the men cried out.

'It's OK," he told them. "We're almost there." Once at the top, he paused to see what artillery activity there was. There was plenty but seemed to be towards the widening gap in the American line forced by the German tanks to create their bulge. He was surprised that the tanks had not seemed to make as much progress as their earlier mad dash had promised. Through rents in the snow, mist and dust thrown up by the artillery strikes he could see immobilized Panzers. He reached the aide station at Vossenach and helped to carry in his wounded, receiving litters in return.

"What's the word on the Germans? They seem to be slowing down," he asked a medic.

"Radio chatter is that the 112th has stopped them. Between the mines, artillery and their own bazookas, they are making the Krauts re-group. But they can't last much longer just sitting there. Somebody's going to blow them all to Hell."

"Maybe some shit-for-brains general will think of that and pull them," Aiken said as he loaded medical supplies for the mill aide station. "Things remain plenty busy in the valley. Bodies and body parts are piling up. This fucking cold at least keeps them from rotting. I'll be back."

Lieutenant Barclay and Sergeant Rosinsky were rounding up as a many warm bodies of the 112th that he could find.

"What's the plan, Lieutenant?" asked Anderson. Howe had long ago learned not to ask.

"We've got them stopped for now. Regiment wants us to counterattack and drive 'em before their infantry catches up. Full ammo loads and as many grenades as you can carry."

"Oh, for the love of God," exploded Howe. "We stopped them, now we're supposed to take 'em out with our bare hands? This is totally FUBAR." Nevertheless, he and Anderson loaded up with grenades and waited to go.

As they waited in their waterlogged foxhole, watching over the stopped Panzer column, Anderson said, "Why aren't they moving? They gotta know the 105s are on the way. They are sitting ducks."

Right on cue, a Panzer was hit. They ducked down expecting a blast but none came.

"What the fuck?" said Howe. "It didn't blow up?"

Then came Barclay's order. "Move out, let's go."

Anderson and Howe sprinted forward to the first undamaged tank. Amazed they were not cut down by the tank's MG34, they climbed on top, Anderson opened the commander's half hatch and Howe dropped in two grenades. Both recoiled off the turret to the snow expecting the fuel tanks to explode. They were on to the second using the same approach, disabling that Panzer as well. Again, no explosion. There was also no fire coming from any of the three remaining tanks.

"What the fuck?" asked Howe.

They cautiously climbed aboard the third tank in line. Anderson dropped inside. There were still shells in the rack, .30 mm ammo belt led to the coaxial gun. In passing, he glanced at the dials and saw the fuel indicator on empty.

"Jesus, Jeff, they're out of gas. That's why they stopped and didn't blow up when we hit them. Son of a bitch, what do you know?"

Herr General der Panzertruppe von Monteuffel and his Fifth Panzerarmee were forced to abandon their tanks, armored cars and even the General's staff car and walk back to where they had started the "Unternehmen Wacht am Rhein" just behind the Siegfried Line. The "Bulge" had been contained after ten days of hard fighting.

#

The weather broke on December 24th, and was celebrated by the roar of Merlin and Alison engines as wave after wave of P51s, P47s followed by B17 s and B24s, all arising from their airfields, Wright-Cyclone, Pratt and Whitney engines joining as the heavy bombers took to the sky, heading east. The safety of the bomber crews depended on their flying tight box formations, the capabilities of the gunners but just as critically, on the ground crews, most of them eighteen-year-olds, responsible for the air-worthiness of the immense, complicated machines, the like of which the world had never seen.

TSgt. Joe Hanover settled in at his spot in the right waist of *The Usual Suspects,* having tested his gun. He fought off sleep by intermittently disconnecting his heated, "Blue Bunny" flight suit from the heat source until he was shivering. This way he could remain alert. The bomber streams were encountering the Luftwaffe less frequently in the months since the arrival of the P51s and their long-range escort capability. Every so often, the German fighter command could still put up a maximum effort with hundreds of 109s, overwhelming both gunners and escorts alike. So as much as he'd like to spend the ten-to-twelve-hour flights dreaming of Virginia, there were reminders that he has still not out of the woods.

The *Suspects* was lead ship once again. They were on their way to Berlin, deep inside Germany. The weather was clear at their cruising altitude of 24,000 feet.

"Bogeys, bogeys, bogeys, eleven o'clock, three and six o'clock. There must be hundreds of them," shouted Payne in the belly turret. Forbes, the co-pilot, chimed in, "Plenty up here as well. There go the Mustangs but stay alert."

Soon, the fighters were swirling and diving, firing and exploding all around the bomber formations. Red whips of .50 caliber fire lashed out from the bombers themselves. Flying Fortresses were being hit as if they were sitting still. Some started smoking, some exploded, some showed no signs of being in trouble except that they began their almost graceful dives to their final landings.

Captain James Wilson, the captain of the *Suspects*, keyed his mic.

"Alright, there are a lot of those sombitches, but we've been through worse than this. Stay sharp, pick your targets and make 'em sorry they fucked with the 100th. Good hunting."

Joe lined up on a fast-approaching 109, the leading edges of his wings aflame with .20 caliber machinegun fire. He depressed the trigger on his .50 caliber and had the satisfaction of watching the Messerschmitt dissolve in flames. The rapid-paced narration of the other gun positions, calling out German fighters, remarking on close calls, reporting the loss of B17s formed an enveloping soundscape to Joe's personal battles with 109 after 109. Despite the continuous attacks against the Luftwaffe, the Reich was still able to produce enough planes to produce a final vicious fight to preserve itself.

"Tighten up, tighten up!" shouted Captain Wilson on the interplane frequencies. The natural tendency to move out of formation, trying to dodge incoming Messerschmitts as well as the distraction caused by the attack, making pilots pay less attention to their slots in the ever-decreasing formations and weakened the protection of a tight box and its combined firepower.

The fighter escort of Mustangs was once again led by Captain Robert Mullen of the 363rd Fighter Squadron. He felt secure in pursuing the first wave of 109s, thinking there was no way the Germans could mount as big a fighter sortie as was now becoming evident. He cursed himself for falling for the German two-pronged attack.

"Where the fuck, did they get all these planes?" he thought. He keyed his mic.

"Return to the bombers, they've been jumped by a second wave of Krauts."

One by one the sleek silver Mustangs peeled off and swept down on the beleaguered bombers. Mullen was able to make an easy kill on a 109 as the German was diving on a smoking B17. It was too late to save the plane and its ten-man crew. The Fortress blew apart, making Mullen fly through the combined flame and smoke of the destroyed plane.

"Ten minutes to the IP." Wilson informed the bomber flight.

"Ten minutes," thought Hanover as he saw his tracers skim over another 109. "Jesus Christ, we aren't even half-way there. There is no fucking way we are getting out of this."

.30 caliber rounds ripped through the *Suspects'* fuselage just aft of Joe's window, through the crew hatch and out the other side.

The re-appearance of the Mustangs was only slightly reassuring for the bombers. The 109s began to take a real beating and far more of them fell out of the sky than B17s or P51s. Over his year of dogfighting with the Germans, Mullen had gained a respect for his adversaries and saw in them pilots equal to himself in terms of skill and lethality. But lately he felt there was a definite decline in the Germans' quality. The planes were as good if not better that he had faced before but the pilots were not as sharp.

"You can make a good plane in a week," he thought, "but it takes time to make a good pilot." He did a barrel roll over a Fortress which brought him on the tail of a now helpless Messerschmitt. He calmly depressed his firing button on his stick and the 109 burst into flames. The Germans disengaged, letting the bombers have a slight respite until they hit the flak batteries surrounding Berlin.

#

Spearheading the last, organized German Panzer attack was what was left of the 116th Panzer, "Der Windhunds". The 272nd Volksgrenadieren Division had been incorporated as Panzergrenadieren to support this final push. Hitler's tactic of holding back his best tanks and men to fuel this operation was successful. It took the Americans completely by surprised due to the week-long cloud cover that blinded the air recon. There had been only selected chatter to be picked up Ultra, lulling the Allies further. Fighting on their home turf had allowed all important communications to be done by land line. Even the name of the operation, "Unternehmen der Rhein: Watch on the Rhine", did not indicate activity. The Germans were finished, everyone knew it and this lack of any activity on their part was taken as proof. Everyone wanted to believe it. The war-weariness was overwhelming. All anyone wanted was to go home in one piece. The Americans believed the end was near.

But that was all blown up by von Kleist's 88s marching down the Monschau Corridor towards the 112th Pennsylvania, the unwitting point of attack for Hitler's final blow.

Howe and Anderson now sheltered in the Panzer IV that minutes before, they had planned to blow up. This was only the third tank they had ever been in and the only one under attack. The rocking caused by near misses, the shrapnel twanging off the turret, the choking smoke and dust beginning to fill their lungs and panic them. Their choice seemed to be staying in the tank and suffocating or bailing out and likely becoming splotches of blood and bone strewn about the ground.

"Christ Almighty, Henry, what the fuck are we going to do?"

"I think our chances are better in the tank. Maybe open up the hatches for some air. Hopefully, the shells will move on down the valley."

"Yeah, then followed by fucking infantry.

"Holy Mary, mother of God..."

"Are you praying, Jeff? I know you're scared when the prayin' starts," teased Anderson. Another near miss seemed to almost lift the tank up. "Maybe you could put in a good word for me."

Both knew the 88s had them bracketed and that time was running out when the next round landed twenty yards away, the next further still.

"Jesus, Jeff, they're moving on. What do you think: stay or go?"

"Stay, just hunker down for now."

Their hearing was beginning to clear only for them to hear German voices: passing troops following up the artillery barrage. They made themselves as small as they could and waited for the "potato-masher" hand grenade to be tossed through the open hatch.

The 272nd GVD moved swiftly by the abandoned Panzers to take advantage of the barrage and its disruption of the 112th Pennsylvania's skirmish line which closed off the Monschau Corridor. Locher, following Schneider's lead, marched grimly forward with their Karabiner 94s, pointed to the front. All the while, Schneider had been slowly angling to the side of the column towards the trees. He had decided to sit this one out. He had fought in two lost wars already. Ernst had been wounded and nearly died already. They had both, he decided, fulfilled their duty to the Fatherland. Let Hitler and Goebbels finish this one off.

The ruse worked. Schneider found a thicket a few yards into the woods and dragged Ernst in with him. He knew full well that just getting them out of the fighting would not save them if they were captured by their own company. They would both be shot as deserters. But he liked the odds better this way.

"Herr Schneider, what are we to do now?" asked a very shaken Ernst Locher. "Where has our company gone?"

"Scattered to the winds," he whispered.

Schneider peered over the snowy rim of the shallow trench they had managed to scrape out with their helmets just inside the thicket. They had front-row seats, not the kind anyone would pay money for, as the German attack and the American counter-attack played out before them.

"Howe, Anderson, come with me," shouted Sergeant Rosinsky.

"What's up, Sarge?" asked Anderson. Howe kept his muttered opinion to himself.

"We've got to check the rest of the Panzers and then do a little recon as to just where their former occupants went."

"It's enough for me that they went," muttered Howe, as he and Anderson scrambled atop the next Panzer. Rosinsky stayed on the ground, his M-1 Garand at the ready. As before, Anderson opened the half hatch and Howe dropped in the grenade. Slamming the hatch closed, they both slithered down the side to re-join Rosinski as the grenade blew the hatch open again. They finished the last two Panzer the same way the huddled under the still warm engine of the disabled tank.

"You know, in a properly run army, we'd be able to knock off for the day," said Howe.

"Yeah, well, we're in this army," replied Rosinsky, "and I know what you think of it. So, let's go see if we can find some Krauts. I've got the radio."

Schneider and Locher watched the Americans destroy the tanks and then head away following the foot prints left in the fresh snow.

"Where are they going?" asked Ernst

"They are probably looking for the rest of us. Say, did they look familiar to you?" Schneider asked.

"Not really," he replied, beginning to shake with the cold.

"I am pretty sure they are the Americans that captured us at Schmidt. They treated us very humanely - got you patched up. Isn't it a small war after all? Come on, let's get deeper in the woods for now."

With Schmidt back in German hands, targeting for von Kleist's 88s was much more accurate and shells began to rain down on the American positions around Vossenach. The clouds showed no sign of breaking. Lt. Alfred Moore's 105s had been pulled back from the Kall valley rim and did not have the range to silence the 88s. Unless the 112th Pennsylvania could drive the Germans back beyond the Kall once again, it was doubtful that the Americans could hold Vossenach. To do that, they would need a lot more than they had.

"Sergeant Davis," Captain Ramsey's voice crackled over the radio.

"Yes, Sir, what can I do for you?"

"I'm going to need your tank platoon to lead in the counterattack with the 112th to continue to drive the Krauts back. I have a three-man recon patrol who have checked out the Panzers and confirm they stopped because they ran out of gas. They are moving forward from just east of Dinant where the Krauts stopped, to see if they can re-establish contact with them. I want you to find them and we'll turn this into a recon in force operation. Sergeant Rosinsky and two of his men are making regular contact with us and I'll patch him through to you.

"Any questions?"

"What about those 88s?

"We can't reach them from here and until the weather breaks, we can't bomb the shit out of them either. So, without air recon we'll have to find the Krauts the old fashion way. Lieutenant Barclay will be in command of the 112th. As soon as you two work out a plan and contact Rosinsky, you can kick off."

"Yes, Sir. We'll let you know. Where's Lieutenant Barclay now?"

"Heading your way, he just left the CP and is organizing the 112th. Won't be long."

Davis in *Hell's Fire* confirmed with his other tank commanders, Soames in *Death Wagon* and Suarez in *Adolph's Nightmare,* that they had the plan. All they needed was to wait on Barclay and the infantry. They buttoned up to stay warm. In less than half-an-hour, Barclay had picked up the field hand set on the back of Davis's tank.

"Sergeant Davis, we have got to stop meeting like this," Barclay's familiar voice came over the intercom.

Davis popped the hatch and slid down the glacis. He was joined with the other two tank commanders.

"Good to see you again, Sir." Barclay extended his hand. "Where are your guys," Davis asked, looking around.

"They will be here shortly."

"How many?"

"That's the tricky part. This last push hit us pretty hard. We're down to about three hundred and half of those are replacements and engineers. But on the bright side, Rosinsky's patrol hasn't turned up any Krauts, just abandoned vehicles, all of them out of gas. It doesn't look like Krauts even tried to disable them or booby trap them. According to Rosinski, they've been climbing on board, dropping in grenades and moving on. No sign of them so far.

"How are you fixed for gas?"

"All topped off, ready to go."

"That's fine, we kick off in fifteen minutes. I'll let Rosinski know the cavalry is on the way."

Rosinski, Howe and Anderson, while not breaking any land speed records, were making reasonable progress down the Monschau corridor away from Dinant and the last of the Panzers. It was still too fast for Howe's liking.

"I don't like this, Sarge", he said in a hoarse whisper.

"Imagine my surprise, Howe", Rosinski answered. "You haven't like anything since we left Altoona."

"No, I mean it. Sure as hell, the Krauts have left behind a rear guard just to knock off dumb fucks like us. I say, we get the rest of the gang up here and then we can do a real recon. And another thing, why is it always us? There's lots of other cannon fodder in the company that can get shot up as good as us. Give someone else a chance at a Purple Heart and heartfelt thanks bullshit."

"It's because we do such a good job. Won't your mother be proud to know you are so highly thought of?"

"You mean when she reads it in the obits."

Rosinski let this pass. “Come on, there is a small rise ahead and if we don’t see them from there, we’ll stop there and phone it in. Satisfied?”

Howe just snorted. Five hundred yards later they saw only the footprints of the retreating Germans slowly filling with snow.

Chapter Twenty-Three: Hope and Fear

Joe Hanover had never known such fear: not with endless Messerschmitt bf109 attacks, planes blowing up all around him, his Fortress on fire and spinning towards the earth, drifting down amidst red and green tracers in a torn parachute; never until the moment he tentatively knocked on the door of the "Foxes and Hens". It was a rare day off for him and the pub was closed to give Mr. Standhope a well- deserved rest.

"We're closed today," Mr. Standhope's disembodied voice came through the door. "Come back tomorrow."

"It's me, Mr. Standhope, Joe."

"Ginnie's not here at the moment, she's off to the village to pick up a few things. She'll be back this afternoon."

"Actually, it is you that I hoped to talk to. Just for a moment. I won't have a chance for a week or so."

He could hear the locks undone and the door creaked open. Horace Standhope's rumpled hair and lined, flushed face appeared around the door.

"Joe, is everything alright? You aren't wounded, are you?"

"No, Sir."

"Well, then come in, sit down. I'll put the kettle on."

Joe was so nervous, he could not sit, in fact, he worried he might get sick. Standhope busied himself in the kitchen and came back with the tea and biscuits. Joe's hands shook as he took the cup and saucer.

"Now, then, son, what's on your mind?"

"I have twenty-five missions done and if they don't raise the number again, I may be able to rotate home in a month or so. I think you know how I feel about Virginia and I hope that she feels the same about me." He drew in a shuddering breath.

"Take your time, son. I know she cares very deeply for you."

"Thank you, sir. So, I have come here to ask you for her hand in marriage. If she'll have me, that is." Joe would have rather faced any number of Messerschmitts or flak bursts then endure the few silent minutes with Virginia's father.

Horace Standhope was unsteady when he got up, not just because of his amputated leg. He pretended to busy himself at the bar and when he turned back to face Joe, there were tears in his eyes.

"Of course, Joe, you have my permission to marry Ginnie. Nothing would make me prouder."

Joe felt the blood return to his clammy hands and he began to breathe again.

"But, not until after the war."

Joe felt as if he was being hollowed out. Never had he gone from such a height to an abysmal low in just a few seconds.

"May I ask why, sir?"

Mr. Standhope saw the color drain from Joe's face and became afraid he might faint.

"Come and sit, my boy." He got him a glass of water and sat down beside him on the bench against the wall.

"You have only to look around the airfield, the burned hulks of your bombers. Those are just the ones that make it back here. I cannot imagine what you must have seen over Germany, all the friends you have lost, who have died horribly."

"But missions are getting so much better. The Krauts are running out of planes and pilots. Our Mustang escorts have greatly decreased our losses. I'm flying with one of the best crews. I don't understand."

"We have enough war widows, Joe." Standhope said softly. "I hear Ginny crying whenever you fly. She only starts to live again when she sees you or hear you've made it back one more time. She has lost her mother, I am next to useless to her, indeed, I am a constant reminder of war's cost. You have given me back my Ginny through her love for you. Marrying you then losing you would end all that.

"When you were shot down and no word came for weeks, I feared she would simply waste away to nothing. I was so selfish that I hoped I would die before she did. Imagine how much worse it would be were she to lose her husband.

"No, Joe, as hard as it is on all of us, I must think the worst and do what I can to lessen it.

"So, after the war it must be and then a lifetime together."

He squeezed Joe's arm. Joe's blank stare, halting breaths and stifled sobs, told Standhope all he needed to know. He hoped that the promise of marriage to Ginny would be the thing that would keep Joe alive. He knew from his days in the trenches in France those moments when it would have been so easy to seek release by simply standing up and taking a bullet – the blessed darkness and silence his death would bring. At those times he saw no need for a future that could exist after the butchery of the war. Indeed, what kind of world would it be that could move on from that pointless, endless slaughter? Would he want to live in it, to move on? What good could he find?

But he found Ginny's mother and the too few years they had together. Her dying gift to him was Ginny which made him cherish her all the more and though he knew it was impossible, to shield her from life's horrors. Living on as Joe's widow would cause her more guilt and remorse than she could stand.

"Trust me, Joe. It is better to wait a while now and have a life time together after the war," he repeated.

"You don't think I am going to make it, do you?"

"I don't know, of course. But you have only to look around your own base, at the burned-out hulks, the faces missing from the morning mess to know that nothing is certain except the unbearable grief your death will cause Ginny. Now, you two know the future is uncertain and have come to a degree to accept that. Marriage is a commitment to a hoped-for future: plans are made, dreams transform into a reality which is far harder to lose. The grief is deeper, darker and changes a person forever. Trust me, I know."

They sat silently, side-by-side in the pub, staring at a shaft of sunlight in which dust motes danced. Their reverie was broken by Ginny returning on her bike from the village store with a few purchases.

"Look, Papa, I have some canned peaches. I haven't seen those in ages." She stopped, backlit by the sun's beam when she saw Joe and her father. They were not quick enough to hide their sad expressions.

"Joe, Papa, what is it?" She dropped her basket and took Joe's hands in hers.

"Nothing, my pet," her father said. "Joe heard they might raise the number of missions again. That's all."

"Yeah, that's right," he said, rising to hold her. "It just means I'll be staying here a little longer."

#

The last sortie of the "Green Hearts of Thuringen" with the loss of von Reidel as well as ten planes and the irreplaceable loss of their pilots, had decimated Staffel III/54. Command fell onto the young shoulders of Lieutenant Joachim Brenner, who became second in command to von Rindel when Griebel was killed. Von Reidel's death meant that now he had command of the Staffel. Although the flight had lost most of its planes when Captain Mullen and his Mustangs had found them on the ground, he felt it important to have some continuity and got permission to resurrect the "Green Hearts."

He looked around at the faces in the make-shift ready room in a barn near the road which served as their runway. Only fear and uncertainty looked back. They were all as new as the Messerschmitts they flew. These lay hidden beneath the trees and two large barns. Only Brenner had any combat experience and that was sparse, mainly against the unescorted B17s. The rate of climb and speed made the 109Gs nearly unhittable. They received their sortie orders via a land line strung tenuously over a mile back to headquarters. The Allies had gotten so good with Ultra that even transmissions of a small unit like theirs could be intercepted. They would refuel at the end of their missions at the main base then disburse in the countryside.

All his planes were the newest G-6 variants of the basic Messerschmitt. The "G" got them the "Gustav" nickname. The main improvement was the more powerful supercharged engine which could out climb the Supermarine Spits and Mustangs. Brenner could hardly wait to test himself against the Americans. The raucous jangle of the field telephone let him know his chance was coming.

"Staffel 54, this is base. We have a mission for you."

"Go ahead, base," answered Brenner. He grabbed a pad and pencil to write down the intercept

coordinates which he would transmit to the rest of the Staffel. He confirmed the information and the "Green Hearts" ran to their planes. Brenner glanced skyward hoping to see the contrails of B17s. He saw only crystalline blue sky. The thirty planes of the 100th Bomb Group had just crossed the Belgian coast and had not made their turn yet. Although their ultimate target was not known, the route to the inland targets was often the same so they could be intercepted before they reached their targets.

Lieutenant Brenner tried to pass on the knowledge he had gotten from von Reidel and Griebel. His days of his first missions were not far behind him. He remembered well the mix of fear and exhilaration as he climbed into the cockpit and looked to follow von Reidel's lead. Now, he knew that his new, young Staffel looked to him. He felt a fraud and hoped only to get most of them through their first sortie.

He keyed his mic. "Green Hearts, remember your training: pick your targets, short bursts and rapid maneuvers. We don't need to shoot them all down at once. Now, we fly to victory."

He turned his bf109G onto the road, immediately accelerating and into the air, followed by his nine planes. As they rose through ten thousand feet, they spotted the B17s another ten thousand feet above them.

Excited shouts came over the radio: "There they are! Good hunting today", and similar remarks of the callow youthful pilots. One peeled off and climbed towards their target. He was followed by a second and then a third.

"No, no, no. Come back," shouted Brenner. "We must coordinate our attack."

Technical Sergeant John Payne, in the belly turret of *The Usual Suspects,* saw them first.

"Bandits, bandits, six o'clock low." He easily rotated his twin .50 caliber guns downward and lined up on the first Gustav. The German had already started firing even though he was not in range. Payne lined up the plane in his sight and depressed his triggers. The plane disappeared in a fireball. The belly turrets on the other bombers picked up their own targets. All of the Staffel was destroyed except for Brenner with only minimal damage to the bombers.

"Gott verdamt." Brenner circled out of range of the B17's guns. He did not know what to do. He was not ready to commit meaningless suicide but to return to base without his Staffel meant court marshal and likely a firing squad. Above him diving down through the lumbering bombers came silver sparks: Mustangs and an honorable death.

"To fly and fight until victory or death", he shouted although there were no "Green Hearts" to hear him. He pulled sharply back on his stick, turned on the supercharger and streaked to meet the Americans.

#

Much to Howe's satisfaction, the three-man recon patrol, now about a mile ahead of the rest of the 112th, stopped at the rise and saw no sign of the retreating Germans, even their tracks had filled in under the unrelenting snow. Rosinsky raised Lieutenant Barclay on the radio.

"We've got nothing up here, Sir. There are only footprints, filling with snow, no signs of any vehicles. If we had some air cover, we might be able to finish them off right here and now."

"That would be nice, Sergeant, but we've got this shitty weather for the next three days at least. Stay put and we'll catch up with you. Good job on the Kraut tanks and the recon. We'll see you soon. Out."

"The plan is ok with you, Howe?" asked Rosinski, sarcastically. Without moving forward and the constant alertness that had sustained the three until now, the penetrating cold was beginning to eat at them. The light breeze began to pick up worsening the shivering that possessed them.

"Won't make no difference to us, will it?" replied Howe. "We'll be nothing but frozen meat sticks by the time they get here."

"The tanks are coming: nice warm ride for us, you'll see," Anderson chimed in.

#

Technical Sergeant Enfield Davis stood through his hatch behind the .50 cal as they made their best speed forward. The rest of the Company E with the ragtag force of replacements and engineers that formed the 112th's remnants could do little better than a slow walk. But after an hour, had caught up to their small recon patrol. Lieutenant Barclay walked with the rest of his men rather than ride in the relative comfort of the tanks which is what made his men have confidence in him. *Hell's Fire* pulled up next to Howe, Anderson and Rosinski. They formed a defensive arc while the rest of the 112th came up. Howe scuttled round the rear of the tank and its warm engine as did clumps of infantrymen behind the other two tanks.

Davis left the warmth of his tank to join with Barclay and Rosinski.

"What do you think, Sergeant?" Barclay asked.

"Well, Sir, I don't see how they can be that far ahead of us. They've got to slog through this shit the same way we do. With our tanks breaking trail and the men following behind, we should be able to catch up with them. Where do you think they are headed?"

"Probably back to their position along the Siegfried Line. That's about twenty or so miles. They are Panzergrenadieren so not so used to walking. They should tire out before we do. I bet you we can catch them before nightfall.

"The tanks will run point on this, the men follow in their tracks so the going should be easier than what the Krauts have. We won't have any aircover and the artillery is probably too far back for any accurate support. So, it looks like it is going to be just us for now.

"We move out in five minutes."

#

"Please, Herr Schneider, can we rest here for a minute? I am so cold and tired. When do you think we will find our company?"

Schneider had not had the heart to tell Ernst Locher that they were not going back to their company. His plan was to surrender to the first available Americans and save their lives that way. But looking at Ernst, Schneider knew that time was running out on that plan. Ernst was slowly freezing to death in the bowels of the Huertgan Forest. They had to find some shelter and some way to get warm if he was going to survive. Ernst's survival had become Schneider's sole reason to survive himself. He saw that as the one good thing he could do. The one good thing to justify his living on while all the comrades that he had had died in his place.

"Come, Kleine, there must be a cabin in these woods somewhere. We will be alright." With that, Schneider put his arm around Ernst and half-dragged him forward deeper into the forest. The sounds of battle slowly receded and they were enveloped in the silence of the forest. Schneider reveled in it. He began to have renewed hope in their futures. But only if he found a place of refuge. The snow was not as deep the further they went into the forest but he had no idea if he was moving toward salvation or freezing to death. Already, Ernst was falling asleep and had to be shaken awake. He had trouble finding his footing and increasingly had to be carried if they were to make any progress at all. Schneider was rapidly losing strength but to stop and rest was to die. Each time he slipped and fell, he thought he would not be able to arise again. Ernst moaned in his sleep, his lips blue, turning grey. He had stopped shivering.

They slipped down an unseen ditch and came to rest with Ernst cradled in Schneider's lap. He looked at the boy's peaceful face, snowflakes melting on his closed eyelids.

"Well, Kleine, I have done all I can. Here is not so bad. We looked to be surrounded by Christmas trees. It is so quiet, like there is no war anymore, anywhere. Our own peace."

He gathered Ernst closer to his chest and slowly rocked, feeling his eyes close. He began to hum "Stille Nacht". There came the sound of a tree branch breaking off from its trunk landing so close to them that the pine needles brushed against his face. He was startled awake and looked around. He sat up straighter and saw he was beside a road. They were sitting in the drainage ditch which ran along side.

"Kleine, Ernst, wake up." Schneider shook the boy violently, "You must wake up. There is a road, it must lead somewhere. Come on." Ernst did awaken enough to call for his mother and sob.

"I am so tired, let me sleep some more then I'll get up and do my chores."

Schneider shook him some more and heaved himself with the boy, using the last of his strength, born of desperation, to gain the road. He had to rest, panting, as he tried to decide which direction to take. The forest gave no clue. He remembered a saying of his father's, "Rechts ist rechts", "Right is right".

"Rechts it is then. Come on, Kleine. We'll see if the old saying is true."

The footing on the snow-covered road was better and the sense of progress buoyed Schneider's spirits. Even Ernst seemed easier to carry. But the new found strength gave out one hundred yards down the road. Schneider fell to his knees, too exhausted to go on.

"I am sorry, Kleine. I can't go on. We'll rest a bit."

He was not sure if he dreamed it, retreating into the past of his time hunting with his father and the campfires they built but he thought he smelled wood smoke. Off to his left he saw the merest suggestion of a path leading into the trees where the smoke seemed to be coming.

"We will not die just yet," he whispered to the unhearing Ernst. Once again, drawing on the strength of desperation, he pulled Ernst onto the path, blindly pushing forward until he collapsed once again.

"Kann Ich hilfen?" asked Hans Rudin who had come upon Ernst and Schneider as he was gathering firewood for the hunter's hut in which he and his mother, Frieda, were taking refuge. Soon, Ernst and Schneider were being drawn back to life with Hans' venison stew, in the "Jager hut" deep in the Huertgen Forest.

"Many thanks, you have saved our lives. Can you tell us where we are? We became separated from our company during the last battle."

"You are not deserters, then?" Hans asked. "Because if you are and are found then we are all dead."

"No, not deserters. Can you tell us where the Americans and our comrades are? Then maybe we can figure out a way to join them again."

Beyond lying about deserting, everything else Schneider was saying was at least within sight of the truth. He left it vague enough without specifying which side he wanted to join. They had been at one time or another with both sides. It was natural for him to ask where the lines were. He hoped Hans was not a Nazi sympathizer but the risk that they were putting him and his mother in would be fatal.

Hans put more wood on the fire. He could see Schneider and Ernst were unarmed but he kept close to his grandfather's WWI Mauser.

"To tell you the truth, my mother and I came here from Aachen. I knew of this hut from hunting with my father. The Americans were advancing on Aachen so we thought to come here until things settled down. We traveled at night, avoiding everyone until we got here. So, I don't know where the Americans or our troops are. We rarely hear any fighting, though, so I guess the lines are fairly far off."

"Can you tell me where the road goes?"

"Going north, back to Aachen, to the west is Liege, east to Duren, but you would have to cross the West Wall. That I think is very dangerous because with the Americans closing in, our boys are likely to shoot you as the enemy or as deserters. The Americans are somewhere to the west but I don't know how far."

"We got separated from our unit when the attack on the Americans began maybe five or six days ago. We don't know what happened with that attack. We got turned around in the forest and wandered until you found us. Many thanks, again."

Frieda, Hans' mother, saw in Ernst what would happen to her boy if the Volkstrum got their hands on him. She fussed over him, rubbed his hands and feet to get some blood back into them and kept him next to their fire. He was soon sleeping, his color back to normal. Schneider dozed off next to him.

"Hans," she said, "they have to stay with us."

"For how long? There is not much game in the woods due to the war. How can we feed them? There is barely enough for us. They are grateful because we saved them but once they get their strength back, who knows what they will be like. They might turn us in for harboring them as deserters to save their own skins. And if the Americans find us first, they will shoot us as collaborators.

"No, we have to convince them to leave when they are stronger. It is the only way to keep us safe."

Chapter Twenty-Four: Stille Nacht

"OK, Howe, let's hear it," said Sergeant Rosinski, "how the US Army has let you down once again. You've been pretty quiet these last few miles, so I'm sure you have got some real gems stored up."

He had led them through the deep snow of the Huertgen Forest, trying to find the road he remembered from the last tactical briefing. He hoped that it would lead them back to the company or at least somewhere recognizable. Failing that, at least some cabin where they could get out of the cold. He was actually relieved when Howe started in: an uncomplaining Howe was a defeated Howe. He knew it was a way to take their minds off the numbing cold and the strength-sapping slog through the snow.

"Well, now that you mention it, Sarge, where the fuck are we anyway? I mean, besides in some fucking forest, up to our asses in snow, when we're not sinking in mud. I haven't heard any of our stuff or theirs, for that matter, for a while yet. For all we know the fucking war is over. We're always the last to fucking know anything about anything."

"Why should our betters include us in their plans?" asked Anderson. "As far as I can see, they have screwed up this war without our input. I suppose we have to trust to that some greater plan is in play," he ended sarcastically.

"You know what I think of their plans," said Howe, viscously slashing at a snow laded pine bough which only made him slip and be covered with more snow.

They had not eaten in a day, not had hot food in a week. The promised rotation back to St. Vith had been crushed by the German offensive which had slashed through their position and cut them off from their company. Rosinski's goal now was to get them out of the snow and possibly warm up somehow. Things did not improve when he slid into a ditch that was concealed by the snow.

"Jesus-fucking-Christ! Help me outta here". Howe and Anderson grabbed him under each arm and hauled him out while slipping in themselves. They finally scrambled onto higher ground but were exhausted. They leaned over, hands on their knees while the caught their breaths. Anderson looked up.

"Hey, Sarge, I think we're on a track or some kind of road. Look ahead."

The flat open, but trackless, path stretched ahead of them.

"This would be good news if we knew where the hell we are," remarked Howe. "Any ideas, Sarge?"

The clouded sky hid the sun, he had no map or compass which made little difference since, as Howe pointed out, they did not know where the hell they were. Rosinski knew that the last storm had blown out of the north. Looking at the trees, he saw there was heavy snow deposited on one side, which he thought was likely to be on their north sides. He was not sure just who, American or German, was to their north but at least it was a direction to go.

"OK, that way is north, I think, so that's where we go," he said.

"Well, shit, why not?" said Howe and the three infantrymen started off once again. They made better, less fatiguing progress as the footing was better and the snow not thigh-high. They trudged forward for half-an-hour before Rosinski called a halt.

"OK, we'll take a breather." Anderson inhaled deeply through his nose.

"Hey, Sarge, do you smell that?"

"What?"

"I think it is wood smoke." All three of them inhaled.

"Yeah, I smell it, too," Howe said.

They readied their rifles, clearing off the snow and advanced with alert urgency.

Anderson saw the path off to their left and felt the smoke was heavier coming from that direction. He signaled to the other two and headed in between the branches. The smoke smell grew and then they saw light from a cabin. The windows were frosted over and no sound came from inside.

"Go ahead," said Rosinski, "we'll cover you."

Anderson, carrying his Garand at the ready in his right arm, pushed the door open with his left.

Hans looked up at the barrel of the rifle and held his hands out to his side.

"Kann Ich helfen?"

Schneider and Ernst were sitting with their backs to the door by the fire. They turned around and stared down the three American gun barrels. They raised their hands as well.

In the stunned silence that followed, the five soldiers individually considered their new situation.

Schneider spoke first. "Wir aufgaben, (we surrender)". He was relieved that his plan for their survival might actually work out.

"This is just fucking great," said Howe, centering his rifle on Schneider. "Now what do we do with these guys, Sarge?"

Rosinski said, "Lower your rifle. Don't we know these guys? Didn't we capture them at Schmidt?"

"Yeah, I think you're right," said Anderson. "We took them over from those tankers and passed them on to the MPs."

"Oh, ferchrissake," exclaimed Howe. "It just goes to show you, we should have shot them when we had the chance. How many of our guys did they shot between now and then?"

Schneider stood in front of Ernst with his hands out to his side. "Wir aufgaben, wir aufgaben," he repeated again. The warmth of the cabin and the scent of venison stew softened the Americans.

"I don't think they represent the best killers the Nazis have to offer," said Anderson. "Besides, it's Christmas, isn't it, or thereabouts? I say we call a truce. They're unarmed and probably just as lost as we are. The German push last couple of days blew through them just like us."

Hans' mother was busy finding enough bowls for her new "guests" and put the steaming stew on the table.

"Bitte stellen Sie Ihre Gewehre Ausserhalb des Hauses auf," and opened the door. She pointed to Anderson's Garand and then outside.

"Ain't no fuckin' way I'm leaving my rifle outside," said Howe. "We don't know how many more Krauts there are wandering around and they see three Garands leaning up against the wall, that's an open invitation for them right there."

"Can't argue with that," said Anderson.

"Alright," said Rosinsky, "we'll lay them down over here." He put his against the far wall, Anderson did so and reluctantly, so did Howe. They settled down to the first hot meal they had had in days. They shared their C-rations with Hans and his mother. Even the hardtack crackers tasted good when dunked in the stew.

In the warmth of the cabin, with their stomachs at least partially filled, Rosinski turned to Scheider.

"How's the kid's shoulder?" pointing to Ernst and grimaced.

"Ach, besser," Schneider replied and told Ernst to open his fatigue shirt.

Rosinski whistled at the long scar, purple in the light. He pulled up his shirt and pointed to his appendectomy scar. "You've got me beat," he said and gave Ernst a pat.

Soon the meal and the warm cabin began to overtake the Americans. Anderson thought he heard Hans, softly singing "Stille Nacht" as he drifted off.

#

The weather broke on Christmas. The inactivity forced on the 100th Bomb Group at Thorpe Abbotts was coming to an end. Despite the extra time Joe Hanover had with Ginnie Standhope at the Fox and Hens, even he was feeling restless. The number of missions before rotation had risen from thirty to thirty-five leaving eleven more missions for Joe. After having secured Horace Standhope's permission and Ginnie's acceptance, Joe was planning on getting permission from his C.O. Although, there were a few obstacles to marrying "locals" officially, doing so with so many combat missions remaining would give the C.O. pause. How could he be sure that she was not marrying a man at high risk for dying just to get his benefits? Hanover was as nervous about meeting with the C.O. of the 349th Bomb Squadron, Lt. Col. Sam Barr as when he asked for Ginnie's hand.

"Come in, Sergeant," said the Colonel. He was known as an airman's commander and had flown fifty missions himself. He also made it a point to know as many of the veteran flyers in his command as possible. Hanover's story was one that the Colonel knew well. Not only did he have one of the best kill totals in the squadron but his return from having been shot down was notable. He felt that men like Hanover who had "done their bit" and lived through their twenty-five missions only to have the requirement raised not once but twice were particularly mistreated. So, he was willing to hear Hanover out.

Joe had on his best class-A uniform and came to rigid attention, snapping off a crisp salute, which his colonel returned.

"Have a seat, Sergeant. What can I do for you?"

Joe gripped the arms of the chair and tried to control his voice. He had never spoken to an officer of higher rank than captain, other than Le May on the one flight he took with the *Bouncing Betty*, and he found it intimidating.

"Thank you for seeing me, Sir. I want to request permission to marry a girl from the village. She has accepted me and I have her father's permission." He faltered to a stop and took a deep breath. He hoped the worse was now over.

"How long have you known her, Sergeant?"

"Not quite a year. We met soon after the bomb group arrived at Thrope Abbotts. Her father owns the 'Fox and Hens' pub in town."

Lt. Col. Barr knew of the pub, mainly through MP reports of dealing with drinking infractions. He had never gone there, being able to commandeer transport into London.

"Excuse me, Sergeant, I don't want to be indelicate but the girl in question is not pregnant?"

"Oh, no, Sir, it's not that. It's just that, her father wants us to wait until the war is over." As Joe relaxed, he became more talkative. "You see, he barely survived the first war. He lost his leg at the Somme. And he, well, they both can see our bombers as they come in, so they know the risks. The thing is, Sir, if I had your permission, that might sway him some."

There was a pause during which Joe gained some hope that his colonel was at least considering his request.

"How many missions do you have left, Sergeant?"

"As it stands now, eleven, Sir. But with the Mustangs escorting us and the Luftwaffe seems to be pretty shot up, I figure the odds are finally turning in our favor."

"What was his reason to wait for the end of the war?"

"He said England had enough war widows."

"I have to agree with him," said Barr. "I'm sorry but we got to finish the job here and then the rest of all our lives can start again.

"Permission denied. You are dismissed."

Joe reeled to his feet, saluted and stumbled out of the orderly room.

Lt. Col. Barr knew there really was not anything he could do if Hanover did marry his girl but he also knew that the chance of his living through the war was less than fifty-fifty. Even if he did survive, as

an enlisted man, the roadblocks to bringing her home when he rotated back to the States were many and severe.

He kept this to himself.

The mission planners had wasted no time in getting the 100th back into the air. They wanted to take advantage of every day of acceptable weather. The next morning at three am, the sergeants came through the tents and dragged the men out to pre-flight briefing. With the C.O.'s denial of his wedding plans, Joe felt that maybe the odds against him marrying Ginnie were insurmountable. Hard as waiting was, leaving her a widow was worse. But with that acceptance of how things were, no possibility of a future with Ginnie, for he knew his odds as well as anyone, Joe resigned himself to dying somewhere over Germany.

The resumption of flying had caused the crews to be confined to their barracks. Joe was relieved and accepted this as well, though he thought himself a coward, unable to face Ginnie now that he saw no future for them.

The Jeeps brought the crews out to the flight line. Joe tossed his kitbag into the plane and with practiced ease swung himself into the dark belly of *The Usual Suspects*. He took his place at the right waist and mechanically completed his pre-flight checks. His squadron, the 349th, was flying lead. They lined up behind the "Judas plane" that would assemble the rest of the groups at Buncher 28, before turning for home, leaving the bombers to fly on to their fate.

Ginnie in her bedroom at the Fox and Hens, heard the rumble of the B17s racing down the runway. She buried her face in her pillow so her sobbing would not waken her father.

#

"Enfield, godammit, where have you been?" The exasperation mixed with relief in Gus Tolliver's voice was not lost on Enfield Davis, tank commander of *Hell's Fire.* Grinning, he came back from the tree line, dragging a two-foot fir sapling behind him. He clambered on board the rear of his tank and stuck the trimmed trunk into the radiator filler vent. "What the fuck is that?" continued Tolliver.

"And a Merry Christmas to you, too, sour puss," replied Davis. "Come on, where's your holiday spirit? Think of it as a little bit of camouflage." Tolliver nearly lost it when Davis proceeded to tie spent fifty caliber shell casings onto the small tree.

"There," Davis said with satisfaction.

"The captain is going to shit a brick when he sees this. What's next, fucking Christmas carols?"

"What a great idea," replied Davis. "Join in." He started a scratchy rendition of "Silent Night".

"You've gone mental, you have. Are you trying for a 'Section Eight'?"

From deep in the bowels of the tank, Emmonds, the driver had been listening to this exchange.

"Tell you what, Enfield, if you do get sectioned, then I'll rig up some fake reindeer for the front. Maybe we can all have a nice Christmas."

"Well, speak of the devil, or maybe, Old St. Nick," said Peters, the loader/radio operator. "It's the captain on the horn for you."

"Davis, where are you?"

"We're on a slight rise just beyond the abandoned Kraut armor with about a hundred guys from the 112th, Captain. Over."

"How are you fixed for fuel and ammo? Over."

"About ninety percent on both. Over"

"Good. You are to continue your recon east to see if you can re-establish contact with the Panzers. We have a flight of Mustangs ready to go if you can find the Krauts while this weather holds. Over"

"Understood. We will keep you informed. Out."

Davis climbed down from the turret and found Lt. Judd Barclay of the 112th. He relayed the new orders.

"Sounds good," Barclay said. He turned to his men huddled against the tanks for warmth. "OK, we're moving out with the tanks and try to find those Panzers. When we do, the Air Force promises to blow hell out of them. Mount up".

"Jesus Christ," groused Howe. "How could he tell I was just getting as warm as I've been in three weeks. Now we've got to slog through more of this fucking snow, just to get our asses shot off."

"Come on, Jeff," said Anderson, "the walk will warm us up and I don't think those Panzer boys will be in any too good shape to cause much trouble. You think you're pissed; those guys were all nice and warm in their cozy tanks only to have to leave them. We could probably get them to surrender for some hot soup."

"My ass," was all Howe could reply.

The three tanks started off, going abreast with the infantry following in their tracks. Barclay walked along side *Hell's Fire* to set the pace. After only going a mile, the small column was brought to a stop by Panzerfausts falling just short of the lead tank.

"Ambush," shouted Barclay. The three tanks returned fire with their main guns and the machine guns. Still firing, they thrust ahead hoping to overrun the hidden Germans. Howe and Anderson with the rest of their company moved forward as best they could.

"Call it in," Howe shouted. "Let the fucking fly-boys do some work for a change."

"Not yet. This is probably just a leave-behind ambush to slow us down. The real column is getting away. Move it!"

"Fine with me," muttered Howe. But he followed Anderson and Barclay. Soon enough, small arms fire started pining off the tanks and whirring by Howe's head.

"Where the fuck are they?" he shouted.

"Just behind the next rise." Barclay pointing. "Return fire."

The men of the 112th raised their Garands and began firing. The volume built steadily, suppressing any German return fire.

"That's got their heads down," yelled Barclay. "Come on." He rose up and firing from the hip sprinted as best he could through the snow.

"I swear, if he yells 'charge', I'll shoot him myself," muttered Howe.

They advanced about one hundred yards before exhausting themselves.

"I think we've found them, Sir. Can we call in the fucking Air Force now?"

"That would be fine, Sergeant."

The radioman soon had the 363rd Fighter Group at Maastricht contacted. He gave them the coordinates of the Panzer group. "Help is on the way," he told Barclay.

Captain Robert Mullen with his ten Mustangs formed the ready reserve at Maastricht. They were not assigned to active patrolling but were held for situations such as the 112th presented them.

They were airborne within ten minutes of receiving the coordinates and in another ten minutes were streaking at two hundred feet above the beleaguered infantrymen.

"Howe, pop smoke," shouted Lt. Barclay.

"My fucking pleasure", he said. He hurled the purple smoke cannister as far as he could towards the German position. Although, there was no direct communication with the Mustangs, the meaning was clear.

Mullen did a barrel roll followed by the rest of his flight and began their strafing runs. The panicked Panzergrenadieren broke and ran. Only those few that made it to the cover of the forest survived. Over the next few days, they straggled to the West Wall and re-joined the 116th Regiment, the "Windhunds" and the remnants of Monteuffel's Fifth Panzerarmee.

After forty days of fighting, tens of thousands of casualties, the Battle of the Bulge ended with the armies back where they began. Eighty years before, the ancestor regiment of the 112th Pennsylvania, the 13th Pennsylvania Reserves, fought in the Battle of the Wilderness in a forest as impenetrable as the Huertgan Forest. It, too, was a battle that irrevocably turned the tide of the war towards victory.

#

"Prosit, Herr Doktor," said Oberstabartz Genter von Stettgen, handing Major Albert Brendt a tin cup with the last of his schnapps. "Frohe Weihnacten, Merry Christmas."

The two surgeons in the mill/aide station on the Kall River were enjoying the first respite in the unending stream of wounded that had peaked with the Battle of the Bulge. The evacuation of their dead and wounded had become more normalized. T.Sergeant Douglas Aiken with his M29 Weasel had had his role extended to the point that he was the main conductor of the operation. Neither of the surgeons could explain why their respective commands had not interfered with the operation of the aide station. Aiken continued to take out the wounded that could be moved and return with supplies. Periodically, the graves registration troops of both sides would remove the frozen dead stacked beyond the walls of the Mestranger Mill.

"Thank you, and Merry Christmas to you," replied Brendt. "Although it seems at least incongruous if not blasphemous to say so."

"We must harvest bits of civilization when we can. It may be our only hope as a species."

"There are certainly times when I doubt the continuation of our kind is such a good idea. The most slack..."

"Excuse me... 'slack'", von Stettgen asked.

"It means benefit of the doubt, leeway. Anyway, the most slack I will give our leaders is that they don't have any idea of what the fuck they are doing. I would like to think that if they came here and spent a day, no, an hour to see what the bottom line, the cost of their grand schemes was that they would stop this madness."

"Perhaps you attribute humanity to those that have so far shown only their lack of it," von Stettgen replied.

They tapped their mess tins and downed the schnapps. Both men seemed to have moved from robust youthful health to gaunt old age in the short month that they had been attending to their own and each other's wounded soldiers. Their revery was broken by the sound of Aiken's Weasel making its way down the eastern bank of the Kall River. They had gotten so attuned to the groan of the engine, the whine of the brakes and the grinding of the gears that they could tell how loaded with wounded he was. The two surgeons used to make bets on how many shattered soldiers Aiken was about to deliver but it was just too sad. They tipped their mess tins back to make sure all of the schnapps had been drunk, then went outside to begin triaging the new arrivals.

Aiken could carry up to six wounded on one trip. With their orderlies helping, the surgeons quickly sorted through the newly shattered lives in front of them. The process was sped along by finding one of the men had died in transit. He went straight to snowbank/morgue outside the walls.

"What's it look like up there," asked Brandt.

"I guess there's about twenty more up there. The poor bastards got hit with those fucking 88s. Everything is so blown to hell there's no cover. The towns are flattened, the trees are burnt to ash, can't dig in the frozen ground before the shelling starts. And the snow don't stop no frags. So, plenty to keep us busy. The shit-for-brains general running this show had better pull us out of there while they've got some living troops."

The orderlies had filled Aiken's Weasel with nominally stabilized wounded from the mill. He started up the western bank towards the aide station at Vossenach. The promised extra Weasels had not arrived.

#

As the seventeen planes that the 100th Bomb Group could mount for the Christmas day raid, gathered at Buncher 28, led by the garishly painted "Judas plane", a non-combat serviceable bomber meant to speed the assembly of the bomber flights. There was understandable grumbling on the intercom.

"Ber-fuckin'-lin, again?!", the disembodied voice said.

"I know, ya think they might be expecting us?'

Joe Hanover was a replacement waist gunner, on a replacement B17. He did not know the rest of the crew, all replacements themselves, and did not join in the generalized moaning and groaning. He had sunk into a state of near despair since his squadron commander had denied his request to marry Ginnie. His eleven remaining sorties before he could rotate home looked like tombstones in his imagination. Going home without her robbed him of his future. A future that ironically now seemed more likely since the near elimination of the Luftwaffe. Escorting Mustangs and Thunderbolts had become rare, even with the deep penetration missions to Berlin. They were used as more nimble bombers attacking troop concentrations, railyards and the few remaining factories.

What had worsened for the 100th BG was the lethality of flak batteries, concentrated around targets like Berlin. The Wehrmacht poured all its fury into stopping the bombers which were speeding up the Allied and Russian ground forces, steadily snuffing out German resistance. As a result, there was little for Joe Hanover to concentrate on other than his misery over losing Ginnie. He no longer hated the black popcorn bursts of flak, sometimes even hoping for an obliterating blast that would end his suffering.

"Ok, boys," Captain Emory Macauliff of the B17F *Special Delivery*, "we've made the IP and will over the target in ten minutes, flak in five. Good luck." From the cockpit, the flak bursts were blooming along their flight path like black roses at a satanic mass. First came the buffeting and jolting of near misses, then the screaming passage of shards of flak through the bodies of the bombers and crew alike. Joe had taken on the role of medic in the crew. He carried extra bandages and tourniquets and did the best he could. He thought if he was going to die, he'd rather die trying to save someone else.

He turned off his mic so that most of the near misses were muffled and he could avoid distractions. He was working on the belly turret gunner who had been dragged into the ship with wounds to his legs. Joe turned to grab his bag when something hit his right leg like hammer. He felt no pain or panic. He was thrown up to the navigator's seat on his back. Sunlight shining through the top gun turret from a cloudless blue sky warmed his face as he slipped into blackness.

Chapter Twenty-Five: Home

"The 100th is coming in," said a breathless Corporal Victor Hume who had run from the control tower with the news. He worked with the chief surgeon, Captain Luther Haynes at the base hospital at Thorpe Abbotts. Haynes was trying to get some sleep after operating all night on the survivors of a raid on Bremen the day before. The 100th Bomb Group had flown over Bremen at 25,000 feet on its way to bomb Berlin.

Haynes had seen the types of wounds change as the Luftwaffe had been largely cleared from the sky. Where the aircrews had been ripped into by 7.92mm machine gun fire and 20mm nose cannons, they were mainly now flak wounds: large shards of hot metal knifing through bombers and bodies alike. Burns remained a constant sorrow. The only thing that had improved was a more efficient evacuation scheme moving the wounded quickly to larger hospitals near London and then Stateside. The Atlantic was safer for the troopships transporting whole young boys to England and returning with shattered old men, aged by the war.

Dr. Haynes felt that his overall work was made somewhat more satisfactory with the advent of more surgeons and nurses, better equipment and techniques. The 100th Bomb Group's arrival always brought with it the air of savage, medieval combat.

"Alright, Victor, I'm awake." Groaning as he rolled out of his cot, still wearing his blood stiffened surgical greens, he pulled on his boots and started back to the base hospital. Glancing to his left, he saw the battered, smoking, actively burning planes barely staying aloft, red flares arcing away from their sides, half-landing, half-crashing onto the runway at Thorpe Abbotts Field. The "Bloody 100th" had returned.

The radar guided flak over Berlin was accurate and severe. Although the occasional 109 Messerschmitt or 190 Focke-Wulf would sortie against the huge bomber streams they were too few and too late. The Me 262 Messerschmitt was a terrifying novelty, too fast for its own effectiveness. The jets would close on the bombers, stodgy in comparison, in excess of five hundred miles per hour, a good 100 miles per hour faster than the Spitfire Mk IX or the Mustang. This allowed one pass on the way up, one on the way down then back to base before running out of gas. Therefore, the defense of the Reich fell to the lowly flak gunner. These batteries were pulled back to defend Berlin as other German cities fell to the Allies.

Joe Hanover's right leg had been torn open by a frag from an 88mm antiaircraft cannon over Berlin. He was the worst of the wounded on *Special Delivery*. He lived only because frag had missed the femur and its attendant blood vessels. His crewmates were able to pack the wound and slow the bleeding. The ambulances from the base hospital arrived and Joe was handed out to their crews as gently as possible through the hole in the fuselage. He remained unconscious throughout and was on Dr. Haynes' operating table within a half hour.

"Are we ready to go?" he asked the anesthetist who nodded.

"Well, Victor, let's see what we've got." Joe's entire leg and groin were washed down with an iodine solution and Haynes began to probe the open wound. "I would have to say, this is one lucky sonuvabitch enlisted man. He has all soft tissue damage, a lot of it, mind you, but he gets to keep his leg and nuts, for now.

"OK, rat-toothed forceps and curved Mayo scissors." For the next hour, Haynes and Victor cut and snipped away the dead and dying muscle of Joe's thigh, dropping chunks of meat into a basin. Bleeders were tied off and the wound, now enlarged by half, was irrigated. Iodine-soaked pads were packed into the wound and Joe was allowed to wake up in a drugged stupor. He drifted in and out of consciousness over the next three weeks, during which time, he had four more surgeries. He moved through the evac chain of hospitals near London, on to a hospital ship and finally by train to Twin Forks, Indiana, and home.

Ginnie Standhope had heard only that his plane had been shot down and crewmen had died but nothing specific about Joe. She assumed he was dead since she heard nothing from him. All who knew of her and Joe and could bring her word were dead. She made the best peace with that reality that she could. After a month, she no longer cried herself to sleep, but she no longer felt any joy in her life. It was the mutual support she gave to her father and he to her that constituted the framework of her life after Joe.

#

Against all odds, Davis's Christmas tree survived stuck in the re-fueling vent on the back of *Hell's Fury.* The engine exhaust and heat dried it out and finally, an errant spark set it on fire.

"Enfield, your tree is alight," said Saurez of *Adolph's Nightmare* over the intercom.

"Shit," said Davis. He clambered out of the turret and kicked the tree off the tank and onto the snow where it sizzled its last. "Well, it was nice while it lasted," he said as he sunk back into his seat in the turret.

"Let's leave blowing us up to the Krauts, shall we?" asked Tolliver.

"That would look better on the after-action report, I suppose," agree Davis. "Meanwhile, we have orders to continue east toward the Siegfried Line and clean up any straggling Germans. We have clear skies for our friends in the Air Force and word is that the Panzers that we passed were the last of their armor in this section. Should be a..."

"Don't you say it," said Grisholm, the driver. "We ain't home yet." And as if to put a finishing point to it, four shells from von Kleist's battery of 88s crashed to their rear.

"And there it is," said Tolliver. "Let's roll." The small patrol of three Shermans lurched into motion towards the pillboxes and dragon's teeth of the last line of German defense: the Siegfried Line. They had gone less than a mile when a single Panzerfaust round hit *Hell's Fire* right track stopping it cold. Immediately MG34, potato masher grenades and Karabiner 98 rounds started to score hits on the tanks.

"Where are they?" shouted Suarez.

"All around us," replied Soames in *Death Wagon*. The tanks began to return fire as they tried to back up only to have another Panzerfaust immobilize *Adolph's Nightmare*.

"Son of a bitch, return fire," shouted Davis. He got on the radio.

"Mayday, mayday, any units. We are surrounded and need assistance." He gave their coordinates then popped up out of the turret to man the .50 cal.

"Goddamit, Enfield, get your ass back in here," commanded Tolliver.

"Rounds on the way," came the most welcome news from the 229th FA's Lt. Alfred Moore. "Button up. We will lay suppressing fire fifty yards around your perimeter."

"I owe you a beer when this is over," shouted Davis. It was over in five minutes.

"I'm on the horn to the company," reported Soames. "They say they are 30 minutes out with a retriever and replacement tanks. Not too shabby, if you ask me."

"If they have all these surplus tanks hanging around, why don't they send a few our way, or do they think we can invade Germany all on our lonesome?" asked Tolliver.

"That's the price you pay for being good and getting noticed, I guess," said Emmonds, *Hell Fire's* driver.

Howe and Anderson were not privy to all this chatter and the arrival of replacement tanks. They and the other members of the 112th Pennsylvania that accompanied the tanks had more than enough to do covering their own asses. Lt. Barclay came up to the huddled troops by the tanks.

"First Platoon, go right and form a perimeter towards the woods. Second go left, the rest of you are on me. Sergeant Rosinski, call in our new positions and see if we can get some air support. OK, let's move out."

Reluctantly, Howe most of all, the 112th moved from the relatively safety of the tanks and out into the snow. There were no clear targets and they were aware of their limited ammo. Rosinsky was back on the horn to the company.

"Hey, along with those tanks, maybe fill them up with ammo, grenades and whatnot. We're running a bit low out here."

"Roger that. Any wounded, yet?"

"Not yet. Transmit our new coordinates to the artillery and have them give us another few rounds." Rosinsky tried to keep his voice calm and steady but he did not know how many Germans they faced, what their armaments were and if they had any air support of their own. All he did know was that they were surrounded with two immobile tanks that were sitting ducks for the Panzerfausts. For now, only Soames in *Death Wagon* could still maneuver but was receiving heavy fire from the tree line. It was too dangerous to be out of the turrets to work the .50 caliber and being unable to turn the two disabled tanks, their .30 caliber machineguns could only fire straight ahead. The turrets could turn and the main guns could fire.

"Soames and Suarez, report what rounds you have left," called Davis over the intercom.

"I've got two smoke, four wooly-pete, four cannister and ten HEAP rounds," reported Soames.

"I got no smoke, two wooly-pete, two cannister and eight HEAP," said Suarez. "I guess we know who's been fightin' this war, right?"

Davis said, "I've got one smoke, four wooly-pete, three cannister and six HEAP. OK, so here's the plan. Load up your cannister rounds and hit the tree line. Soames on the left, I'll take the center and Suarez on the left. Fire all you've got followed by the wooly-pete. That ought to keep their heads down or get them running. We'll see what kind of return fire they can muster. We fire in one minute. Any questions?"

There were none.

"Fire!"

The three tanks unleashed all they had and after ten minutes of sustained fire, the ensuing quiet fell like the end of the world.

Davis popped up to man the .50 cal and received no fire from the tree line.

"Alright, 112th," shouted Barclay, "move out." He led the remains of the regiment, now reduced to less than three hundred men, into the smoldering tree line and found only dead and dying Germans.

"Rosinsky, call the artillery and tell them we won't be needing their fire mission for now."

In the quiet, the low rumble of Aiken's M-29 Weasel could be heard approaching. He carried ammo for the infantry and some shells for the tanks. The replacement tanks soon arrived.

#

The commander of the 116th Panzers, the "Windhunds", had lived longer into the war then he ever expected: longer than his tanks which he had to leave when they ran out of fuel; longer than eighty percent of his men, not counting his losses in North Africa and Kursk and the fighting retreat up the Italian boot and across Germany to land at the Siegfried Line facing the limitless number of American Shermans.

"Was it only two months," Col. Hinman thought ruefully, "since I sat in my Panzer IV on the eve of overrunning Bastogne? Except, we didn't take Bastogne, did we? Patton saw to that. Our best weapon against the Americans was actually their rapid advance, stretching and breaking their supply lines. Lack of fuel was the only thing that stopped them. Just like it has stopped us. But then the Brits took Antwerp before we could and that is it: the end. They have unlimited fuel and we have 'Scheiss.'"

"Now we are little more than foot soldiers, throwing rocks at their tanks."

"All I hope to do now is get as many of my men and myself back home to our families and hopefully, peace."

"Herr Colonel," his sergeant reported. "The Americans' replacement tanks have arrived and they are on the move."

"Where to?"

"They are heading north. It looks like they mean to flank us and advance through the Aachen Gap."

"That is certainly what I would do in their place. Very well, leave two men per bunker and bring the rest with all the panzerfausts we have left. We will do our duty to the Fatherland to the end."

The remaining pillboxes were taken out with flamethrowers and bangalore torpedoes. Colonel Hinman realized that he faced overwhelming odds and he surrendered his men. The "Windhunds" would not live to fight another day but they would live to see home.

#

This was the last major combat action that the 112th and the 707th Tanks were engaged in. With the rest of the First Army, they swung north of the Siegfried Line, through the Aachen Gap and helped to invest Aachen. Howe, Anderson and Rosinski were on guard duty, but mostly relaxing and staying warm in one of the pillboxes that had been abandoned and was relatively clean. They had passed on several that had burned corpses of the former occupants. Their days were spent blasting the remaining "dragons' teeth" tank traps, clearing the way for the 707th's tanks. Now that the regiment was more stationary, their re-supply was much improved and for Thanksgiving, the Quartermaster Corps had been able to being in turkeys which they were happy to share with the tankers.

Dr. Alfred Brandt had left the Mestranger Mill aide station to serve as the 112th's medical officer. He had tried to convince Dr. von Stettgen to join him but he held true to his oath to, serve not the Fuhrer, but his men. Addresses were exchanged for "after the war" but neither man felt it likely to see the other again.

He caught up with Co. E just as they were about to lay into their turkey dinner.

"Hang on, boys," he said, "you might want to give that bird the sniff test. I've had reports of bad turkey: salmonella and the like, so I'd cook that a bit longer."

"What's salmonella?" asked Howe.

"Food poisoning, basically. It can cause some nasty diarrhea, sometimes bloody, fever, abdominal pain."

"Hell, I've got that already," Howe said. "I haven't had a solid shit since we left St. Vith which is also just about as long as I've had anything to eat except Spam and hard tack. So, I think I'll take my chances."

The smell of warm turkey filled their pillbox and for the first time since landing on Normandy, they allowed themselves thoughts of home.

"I tell you what," began Anderson, "it's probably not that unusual, but turkey-day was always the favorite holiday at my house – bigger than Christmas, even. I think the Anderson family made up about a third of the population around Altoona, least it seemed like that from all the people who showed up. There were aunts, uncles, cousins, nephews, nieces, grandparents – so many that I didn't recognize a lot of them. It was like the word got out: "The Anderson feedbag is open for business. Lord, everybody brought something. My mom didn't have to shop or cook or even clean up, the house was too full of people that nobody could see the floor anyway. All we did was supply the electricity. I used to not eat for two days before just to make room. After dinner, no one could move for the rest of the day.

"The last Thanksgiving was '41, days before Pearl Harbor. Little did we know. Within a week all of the men in the family enlisted in one of the services. I don't know where anyone is or who is still alive. I guess it will have to be Thanksgiving after the war to find that out. A mixed Thanksgiving if there ever will be one."

"Yeah," said Howe, "I remember your parties. We had a much smaller time of it. I even thought of sneaking into yours figuring no one would notice us."

"You would have been and will be welcome anytime," replied Anderson.

"How about you, Sarge? Big doings at the Rosinsky house for the holiday?"

"We were pretty much just off the boat," he began. "So, not so much turkey but feet of kielbasa, mulled beer, leek and apple salad, cabbage and mushroom pie, pumpkin pierogi and kopytka which are little potato dumplings, potato cake. Same thing as you: family from all over, all speaking Polish, bringing their favorite dishes, eating for days."

The men were silent, thinking about their homes and if they were ever going to see them again.

'Fuckin' Krauts," said Howe. "How much longer can they go? And why? They must be able to see this killing is pointless. They have no air power, we're fighting boys and old men, their industry is bombed all to shit, they had to abandon a fuck-load of armor because they ran out of gas, Antwerp's gone. What are they thinking?'

"It's the Fuhrer, man. He's a homicidal crazy motherfucker," said Anderson.

"Yeah, but are his generals? Maybe those SS sons of bitches, but they can't all be like that, can they?"

Rosinsky, cleared his throat. "It's maybe mass hysteria or they've got nothing else at this point. The Germans are a pretty militaristic society and to against their leader would be seen as cowardice and betrayal."

"So, they are willing to die, have their children die, their country bombed into the Stone Age just so they don't disappoint Hitler? That is truly fucked up," said Howe.

"Well, look at us, solving the problems of the world when we should be getting some shut-eye. Anderson, you take the first watch. Wake me up in two," Rosinsky said.

But unfortunately, their sleep was delayed by the first grumbling cramps in their guts caused by the spoiled Thanksgiving turkey.

"Shit, but I guess the Quartermasters meant well," said Rosinsky as he scrambled out of the pillbox and behind the nearest dragon's tooth.

The three friends from Altoona did make it home four months later, to pick up their lives and make the best of them.

#

The next two months of the war for the 707th Tank Battalion spent with the 112th Pennsylvania National Guard, were a kind of reverse "Wacht am Rhine" that Hitler could not have imagined. They secured the bridges crossing the Rhine as the engineers re-built them. There were a few harassing rounds from Lt. von Kleist's remaining 88s still two ridges away but well into Germany, beyond the 707th's 76mm cannon but there were Captain Robert Mullens' P-51 Mustangs from the 363rd squadron on ready call to suppress the incoming rounds. Mullens was happy for the work, there being no Messerschmitts left to deal with.

With the final defeat of Germany in May, 1945, the pressure to bring the troops home grew exponentially. In a bureaucratic boondoggle born out of trying to be fair, a points system was devised that assigned points for a bewildering number of categories which left every one frustrated. There were mutinies, marches by soldiers and their families demanding faster demobilization. The pervading sentiment was that they "sure as hell got them over there fast enough, why can't they get them home the same way." There were, of course, global considerations such as keeping our former allies, the Russians in check, defeating the Japanese in the Pacific which required maintaining significant number of service men in uniform. Those considerations came to an end with Hiroshima and Nagasaki.

By July, 1945, Technical Sergeant Enfield Davis parked *Hell's Fire* at the port of Antwerp to be transported home with his crew. The men from Co. E, 112th Pennsylvania National Guard, Barclay, Howe, Anderson and Rosinski, having against all odds, fulfilled that often promised but usually missed goal of being home by Christmas.

Epilogue:
Thorpe Abbotts

"You are doing so much better, Joey", said Myrna Hanover, his mother, welcoming him back from his walk down the hill to the quay at the confluence of the Ohio and Wabash rivers, giving the southern Indiana town its name of Twin Forks. His recovery from being wounded over Berlin had been slow, painful and wracked with a sense of guilt having survived alone from all his fellow crew members. He was the most highly decorated of all the sons of Twin Forks who had gone off to war. This made him all the more guilt-ridden so that he barely acknowledged the waves and shouted hellos of his neighbors. The walks and the returning strength he felt was a small ray of hope in the spring of 1946. But home for him was divided between Twin Forks and Thorpe Abbotts, Norfolk County, England, where he had left Virginia Standhope. She still assumed him to be dead as she had heard nothing from him since his last mission to Berlin.

He put down his cane and sagged heavily into the wicker chair on the porch. His mother brought him some fresh squeezed lemon aide which he accepted with a wan smile and placed on the side table.

"Joey," she began brightly, "there's going to be a dinner dance at the VFW hall this weekend..."

"No."

"But there is," she said not understanding his meaning.

"I am not going to any dinner dance," he shouted. He picked up the lemon aide glass and threw onto the walkway where it shattered. He instantly regretted doing it but was too proud to explain or apologize.

"But our friends, people who have known you all your life and are so proud of you, they only want to say hello."

"Mother, I am going back to England as soon as I can. I cannot stay here and be gawked at like some prize heifer. I did nothing special but to survive through luck or cowardice. I did my job like thousands of other guys. I am no hero," he said softly emphasizing each word.

The 88 shell that crippled his B17 ripped through his right thigh had nearly killed him. Only through the heroics of his crew did he live long enough to be patched up at the aide station at Thorpe Abbotts and eventually get home. The wound was scarred over and beginning to contract so that it was only with the greatest of painful effort, that he had trained himself to keep walking upright. He had sworn that he would return to Ginny but not as a cripple. Now, he was nearly there. He had not written to her fearing that at any time on his return journey to her, he would lose his nerve and go back home to the coward's life he thought he deserved. It was better she had no expectations. The thought of her needlessly grieving for him did not enter his thoughts. Why would she? He was nothing special.

He had the money, saved from his mustering out pay, and the $45 dollars per month for being wounded and had booked passage on a tramp steamer from New York to Liverpool. The ocean voyage was slower but Joe had enough of flying.

He made port at Liverpool and took the train from there to Norwich and on to Diss, six miles from Thorpe Abbotts. From the bus window, he saw the hedge rows and even the gate through which he and Ginny had ridden their bicycles for their picnics. Unconsciously, he rose in his seat to catch the earliest glimpse of the round tower of All Saints church. The bus stopped at the post office. The long trip had stiffened him and he had difficulty navigating to narrow aisle to the steep steps.

One hundred yards down the main street, he saw, swinging in the breeze, the sign for the "Fox and Hens". His heart pounding, his nerve threatened failing as he limped slowly towards the pub. To his right he knew was the airfield and the burned hulks of the "Bloody 100th".

A small boy carrying newspapers for the pub impatiently brushed by him, causing him to stumble. But he righted himself and with a deep breath stepped into the busy lunch time pub. He stood before the sun streamed window and watched Ginny handle the lunch trade at the bar. She glanced up briefly at him then again for a longer time.

"Joe?"

Then again, "Joe? Oh my God, Joe!" and rushed to embrace him.

"I'm back, Ginny, if you'll have me."

The End

www.ingramcontent.com/pod-product-compliance
Lightning Source LLC
Chambersburg PA
CBHW071715210925
32774CB00018B/124

9781959621454